## Books by Susan Hill

THE ENCLOSURE
DO ME A FAVOUR
GENTLEMAN AND LADIES
A CHANGE FOR THE BETTER
I'M THE KING OF THE CASTLE
THE ALBATROSS AND OTHER STORIES
STRANGE MEETING
THE BIRD OF NIGHT
A BIT OF SINGING AND DANCING
IN THE SPRINGTIME OF THE YEAR
THE MAGIC APPLE TREE
THE WOMAN IN BLACK

*Ghost Stories*

# *Ghost Stories*

Selected by Susan Hill

Hamish Hamilton · London

First published in Great Britain 1983
by Hamish Hamilton Ltd
Garden House, 57-59 Long Acre, London WC2E 9JZ



British Library Cataloguing in Publication Data

Ghost stories.
1. Ghost stories, English
I. Hill, Susan
823'.01'.08375[FS] PR1309.G5

ISBN 0-241-11102-1

Photoset in Great Britain by
Rowland Phototypesetting Ltd, Bury St Edmunds, Suffolk
and printed by St Edmundsbury Press
Bury St Edmunds, Suffolk

# Contents

Acknowledgements .................................................. 7

Introduction .................................................. 9

Keeping His Promise ............. Algernon Blackwood 17
The Demon Lover ......................... Elizabeth Bowen 31
The Man with the Nose ............... Rhoda Broughton 39
The Dream Woman ........................... Wilkie Collins 55
The Signal-Man .............................. Charles Dickens 79
The Old Nurse's Story .................. Elizabeth Gaskell 91
Sir Edmund Orme .............................. Henry James 112
'Oh, Whistle, and I'll Come to
You, My Lad' .................................. M. R. James 139
'They' ........................................... Rudyard Kipling 159
Green Tea ......................................... J. S. Le Fanu 179
The White Cat of Drumgunniol ........... J. S. Le Fanu 209
The Story of the
Inexperienced Ghost .......................... H. G. Wells 220
All Souls .......................................... Edith Wharton 233

# *Acknowledgements*


*Keeping His Promise* by Algernon Blackwood was first published in *The Empty House*, London 1906

*The Demon Lover* by Elizabeth Bowen was first published in *The Listener*, 1941. © 1946 and renewed 1974 *The Demon Lover* by Elizabeth Bowen by permission of Alfred Knopf Inc.

*The Man with the Nose* by Rhoda Broughton was first published in Temple Bar, New York, 1872

*The Dream Woman* by Wilkie Collins was first published as *The Ostler* in the Christmas edition of *Household Words*, London 1855

*The Signal Man* by Charles Dickens was first published as part of *Mugby Junction* in the Christmas number of *All the Year Round*, London 1866

*The Old Nurse's Story* by Mrs Gaskell was first published in *A Round of Christmas Stories by the Fire*, the Christmas Supplement to *Household Words*, London 1852

*Sir Edmund Orme* by Henry James was first published in *Black and White*, 1891

*Oh, Whistle . . .* by M. R. James was first published in *Ghost Stories of an Antiquary*, London 1904

*They* by Rudyard Kipling was first published in *Scribner's Magazine*, New York 1904

*The White Cat of Drumguinnol* by Sheridan Le Fanu was first published in *All the Year Round*, London 1870

*Green Tea* by Sheridan Le Fanu was first published in *All the Year Round*, London 1869

*The Story of the Inexperienced Ghost* by H. G. Wells was first published in *The Strand Magazine*, London 1902

*All Souls* by Edith Wharton was first published in *Ghosts*, New York 1937. © 1937 d Appleton-Century Co.; renewal copyright © 1965 William R. Tyler.

Susan Hill gratefully acknowledges the permission given by the following:

Jonathan Cape Ltd on behalf of the Elizabeth Bowen Estate for *The Demon Lover* from *The Demon Lover* published by Jonathan Cape Ltd

The National Trust and Macmillan, London, Ltd for *They* from *Traffics and Discoveries* by Rudyard Kipling published by Macmillan, London, Ltd

The Executors of the Estate of H. G. Wells for *The Inexperienced Ghost* by H. G. Wells from *The Short Stories of H. G. Wells*

Constable Publishers for *All Souls* by Edith Wharton from *The Ghost Stories of Edith Wharton*

# *Introduction*

The traditional, classic English ghost story, like the traditional classic English detective story, has its origins in the nineteenth century. Of course, it is possible to trace elements that are essential to both back much further, to early mythological literature, and folk-lore. Nevertheless, as wc recognise the forms, they were really Victorian; that period was when they were formed, that was when every self-respecting writer, good and bad, turned his or her hand to one, or both.

But, since the nineteenth century, the detective story has carried on its familiar way; although there have been various sub-divisions – the thriller, the spy-story – a great many of the detective novels that are still being published in such large numbers are cast in exactly the same mould as those written in the 1880s or the 1920s and '30s. Moreover, the detective story has gained, on the way, an intellectual snob-value – it is a form much dabbled in by dons. It is no shame – rather the contrary – to admit to being an addict, or a writer, of detective stories. But what about the ghost story? What about that once phenomenally popular form, without several examples of which no journal or magazine used to be complete? What happened to that?

Browse along the shelves of any public library which has a decent backstock, and you will find all manner of out-of-print collections, by individual, or assorted authors, most of them long-forgotten, of classic ghost stories. But browse in any bookshop and you will find, apart from the complete works of a very few masters of the form, like J. S. Le Fanu, nothing of the sort. You may be misled by paperbacks with lurid covers and titles that seem to be leading you in the right direction; Tales of Horror, the Uncanny, the Supernatural, and Terror, will be their general style. Inside, you may possibly find one or two true ghost stories. But, on the whole, they will be something quite other, for the classic ghost story has gone a long way (and many would say downhill) in the direction of the gruesome, the crudely horrible, the weird, outlandish and fantastic. One of the first questions I was obliged to confront when I began to compile this anthology was, 'When is a ghost story not a ghost story?', and so far as anything written since the 1930s went I had to reply, 'Most of the time.'

So – what is *not* a ghost story? What did I rigorously exclude? Anything to do with werewolves, witches, vampires and monsters; anything science-fictional or about fantasy other-worlds inhabited by alien beings, however wraith-like their mere appearance might be; anything involving frightening occurrences which were bizarre, odd, inexplicable, in any ordinary, human terms, and yet which did not, apparently, involve 'ghosts' or, at least, ghostly phenomena. There is a masterly story of the macabre by Wilkie Collins, called 'A Terribly Strange Bed', in which a young man in nineteenth-century Paris visits a gambling house and is drugged and dragged upstairs by a crew of villains who have parted a good many other foolish young men from their money in this way; after robbing them, they murder them, as they almost murder the young narrator, by means of a bed which is built so that its canopy moves, by remote control, downwards, at the same time as its sides move inwards, to crush the sleeping victim to death beneath.

It is a sinister, heart-stopping tale, brilliant in its pacing, and its use of macabre detail. But it is not a ghost story. There is a practical, this-worldly explanation for every horrible happening.

The result of the rise of the tale of terror and horror was the decline in popularity of the classic ghost story. It was, at first, deemed not frightening enough. Worse, far worse, must happen, grim and dreadful and hair-raising incidents must be piled one on top of the other; blood must flow and be seen to flow, wounds must gape and stakes be driven through hearts. It was said that, as readers became more sophisticated and more informed about real, horrifying events in this world – and, also, as they distanced themselves from superstitions and belief in a supernatural order – they became far less easily frightened, and so more and more grotesque and savage tales had to be fabricated before any flesh could be made to creep.

Virginia Woolf said as much, in her essay on 'Henry James's Ghost Stories' in 1921:

> The truth is perhaps that we have become fundamentally sceptical. Mrs Radcliffe amused our ancestors because they were our ancestors; because they lived with very few books, an occasional post, a newspaper superannuated before it reached them, in the depths of the country or in a town which resembled the more modest of our villages, with long hours to spend sitting over the fire drinking wine by the light of half a dozen candles. Nowadays we breakfast upon a richer feast of horror than served them for a twelvemonth. We are tired of violence; we suspect mystery.

And, a little further on in the same essay, she tells a writer of them that 'your ghosts will only make us laugh'.

In fact, laughter is precisely what is provoked by the horror film. As the incredible, grisly incidents are multiplied and become ever more fantastic and divorced from imaginable reality, the audience finds its release in mockery and gales of derisive laughter, rather than in shudders of fear.

Yet the classic ghost story still has tremendous power to chill and alarm, to make us turn our heads to look behind us and dread to walk up the dark staircase to bed at night. That is partly because its strength lies in under- not over-statement. Its art is the art of omission, of suggestion, not of crude and explicit description. But, even more important, it is frightening because it has its roots in the real world, the world we ourselves know and see and smell and touch and move about in, the world of houses, of furnished rooms, of tables and chairs, busy streets, of eating and drinking and conversation. And also because it strikes a chord with us of suspicion, of belief. We simply cannot, and do not, believe in werewolves and vampires, any more than we now believe in gorgons and dragons. But ghosts we can, and do – perhaps, indeed, *must* – believe in, however much we may say, in public, that we do not. Even if we do not believe in the external existence of a ghostly spirit of some person, now dead, who is appearing to us, in spectral shape, we believe in evil, and in forces within ourselves which can be externalised, actually or, at the very least, symbolically.

Investigations into psychic phenomena, including hauntings, became popular and widespread, with the ghost stories themselves, in the nineteenth century and they continue today, on a careful, scientific basis. Even if you discount ninety-nine per cent of them all, even if as many as that admit of some perfectly natural explanation, and even if one applies the principle of Occam's razor most rigorously, there is nevertheless that one per cent, that hard core of 'occurrences' which cannot be explained away. Ghosts exist. Certain places are haunted. Evil is sometimes made manifest and has power over certain individuals, circumstances, events.

But still, the ghost story, the tale of a quiet haunting, has declined in popularity, and, although it is certainly still written occasionally today, could scarcely be said to be thriving vigorously, as is the detective story.

One reason may be rather a mundane one. There have been a few outstanding examples of the ghost novel – *A Christmas Carol*, Henry James's *The Turn of the Screw* – but, on the whole, it is a short form, and very difficult to sustain over more than, say, ten thousand words or so. And short stories – individually or in collections – are simply not as popular as they were. Victorian readers devoured them by the dozen, in their variety of periodicals. But, since the last war, the number of magazines publishing them has gone on declining. And any novelist, however popular, who produces a collection of short stories, will notice a lower level of sales for these than for their full-length fiction.

Yet, just because it can, in its quiet, simple way, arouse such an extraordinary response, the time would now seem to be ripe for a revival of the classic ghost story, in a world where an overkill of horror has begun to provoke a reaction of mere hilarity and boredom.

Charles Dickens was by no means the first nineteenth-century writer of ghost stories, but he was certainly its major populariser, responsible not only for writing a large number himself, but also for commissioning and publishing many others, in the magazines he edited. And the link between Dickens and the ghost story is strengthened by a further link between them both and the season of Christmas, which became the traditional time for the telling of ghost stories. The appearance of ghosts has long been associated, in legend and in religious mythology, with Christmas – though not, of course, exclusively so. The setting of the old house in the country, and the assembled company around a roaring fire, and the telling of a ghost story on Christmas Eve, became a classic one. M. R. James used to read aloud one of his own ghost stories to a group of friends, gathered together, in the light of a single candle; *The Turn of the Screw* opens in just such a setting.

It all works so well because what the ghost story writer must conjure up above all is atmosphere – his art relies almost exclusively upon it for its effect. The ghost story must impart a strong sense of place, of mood, of the season, of the elements, and so the traditional, haunted settings – old isolated houses, lonely churchyards, castles and convents and empty, narrow streets at night – are heavily relied upon. The worst writers of the Victorian ghost story, of course, simply piled on every spooky detail indiscriminately, in an effort to send shudders up the spine of the reader. The best writers are very carefully selective. For the history of the ghost story is precisely the history of an extraordinary mixture of the best and the worst of English fictional writing.

Before Dickens, there was Sir Walter Scott, whose fine ghost story 'Wandering Willie's Tale', in dialect, originally formed part of the novel *Redgauntlet*, and who wrote an essay on the supernatural in fiction which is one of the relatively few pieces of critical commentary on the form. Mrs Gaskell and Robert Louis Stevenson, Oscar Wilde and Henry James, Rudyard Kipling and H. G. Wells and Walter de la Mare, all wrote excellent ghost stories. More recently, Daphne du Maurier and Kingsley Amis have added beautifully to the repertoire, and Penelope Lively and Leon Garfield have made a corner all their own in the writing of ghost stories for children. But when I came to make my selection for this anthology it quickly became obvious that most of the entries would be from the period more than fifty and, in many cases, more than a hundred years ago.

In terms of literary quality, the stories chose themselves, though it was not easy, for example, to select finally between several equally good stories by Henry James or Kipling. But I made my definition of the classic ghost story very strict, and so a number of stories, excellent in themselves, did not fulfil all my conditions (including, for example, Thomas Hardy's 'The Withered Arm', and D. H. Lawrence's 'The Rocking Horse Winner', though both of them are brilliant stories of the supernatural).

Quite simply, I decided that a ghost story must have a ghost, and that the ghost must appear, or at least be heard, smelled or otherwise sensed. 'A ghost' was the spirit of some person, now dead, or else an embodiment of an evil force, or a strong emotion, such as distress or terror. It was not a demon, a dragon or Dracula.

On the other hand, the ghost might be seen as the projection of the (living) narrator's own psyche. (All Henry James's ghost stories fall into this category.) Nevertheless, they take external form and are described and seen as 'ghosts'.

I excluded stories in which the narrator or central figure saw his ghost while under the influence of drink, drugs or delirium; perhaps, in this, I was being a little over-scrupulous, but these do not seem to me to be true, ghostly apparitions, but hallucinations, which admit of real, medical or psychological explanations and do not 'exist' in any independent sense.

There are several writers known chiefly – or, indeed, only – as the authors of ghost stories: M. R. James, Arthur Machen, J. S. Le Fanu. Out of the works of the latter, who is perhaps the greatest ghost story writer of them all, it was particularly difficult to choose, but the two here are typical representatives of their genre, as well as being good in their own right. 'Green Tea' is a masterpiece, and 'The White Cat of Drumgunniol' can stand for a large number of stories about an apparition as a portent of death.

From that to Henry James's eminently civilised and even rather amusing and unfrightening ghost, 'Sir Edmund Orme', is a large step. A lot of writers worked more seriously in other forms, and treated their ghost stories as fun, but nothing Henry James wrote was ever irrelevant to his consistently serious, artistic purpose – the investigation and understanding and complex portrayal of the human individual, in the context of his society. His ghost stories are serious, they are never pot-boilers, and neither are they ever written merely to make the reader's flesh creep. The effect they have is deeper and more permanent than that.

Rarely, at the other extreme, does a ghost story make one laugh. But Rhoda Broughton's curious tale of 'The Man with the Nose' is funny, to begin with at least, before the dreadful denouement, which foreshadows the much more chilling story of a ghostly abduction, Elizabeth Bowen's 'The Demon Lover'. And, until its final paragraphs, H. G. Wells makes us laugh, too, though increasingly hollowly and falteringly, at 'The Story of the Inexperienced Ghost'.

Kipling's story, 'They', moves one not to terror but to tears –

indeed, it hovers on the edge of sentimentality but does not quite topple over and it is a particularly distinctive example of a common ghost story theme, a haunting by or of children. So is Mrs Gaskell's only excursion into the genre, 'The Old Nurse's Story', which is also rather moving.

There are several isolated houses here, but the most eerily unforgettable, the most atmospheric and unnerving, is surely Edith Wharton's Whitegates, cut off from the outside world by thick snow, on All Souls' Eve. Sense of place is also strong in M. R. James's classic, 'Oh, Whistle, and I'll Come to You, My Lad' – lonely shingle-shore and flat, open marshland will never seem the same to anyone who visits them, after reading it.

In a sense, every story is included here both for itself, and because it is a representative of many others. None of them is obscure, none has been dug out of long-lost Victorian periodicals, all are by well-known authors. What I wanted to assemble was simply a selection of the very best – best imagined, best written, best constructed – of a minor yet unjustly neglected English literary form. Ghost stories tell us a great deal about ghosts, and about living human beings, too, and about the relationship between them, and between the seen and the unseen worlds, the real and the supernatural, as well as between good and evil. They tell us about things that lie hidden within all of us, and which lurk outside all around us. They show human beings in the grip of the extremes of powerful emotions, at key moments and turning points in their lives. They also frighten delightfully, give shape, form and substance to our darkest and most primitive and child-like fears and imaginings, and, perhaps most importantly of all, they entertain and, like all good stories, hold 'children from play and old men from the chimney corner'.

Susan Hill

# *Keeping His Promise*

Algernon Blackwood

It was eleven o'clock at night, and young Marriott was locked into his room, cramming as hard as he could cram. He was a Fourth Year Man at Edinburgh University and he had been ploughed for this particular examination so often that his parents had positively declared they could no longer supply the funds to keep him there.

His rooms were cheap and dingy, but it was the lecture fees that took the money. So Marriott pulled himself together at last and definitely made up his mind that he would pass or die in the attempt, and for some weeks now he had been reading as hard as mortal man can read. He was trying to make up for lost time and money in a way that showed conclusively he did not understand the value of either. For no ordinary man – and Marriott was in every sense an ordinary man – can afford to drive the mind as he had lately been driving his, without sooner or later paying the cost.

Among the students he had few friends or acquaintances, and these few had promised not to disturb him at night, knowing he was at last reading in earnest. It was, therefore, with feelings a good deal stronger than mere surprise that he heard his doorbell ring on this particular night and realized that he was to have a visitor. Some men would simply have muffled the bell and gone on quietly with their work. But Marriott was not this sort. He was nervous. It would have bothered and pecked at his mind all night long not to know who the visitor was and what he wanted. The only thing to do, therefore, was to let him in – and out again – as quickly as possible.

The landlady went to bed at ten o'clock punctually, after

which hour nothing would induce her to pretend she heard the bell, so Marriott jumped up from his books with an exclamation that augured ill for the reception of his caller, and prepared to let him in with his own hand.

The streets of Edinburgh town were very still at this late hour – it was late for Edinburgh – and in the quiet neighbourhood of F—— Street, where Marriott lived on the third floor, scarcely a sound broke the silence. As he crossed the floor, the bell rang a second time, with unnecessary clamour, and he unlocked the door and passed into the little hall-way with considerable wrath and annoyance in his heart at the insolence of the double interruption.

'The fellows all know I'm reading for this exam. Why in the world do they come to bother me at such an unearthly hour?'

The inhabitants of the building, with himself, were medical students, general students, poor Writers to the Signet, and some others whose vocations were perhaps not so obvious. The stone staircase, dimly lighted at each floor by a gas jet that would not turn above a certain height, wound down to the level of the street with no pretence at carpet or railing. At some levels it was cleaner than at others. It depended on the landlady of the particular level.

The acoustic properties of a spiral staircase seem to be peculiar. Marriott, standing by the open door, book in hand, thought every moment the owner of the footsteps would come into view. The sound of the boots was so close and so loud that they seemed to travel disproportionately in advance of their cause. Wondering who it could be, he stood ready with all manner of sharp greetings for the man who dared thus to disturb his work. But the man did not appear. The steps sounded almost under his nose, yet no one was visible.

A sudden queer sensation of fear passed over him – a faintness and a shiver down the back. It went, however, almost as soon as it came, and he was just debating whether he would call aloud to his invisible visitor, or slam the door and return to his books, when the cause of the disturbance turned the corner very slowly and came into view.

It was a stranger. He saw a youngish man, short of figure and very broad. His face was the colour of a piece of chalk, and the eyes, which were very bright, had heavy lines underneath them. Though the cheeks and chin were unshaven and the general appearance unkempt, the man was evidently a gentleman, for he was well dressed and bore himself with a certain air. But, strangest of all, he wore no hat, and carried none in his hand, and although rain had been falling steadily all the evening, he appeared to have neither overcoat nor umbrella.

A hundred questions sprang up in Marriott's mind and rushed to his lips, chief among which was something like 'Who in the world are you?' and 'What in the name of Heaven do you come to me for?' But none of these questions found time to express themselves in words, for almost at once the caller turned his head a little so that the gaslight in the hall fell upon his features from a new angle. Then in a flash Marriott recognized him.

'Field! Man alive! Is it you?' he gasped.

The Fourth Year Man was not lacking in intuition, and he perceived at once that here was a case for delicate treatment. He divined, without any actual process of thought, that the catastrophe often predicted had come at last, and that this man's father had turned him out of the house. They had been at a private school together years before, and though they had hardly met once since, the news had not failed to reach him from time to time with considerable detail, for the family lived near his own, and between certain of the sisters there was great intimacy. Young Field had gone wild later, he remembered hearing about it all – drink, a woman, opium, or something of the sort – he could not exactly call to mind.

'Come in,' he said at once, his anger vanishing. 'There's been something wrong, I can see. Come in, and tell me all about it and perhaps I can help –' He hardly knew what to say, and stammered a lot more besides. The dark side of life, and the horror of it, belonged to a world that lay remote from his own select little atmosphere of books and dreamings. But he had a man's heart for all that.

He led the way across the hall, shutting the front door carefully behind him, and noticed as he did so that the other, though certainly sober, was unsteady on his legs, and evidently much exhausted. Marriott might not be able to pass his examinations, but he at least knew the symptoms of starvation – acute starvation, unless he was much mistaken – when they stared him in the face.

'Come along,' he said cheerfully, and with genuine sympathy in his voice. 'I'm glad to see you. I was going to have a bite of something to eat, and you're just in time to join me.'

The other made no audible reply, and shuffled so feebly with his feet that Marriott took his arm by way of support. He noticed for the first time that the clothes hung on him with pitiful looseness. The broad frame was literally hardly more than a frame. He was as thin as a skeleton. But, as he touched him, the sensation of faintness and dread returned. It only lasted a moment, and then passed off, and he ascribed it not unnaturally to the distress and shock of seeing a former friend in such a pitiful plight.

'Better let me guide you. It's shamefully dark – this hall. I'm always complaining,' he said lightly, recognizing by the weight upon his arm that the guidance was sorely needed, 'but the old cat never does anything except promise.' He led him to the sofa, wondering all the time where he had come from and how he had found out the address. It must be at least seven years since those days at the private school when they used to be such close friends.

'Now, if you'll forgive me for a minute,' he said, 'I'll get supper ready – such as it is. And don't bother to talk. Just take it easy on the sofa. I see you're dead tired. You can tell me about it afterwards, and we'll make plans.'

The other sat down on the edge of the sofa and stared in silence, while Marriott got out the brown loaf, scones and a huge pot of marmalade that Edinburgh students always keep in their cupboards. His eyes shone with a brightness that suggested drugs, Marriott thought, stealing a glance at him from behind the cupboard door. He did not like yet to take a full square look. The fellow was in a bad way, and it would have been so like an examination to stare and wait for explanations. Besides, he was evidently almost too exhausted to speak. So, for reasons of delicacy – and for another reason as well which he could not exactly formulate to himself – he let his visitor rest apparently unnoticed, while he busied himself with the supper. He lit the spirit-lamp to make cocoa, and when the water was boiling he drew up the table with the good things to the sofa, so that Field need not have even the trouble of moving to a chair.

'Now, let's tuck in,' he said, 'and afterwards we'll have a pipe and a chat. I'm reading for an exam, you know, and I always have something about this time. It's jolly to have a companion.'

He looked up and caught his guest's eyes directed straight

upon his own. An involuntary shudder ran through him from head to foot. The face opposite him was deadly white and wore a dreadful expression of pain and mental suffering.

'By gad!' he said, jumping up, 'I quite forgot. I've got some whisky somewhere. What an ass I am. I never touch it myself when I'm working like this.'

He went to the cupboard and poured out a stiff glass which the other swallowed at a single gulp and without any water. Marriott watched him while he drank it, and at the same time noticed something else as well – Field's coat was all over dust, and on one shoulder was a bit of cobweb. It was perfectly dry; Field arrived on a soaking wet night without hat, umbrella or overcoat, and yet perfectly dry, even dusty. Therefore he had been under cover. What did it all mean? Had he been hiding in the building?. . .

It was very strange. Yet he volunteered nothing; and Marriott had pretty well made up his mind by this time that he would not ask any questions until he had eaten and slept. Food and sleep were obviously what the poor devil needed most and first – he was pleased with his powers of ready diagnosis – and it would not be fair to press him till he had recovered a bit.

They ate their supper together while the host carried on a running one-sided conversation, chiefly about himself and his exams and his 'old cat' of a landlady, so that the guest need not utter a single word unless he really wished to – which he evidently did not! But, while he toyed with his food, feeling no desire to eat, the other ate voraciously. To see a hungry man devour cold scones, stale oatcake, and brown bread laden with marmalade was a revelation to this inexperienced student who had never known what it was to be without at least three meals a day. He watched in spite of himself, wondering why the fellow did not choke in the process.

But Field seemed to be as sleepy as he was hungry. More than once his head dropped and he ceased to masticate the food in his mouth. Marriott had positively to shake him before he would go on with his meal. A stronger emotion will overcome a weaker, but this struggle between the sting of real hunger and the magical opiate of overpowering sleep was a curious sight to the student, who watched it with mingled astonishment and alarm. He had heard of the pleasure it was to feed hungry men, and watch them eat, but he had never actually witnessed it, and he had no idea it was like this. Field ate like an animal – gobbled, stuffed, gorged. Marriott forgot his reading, and began to feel something very much like a lump in his throat.

'Afraid there's been awfully little to offer you, old man,' he managed to blurt out when at length the last scone had disappeared, and the rapid, one-sided meal was at an end. Field still made no reply, for he was almost asleep in his seat. He merely looked up wearily and gratefully.

'Now you must have some sleep, you know,' he continued, 'or you'll go to pieces. I shall be up all night reading for this blessed exam. You're more than welcome to my bed. To-morrow we'll have a late breakfast and – and see what can be done – and make plans – I'm awfully good at making plans, you know,' he added with an attempt at lightness.

Field maintained his 'dead sleepy' silence, but appeared to acquiesce, and the other led the way into the bedroom, apologizing as he did so to this half-starved son of a baronet – whose own home was almost a palace – for the size of the room. The weary guest, however, made no pretence of thanks or politeness. He merely steadied himself on his friend's arm as he staggered across the room, and then, with all his clothes on, dropped his exhausted body on the bed. In less than a minute he was to all appearances sound asleep.

For several minutes Marriott stood in the open door and watched him; praying devoutly that he might never find himself in a like predicament, and then fell to wondering what he would do with his unbidden guest on the morrow. But he did not stop long to think, for the call of his books was imperative, and happen what might, he must see to it that he passed that examination.

Having again locked the door into the hall, he sat down to his books and resumed his notes on *materia medica* where he had left off when the bell rang. But it was difficult for some time to concentrate his mind on the subject. His thoughts kept wandering to the picture of that white-faced, strange-eyed fellow, starved and dirty, lying in his clothes and boots on the bed. He recalled their schooldays together before they had drifted apart, and how they had vowed eternal friendship – and all the rest of it. And now! What horrible straits to be in. How could any man let the love of dissipation take such hold upon him?

But one of their vows together Marriott, it seemed, had

completely forgotten. Just now, at any rate, it lay too far in the background of his memory to be recalled.

Through the half-open door – the bedroom led out of the sitting-room and had no other door – came the sound of deep, long-drawn breathing, the regular steady breathing of a tired man, so tired that even to listen to it made Marriott almost want to go to sleep himself.

'He needed it,' reflected the student, 'and perhaps it came only just in time!'

Perhaps so; for outside the bitter wind from across the Forth howled cruelly and drove the rain in cold streams against the window-panes, and down the deserted streets. Long before Marriott settled down again properly to his reading, he heard distinctly, as it were, through thc sentences of the book, the heavy, deep breathing of the sleeper in the next room.

A couple of hours later, when he yawned and changed his books, he still heard the breathing, and went cautiously up to the door to look round.

At first the darkness of the room must have deceived him, or else his eyes were confused and dazzled by the recent glare of the reading-lamp. For a minute or two he could make out nothing at all but dark lumps of furniture, the mass of the chest of drawers by the wall, and the white patch where his bath stood in the centre of the floor.

Then the bed came slowly into view. And on it he saw the outline of the sleeping body gradually take shape before his eyes, growing up strangely into the darkness, till it stood out in marked relief – the long black form against the white counterpane.

He could hardly help smiling. Field had not moved an inch. He watched him a moment or two and then returned to his books. The night was full of the singing voices of the wind and rain. There was no sound of traffic; no hansoms clattered over the cobbles, and it was still too early for the milk-carts. He worked on steadily and conscientiously, only stopping now and again to change a book, or to sip some of the poisonous stuff that kept him awake and made his brain so active, and on these occasions Field's breathing was always distinctly audible in the room. Outside, the storm continued to howl, but inside the house all was stillness. The shade of the reading-lamp threw all the light upon the littered table, leaving the other end of the room in comparative darkness. The bedroom door was exactly opposite him where he sat. There was nothing to disturb the worker, nothing but an occasional rush of wind against the windows, and a slight pain in his arm.

This pain, however, which he was unable to account for, grew once or twice very acute. It bothered him; and he tried to remember how, and when, he could have bruised himself so severely, but without success.

At length the page before him turned from yellow to grey, and there were sounds of wheels in the street below. It was four o'clock. Marriott leaned back and yawned prodigiously. Then he drew back the curtains. The storm had subsided and the Castle Rock was shrouded in mist. With another yawn he turned away from the dreary outlook and prepared to sleep the remaining few hours till breakfast on the sofa. Field was still breathing heavily in the next room, and he first tiptoed across the floor to take another look at him.

Peering cautiously round the half-opened door his first glance fell upon the bed now plainly discernible in the grey light of morning. He stared hard. Then he rubbed his eyes. Then he rubbed his eyes again and thrust his head farther round the edge of the door. With fixed eyes, he stared harder still, and harder.

But it made no difference at all. He was staring into an empty room.

The sensation of fear he had felt when Field first appeared upon the scene returned suddenly, but with much greater force. He became conscious, too, that his left arm was throbbing violently and causing him great pain. He stood wondering, and staring, and trying to collect his thoughts. He was trembling from head to foot.

By a great effort of the will he left the support of the door and walked forward boldly into the room.

There, upon the bed, was the impress of a body, where Field had lain and slept. There was the mark of the head on the pillow, and the slight indentation at the foot of the bed where the boots had rested on the counterpane. And there, plainer than ever – for he was closer to it – was *the breathing*!

Marriott tried to pull himself together. With a great effort he found his voice and called his friend aloud by name!

'Field! Is that you? Where are you?'

There was no reply; but the breathing continued without interruption, coming directly from the bed. His voice had such an unfamiliar sound that Marriott did not care to repeat his questions, but he went down on his knees and examined the bed above and below, pulling the mattress off finally, and taking the coverings away separately one by one. But though the sounds continued there was no visible sign of Field, nor was there any space in which a human being, however small, could have concealed itself. He pulled the bed out from the wall, but the sound *stayed where it was*. It did not move with the bed.

Marriott, finding self-control a little difficult in his weary condition, at once set about a thorough search of the room. He went through the cupboard, the chest of drawers, the little alcove where the clothes hung – everything. But there was no sign of anyone. The small window near the ceiling was closed; and, anyhow, was not large enough to let a cat pass. The sitting-room door was locked on the inside; he could not have got out that way. Curious thoughts began to trouble Marriott's mind, bringing in their train unwelcome sensations. He grew more and more excited; he searched the bed again till it resembled the scene of a pillow fight; he searched both rooms, knowing all the time it was useless – and then he searched again. A cold perspiration broke out all over his body; and the sound of heavy breathing, all this time, never ceased to come from the corner where Field had lain down to sleep.

Then he tried something else. He pushed the bed back exactly into its original position – and himself lay down upon it just where his guest had lain. But the same instant he sprang up again in a single bound. The breathing was close beside him, almost on his cheek, and between him and the wall! Not even a child could have squeezed into the space.

He went back into his sitting-room, opened the windows, welcoming all the light and air possible, and tried to think the whole matter over quietly and clearly. Men who read too hard, and slept too little, he knew, were sometimes troubled with very vivid hallucinations. Again he calmly reviewed every incident of the night: his accurate sensations; the vivid details; the emotions stirred in him; the dreadful feast – no single hallucination could ever combine all these and cover so long a period of time. But with less satisfaction he thought of the recurring faintness, and curious sense of horror that had once or twice come over him, and then of the violent pains in his arm. These were quite unaccountable.

Moreover, now that he began to analyse and examine, there was one other thing that fell upon him like a sudden revelation: *during the whole time Field had not actually uttered a single word!* Yet, as though in mockery upon his reflections, there came ever from that inner room the sound of the breathing, long-drawn, deep and regular. The thing was incredible. It was absurd.

Haunted by visions of brain fever and insanity, Marriott put on his cap and mackintosh and left the house. The morning air on Arthur's Seat would blow the cobwebs from his brain; the scent of the heather, and above all, the sight of the sea. He roamed over the wet slopes above Holyrood for a couple of hours, and did not return until the exercise had shaken some of the horror out of his bones, and given him a ravening appetite into the bargain.

As he entered he saw that there was another man in the room, standing against the window with his back to the light. He recognized his fellow-student, Greene, who was reading for the same examination.

'Read hard all night, Marriott,' he said, 'and thought I'd drop in here to compare notes and have some breakfast. You're out early?' he added, by way of a question. Marriott said he had a headache and a walk had helped it, and Greene nodded and said, 'Ah!' But when the girl had set the steaming porridge on the table and gone out again, he went on with rather a forced tone, 'Didn't know you had any friends who drank, Marriott?'

This was obviously tentative, and Marriott replied dryly that he did not know it either.

'Sounds just as if some chap were "sleeping it off" in there, doesn't it, though?' persisted the other, with a nod in the direction of the bedroom, and looking curiously at his friend. The two men stared steadily at each other for several seconds, and then Marriott said earnestly:

'Then you hear it too, thank God!'

'Of course I hear it. The door's open. Sorry if I wasn't meant to.'

'Oh, I don't mean that,' said Marriott, lowering his voice. 'But I'm awfully relieved. Let me explain. Of course, if you hear it too, then it's all right; but really it frightened me more than I can tell you. I thought I was going to have brain fever, or something, and you know what a lot depends on this exam. It always begins with sounds, or visions, or some sort of beastly hallucination, and I –'

'Rot!' ejaculated the other impatiently. 'What *are* you talking about?'

'Now, listen to me, Greene,' said Marriott, as calmly as he could, for the breathing man was still plainly audible, 'and I'll tell you what I mean, only don't interrupt.' And thereupon he related exactly what had happened during the night, telling everything, even down to the pain in his arm. When it was over he got up from the table and crossed the room.

'You hear the breathing now plainly, don't you?' he said. Greene said he did. 'Well, come with me, and we'll search the room together.' The other, however, did not move from his chair.

'I've been in already,' he said sheepishly; 'I heard the sounds and thought it was you. The door was ajar – so I went in.'

Marriott made no comment, but pushed the door open as wide as it would go. As it opened, the sound of breathing grew more and more distinct.

'*Someone* must be in there,' said Greene under his breath.

'*Someone* is in there, but *where*?' said Marriott. Again he urged his friend to go in with him. But Greene refused point-blank; said he had been in once and had searched the room and there was nothing there. He would not go in again for a good deal.

They shut the door and retired into the other room to talk it all over with many pipes. Greene questioned his friend very closely, but without illuminating result, since questions cannot alter facts.

'The only thing that ought to have a proper, logical explanation is the pain in my arm,' said Marriott, rubbing that member with an attempt at a smile. 'It hurts so infernally and aches all the way up. I can't remember bruising it, though.'

'Let me examine it for you,' said Greene. 'I'm awfully good at bones in spite of the examiners' opinion to the contrary.' It was a relief to play the fool a bit and Marriott took his coat off and rolled up his sleeve.

'By George, though, I'm bleeding!' he exclaimed. 'Look here! What on earth is this?'

On the forearm, quite close to the wrist, was a thin red line. There was a tiny drop of apparently fresh blood on it. Greene came over and looked closely at it for some minutes. Then he sat back in his chair, looking curiously at his friend's face.

'You've scratched yourself without knowing it,' he said presently.

'There's no sign of a bruise. It must be something else that made the arm ache.'

Marriott sat very still, staring silently at his arm as though the solution of the whole mystery lay there actually written upon the skin.

'What's the matter? I see nothing very strange about a scratch,' said Greene, in an unconvincing sort of voice. 'It was your cuff-links probably. Last night in your excitement –'

But Marriott, white to the very lips, was trying to speak. The sweat stood in great beads on his forehead. At last he leaned forward close to his friend's face.

'Look,' he said, in a low voice that shook a little. 'Do you see that red mark? I mean *underneath* what you call the scratch?'

Greene admitted he saw something or other, and Marriott wiped the place clean with his handkerchief and told him to look again more closely.

'Yes, I see,' returned the other lifting his head after a moment's careful inspection. 'It looks like an old scar.'

'It *is* an old scar,' whispered Marriott, his lips trembling. '*Now* it all comes back to me.'

'All what?' Greene fidgeted on his chair. He tried to laugh, but without success. His friend seemed bordering on collapse.

'Hush! Be quiet, and – I'll tell you,' he said. '*Field made that scar.*'

For a whole minute the two men looked each other full in the face without speaking.

'Field made that scar!' repeated Marriott at length in a louder voice.

'Field! You mean – last night?'

'No, not last night. Years ago – at school, with his knife. And I made a scar in his arm with mine.' Marriott was talking rapidly now.

'We exchanged drops of blood in each other's cuts. He put a drop into my arm and I put one into his –'

'In the name of heaven, what for?'

'It was a boys' compact. We made a sacred pledge, a bargain. I remember it all perfectly now. We had been reading some dreadful book and we swore to appear to one another – I mean, whoever died first swore to show himself to the other.

And we sealed the compact with each other's blood. I remember it all so well – the hot summer afternoon in the playground, seven years ago – and one of the masters caught us and confiscated the knives – and I have never thought of it again to this day –'

'And you mean –' stammered Greene.

But Marriott made no answer. He got up and crossed the room and lay down wearily upon the sofa, hiding his face in his hands.

Greene himself was a bit nonplussed. He left his friend alone for a little while, thinking it all over again. Suddenly an idea seemed to strike him. He went over to where Marriott still lay motionless on the sofa and roused him. In any case it was better to face the matter, whether there was an explanation or not. Giving in was always the silly exit.

'I say, Marriott,' he began, as the other turned his white face up to him. 'There's no good being so upset about it. I mean – if it's all a hallucination we know what to do. And if it isn't – well, we know what to think, don't we?'

'I suppose so. But it frightens me horribly for some reason,' returned his friend in a hushed voice. 'And that poor devil –'

'But, after all, if the worst is true and – and that chap *has* kept his promise – well, he has; that's all, isn't it?'

Marriott nodded.

'There's only one thing that occurs to me,' Greene went on, 'and that is, are you quite sure that – that he really ate like that – I mean that he actually *ate anything at all*?' he finished, blurting out all his thought.

Marriott stared at him for a moment and then said he could easily make certain. He spoke quietly. After the main shock no lesser surprise could affect him.

'I put the things away myself,' he said, 'after we had finished. They are on the third shelf in that cupboard. No one's touched 'em since.'

He pointed without getting up, and Greene took the hint and went over to look.

'Exactly,' he said, after a brief examination; 'just as I thought. It was partly hallucination, at any rate. The things haven't been touched. Come and see for yourself.'

Together they examined the shelf. There was the brown loaf, the plate of stale scones, the oatcake, all untouched. Even the glass of whisky Marriott had poured out stood there with the whisky still in it.

'You were feeding – no one,' said Greene. 'Field ate and drank nothing. He was not there at all!'

'But the breathing?' urged the other in a low voice, staring with a dazed expression on his face.

Greene did not answer. He walked over to the bedroom, while Marriott followed him with his eyes. He opened the door, and listened. There was no need for words. The sound of deep, regular breathing came floating through the air. There was no hallucination about that, at any rate. Marriott could hear it where he stood on the other side of the room.

Greene closed the door and came back. 'There's only one thing to do,' he declared with decision. 'Write home and find out about him, and meanwhile come and finish your reading in my rooms. I've got an extra bed.'

'Agreed,' returned the Fourth Year Man; 'there's no hallucination about that exam; I must pass that whatever happens.'

And this was what they did.

It was about a week later when Marriott got the answer from his sister. Part of it he read out to Greene:

'It is curious,' she wrote, 'that in your letter you should have enquired after Field. It seems a terrible thing, but you know only a short while ago Sir John's patience became exhausted, and he turned him out of the house, they say without a penny. Well, what do you think? He has killed himself. At least, it looks like a suicide. Instead of leaving the house, he went down into the cellar and simply starved himself to death . . . They're trying to suppress it, of course, but I heard it all from my maid, who got it from their footman . . . They found the body on the 14th, and the doctor said he had died about twelve hours before . . . He was dreadfully thin . . .'

'Then he died on the 13th,' said Greene.

Marriott nodded.

'That's the very night he came to see you.'

Marriott nodded again.

# *The Demon Lover*

Elizabeth Bowen

Towards the end of her day in London Mrs Drover went round to her shut-up house to look for several things she wanted to take away. Some belonged to herself, some to her family, who were by now used to their country life. It was late August; it had been a steamy, showery day: at the moment the trees down the pavement glittered in an escape of humid yellow afternoon sun. Against the next batch of clouds, already piling up ink-dark, broken chimneys and parapets stood out. In her once familiar street, as in any unused channel, an unfamiliar queerness had silted up; a cat wove itself in and out of railings, but no human eye watched Mrs Drover's return. Shifting some parcels under her arm, she slowly forced round her latchkey in an unwilling lock, then gave the door, which had warped, a push with her knee. Dead air came out to meet her as she went in.

The staircase window having been boarded up, no light came down into the hall. But one door, she could just see, stood ajar, so she went quickly through into the room and unshuttered the big window in there. Now the prosaic woman, looking about her, was more perplexed than she knew by everything that she saw, by traces of her long former habit of life – the yellow smoke-stain up the white marble mantelpiece, the ring left by a vase on the top of the escritoire; the bruise in the wallpaper where, on the door being thrown open widely, the china handle had always hit the wall. The piano, having gone away to be stored, had left what looked like claw-marks on its part of the parquet. Though not much dust had seeped in, each object wore a film of another kind; and, the only ventilation being the chimney, the whole drawing-room smelled of the cold hearth. Mrs Drover put down her parcels on the escritoire and left the room to proceed upstairs; the things she wanted were in a bedroom chest.

She had been anxious to see how the house was – the part-time caretaker she shared with some neighbours was away this week on his holiday, known to be not yet back. At the best of times he did not look in often, and she was never sure that she trusted him. There were some cracks in the structure, left by the last bombing, on which she was anxious to keep an eye. Not that one could do anything –

A shaft of refracted daylight now lay across the hall. She stopped dead and stared at the hall table – on this lay a letter addressed to her.

She thought first – then the caretaker *must* be back. All the same, who, seeing the house shuttered, would have dropped a letter in at the box? It was not a circular, it was not a bill. And the post office redirected, to the address in the country, everything for her that came through the post. The caretaker (even if he *were* back) did not know she was due in London to-day – her call here had been planned to be a surprise – so his negligence in the manner of this letter, leaving it to wait in the dusk and the dust, annoyed her. Annoyed, she picked up the letter, which bore no stamp. But it cannot be important, or they would know . . . She took the letter rapidly upstairs with her, without a stop to look at the writing till she reached what had been her bedroom, where she let in light. The room looked over the garden and other gardens: the sun had gone in; as the clouds sharpened and lowered, the trees and rank lawns seemed already to smoke with dark. Her reluctance to look again at the letter came from the fact that she felt intruded upon – and by someone contemptuous of her ways. However, in the tenseness preceding the fall of rain she read it: it was a few lines.

DEAR KATHLEEN,

You will not have forgotten that to-day is our anniversary, and the day we said. The years have gone by at once slowly and fast. In view of the fact that nothing has changed, I shall rely upon you to keep your promise. I was sorry to see you leave London, but was satisfied that you would be back in time. You may expect me, therefore, at the hour arranged.

Until then . . .

K.

Mrs Drover looked for the date: it was to-day's. She dropped the letter on to the bed-springs, then picked it up to see the writing again – her lips, beneath the remains of lipstick, beginning to go white. She felt so much the change in her own face that she went to the mirror, polished a clear patch in it and looked at once urgently and stealthily in. She was confronted by a woman of forty-four, with eyes starting out under a hat-brim that had been rather carelessly pulled down. She had not put on any more powder since she left the shop where she ate her solitary tea. The pearls her husband had given her on their marriage hung loose round her now rather thinner throat, slipping into the V of the pink wool jumper her sister knitted last autumn as they sat round the fire. Mrs Drover's most normal expression was one of controlled worry, but of assent. Since the birth of the third of her little boys, attended by a quite serious illness, she had had an intermittent muscular flicker to the left of her mouth, but in spite of this she could always sustain a manner that was at once energetic and calm.

Turning from her own face as precipitately as she had gone to meet it, she went to the chest where the things were, unlocked it, threw up the lid and knelt to search. But as rain began to come crashing down she could not keep from looking over her shoulder at the stripped bed on which the letter lay. Behind the blanket of rain the clock of the church that still stood struck six – with rapidly heightening apprehension she counted each of the slow strokes. 'The hour arranged . . . My God,' she said, '*what* hour? How should I . . .? After twenty-five years. . . .'

The young girl talking to the soldier in the garden had not ever completely seen his face. It was dark; they were saying good-bye under a tree. Now and then – for it felt, from not seeing him at this intense moment, as though she had never seen him at all – she verified his presence for these few moments longer by putting out a hand, which he each time pressed, without very much kindness, and painfully, on to one of the breast buttons of his uniform. That cut of the button on the palm of her hand was, principally, what she was to carry away. This was so near the end of a leave from France that she could only wish him already gone. It was August 1916. Being not kissed, being drawn away from and looked at intimidated Kathleen till she imagined spectral glitters in the place of his eyes. Turning away and looking back up the lawn she saw, through branches of trees, the drawing-room window alight: she caught a breath for the moment when she could go running back there into the safe arms of her mother and sister, and cry: 'What shall I do, what shall I do? He has gone.'

Hearing her catch her breath, her fiancé said, without feeling: 'Cold?'

'You're going away such a long way.'

'Not so far as you think.'

'I don't understand?'

'You don't have to,' he said. 'You will. You know what we said.'

'But that was – suppose you – I mean, suppose.'

'I shall be with you,' he said, 'sooner or later. You won't forget that. You need do nothing but wait.'

Only a little more than a minute later she was free to run up the silent lawn. Looking in through the window at her mother and sister, who did not for the moment perceive her, she already felt that unnatural promise drive down between her and the rest of all human kind. No other way of having given herself could have made her feel so apart, lost and foresworn. She could not have plighted a more sinister troth.

Kathleen behaved well when, some months later, her fiancé was reported missing, presumed killed. Her family not only supported her but were able to praise her courage without stint because they could not regret, as a husband for her, the man they knew almost nothing about. They hoped she would, in a year or two, console herself – and had it been only a question of consolation things might have gone much straighter ahead. But her trouble, behind just a little grief, was a complete dislocation from everything. She did not reject other lovers, for these failed to appear: for years she failed to attract men – and with the approach of her 'thirties she became natural enough to share her family's anxiousness on this score. She began to put herself out, to wonder; and at thirty-two she was very greatly relieved to find herself being courted by William Drover. She married him, and the two of them settled down in this quiet, arboreal part of Kensington: in this house the years piled up, her children were born and they all lived till they were driven out by the bombs of the next war. Her movements as Mrs Drover were circumscribed, and she dismissed any idea that they were still watched.

As things were – dead or living the letter-writer sent her only a threat. Unable, for some minutes, to go on kneeling with her back exposed to the empty room, Mrs Drover rose from the chest to sit on an upright chair whose back was firmly against the wall. The desuetude of her former bedroom, her married London home's whole air of being a cracked cup from which memory, with its reassuring power, had either evaporated or leaked away, made a crisis – and at just this crisis the letter-writer had, knowledgeably, struck. The hollowness of the house this evening cancelled years on years of voices, habits and steps. Through the shut windows she only heard rain fall on the roofs around. To rally herself, she said she was in a mood – and, for two or three seconds shutting her eyes, told herself that she had imagined the letter. But she opened them – there it lay on the bed.

On the supernatural side of the letter's entrance she was not permitting her mind to dwell. Who, in London, knew she meant to call at the house to-day? Evidently, however, this has been known. The caretaker, *had* he come back, had had no cause to expect her: he would have taken the letter in his pocket, to forward it, at his own time, through the post. There was no other sign that the caretaker had been in – but, if not? Letters dropped in at doors of deserted houses do not fly or walk to tables in halls. They do not sit on the dust of empty tables with the air of certainty that they will be found. There is needed some human hand – but nobody but the caretaker had a key. Under circumstances she did not care to consider, a house can be entered without a key. It was possible that she was not alone now. She might be being waited for, downstairs. Waited for – until when? Until 'the hour arranged'. At least that was not six o'clock: six has struck.

She rose from the chair and went over and locked the door.

The thing was, to get out. To fly? No, not that: she had to catch her train. As a woman whose utter dependability was the keystone of her family life she was not willing to return to the country, to her husband, her little boys and her sister, without the objects she had come up to fetch. Resuming work at the chest she set about making up a number of parcels in a rapid, fumbling-decisive way. These, with her shopping parcels, would be too much to carry; these meant a taxi – at the thought of the taxi her heart went up and her normal breathing resumed. I will ring up the taxi now; the taxi cannot come too soon: I shall hear the taxi out there running its engine, till I walk calmly down to it through the hall. I'll ring up – But no: the telephone is cut off . . . She tugged at a knot she had tied wrong.

The idea of flight . . . He was never kind to me, not really. I don't remember him kind at all. Mother said he never considered me. He was set on me, that was what it was – not love. Not love, not meaning a person well. What did he do, to make me promise like that? I can't remember – But she found that she could.

She remembered with such dreadful acuteness that the twenty-five years since then dissolved like smoke and she instinctively looked for the weal left by the button on the palm of her hand. She remembered not only all that he said and did but the complete suspension of *her* existence during that August week. I was not myself – they all told me so at the time. She remembered – but with one white burning blank as where acid has dropped on a photograph: *under no conditions* could she remember his face.

So, wherever he may be waiting, I shall not know him. You have no time to run from a face you do not expect.

The thing was to get to the taxi before any clock struck what could be the hour. She would slip down the street and round the side of the square to where the square gave on the main road. She would return in the taxi, safe, to her own door, and bring the solid driver into the house with her to pick up the parcels from room to room. The idea of the taxi driver made her decisive, bold: she unlocked her door, went to the top of the staircase and listened down.

She heard nothing – but while she was hearing nothing the *passé* air of the staircase was disturbed by a draught that travelled up to her face. It emanated from the basement: down there a door or window was being opened by someone who chose this moment to leave the house.

The rain had stopped; the pavements steamily shone as Mrs Drover let herself out by inches from her own front door into the empty street. The unoccupied houses opposite continued to meet her look with their damaged stare. Making towards the thoroughfare and the taxi, she tried not to keep looking behind. Indeed, the silence was so intense – one of those creeks of London silence exaggerated this summer by the damage of war – that no tread could have gained on hers unheard. Where her street debouched on the square where people went on living, she grew conscious of, and checked, her unnatural pace. Across the open end of the square two buses impassively passed each other: women, a perambulator, cyclists, a man wheeling a barrow signalized, once again, the ordinary flow of life. At the square's most populous corner should be – and was – the short taxi rank. This evening, only one taxi – but this, although it presented its blank rump, appeared already to be alertly waiting for her. Indeed, without looking round the driver started his engine as she panted up from behind and put her hand on the door. As she did so, the clock struck seven. The taxi faced the main road: to make the trip back to her house it would have to turn – she had settled back on the seat and the taxi *had* turned before she, surprised by its knowing movement, recollected that she had not 'said where'. She leaned forward to scratch at the glass panel that divided the driver's head from her own.

The driver braked to what was almost a stop, turned round and slid the glass panel back: the jolt of this flung Mrs Drover forward till her face was almost into the glass. Through the aperture driver and passenger, not six inches between them, remained for an eternity eye to eye. Mrs Drover's mouth hung open for some seconds before she could issue her first scream. After that she continued to scream freely and to beat with her gloved hands on the glass all round as the taxi, accelerating without mercy, made off with her into the hinterland of deserted streets.

# *The Man With The Nose*

Rhoda Broughton

*(The details of this little story are, of course, imaginary, but the main incidents are, to the best of my belief, facts. They happened twenty, or more than twenty years ago.)*

CHAPTER I

'Let us get a map and see what places look pleasantest?' says she.

'As for that,' reply I, 'on a map most places look equally pleasant.'

'Never mind; get one!'

I obey.

'Do you like the seaside?' asks Elizabeth, lifting her little brown head and her small happy white face from the English sea-coast along which her forefinger is slowly travelling.

'Since you ask me, distinctly *no*,' reply I, for once venturing to have a decided opinion of my own, which during the last few weeks of imbecility I can be hardly said to have had. 'I broke my last wooden spade five and twenty years ago. I have but a poor opinion of cockles – sandy red-nosed things, are not they? and the air always makes me bilious.'

'Then we certainly will not go there,' says Elizabeth, laughing. 'A bilious bridegroom! alliterative but horrible! None of our friends show the least eagerness to lend us their country house.'

'Oh that God would put it into the hearts of men to take their wives straight home, as their fathers did!' say I with a cross groan.

'It is evident, therefore, that we must go somewhere,' returns she, not heeding the aspiration contained in my last speech, making her fore-finger resume its employment, and reaching Torquay.

'I suppose so,' say I, with a sort of sigh; 'for once in our lives we must resign ourselves to having the finger of derision pointed at us by waiters and landlords.'

'You shall leave your new portmanteau at home, and I will leave all my best clothes, and nobody will guess that we are bride and bridegroom; they will think that we have been married – oh, ever since the world began' (opening her eyes very wide).

I shake my head. 'With an old portmanteau and in rags we shall still have the mark of the beast upon us.'

'Do you mind much? do you hate being ridiculous?' asks Elizabeth, meekly, rather depressed by my view of the case; 'because if so, let us go somewhere out of the way, where there will be very few people to laugh at us.'

'On the contrary,' return I, stoutly, 'we will betake ourselves to some spot where such as we do chiefly congregate – where we shall be swallowed up and lost in the multitude of our fellow-sinners.' A pause devoted to reflection. 'What do you say to Killarney?' say I cheerfully.

'There are a great many fleas there, I believe,' replied Elizabeth, slowly; 'flea-bites make large lumps on me; you would not like me if I were covered with large lumps.'

At the hideous ideal picture thus presented to me by my little beloved I relapse into inarticulate idiocy; emerging from which by-and-by, I suggest 'The Lakes?' My arm is round her, and I feel her supple body shiver though it is mid July and the bees are booming about in the still and sleepy noon garden outside.

'Oh – no – no – not *there*!'

'Why such emphasis?' I ask gaily; 'more fleas? At this rate, and with this *sine quâ non*, our choice will grow limited.'

'Something dreadful happened to me there,' she says, with another shudder. 'But indeed I did not think there was any harm in it – I never thought anything would come of it.'

'What the devil was it?' cry I, in a jealous heat and hurry; 'what the mischief *did* you do, and why have not you told me about it before?'

'I did not *do* much,' she answers meekly, seeking for my hand, and when found kissing it in timid deprecation of my wrath; 'but I was ill – very ill – there; I had a nervous fever. I was in a bed hung with a chintz with a red and green fern-leaf pattern on it. I have always hated red and green fern-leaf chintzes ever since.'

'It would be possible to avoid the obnoxious bed, would not it?' say I, laughing a little. 'Where does it lie? Windermere? Ulleswater? Wastwater? Where?'

'We were at Ulleswater,' she says, speaking rapidly, while a hot colour grows on her small white cheeks – 'Papa, mamma, and I; and there came a mesmeriser to Penrith, and we went to see him – everybody did – and he asked leave to mesmerise me – he said I should be such a good medium – and – and – I did not know what it was like. I thought it would be quite good fun – and – and – I let him.'

She is trembling exceedingly; even the loving pressure of my arms cannot abate her shivering.

'Well?'

'And after that I do not remember anything – I believe I did all sorts of extraordinary things that he told me – sang and danced, and made a fool of myself – but when I came home I was very ill, very – I lay in bed for five whole weeks, and – and was off my head, and said odd and wicked things that you would not have expected me to say – that dreadful bed! shall I ever forget it?'

'We will *not* go to the Lakes,' I say, decisively, 'and we will not talk any more about mesmerism.'

'That is right,' she says, with a sigh of relief, 'I try to think about it as little as possible; but sometimes, in the dead black of the night, when God seems a long way off, and the devil near, it comes back to me so strongly – I feel, do not you know, as if he were *there* somewhere in the room, and I *must* get up and follow him.'

'Why should not we go abroad?' suggest I, abruptly turning the conversation.

'Why, indeed?' cries Elizabeth, recovering her gaiety, while her pretty blue eyes begin to dance. 'How stupid of us not to have thought of it before; only *abroad* is a big word. *What* abroad?'

'We must be content with something short of Central Africa,' I say, gravely, 'as I think our one hundred and fifty pounds would hardly take us that far.'

'Wherever we go, we must buy a dialogue book,' suggests

my little bride-elect, 'and I will learn some phrases before we start.'

'As for that, the Anglo-Saxon tongue takes one pretty well round the world,' reply I, with a feeling of complacent British swagger, putting my hands in my breeches pockets.

'Do you fancy the Rhine?' says Elizabeth, with a rather timid suggestion; 'I know it is the fashion to run it down nowadays, and call it a cocktail river; but – but – after all it cannot be so *very* contemptible, or Byron could not have said such noble things about it.'

' "The castled crag of Drachenfels
Frowns o'er the wide and winding Rhine,
Whose breast of waters broadly swells
Between the banks which bear the vine," '

say I, spouting. 'After all, that proves nothing, for Byron could have made a silk purse out of a sow's ear.'

'The Rhine will not do then?' says she resignedly, suppressing a sigh.

'On the contrary, it will do admirably: it *is* a cocktail river, and I do not care who says it is not,' reply I, with illiberal positiveness; 'but everybody should be able to say so from their own experience, and not from hearsay: the Rhine let it be, by all means.'

So the Rhine it is.

## CHAPTER II

I have got over it; we have both got over it, tolerably, creditably; but after all, it is a much severer ordeal for a man than a woman, who, with a bouquet to occupy her hands, and a veil to gently shroud her features, need merely be prettily passive. I am alluding, I need hardly say, to the religious ceremony of marriage, which I flatter myself I have gone through with a stiff sheepishness not unworthy of my country. It is a three-days-old event now, and we are getting used to belonging to one another, though Elizabeth still takes off her ring twenty times a day to admire its bright thickness; still laughs when she hears herself called 'Madame'. Three days ago, we kissed all our friends, and left them to make themselves ill on our cake, and criticise our bridal behaviour, and now we are at Brussels, she and I, feeling oddly, joyfully free from any chaperone. We have been mildly sightseeing – very mildly most people would say, but we have resolved not to take our pleasure with the railway speed of Americans, or the hasty sadness of our fellow Britons. Slowly and gaily we have been taking ours. Today we have been to visit Wiertz's pictures. Have you ever seen them, oh reader? They are known to comparatively few people, but if you have a taste for the unearthly terrible – if you wish to sup full of horrors, hasten thither, we have been peering through the appointed peep-hole at the horrible cholera picture – the man buried alive by mistake, pushing up the lid of his coffin, and stretching a ghastly face and livid hands out of his winding sheet towards you, while awful grey-blue coffins are piled around, and noisome toads and giant spiders crawl damply about. On first seeing it, I have reproached myself for bringing one of so nervous a temperament as Elizabeth to see so haunting and hideous a spectacle; but she is less impressed than I expected – less impressed than I myself am.

'He is very lucky to be able to get his lid up,' she says, with a half-laugh; 'we should find it hard work to burst our brass nails, should not we? When you bury me, dear, fasten me down very slightly, in case there may be some mistake.'

And now all the long and quiet July evening we have been prowling together about the streets. Brussels is the town of towns for *flâner*-ing – have been flattening our noses against the shop windows, and making each other imaginary presents. Elizabeth has not confined herself to imagination, however; she has made me buy her a little bonnet with feathers – 'in order to look married,' as she says, and the result is such a delicious picture of a child playing at being grown up, having practised a theft on its mother's wardrobe, that for the last two hours I have been in a foolish ecstasy of love and laughter over her and it. We are at the 'Bellevue,' and have a fine suite of rooms, *au premier*, evidently specially devoted to the English, to the gratification of whose well-known loyalty the Prince and Princess of Wales are simpering from the walls. Is there any one in the three kingdoms who knows his own face as well as he knows the faces of Albert Victor and Alexandra? The long evening has at last slidden into night – night far advanced – night melting into earliest day. All Brussels is asleep. One moment ago I also was asleep, soundly as any log. What is it that has made me take this sudden, headlong plunge out of sleep into wakefulness? Who is it that is clutching at and calling upon me? What is it that is making me struggle mistily up into a sitting posture, and try to revive my sleep-numbed senses? A summer night is never wholly dark; by the half light that steals through the closed *persiennes* and open windows I see my wife standing beside my bed; the extremity of terror on her face, and her fingers digging themselves with painful tenacity into my arm.

'Tighter, tighter!' she is crying, wildly. 'What are you thinking of? You are letting me go!'

'Good heavens!' say I, rubbing my eyes, while my muddy brain grows a trifle clearer. 'What is it? What has happened? Have you had a nightmare?'

'You saw him,' she says, with a sort of sobbing breathlessness; 'you know you did! You saw him as well as I.'

'I!' cry I, incredulously – 'not I! Till this second I have been fast asleep. *I* saw nothing.'

'You did!' she cries, passionately. 'You know you did. Why do you deny it? You were as frightened as I.'

'As I live,' I answer, solemnly, 'I know no more than the dead what you are talking about; till you woke me by calling and catching hold of me, I was as sound asleep as the seven sleepers.'

'Is it possible that it can have been a *dream*?' she says, with a long sigh, for a moment loosing my arm, and covering her face with her hands. 'But no – in a dream I should have been somewhere else, but I was here – *here* – on that bed, and he stood *there*,' pointing with her forefinger, 'just *there*, between the foot of it and the window!'

She stops, panting.

'It is all that brute Wiertz,' say I, in a fury. 'I wish I had been buried alive myself before I had been fool enough to take you to see his beastly daubs.'

'Light a candle,' she says, in the same breathless way, her teeth chattering with fright. 'Let us make sure he is not hidden somewhere in the room.'

'How could he be?' say I, striking a match; 'the door is locked.'

'He might have got in by the balcony,' she answers, still trembling violently.

'He would have had to have cut a very large hole in the *persiennes*,' say I, half mockingly. 'See, they are intact, and well fastened on the inside.'

She sinks into an arm-chair, and pushes her loose soft hair from her white face.

'It *was* a dream then, I suppose?'

She is silent for a moment or two, while I bring her a glass of water, and throw a dressing-gown round her cold and shrinking form.

'Now tell me, my little one,' I say coaxingly, sitting down at her feet, 'what it was – what you thought you saw?'

'*Thought* I saw!' echoes she, with indignant emphasis, sitting upright, while her eyes sparkle feverishly. 'I am as certain that I saw him standing there as I am that I see that candle burning – that I see this chair – that I see you.'

'*Him*! but who is *him*?'

She falls forward on my neck, and buries her face in my shoulder.

'That – dreadful – man!' she says, while her whole body is one tremor.

'*What* dreadful man?' cry I impatiently.

She is silent.

'Who was he?'

'I do not know.'

'Did you ever see him before?'

'Oh, no – no, never! I hope to God I may never see him again!'

'What was he like?'

'Come closer to me,' she says, laying hold of my hand with her small and chilly fingers; 'stay *quite* near me, and I will tell you,' – after a pause – 'he had a *nose*!'

'My dear soul,' cry I, bursting out into a loud laugh in the silence of the night, 'do not most people have noses? Would not he have been much more dreadful if he had had *none*?'

'But it was *such* a nose!' she says, with perfect trembling gravity.

'A bottle nose?' suggest I, still cackling.

'For heaven's sake, don't laugh!' she says nervously; 'if you had seen his face, you would have been as little disposed to laugh as I.'

'But his nose?' return I, suppressing my merriment, 'what kind of nose was it? See, I am as grave as a judge.'

‘It was very prominent,’ she answers, in a sort of awe-struck half-whisper, ‘and very sharply chiselled; the nostrils very much cut out.’ A little pause. ‘His eyebrows were one straight black line across his face, and under them his eyes burnt like dull coals of fire, that shone and yet did not shine; they looked like dead eyes, sunken, half extinguished, and yet sinister.’

‘And what did he do?’ asked I, impressed, despite myself, by her passionate earnestness; ‘when did you first see him?’

‘I was asleep,’ she said – ‘at least, I thought so – and suddenly I opened my eyes, and he was *there* – *there*’ – pointing again with trembling finger – ‘between the window and the bed.’

‘What was he doing? Was he walking about?’

‘He was standing as still as stone – I never saw any live thing so still – *looking* at me; he never called or beckoned, or moved a finger, but his eyes *commanded* me to come to him, as the eyes of the mesmeriser at Penrith did.’ She stops, breathing heavily. I can hear her heart’s loud and rapid beats.

‘And you?’ I say, pressing her more closely to my side, and smoothing her troubled hair.

‘I *hated* it,’ she cries, excitedly; ‘I loathed it – abhorred it. I was ice-cold with fear and horror, but – I *felt* myself going to him.’

‘Yes?’

‘And then I shrieked out to you, and you came running, and caught fast hold of me, and held me tight at first – quite tight – but presently I felt your hold slacken – slacken – and though I *longed* to stay with you, though I was *mad* with fright, yet I felt myself pulling strongly away from you – going to him; and he – he stood there always looking – looking – and then I gave one last loud shriek, and I suppose I awoke – and it was a dream!’

‘I never heard of a clearer case of nightmare,’ say I, stoutly, ‘that vile Wiertz! I should like to see his whole *Musée* burnt by the hands of the hangman tomorrow.’

She shakes her head. ‘It had nothing to say to Wiertz; what it meant I do not know, but – ’

‘It meant nothing,’ I answer, reassuringly, ‘except that for the future we will go and see none but good and pleasant sights, and steer clear of charnel-house fancies.’

## CHAPTER III

Elizabeth is now in a position to decide whether the Rhine is a cocktail river or no, for she is on it, and so am I. We are sitting, with an awning over our heads, and little wooden stools under our feet. Elizabeth has a small sailor's hat and blue ribbon on her head. The river breeze has blown it rather awry; has tangled her plenteous hair; has made a faint pink stain on her pale cheeks. It is some fête day, and the boat is crowded. Tables, countless camp stools, volumes of black smoke pouring from the funnel, as we steam along. 'Nothing to the Caledonian Canal!' cries a burly Scotchman in leggings, speaking with loud authority, and surveying with an air of contempt the eternal vine-clad slopes, that sound so well, and look so *sticky* in reality. 'Cannot hold a candle to it!' A rival bride and bridegroom opposite, sitting together like love-birds under an umbrella, looking into each other's eyes instead of at the Rhine scenery.

'They might as well have stayed at home, might not they?' says my wife, with a little air of superiority. 'Come, we are not so bad as that, are we?'

A storm comes on: hailstones beat slantwise and reach us – stone and sting us right under our awning. Everybody rushes down below, and takes the opportunity to feed ravenously. There are few actions more disgusting than eating *can* be made. A handsome girl close to us – her immaturity evidenced by the two long tails of black hair down her back – is thrusting her knife halfway down her throat.

'Come on deck again,' says Elizabeth, disgusted and frightened at this last sight. 'The hail was much better than this!'

So we return to our camp stools, and sit alone under one mackintosh in the lashing storm, with happy hearts and empty stomachs.

'Is not this better than any luncheon?' asks Elizabeth, triumphantly, while the rain-drops hang on her long and curled lashes.

'Infinitely better,' reply I, madly struggling with the umbrella to prevent its being blown inside out, and gallantly ignoring a species of gnawing sensation at my entrails.

The squall clears off by-and-by, and we go steaming, steaming on past the unnumbered little villages by the water's edge with church spires and pointed roofs, past the countless rocks with their little pert castles perched on the top of them, past the tall, stiff poplar rows. The church bells are ringing gaily as we go by. A nightingale is singing from a wood. The black eagle of Prussia droops on the stream behind us, swish-swish through the dull green water. A fat woman who is interested in it, leans over the back of the boat, and by some happy effect of crinoline, displays to her fellow-passengers two yards of thick white cotton legs. She is, fortunately for herself, unconscious of her generosity.

The day steals on; at every stopping place more people come on. There is hardly elbow room; and, what is worse, almost everybody is drunk. Rocks, castles, villages, poplars, slide by, while the paddles churn always the water, and the evening draws greyly on. At Bingen a party of big blue Prussian soldiers, very drunk, 'glorious' as Tam o' Shanter, come and establish themselves close to us. They call for Lager Beer; talk at the tip-top of their strong voices; two of them begin to spar; all seem inclined to sing. Elizabeth is frightened. We are two hours late in arriving at Biebrich. It is half an hour more before we can get ourselves and our luggage into a carriage and set off along the winding road to Wiesbaden. 'The night is chilly, but not dark.' There is only a little shabby bit of a moon, but it shines as hard as it can. Elizabeth is quite worn out, her tired head droops in uneasy sleep on my shoulder. Once she wakes up with a start.

'Are you sure that it meant nothing?' she asks, looking me eagerly in my face; 'do people often have such dreams?'

'Often, often,' I answer, reassuringly.

'I am always afraid of falling asleep now,' she says, trying to sit upright and keep her heavy eyes open, 'for fear of seeing him standing there again. Tell me, do you think I shall? Is there any chance, any probability of it?'

'None, none!'

We reach Wiesbaden at last, and drive up to the Hôtel des Quatre Saisons. By this time it is full midnight. Two or three men are standing about the door. Morris, the maid, has gone out – so have I, and I am holding out my hand to Elizabeth when I hear her give one piercing scream, and see her with ash-white face and starting eyes point with her fore-finger –

'There he is! – there! – there!'

I look in the direction indicated, and just catch a glimpse of a tall figure standing half in the shadow of the night, half in the gas-light from the hotel. I have not time for more than one cursory glance, as I am interrupted by a cry from the bystanders, and turning quickly round, am just in time to catch my wife, who falls in utter insensibility into my arms. We carry her into a room on the ground floor; it is small, noisy, and hot, but it is the nearest at hand. In about an hour she re-opens her eyes. A strong shudder makes her quiver from head to foot.

'Where is he?' she says, in a terrified whisper, as her senses come slowly back. 'He is somewhere about – somewhere near. I feel that he is!'

'My dearest child, there is no one here but Morris and me,' I answer soothingly. 'Look for yourself. See.'

I take one of the candles and light up each corner of the room in succession.

'You saw him!' she says, in trembling hurry, sitting up and clenching her hands together. 'I know you did – I pointed him out to you – you *cannot* say that it was a dream *this* time.'

'I saw two or three ordinary-looking men as we drove up,' I answer, in a commonplace, matter-of-fact tone. 'I did not notice anything remarkable about any of them; you know, the fact is, darling, that you have had nothing to eat all day, nothing but a biscuit, and you are overwrought, and fancy things.'

'Fancy!' echoes she, with strong irritation. 'How you talk! Was I ever one to fancy things! I tell you that as sure as I sit here – as sure as you stand there – I saw him – *him* – the man I saw in my dream, if it was a dream. There was not a hair's breadth of difference between them – and he was looking at me – looking –'

She breaks off into hysterical sobbing.

'My dear child!' say I, thoroughly alarmed, and yet half angry, 'for God's sake do not work yourself up into a fever: wait till tomorrow, and we will find out who he is, and all about him; you yourself will laugh when we discover that he is some harmless bagman.'

'Why not *now*?' she says, nervously; 'why cannot you find out *now – this minute*?'

'Impossible! Everybody is in bed! Wait till tomorrow, and all will be cleared up.'

The morrow comes, and I go about the hotel, inquiring. The house is so full, and the data I have to go upon are so small, that for some time I have great difficulty in making it understood to whom I am alluding. At length one waiter seems to comprehend.

'A tall and dark gentleman, with a pronounced and very peculiar nose? Yes; there has been such a one, certainly, in the hotel, but he left at "grand matin" this morning; he remained only one night.'

'And his name?'

The garçon shakes his head. 'That is unknown, monsieur; he did not inscribe it in the visitors' book.'

'What countryman was he?'

Another shake of the head. 'He spoke German, but it was with a foreign accent.'

'Whither did he go?'

That also is unknown. Nor can I arrive at any more facts about him.

## CHAPTER IV

A fortnight has passed; we have been hither and thither; now we are at Lucerne. Peopled with better inhabitants, Lucerne might well do for Heaven. It is drawing towards eventide, and Elizabeth and I are sitting hand in hand on a quiet bench, under the shady linden trees, on a high hill up above the lake. There is nobody to see us, so we sit peaceably hand in hand. Up by the still and solemn monastery we came, with its small and narrow windows, calculated to hinder the holy fathers from promenading curious eyes on the world, the flesh, and the devil, tripping past them in blue gauze veils: below us grass and green trees, houses with high-pitched roofs, little dormer-windows, and shutters yet greener than the grass; below us the lake in its rippleless peace, calm, quiet, motionless as Bethesda's pool before the coming of the troubling angel.

'I said it was too good to last,' say I, doggedly, 'did not I, only yesterday? Perfect peace, perfect sympathy, perfect freedom from nagging worries – when did such a state of things last more than two days?'

Elizabeth's eyes are idly fixed on a little steamer, with a stripe of red along its side, and a tiny puff of smoke from its funnel, gliding along and cutting a narrow white track on Lucerne's sleepy surface.

'This is the fifth false alarm of the gout having gone to his stomach within the last two years,' continue I resentfully. 'I declare to Heaven, that if it has not really gone there this time, I'll cut the whole concern.'

Let no one cast up their eyes in horror, imagining that it is my father to whom I am thus alluding; it is only a great-uncle by marriage, in consideration of whose wealth and vague promises I have dawdled professionless through twenty-eight years of my life.

'You *must* not go,' says Elizabeth, giving my hand an imploring squeeze. 'The man in the Bible said, "I have married a wife, and therefore I cannot come;" why should it be a less valid excuse nowadays?'

'If I recollect rightly, it was considered rather a poor one even then,' reply I, dryly.

Elizabeth is unable to contradict this; she therefore only lifts two pouted lips (Monsieur Taine objects to the redness of English women's mouths, but I do not) to be kissed, and says, 'Stay.' I am good enough to comply with her unspoken request, though I remain firm with regard to her spoken one.

'My dearest child,' I say, with an air of worldly experience and superior wisdom, 'kisses are very good things – in fact, there are few better – but one cannot live upon them.'

'Let us try,' she says coaxingly.

'I wonder which would get tired first?' I say, laughing. But she only goes on pleading, 'Stay, stay.'

'How *can* I stay?' I cry impatiently; 'you talk as if I *wanted* to go! Do you think it is any pleasanter to me to leave you than to you to be left? But you know his disposition, his rancorous resentment of fancied neglects. For the sake of two days' indulgence, must I throw away what will keep us in ease and plenty to the end of our days?'

'I do not care for plenty,' she says, with a little petulant gesture. 'I do not see that rich people are any happier than poor ones. Look at the St. Clairs; they have £40,000 a year, and she is a miserable woman, perfectly miserable, because her face gets red after dinner.'

'There will be no fear of *our* faces getting red after dinner,' say I, grimly, 'for we shall have no dinner for them to get red after.'

A pause. My eyes stray away to the mountains. Pilatus on the right, with his jagged peak and slender snow-chains about his harsh neck; hill after hill rising silent, eternal, like guardian spirits standing hand in hand around their child, the lake. As I look, suddenly they have all flushed, as at some noblest thought, and over all their sullen faces streams an ineffable rosy joy – a solemn and wonderful effulgence, such as Israel saw reflected from the features of the Eternal in their prophet's transfigured eyes. The unutterable peace and stainless beauty of earth and sky seemed to lie softly on my soul. 'Would God I could stay! Would God all life could be like this!' I say, devoutly, and the aspiration has the reverent earnestness of a prayer.

'Why do you say, "*Would God*!" ' she cries passionately, 'when it lies with yourself? Oh my dear love,' gently sliding her hand through my arm, and lifting wetly-beseeching eyes to my face, 'I do not know why I insist upon it so much – I cannot tell you myself – I dare say I seem selfish and unreasonable – but I feel as if your going now would be the end of all things – as if – ' She breaks off suddenly.

'My child,' say I, thoroughly distressed, but still determined to have my own way, 'you talk as if I were going for ever and a day; in a week, at the outside, I shall be back, and then you will thank me for the very thing for which you now think me so hard and disobliging.'

'Shall I?' she answers, mournfully. 'Well, I hope so.'

'You will not be alone, either; you will have Morris.'

'Yes.'

'And every day you will write me a long letter, telling me every single thing that you do, say, and think.'

'Yes.'

She answers me gently and obediently; but I can see that she is still utterly unreconciled to the idea of my absence.

'What is it that you are afraid of?' I ask, becoming rather irritated. 'What do you suppose will happen to you?'

She does not answer; only a large tear falls on my hand, which she hastily wipes away with her pocket handkerchief, as if afraid of exciting my wrath.

'Can you give me any good reason why I *should* stay?' I ask, dictatorially.

'None – none – only – stay – stay!'

But I am resolved *not* to stay. Early the next morning I set off.

## CHAPTER V

This time it is not a false alarm; this time it really has gone to his stomach, and, declining to be dislodged thence, kills him. My return is therefore retarded until after the funeral and the reading of the will. The latter is so satisfactory, and my time is so fully occupied with a multiplicity of attendant business, that I have no leisure to regret the delay. I write to Elizabeth, but receive no letters from her. This surprises and makes me rather angry, but does not alarm me. 'If she had been ill, if anything had happened, Morris would have written. She never was great at writing, poor little soul. What dear little babyish notes she used to send me during our engagement! Perhaps she wishes to punish me for my disobedience to her wishes. Well, *now* she will see who was in the right.' I am drawing near her now; I am walking up from the railway station at Lucerne. I am very joyful as I march along under an umbrella, in the grand broad shining of the summer afternoon. I think with pensive passion of the last glimpse I had of my beloved – her small and wistful face looking out from among the thick fair fleece of her long hair – winking away her tears and blowing kisses to me. It is a new sensation to me to have anyone looking tearfully wistful over my departure. I draw near the great glaring Schweizerhof, with its colonnaded tourist-crowded porch; here are all the pomegranates as I left them, in their green tubs, with their scarlet blossoms, and the dusty oleanders in a row. I look up at our windows: nobody is looking out from them; they are open, and the curtains are alternately swelled out and drawn in by the softly-playful wind. I run quickly upstairs and burst noisily into the sitting-room. Empty, perfectly empty! I open the adjoining door into the bedroom, crying 'Elizabeth! Elizabeth!' but I receive no answer. Empty too. A feeling of indignation creeps over me as I think, 'Knowing the time of my return, she might have managed to be indoors.' I have returned to the silent sitting-room, where the only noise is the wind still playing hide-and-seek with the curtains. As I look vacantly round my eye catches sight of a letter lying on the table. I pick it up mechanically and look at the address. Good heavens! what can this mean? It is my own, that I sent her two days ago, unopened, with the seal unbroken. Does she carry her resentment so far as not even to open my letters? I spring at the bell and violently ring it. It is answered by the waiter who has always specially attended us.

'Is madame gone out?'

The man opens his mouth and stares at me.

'Madame! Is monsieur then not aware that madame is no longer at the hotel?'

'*What*?'

'On the same day as monsieur, madame departed.'

'*Departed*! Good God! what are you talking about?'

'A few hours after monsieur's departure – I will not be positive as to the exact time, but it must have been between one and two o'clock as the midday *table d'hôte* was in progress – a gentleman came and asked for madame –'

'Yes – be quick.'

'I demanded whether I should take up his card, but he said "No," that was unnecessary, as he was perfectly well known to madame; and, in fact, a short time afterwards, without saying anything to anyone, she departed with him.'

'And did not return in the evening?'

'No, monsieur; madame has not returned since that day.'

I clench my hands in an agony of rage and grief. 'So this is it! With that pure child-face, with that divine ignorance – only three weeks married – this is the trick she has played me!' I am recalled to myself by a compassionate suggestion from the garçon.

'Perhaps it was the brother of madame.'

Elizabeth has no brother, but the remark brings back to me the necessity of self-command. 'Very probably,' I answer, speaking with infinite difficulty. 'What sort of looking gentleman was he?'

'He was a very tall and dark gentleman with a most peculiar nose – not quite like any nose that I ever saw before – and most singular eyes. Never have I seen a gentleman who at all resembled him.'

I sink into a chair, while a cold shudder creeps over me as I think of my poor child's dream – of her fainting fit at Wiesbaden – of her unconquerable dread of and aversion from my departure. And this happened twelve days ago! I catch up my hat, and prepare to rush like a madman in pursuit.

'How did they go?' I ask incoherently; 'by train? – driving? – walking?'

'They went in a carriage.'

'What direction did they take? Whither did they go?'

He shakes his head. 'It is not known.'

'It *must* be known,' I cry, driven to frenzy by every second's delay. 'Of course the driver could tell; where is he? – where can I find him?'

'He did not belong to Lucerne, neither did the carriage; the gentleman brought them with him.'

'But madame's maid,' say I, a gleam of hope flashing across my mind; 'did she go with her?'

'No, monsieur, she is still here; she was as much surprised as monsieur at madame's departure.'

'Send her at once,' I cry eagerly; but when she comes I find that she can throw no light on the matter. She weeps noisily and says many irrelevant things, but I can obtain no information from her beyond the fact that she was unaware of her mistress's departure until long after it had taken place, when, surprised at not being rung for at the usual time, she had gone to her room and found it empty, and on inquiring in the hotel, had heard of her sudden departure; that, expecting her to return at night, she had sat up waiting for her till two o'clock in the morning, but that, as I knew, she had not returned, neither had anything since been heard of her.

Not all my inquiries, not all my cross-questionings of the whole staff of the hotel, of the visitors, of the railway officials, of nearly all the inhabitants of Lucerne and its environs, procure me a jot more knowledge. On the next few weeks I look back as on a hellish and insane dream. I can neither eat nor sleep; I am unable to remain one moment quiet; my whole existence, my nights and my days, are spent in seeking, seeking. Everything that human despair and frenzied love can do is done by me. I advertise, I communicate with the police, I employ detectives; but that fatal twelve days' start for ever baffles me. Only on one occasion do I obtain one tittle of information. In a village a few miles from Lucerne the peasants, on the day in question, saw a carriage driving rapidly through their little street. It was closed, but through the windows they could see the occupants – a dark gentleman, with the peculiar physiognomy which has been so often described, and on the opposite seat a lady lying apparently in a state of utter insensibility. But even this leads to nothing.

Oh, reader, these things happened twenty years ago; since then I have searched sea and land, but never have I seen my little Elizabeth again.

# *The Dream-Woman*

Wilkie Collins

## CHAPTER I

I had not been settled much more than six weeks in my country practice, when I was sent for to a neighbouring town, to consult with the resident medical man there on a case of very dangerous illness.

My horse had come down with me at the end of a long ride the night before, and had hurt himself, luckily, much more than he had hurt his master. Being deprived of the animal's services, I started for my destination by the coach (there were no railways at that time), and I hoped to get back again, towards the afternoon, in the same way.

After the consultation was over, I went to the principal inn of the town to wait for the coach. When it came up it was full inside and out. There was no resource left me but to get home as cheaply as I could by hiring a gig. The price asked for this accommodation struck me as being so extortionate that I determined to look out for an inn of inferior pretensions, and to try if I could not make a better bargain with a less prosperous establishment.

I soon found a likely-looking house, dingy and quiet, with an old-fashioned sign, that had evidently not been repainted for many years past. The landlord, in this case, was not above making a small profit, and as soon as we came to terms he rang the yard-bell to order the gig.

'Has Robert not come back from that errand?' asked the landlord, appealing to the waiter who answered the bell.

'No, sir, he hasn't.'

'Well, then, you must wake up Isaac.'

'Wake up Isaac!' I repeated; 'that sounds rather odd. Do your ostlers go to bed in the daytime?'

'This one does,' said the landlord, smiling to himself in rather a strange way.

'And dreams too,' added the waiter; 'I shan't forget the turn it gave me the first time I heard him.'

'Never you mind about that,' retorted the proprietor; 'you go and rouse Isaac up. The gentleman's waiting for his gig.'

The landlord's manner and the waiter's manner expressed a great deal more than they either of them said. I began to suspect that I might be on the trace of something professionally interesting to me as a medical man, and I thought I should like to look at the ostler before the waiter awakened him.

'Stop a minute,' I interposed; 'I have rather a fancy for seeing this man before you wake him up. I'm a doctor; and if this queer sleeping and dreaming of his comes from anything wrong in his brain, I may be able to tell you what to do with him.'

'I rather think you will find his complaint past all doctoring, sir,' said the landlord; 'but if you would like to see him, you're welcome, I'm sure.'

He led the way across a yard and down a passage to the stables, opened one of the doors, and, waiting outside himself, told me to look in.

I found myself in a two-stall stable. In one of the stalls a horse was munching his corn; in the other an old man was lying asleep on the litter.

I stooped and looked at him attentively. It was a withered, woebegone face. The eyebrows were painfully contracted; the mouth was fast set, and drawn down at the corners. The hollow wrinkled cheeks, and the scanty grizzled hair, told their own tale of some past sorrow or suffering. He was drawing his breath convulsively when I first looked at him, and in a moment more he began to talk in his sleep.

'Wake up!' I heard him say, in a quick whisper, through his clenched teeth. 'Wake up there! Murder!'

He moved one lean arm slowly till it rested over his throat, shuddered a little, and turned on his straw. Then the arm left his throat, the hand stretched itself out, and clutched at the side towards which he had turned, as if he fancied himself to be grasping at the edge of something. I saw his lips move, and bent lower over him. He was still talking in his sleep.

'Light grey eyes,' he murmured, 'and a droop in the left eyelid; flaxen hair, with a gold-yellow streak in it – all right, mother – fair white arms, with a down on them – little lady's hand, with a reddish look under the finger-nails. The knife – always the cursed knife – first on one side, then on the other. Aha! you she-devil, where's the knife?'

At the last word his voice rose, and he grew restless on a sudden. I saw him shudder on the straw; his withered face became distorted, and he threw up both his hands with a quick hysterical gasp. They struck against the bottom of the manger under which he lay, and the blow awakened him. I had just time to slip through the door and close it before his eyes were fairly open, and his senses his own again.

'Do you know anything about that man's past life?' I said to the landlord.

'Yes, sir, I know pretty well all about it,' was the answer, 'and an uncommon queer story it is. Most people don't believe it. It's true, though, for all that. Why, just look at him,' continued the landlord, opening the stable door again. 'Poor devil! he's so worn out with his restless nights that he's dropped back into his sleep already.'

'Don't wake him,' I said. 'I'm in no hurry for the gig. Wait till the other man comes back from his errand; and, in the meantime, suppose I have some lunch and a bottle of sherry, and suppose you come and help me to get through it?'

The heart of mine host, as I had anticipated, warmed to me over his own wine. He soon became communicative on the subject of the man asleep in the stable, and by little and little I drew the whole story out of him. Extravagant and incredible as the events must appear to everybody, they are related here just as I heard them and just as they happened.

## CHAPTER II

Some years ago there lived in the suburbs of a large seaport town on the west coast of England a man in humble circumstances, by name Isaac Scatchard. His means of subsistence were derived from any employment that he could get as an ostler, and occasionally, when times went well with him, from temporary engagements in service as stable-helper in private houses. Though a faithful, steady, and honest man, he got on badly in his calling. His ill luck was proverbial among his neighbours. He was always missing good opportunities by no fault of his own, and always living longest in service with amiable people who were not punctual payers of wages. 'Unlucky Isaac' was his nickname in his own neighbourhood, and no one could say that he did not richly deserve it.

With far more than one man's fair share of adversity to endure, Isaac had but one consolation to support him, and that was of the dreariest and most negative kind. He had no wife and children to increase his anxieties and add to the bitterness of his various failures in life. It might have been from mere insensibility, or it might have been from generous unwillingness to involve another in his own unlucky destiny; but the fact undoubtedly was, that he had arrived at the middle term of life without marrying, and, what is much more remarkable, without once exposing himself, from eighteen to eight-and-thirty, to the genial imputation of ever having had a sweetheart.

When he was out of service he lived alone with his widowed mother. Mrs Scatchard was a woman above the average in her lowly station as to capacity and manners. She had seen better days, as the phrase is, but she never referred to them in the presence of curious visitors; and, though perfectly polite to everyone who approached her, never cultivated any intimacies among her neighbours. She contrived to provide, hardly enough, for her simple wants by doing rough work for the tailors, and always managed to keep a decent home for her son to return to whenever his ill luck drove him out helpless into the world.

One bleak autumn, when Isaac was getting on fast towards forty, and when he was, as usual, out of place through no fault of his own, he set forth from his mother's cottage on a long walk inland to a gentleman's seat where he had heard that a stable-helper was required.

It wanted then but two days of his birthday; and Mrs Scatchard, with her usual fondness, made him promise, before he started, that he would be back in time to keep that anniversary with her, in as festive a way as their poor means would allow. It was easy for him to comply with this request, even supposing he slept a night each way on the road.

He was to start from home on Monday morning, and, whether he got the new place or not, he was to be back for his birthday dinner on Wednesday at two o'clock.

Arriving at his destination too late on the Monday night to make application for the stable-helper's place, he slept at the village inn, and in good time on the Tuesday morning presented himself at the gentleman's house to fill the vacant situation. Here again his ill luck pursued him as inexorably as ever. The excellent written testimonials to his character which he was able to produce availed him nothing; his long walk had been taken in vain: only the day before the stable-helper's place had been given to another man.

Isaac accepted this new disappointment resignedly and as a matter of course. Naturally slow in capacity, he had the bluntness of sensibility and phlegmatic patience of disposition which frequently distinguish men with sluggishly-working mental powers. He thanked the gentleman's steward with his usual quiet civility for granting him an interview, and took his departure with no appearance of unusual depression in his face or manner.

Before starting on his homeward walk, he made some inquiries at the inn, and ascertained that he might save a few miles on his return by following a new road. Furnished with full instructions, several times repeated, as to the various turnings he was to take, he set forth on his homeward journey, and walked on all day with only one stoppage for bread and cheese. Just as it was getting towards dark, the rain came on and the wind began to rise, and he found himself, to make matters worse, in a part of the country with which he was entirely unacquainted, though he knew himself to be some fifteen miles from home. The first house he found to inquire at was a lonely roadside inn standing on the outskirts of a thick wood. Solitary as the place looked, it was welcome to a lost man who was also hungry, thirsty, footsore, and wet. The landlord was civil and respectable-looking, and the price he asked for a bed was reasonable enough. Isaac therefore decided on stopping comfortably at the inn for that night.

He was constitutionally a temperate man. His supper consisted of two rashers of bacon, a slice of home-made bread, and a pint of ale. He did not go to bed immediately after this moderate meal, but sat up with the landlord, talking about his bad prospects and his long run of ill luck, and diverging from these topics to the subjects of horse-flesh and racing. Nothing was said either by himself, his host, or the few labourers who strayed into the taproom, which could, in the slightest degree, excite the very small and very dull imaginative faculty which Isaac Scatchard possessed.

At a little after eleven the house was closed. Isaac went round with the landlord and held the candle while the doors and lower windows were being secured. He noticed with surprise the strength of the bolts and bars, and iron-sheathed shutters.

'You see, we are rather lonely here,' said the landlord. 'We never have had any attempts made to break in yet, but it's always as well to be on the safe side. When nobody is sleeping here, I am the only man in the house. My wife and daughter are timid, and the servant-girl takes after her missuses. Another glass of ale before you turn in? No! Well, how such a sober man as you comes to be out of place is more than I can make out, for one. Here's where you're to sleep. You're our only lodger to-night, and I think you'll say my missus has done her best to make you comfortable. You're quite sure you won't have another glass of ale? Very well. Good night.'

It was half-past eleven by the clock in the passage as they went upstairs to the bedroom, the window of which looked on to the wood at the back of the house.

Isaac locked the door, set his candle on the chest of drawers, and wearily got ready for bed. The bleak autumn wind was still blowing, and the solemn, monotonous surging, moan of it in the wood was dreary and awful to hear through the night-silence. Isaac felt strangely wakeful. He resolved, as he lay down in bed, to keep the candle alight until he began to grow sleepy, for there was something unendurably depressing in the bare idea of lying awake in the darkness, listening to the dismal, ceaseless moaning of the wind in the wood.

Sleep stole on him before he was aware of it. His eyes closed, and he fell off insensibly to rest without having so much as thought of extinguishing the candle.

The first sensation of which he was conscious after sinking into slumber was a strange shivering that ran through him suddenly from head to foot, and a dreadful sinking pain at the heart, such as he had never felt before. The shivering only disturbed his slumbers; the pain woke him instantly. In one moment he passed from a state of sleep to a state of wakefulness – his eyes wide open – his mental perceptions cleared on a sudden, as if by a miracle.

The candle had burnt down nearly to the last morsel of

tallow, but the top of the unsnuffed wick had just fallen off, and the light in the little room was, for the moment, fair and full.

Between the foot of his bed and the closed door there stood a woman with a knife in her hand, looking at him.

He was stricken speechless with terror, but he did not lose the preternatural clearness of his faculties, and he never took his eyes off the woman. She said not a word as they stared each other in the face, but she began to move slowly towards the left-hand side of the bed.

His eyes followed her. She was a fair, fine woman, with yellowish flaxen hair and light grey eyes, with a droop in the left eyelid. He noticed those things and fixed them on his mind before she was round at the side of the bed. Speechless, with no expression in her face, with no noise following her footfall, she came closer and closer – stopped – and slowly raised the knife. He laid his right arm over his throat to save it; but, as he saw the knife coming down, threw his hand across the bed to the right side, and jerked his body over that way just as the knife descended on the mattress within an inch of his shoulder.

His eyes fixed on her arm and hand as she slowly drew her knife out of the bed: a white, well-shaped arm, with a pretty down lying lightly over the fair skin – a delicate lady's hand, with the crowning beauty of a pink flush under and round the finger nails.

She drew the knife out, and passed back again slowly to the foot of the bed; stopped there for a moment looking at him; then came on – still speechless, still with no expression on the blank beautiful face, still with no sound following the stealthy footfalls – came on to the right side of the bed, where he now lay.

As she approached she raised the knife again, and he drew himself away to the left side. She struck, as before, right into the mattress, with a deliberate perpendicularly-downward action of the arm. This time his eyes wandered from her to the knife. It was like the large clasp-knives which he had often seen labouring men use to cut their bread and bacon with. Her delicate little fingers did not conceal more than two thirds of the handle: he noticed that it was made of buck-horn, clean and shining as the blade was, and looking like new.

For the second time she drew the knife out, concealed it in the wide sleeve of her gown, then stopped by the bedside, watching him. For an instant he saw her standing in that position, then the wick of the spent candle fell over into the socket; the flame diminished to a little blue point, and the room grew dark.

A moment, or less, if possible, passed so, and then the wick flamed up, smokingly, for the last time. His eyes were still looking eagerly over the right-hand side of the bed when the final flash of light came, but they discerned nothing. The fair woman with the knife was gone.

The conviction that he was alone again weakened the hold of the terror that had struck him dumb up to this time. The preternatural sharpness which the very intensity of his panic had mysteriously imparted to his faculties left them suddenly. His brain grew confused – his heart beat wildly – his ears opened for the first time since the appearance of the woman to a sense of the woeful ceaseless moaning of the wind among the trees. With the dreadful conviction of the reality of what he had seen still strong within him, he leaped out of bed, and screaming 'Murder! Wake up, there! wake up!' dashed headlong through the darkness to the door.

It was fast locked, exactly as he had left it on going to bed.

His cries on starting up had alarmed the house. He heard the terrified, confused exclamations of women; he saw the master of the house approaching along the passage with his burning rush candle in one hand and his gun in the other.

'What is it?' asked the landlord breathlessly.

Isaac could only answer in a whisper. 'A woman, with a knife in her hand,' he gasped out. 'In my room – a fair, yellow-haired woman; she jobbed at me with the knife twice over.'

The landlord's pale cheeks grew paler. He looked at Isaac eagerly by the flickering light of his candle, and his face began to get red again; his voice altered, too, as well as his complexion. 'She seems to have missed you twice,' he said.

'I dodged the knife as it came down,' Isaac went on, in the same scared whisper. 'It struck the bed each time.'

The landlord took his candle into the bedroom immediately. In less than a minute he came out again into the passage in a violent passion.

'The devil fly away with you and your woman with the knife! There isn't a mark in the bedclothes anywhere. What do you mean by coming into a man's place, and frightening his family out of their wits about a dream?'

'I'll leave your house,' said Isaac faintly. 'Better out on the road, in rain and dark, on my road home, than back again in that room, after what I've seen in it. Lend me a light to get my clothes by, and tell me what I'm to pay.'

'Pay!' cried the landlord, leading the way with his light sulkily into the bedroom. 'You'll find your score on the slate when you go downstairs. I wouldn't have taken you in for all the money you've got about you if I'd known your dreaming, screeching ways beforehand. Look at the bed. Where's the cut of a knife in it? Look at the window – is the lock bursted? Look at the door (which I heard you fasten yourself) – is it broke in? A murdering woman with a knife in my house! You ought to be ashamed of yourself!'

Isaac answered not a word. He huddled on his clothes, and then they went downstairs together.

'Nigh on twenty minutes past two!' said the landlord, as they passed the clock. 'A nice time in the morning to frighten honest people out of their wits!'

Isaac paid his bill, and the landlord let him out at the front door, asking, with a grin of contempt, as he undid the strong fastenings, whether 'the murdering woman got in that way'.

They parted without a word on either side. The rain had ceased, but the night was dark, and the wind bleaker than ever. Little did the darkness, or the cold, or the uncertainty about the way home matter to Isaac. If he had been turned out into a wilderness in a thunderstorm, it would have been a relief after what he had suffered in the bedroom of the inn.

What was the fair woman with the knife? The creature of a dream, or that other creature from the unknown world called among men by the name of ghost? He could make nothing of the mystery – had made nothing of it, even when it was midday on Wednesday, and when he stood, at last, after many times missing his road, once more on the doorstep of home.

## CHAPTER III

His mother came out eagerly to receive him. His face told her in a moment that something was wrong.

'I've lost the place; but that's my luck. I dreamed an ill dream last night, mother – or maybe I saw a ghost. Take it either way, it scared me out of my senses, and I'm not my own man again yet.'

'Isaac, your face frightens me. Come in to the fire – come in, and tell mother all about it.'

He was as anxious to tell as she was to hear; for it had been his hope all the way home, that his mother, with her quicker capacity and superior knowledge, might be able to throw some light on the mystery which he could not clear up for himself. His memory of the dream was still mechanically vivid, though his thoughts were entirely confused by it.

His mother's face grew paler and paler as he went on. She never interrupted him by so much as a single word; but when he had done, she moved her chair close to his, put her arm round his neck, and said to him,

'Isaac, you dreamed your ill dream on this Wednesday morning. What time was it when you saw the fair woman with the knife in her hand?'

Isaac reflected on what the landlord had said when they had passed by the clock on his leaving the inn; allowed as nearly as he could for the time that must have elapsed between the unlocking of his bedroom door and the paying of his bill just before going away, and answered,

'Somewhere about two o'clock in the morning.'

His mother suddenly quitted her hold of his neck, and struck her hands together with a gesture of despair.

'This Wednesday is your birthday, Isaac, and two o'clock in the morning was the time when you were born.'

Isaac's capacities were not quick enough to catch the infection of his mother's superstitious dread. He was amazed, and a little startled also, when she suddenly rose from her chair, opened her old writing-desk, took pen, ink, and paper and then said to him,

'Your memory is but a poor one, Isaac, and now I'm an old woman, mine's not much better. I want all about this dream of yours to be as well known to both of us, years hence, as it is now. Tell me over again all you told me a minute ago, when you spoke of what the woman with the knife looked like.'

Isaac obeyed, and marvelled much as he saw his mother carefully set down on paper the very words that he was saying.

'Light grey eyes,' she wrote, as they came to the descriptive part, 'with a droop in the left eyelid; flaxen hair, with gold-yellow streak in it; white arms, with a down upon them; little lady's hand, with a reddish look about the finger-nails; clasp-knife with a buckhorn handle, that seemed as good as new.' To these particulars Mrs Scatchard added the year, month, day of the week, and time in the morning when the woman of the dream appeared to her son. She then locked up the paper carefully in her writing-desk.

Neither on that day nor on any day after could her son induce her to return to the matter of the dream. She obstinately kept her thoughts about it to herself, and even refused to refer again to the paper in her writing-desk. Ere long Isaac grew weary of attempting to make her break her resolute silence; and time, which sooner or later wears out all things, gradually wore out the impression produced on him by the dream. He began by thinking of it carelessly, and he ended by not thinking of it at all.

The result was the more easily brought about by the advent of some important changes for the better in his prospects which commenced not long after his terrible night's experience at the inn. He reaped at last the reward of his long and patient suffering under adversity by getting an excellent place, keeping it for seven years, and leaving it, on the death of his master, not only with an excellent character, but also with a comfortable annuity bequeathed to him as a reward for saving his mistress's life in a carriage accident. Thus it happened that Isaac Scatchard returned to his old mother, seven years after the time of the dream at the inn, with an annual sum of money at his disposal sufficient to keep them both in ease and independence for the rest of their lives.

The mother, whose health had been bad of late years, profited so much by the care bestowed on her and by freedom from money anxieties, that when Isaac's birthday came round she was able to sit up comfortably at table and dine with him.

On that day, as the evening drew on, Mrs Scatchard discovered that a bottle of tonic medicine which she was accustomed to take, and in which she had fancied that a dose or more was still left, happened to be empty. Isaac immediately volunteered to go to the chemist's and get it filled again. It was as rainy and bleak an autumn night as on the memorable past occasion when he lost his way and slept at the road-side inn.

On going into the chemist's shop he was passed hurriedly by

a poorly-dressed woman coming out of it. The glimpse he had of her face struck him, and he looked back after her as she descended the doorsteps.

'You're noticing that woman?' said the chemist's apprentice behind the counter. 'It's my opinion there's something wrong with her. She's been asking for laudanum to put to a bad tooth. Master's out for half an hour, and I told her I wasn't allowed to sell poison to strangers in his absence. She laughed in a queer way, and said she would come back in half an hour. If she expects master to serve her, I think she'll be disappointed. It's a case of suicide, sir, if ever there was one yet.'

These words added immeasurably to the sudden interest in the woman which Isaac had felt at the first sight of her face. After he had got the medicine-bottle filled, he looked about anxiously for her as soon as he was out in the street. She was walking slowly up and down on the opposite side of the road. With his heart, very much to his own surprise, beating fast, Isaac crossed over and spoke to her.

He asked if she was in any distress. She pointed to her torn shawl, her scanty dress, her crushed, dirty bonnet; then moved under a lamp so as to let the light fall on her stern, pale, but still most beautiful face.

'I look like a comfortable, happy woman, don't I?' she said, with a bitter laugh.

She spoke with a purity of intonation which Isaac had never heard before from other than ladies' lips. Her slightest actions seemed to have the easy, negligent grace of a thorough-bred woman. Her skin, for all its poverty-stricken paleness, was as delicate as if her life had been passed in the enjoyment of every social comfort that wealth can purchase. Even her small, finely-shaped hands, gloveless as they were, had not lost their whiteness.

Little by little, in answer to his questions, the sad story of the woman came out. There is no need to relate it here; it is told over and over again in police reports and paragraphs about attempted suicides.

'My name is Rebecca Murdoch,' said the woman, as she ended. 'I have ninepence left, and I thought of spending it at the chemist's over the way in securing a passage to the other world. Whatever it is, it can't be worse to me than this, so why should I stop here?'

Besides the natural compassion and sadness moved in his

heart by what he heard, Isaac felt within him some mysterious influence at work all the time the woman was speaking which utterly confused his ideas and almost deprived him of his powers of speech. All that he could say in answer to her last reckless words was that he would prevent her from attempting her own life, if he followed her about all night to do it. His rough, trembling earnestness seemed to impress her.

'I won't occasion you that trouble,' she answered, when he repeated his threat. 'You have given me a fancy for living by speaking kindly to me. No need for the mockery of protestations and promises. You may believe me without them. Come to Fuller's Meadow to-morrow at twelve, and you will find me alive, to answer for myself – No! – no money. My ninepence will do to get me as good a night's lodging as I want.'

She nodded and left him. He made no attempt to follow – he felt no suspicion that she was deceiving him.

'It's strange, but I can't help believing her,' he said to himself, and walked away, bewildered, towards home.

On entering the house, his mind was still so completely absorbed by its new subject of interest that he took no notice of what his mother was doing when he came in with the bottle of medicine. She had opened her old writing-desk in his absence, and was now reading a paper attentively that lay inside it. On every birthday of Isaac's since she had written down the particulars of his dream from his own lips, she had been accustomed to read that same paper, and ponder over it in private.

The next day he went to Fuller's Meadow.

He had done only right in believing her so implicitly. She was there, punctual to a minute, to answer for herself. The last-left faint defences in Isaac's heart against the fascination which a word or look from her began inscrutably to exercise over him sank down and vanished before her for ever on that memorable morning.

When a man previously insensible to the influence of women forms an attachment in middle life, the instances are rare indeed, let the warning circumstances be what they may, in which he is found capable of freeing himself from the tyranny of the new ruling passion. The charm of being spoken to familiarly, fondly, and gratefully by a woman whose language and manners still retained enough of their early refinement to hint at the high social station that she had lost, would have been a dangerous luxury to a man of Isaac's rank at the age of twenty. But it was far more than that – it was certain ruin to him – now that his heart was opening unworthily to a new influence at that middle time of life when strong feelings of all kinds, once implanted, strike root most stubbornly in a man's moral nature. A few more stolen interviews after that first morning in Fuller's Meadow completed his infatuation. In less than a month from the time when he first met her, Isaac Scatchard had consented to give Rebecca Murdoch a new interest in existence, and a chance of recovering the character she had lost by promising to make her his wife.

She had taken possession, not of his passions only, but of his faculties as well. All the mind he had he put into her keeping. She directed him on every point – even instructing him how to break the news of his approaching marriage in the safest manner to his mother.

'If you tell her how you met me and who I am at first,' said the cunning woman, 'she will move heaven and earth to prevent our marriage. Say I am the sister of one of your fellow-servants – ask her to see me before you go into any more particulars – and leave it to me to do the rest. I mean to make her love me next best to you, Isaac, before she knows anything of who I really am.'

The motive of the deceit was sufficient to sanctify it to Isaac. The stratagem proposed relieved him of his one great anxiety, and quieted his uneasy conscience on the subject of his mother. Still, there was something wanting to perfect his happiness, something that he could not realize, something mysteriously untraceable, and yet something that perpetually made itself felt; not when he was absent from Rebecca Murdoch, but, strange to say, when he was actually in her presence! She was kindness itself with him. She never made him feel his inferior capacities and inferior manners. She showed the sweetest anxiety to please him in the smallest trifles; but, in spite of all these attractions, he never could feel quite at his ease with her. At their first meeting, there had mingled with his admiration, when he looked in her face, a faint, involuntary feeling of doubt whether that face was entirely strange to him. No after familiarity had the slightest effect on this inexplicable, wearisome uncertainty.

Concealing the truth as he had been directed, he announced his marriage engagement precipitately and confusedly to his mother on the day when he contracted it. Poor Mrs Scatchard showed her perfect confidence in her son by flinging her arms round his neck, and giving him joy of having found at last, in the sister of one of his fellow-servants, a woman to comfort and care for him after his mother was gone. She was all eagerness to see the woman of her son's choice, and the next day was fixed for the introduction.

It was a bright sunny morning, and the little cottage parlour was full of light as Mrs Scatchard, happy and expectant, dressed for the occasion in her Sunday gown, sat waiting for her son and her future daughter-in-law.

Punctual to the appointed time, Isaac hurriedly and nervously led his promised wife into the room. His mother rose to receive her – advanced a few steps, smiling – looked Rebecca full in the eyes, and suddenly stopped. Her face, which had been flushed the moment before, turned white in an instant; her eyes lost their expression of softness and kindness, and assumed a blank look of terror; her outstretched hands fell to her sides, and she staggered back a few steps with a low cry to her son.

'Isaac,' she whispered, clutching him fast by the arm when he asked alarmedly if she was taken ill, 'Isaac, does that woman's face remind you of nothing?'

Before he could answer – before he could look round to where Rebecca stood, astonished and angered by her reception, at the lower end of the room, his mother pointed impatiently to her writing-desk, and gave him the key.

'Open it,' she said, in a quick, breathless whisper.

'What does this mean? Why am I treated as if I had no business here? Does your mother want to insult me?' asked Rebecca angrily.

'Open it, and give me the paper in the left-hand drawer. Quick! quick, for Heaven's sake!' said Mrs Scatchard, shrinking farther back in terror.

Isaac gave her the paper. She looked it over eagerly for a moment, then followed Rebecca, who was now turning away haughtily to leave the room, and caught her by the shoulder – abruptly raised the long, loose sleeve of her gown, and glanced at her hand and arm. Something like fear began to steal over the angry expression of Rebecca's face as she shook herself free from the old woman's grasp. 'Mad!' she said to herself; 'and Isaac never told me.' With these few words she left the room.

Isaac was hastening after her when his mother turned and stopped his farther progress. It wrung his heart to see the misery and terror in her face as she looked at him.

'Light grey eyes,' she said, in low, mournful, awestruck tones, pointing towards the open door; 'a droop in the left eyelid; flaxen hair, with a gold-yellow streak in it; white arms, with a down upon them; little lady's hand, with a reddish look under the fingernails – *The Dream-Woman*, Isaac, the Dream-Woman!'

The faint cleaving doubt which he had never been able to shake off in Rebecca Murdoch's presence, was fatally set at rest for ever. He *had* seen her face, then, before – seven years before, on his birthday, in the bedroom of the lonely inn.

'Be warned! oh, my son, be warned! Isaac, Isaac, let her go, and do you stop with me!'

Something darkened the parlour window as those words were said. A sudden chill ran though him, and he glanced sidelong at the shadow. Rebecca Murdoch had come back. She was peering in curiously at them over the low window-blind.

'I have promised to marry, mother,' he said, 'and marry I must.'

The tears came into his eyes as he spoke and dimmed his sight, but he could just discern the fatal face outside moving away again from the window.

His mother's head sank lower.

'Are you faint?' he whispered.

'Broken-hearted, Isaac.'

He stooped down and kissed her. The shadow, as he did so, returned to the window, and the fatal face peered in curiously once more.

## CHAPTER IV

Three weeks after that day Isaac and Rebecca were man and wife. All that was hopelessly dogged and stubborn in the man's moral nature seemed to have closed round his fatal passion, and to have fixed it unassailably in his heart.

After that first interview in the cottage parlour no consideration would induce Mrs Scatchard to see her son's wife again, or even to talk of her when Isaac tried hard to plead her cause after their marriage.

This course of conduct was not in any degree occasioned by a discovery of the degradation in which Rebecca had lived. There was no question of that between mother and son. There was no question of anything but the fearfully-exact resemblance between the living, breathing woman, and the spectre-woman of Isaac's dream.

Rebecca, on her side, neither felt nor expressed the slightest sorrow at the estrangement between herself and her mother-in-law. Isaac, for the sake of peace, had never contradicted her first idea that age and long illness had affected Mrs Scatchard's mind. He even allowed his wife to upbraid him for not having confessed this to her at the time of their marriage engagement, rather than risk anything by hinting at the truth. The sacrifice of his integrity before his one all-mastering delusion seemed but a small thing, and cost his conscience but little after the sacrifices he had already made.

The time of waking from this delusion – the cruel and the rueful time – was not far off. After some quiet months of married life, as the summer was ending, and the year was getting on towards the month of his birthday, Isaac found his wife altering towards him. She grew sullen and contemptuous; she formed acquaintances of the most dangerous kind in defiance of his objections, his entreaties, and his commands; and, worst of all, she learned, ere long, after every fresh difference with her husband, to seek the deadly self-oblivion of drink. Little by little, after the first miserable discovery that his wife was keeping company with drunkards, the shocking certainty forced itself on Isaac that she had grown to be a drunkard herself.

He had been in a sadly desponding state for some time before the occurrence of these domestic calamities. His mother's health, as he could but too plainly discern every time he went to see her at the cottage, was failing fast, and he upbraided himself in secret as the cause of the bodily and mental suffering she endured. When to his remorse on his mother's account was added the shame and misery occasioned by the discovery of his wife's degradation, he sank under the double trial – his face began to alter fast, and he looked what he was, a spirit-broken man.

His mother, still struggling bravely against the illness that was hurrying her to the grave, was the first to notice the sad alteration in him, and the first to hear of his last worst trouble with his wife. She could only weep bitterly on the day when he made his humiliating confession, but on the next occasion when he went to see her she had taken a resolution in reference to his domestic afflictions which astonished and even alarmed him. He found her dressed to go out, and on asking the reason received this answer:

'I am not long for this world, Isaac,' she said, 'and I shall not feel easy on my death-bed unless I have done my best to the last to make my son happy. I mean to put my own fears and my own feelings out of the question, and to go with you to your wife, and try what I can do to reclaim her. Give me your arm, Isaac, and let me do the last thing I can in this world to help my son before it is too late.'

He could not disobey her, and they walked together slowly towards his miserable home.

It was only one o'clock in the afternoon when they reached the cottage where he lived. It was their dinner-hour, and Rebecca was in the kitchen. He was thus able to take his mother quietly into the parlour, and then prepare his wife for the interview. She had fortunately drunk but little at that early hour, and she was less sullen and capricious than usual.

He returned to his mother with his mind tolerably at ease. His wife soon followed him into the parlour, and the meeting between her and Mrs Scatchard passed off better than he had ventured to anticipate, though he observed with secret apprehension that his mother, resolutely as she controlled herself in other respects, could not look his wife in the face when she spoke to her. It was a relief to him, therefore, when Rebecca began to lay the cloth.

She laid the cloth, brought in the bread-tray, and cut a slice from the loaf for her husband, then returned to the kitchen. At that moment, Isaac, still anxiously watching his mother, was startled by seeing the same ghastly change pass over her face which had altered it so awfully on the morning when Rebecca and she first met. Before he could say a word, she whispered, with a look of horror,

'Take me back – home, home again, Isaac. Come with me, and never go back again.'

He was afraid to ask for an explanation; he could only sign to her to be silent, and help her quickly to the door. As they passed the bread-tray on the table she stopped and pointed to it. 'Did you see what your wife cut your bread with?' she asked, in a low whisper.

'No, mother – I was not noticing – what was it?'

'Look!'

He did look. A new clasp-knife, with a buck-horn handle, lay with the loaf in the bread-tray. He stretched out his hand shudderingly to possess himself of it; but, at the same time, there was a noise in the kitchen, and his mother caught at his arm.

'The knife of the dream! Isaac, I'm faint with fear. Take me away before she comes back.'

He was hardly able to support her. The visible, tangible reality of the knife struck him with a panic, and utterly destroyed any faint doubts that he might have entertained up to this time in relation to the mysterious dream-warning of nearly eight years before. By a last desperate effort, he summoned self-possession enough to help his mother out of the house – so quietly that the 'Dream-woman' (he thought of her by that name now) did not hear them departing from the kitchen.

'Don't go back, Isaac – don't go back!' implored Mrs Scatchard, as he turned to go away, after seeing her safely seated again in her own room.

'I must get the knife,' he answered, under his breath. His mother tried to stop him again, but he hurried out without another word.

On his return he found that his wife had discovered their secret departure from the house. She had been drinking, and was in a fury of passion. The dinner in the kitchen was flung under the grate; the cloth was off the parlour table. Where was the knife?

Unwisely, he asked for it. She was only too glad of the opportunity of irritating him which the request afforded her. 'He wanted the knife, did he? Could he give her a reason why? No! Then he should not have it – not if he went down on his knees to ask for it.' Further recriminations elicited the fact that she had bought it a bargain, and that she considered it her own especial property. Isaac saw the uselessness of attempting to get the knife by fair means, and determined to search for it, later in the day, in secret. The search was unsuccessful. Night came on, and he left the house to walk about the streets. He was afraid now to sleep in the same room with her.

Three weeks passed. Still sullenly enraged with him, she would not give up the knife; and still that fear of sleeping in the same room with her possessed him. He walked about at night, or dozed in the parlour, or sat watching by his mother's bedside. Before the expiration of the first week in the new month his mother died. It wanted then but ten days of her son's birthday. She had longed to live till that anniversary. Isaac was present at her death, and her last words in this world were addressed to him:

'Don't go back, my son, don't go back!'

He was obliged to go back, if it were only to watch his wife. Exasperated to the last degree by his distrust of her, she had revengefully sought to add a sting to his grief, during the last days of his mother's illness, by declaring that she would assert her right to attend the funeral. In spite of all that he could do or say, she held with wicked pertinacity to her word, and on the day appointed for the burial forced herself – inflamed and shameless with drink – into her husband's presence, and declared that she would walk in the funeral procession to his mother's grave.

This last worst outrage, accompanied by all that was most insulting in word and look, maddened him for the moment. He struck her.

The instant the blow was dealt he repented it. She crouched down, silent, in a corner of the room, and eyed him steadily; it was a look that cooled his hot blood and made him tremble. But there was no time now to think of a means of making atonement. Nothing remained but to risk the worst till the funeral was over. There was but one way of making sure of her. He locked her into her bedroom.

When he came back some hours after, he found her sitting, very much altered in look and bearing, by the bedside, with a bundle on her lap. She rose, and faced him quietly, and spoke with a strange stillness in her voice, a strange repose in her eyes, a strange composure in her manner.

'No man has ever struck me twice,' she said, 'and my husband shall have no second opportunity. Set the door open and let me go. From this day forth we see each other no more.'

Before he could answer she passed him and left the room. He saw her walk away up the street.

Would she return?

All that night he watched and waited, but no footstep came

near the house. The next night, overpowered by fatigue, he lay down in bed in his clothes, with the door locked, the key on the table, and the candle burning. His slumber was not disturbed. The third night, the fourth, the fifth, the sixth passed, and nothing happened. He lay down on the seventh, still in his clothes, still with the door locked, the key on the table, and the candle burning, but easier in his mind.

Easier in his mind, and in perfect health of body when he fell off to sleep. But his rest was disturbed. He woke twice without any sensation of uneasiness. But the third time it was that never-to-be-forgotten shivering of the night at the lonely inn, that dreadful sinking pain at the heart, which once more aroused him in an instant.

His eyes opened towards the left-hand side of the bed, and there stood –

The Dream-Woman again? No! His wife; the living reality, with the dream-spectre's face, in the dream-spectre's attitude; the fair arm up, the knife clasped in the delicate white hand.

He sprang upon her almost at the instant of seeing her, and yet not quickly enough to prevent her from hiding the knife. Without a word from him – without a cry from her – he pinioned her in a chair. With one hand he felt up her sleeve, and there, where the Dream-Woman had hidden the knife, his wife had hidden it – the knife with the buck-horn handle, that looked like new.

In the despair of that fearful moment his brain was steady, his heart was calm. He looked at her fixedly with the knife in his hand, and said these last words:

'You told me we should see each other no more, and you have come back. It is my turn now to go, and to go for ever. I say that we shall see each other no more, and *my* word shall not be broken.'

He left her, and set forth into thc night. There was a bleak wind abroad, and the smell of recent rain was in the air. The distant church-clocks chimed the quarter as he walked rapidly beyond the last houses in the suburb. He asked the first policeman he met what hour that was of which the quarter past had just struck.

The man referred sleepily to his watch, and answered, 'Two o'clock.' Two in the morning. What day of the month was this day that had just begun? He reckoned it up from the date of his mother's funeral. The fatal parallel was complete: it was his birthday!

Had he escaped the mortal peril which his dream foretold? or had he only received a second warning?

As that ominous doubt forced itself on his mind, he stopped, reflected, and turned back again towards the city. He was still resolute to hold to his word, and never to let her see him more, but there was a thought now in his mind of having her watched and followed. The knife was in his possession; the world was before him; but a new distrust of her – a vague, unspeakable, superstitious dread had overcome him.

'I must know where she goes, now she thinks I have left her,' he said to himself, as he stole back wearily to the precincts of his house.

It was still dark. He had left the candle burning in the bedchamber; but when he looked up to the window of the room now, there was no light in it. He crept cautiously to the house door. On going away, he remembered to have closed it; on trying it now, he found it open.

He waited outside, never losing sight of the house, till day-light. Then he ventured indoors – listened, and heard nothing – looked into kitchen, scullery, parlour, and found nothing; went up, at last, into the bedroom – it was empty. A picklock lay on the floor, betraying how she had gained entrance in the night, and that was the only trace of her.

Whither had she gone? That no mortal tongue could tell him. The darkness had covered her flight; and when the day broke, no man could say where the light found her.

Before leaving the house and the town for ever, he gave instructions to a friend and neighbour to sell his furniture for anything that it would fetch, and apply the proceeds to employing the police to trace her. The directions were honestly followed and the money was all spent, but the inquiries led to nothing. The picklock on the bedroom floor remained the one last useless trace of the Dream-Woman.

At this point of the narrative the landlord paused, and, turning towards the window of the room in which we were sitting, looked in the direction of the stableyard.

'So far,' he said, 'I tell you what was told to me. The little that remains to be added lies within my own experience. Between two and three months after the events I have just been relating, Isaac Scatchard came to me, withered and old-looking before his time, just as you saw him to-day. He had his testimonials to character with him, and he asked for employment here. Knowing that my wife and he were distantly related, I gave him a trial in consideration of that relationship, and liked him in spite of his queer habits. He is as sober, honest, and willing a man as there is in England. As for his restlessness at night, and his sleeping away his leisure time in the day, who can wonder at it after hearing his story? Besides, he never objects to being roused up when he's wanted, so there's not much inconvenience to complain of, after all.'

'I suppose he is afraid of a return of that dreadful dream, and of waking out of it in the dark?' said I.

'No,' returned the landlord. 'The dream comes back to him so often that he has got to bear with it by this time resignedly enough. It's his wife keeps him waking at night, as he has often told me.'

'What! Has she never been heard of yet?'

'Never. Isaac himself has the one perpetual thought about her, that she is alive and looking for him. I believe he wouldn't let himself drop off to sleep towards two in the morning for a king's ransom. Two in the morning, he says, is the time she will find him, one of these days. Two in the morning is the time all the year round when he likes to be most certain that he has got that claspknife safe about him. He does not mind being alone as long as he is awake, except on the night before his birthday, when he firmly believes himself to be in peril of his life. The birthday has only come round once since he has been here, and then he sat up along with the night-porter. 'She's looking for me,' is all he says when anybody speaks to him about the one anxiety of his life; 'she's looking for me.' He may be right. She *may* be looking for him. Who can tell?'

'Who can tell?' said I.

# *The Signal-Man*

## Charles Dickens

'Halloa! Below there!'

When he heard a voice thus calling to him, he was standing at the door of his box, with a flag in his hand, furled round its short pole. One would have thought, considering the nature of the ground, that he could not have doubted from what quarter the voice came; but, instead of looking up to where I stood on the top of the steep cutting nearly over his head, he turned himself about and looked down the Line. There was something remarkable in his manner of doing so, though I could not have said, for my life, what. But, I know it was remarkable enough to attract my notice, even though his figure was foreshortened and shadowed, down in the deep trench, and mine was high above him, so steeped in the glow of an angry sunset that I had shaded my eyes with my hand before I saw him at all.

'Halloa! Below!'

From looking down the Line, he turned himself about again, and, raising his eyes, saw my figure high above him.

'Is there any path by which I can come down and speak to you?'

He looked up at me without replying, and I looked down at him without pressing him too soon with a repetition of my idle question. Just then, there came a vague vibration in the earth and air, quickly changing into a violent pulsation, and an oncoming rush that caused me to start back, as though it had force to draw me down. When such vapour as rose to my height from this rapid train had passed me and was skimming away over the landscape, I looked down again, and saw him re-furling the flag he had shown while the train went by.

I repeated my enquiry. After a pause, during which he

seemed to regard me with fixed attention, he motioned with his rolled-up flag towards a point on my level, some two or three hundred yards distant. I called down to him, 'All right!' and made for that point. There, by dint of looking closely about me, I found a rough zigzag descending path notched out, which I followed.

The cutting was extremely deep, and unusually precipitate. It was made through a clammy stone that became oozier and wetter as I went down. For these reasons, I found the way long enough to give me time to recall a singular air of reluctance or compulsion with which he had pointed out the path.

When I came down low enough upon the zigzag descent to see him again, I saw that he was standing between the rails on the way by which the train had lately passed, in an attitude as if he were waiting for me to appear. He had his left hand at his chin, and that left elbow rested on his right hand crossed over his breast. His attitude was one of such expectation and watchfulness, that I stopped a moment, wondering at it.

I resumed my downward way, and stepping out upon the level of the railroad and drawing nearer to him, saw that he was a dark sallow man, with a dark beard and rather heavy eyebrows. His post was in as solitary and dismal a place as ever I saw. On either side, a dripping wet wall of jagged stone, excluding all view but a strip of sky; the perspective one way, only a crooked prolongation of this great dungeon; the shorter perspective in the other direction, terminating in a gloomy red light, and the gloomier entrance to a black tunnel, in whose massive architecture there was a barbarous, depressing and forbidding air. So little sunlight ever found its way to this spot, that it had an earthy, deadly smell; and so much cold wind rushed through it, that it struck chill to me, as if I had left the natural world.

Before he stirred, I was near enough to him to have touched him. Not even then removing his eyes from mine, he stepped back one step, and lifted his hand.

This was a lonesome post to occupy (I said), and it had riveted my attention when I looked down from up yonder. A visitor was a rarity, I should suppose; not an unwelcome rarity, I hoped? In me, he merely saw a man who had been shut up within narrow limits all his life, and who, being at last set free, had a newly awakened interest in these great works. To such purpose I spoke to him; but I am far from sure of the terms I used, for, besides that I am not happy in opening any conversation, there was something in the man that daunted me.

He directed a most curious look towards the red light near the tunnel's mouth, and looked all about it, as if something were missing from it, and then looked at me.

That light was part of his charge? Was it not?

He answered in a low voice: 'Don't you know it is?'

The monstrous thought came into my mind as I perused the fixed eyes and the saturnine face, that this was a spirit, not a man. I have speculated since, whether there may have been infection in his mind.

In my turn, I stepped back. But in making the action, I detected in his eyes some latent fear of me. This put the monstrous thought to flight.

'You look at me,' I said, forcing a smile, 'as if you had a dread of me.'

'I was doubtful,' he returned, 'whether I had seen you before.'

'Where?'

He pointed to the red light he had looked at.

'There?' I said.

Intently watchful of me, he replied (but without sound), 'Yes.'

'My good fellow, what should I do there? However, be that as it may, I never was there, you may swear.'

'I think I may,' he rejoined. 'Yes. I am sure I may.'

His manner cleared, like my own. He replied to my remarks with readiness, and in well chosen words. Had he much to do there? Yes; that was to say, he had enough responsibility to bear; but exactness and watchfulness were what was required of him, and of actual work – manual labour he had next to none. To change that signal, to trim those lights, and to turn this iron handle now and then, was all he had to do under that head. Regarding those many long and lonely hours of which I seemed to make so much, he could only say that the routine of his life had shaped itself into that form, and he had grown used to it. He had taught himself a language down here – if only to know it by sight, and to have formed his own crude ideas of its pronunciation, could be called learning it. He had also worked at fractions and decimals, and tried a little algebra; but he was, and had been as a boy, a poor hand at figures. Was it necessary for him when on duty always to remain in that channel of damp air, and could he never rise into the sunshine from between those high stone walls? Why, that depended upon times and circumstances. Under some conditions there would be less upon the Line than under others, and the same held good as to certain hours of the day and night. In bright weather, he did choose occasions for getting a little above these lower shadows; but, being at all times liable to be called by his electric bell, and at such times listening for it with redoubled anxiety, the relief was less than I would suppose.

He took me into his box, where there was a fire, a desk for an official book in which he had to make certain entries, a telegraphic instrument with its dial face and needles, and the little bell of which he had spoken. On my trusting that he would excuse the remark that he had been well educated, and (I hoped I might say without offence), perhaps educated above that station, he observed that instances of slight incongruity in such-wise would rarely be found wanting among large bodies of men; that he had heard it was so in workhouses, in the police force, even in that last desperate resource, the army; and that he knew it was so, more or less, in any great railway staff. He had been, when young (if I could believe it, sitting in that hut; he scarcely could), a student of natural philosophy, and had attended lectures; but he had run wild, misused his opportunities, gone down, and never risen again. He had no complaint to offer about that. He had made his bed, and he lay upon it. It was far too late to make another.

All that I have here condensed, he said in a quiet manner, with his grave dark regards divided between me and the fire. He threw in the word 'Sir' from time to time, and especially when he referred to his youth: as though to request me to understand that he claimed to be nothing but what I found him. He was several times interrupted by the little bell, and had to read off messages, and send replies. Once, he had to stand without the door, and display a flag as a train passed, and make some verbal communication to the driver. In the discharge of his duties I observed him to be remarkably exact and vigilant, breaking off his discourse at a syllable, and remaining silent until what he had to do was done.

In a word, I should have set this man down as one of the safest of men to be employed in that capacity, but for the circumstance that while he was speaking to me he twice broke off with a fallen colour, turned his face towards the little bell when it did *not* ring, opened the door of the hut (which was kept shut to exclude the unhealthy damp), and looked out towards the red light near the mouth of the tunnel. On both those occasions, he came back to the fire with the inexplicable air upon him which I had remarked, without being able to define, when we were so far asunder.

Said I when I rose to leave him: 'You almost made me think that I have met with a contented man.'

(I am afraid I must acknowledge that I said it to lead him on.)

'I believe I used to be so,' he rejoined, in the low voice in which he had first spoken; 'but I am troubled, sir, I am troubled.'

He would have recalled the words if he could. He had said them, however, and I took them up quickly.

'With what? What is your trouble?'

'It is very difficult to impart, sir. It is very, very difficult to speak of. If ever you make me another visit, I will try to tell you.'

'But I expressly intend to make you another visit. Say, when shall it be?'

'I go off early in the morning, and I shall be on again at ten tomorrow night, sir.'

'I will come at eleven.'

He thanked me, and went out at the door with me. 'I'll show my white light, sir,' he said, in his peculiar low voice, 'till you have found the way up. When you have found it, don't call out! And when you are at the top, don't call out!'

His manner seemed to make the place strike colder to me, but I said no more than 'Very well.'

'And when you come down tomorrow night, don't call out! Let me ask you a parting question. What made you cry "Halloa! Below there!" tonight?'

'Heaven knows,' said I. 'I cried something to that effect –'

'Not to that effect, sir. Those were the very words. I know them well.'

'Admit those were the very words. I said them, no doubt, because I saw you below.'

'For no other reason?'

'What other reason could I possibly have?'

'You had no feeling that they were conveyed to you in any supernatural way?'

'No.'

He wished me goodnight, and held up his light. I walked by the side of the down Line of rails (with a very disagreeable sensation of a train coming behind me), until I found the path. It was easier to mount than to descend, and I got back to my inn without any adventure.

Punctual to my appointment, I placed my foot on the first notch of the zigzag next night, as the distant clocks were striking eleven. He was waiting for me at the bottom, with his white light on. 'I have not called out,' I said, when we came close together; 'may I speak now?' 'By all means, sir.' 'Goodnight then, and here's my hand.' 'Goodnight, sir, and here's mine.' With that, we walked side by side to his box, entered it, closed the door, and sat down by the fire.

'I have made up my mind, sir,' he began, bending forward as soon as we were seated, and speaking in a tone but a little above a whisper, 'that you shall not have to ask me twice what troubles me. I took you for someone else yesterday evening. That troubles me.'

'That mistake?'

'No. That someone else.'

'Who is it?'

'I don't know.'

'Like me?'

'I don't know. I never saw the face. The left arm is across the face, and the right arm is waved. Violently waved. This way.'

I followed his action with my eyes, and it was the action of an arm gesticulating with the utmost passion and vehemence: 'For God's sake clear the way!'

'One moonlit night,' said the man, 'I was sitting here, when I heard a voice cry "Halloa! Below there!" I stared up, looked from that door, and saw this someone else standing by the red light near the tunnel, waving as I just now showed you. The voice seemed hoarse with shouting, and it cried, "Look out! Look out!" And then again "Halloa! Below there! Look out!" I caught up my lamp, turned it on red, and ran towards the figure, calling, 'What's wrong? What has happened? Where?" It stood just outside the blackness of the tunnel. I advanced so close upon it that I wondered at its keeping the sleeve across its eyes. I ran right up at it, and had my hand stretched out to pull the sleeve away, when it was gone.'

'Into the tunnel,' said I.

'No. I ran on into the tunnel, five hundred yards. I stopped and held my lamp above my head, and saw the figures of the measured distance, and saw the wet stains stealing down the walls and trickling through the arch. I ran out again, faster than I had run in (for I had a mortal abhorrence of the place upon me), and I looked all round the red light with my own red light, and I went up the iron ladder to the gallery atop of it, and I came down again, and ran back here. I telegraphed both ways, "An alarm has been given. Is anything wrong?" The answer came back, both ways: "All well."'

Resisting the slow touch of a frozen finger tracing out my spine, I showed him how that this figure must be a deception of his sense of sight, and how that figures, originating in disease of the delicate nerves that minister to the functions of the eye, were known to have often troubled patients, some of whom had become conscious of the nature of their affliction, and had even proved it by experiments upon themselves. 'As to an imaginary cry,' said I, 'do but listen for a moment to the wind in this unnatural valley while we speak so low, and to the wild harp it makes of the telegraph wires!'

That was all very well, he returned, after we had sat listening for a while, and he ought to know something of the wind and the wires, he who so often passed long winter nights there, alone and watching. But he would beg to remark that he had not finished.

I asked his pardon, and he slowly added these words, touching my arm:

'Within six hours after the appearance, the memorable accident on this Line happened, and within ten hours the dead and wounded were brought along through the tunnel over the spot where the figure had stood.'

A disagreeable shudder crept over me, but I did my best against it. It was not to be denied, I rejoined, that this was a remarkable coincidence, calculated deeply to impress his mind. But it was unquestionable that remarkable coincidences did continually occur, and they must be taken into account in dealing with such a subject. Though to be sure I must admit, I added (for I thought I saw that he was going to bring the objection to bear upon me), men of common sense did not allow much for coincidences in making the ordinary calculations of life.

He again begged to remark that he had not finished.

I again begged his pardon for being betrayed into interruptions.

'This,' he said, again laying his hand upon my arm, and glancing over his shoulder with hollow eyes, 'was just a year ago. Six or seven months passed, and I had recovered from the surprise and shock, when one morning, as the day was breaking, I, standing at that door, looked towards the red light, and saw the spectre again.' He stopped, with a fixed look at me.

'Did it cry out?'

'No. It was silent.'

'Did it wave its arm?'

'No. It leaned against the shaft of the light, with both hands before the face. Like this.'

Once more, I followed his action with my eyes. It was an action of mourning. I have seen such an attitude in stone figures on tombs.

'Did you go up to it?'

'I came in and sat down, partly to collect my thoughts, partly because it had turned me faint. When I went to the door again, daylight was above me, and the ghost was gone.'

'But nothing followed? Nothing came of this?'

He touched me on the arm with his forefinger twice or thrice, giving a ghastly nod each time:

'That very day, as a train came out of the tunnel, I noticed, at a carriage window on my side, what looked like a confusion of hands and heads, and something waved. I saw it, just in time to signal the driver, Stop! He shut off, and put his brake on, but the train drifted past here a hundred and fifty yards or more. I ran after it, and, as I went along, heard terrible screams and cries. A beautiful young lady had died instantaneously in one of the compartments, and was brought in here, and laid down on this floor between us.'

Involuntarily, I pushed my chair back, as I looked from the boards at which he pointed, to himself.

'True, sir. True. Precisely as it happened, so I tell it you.'

I could think of nothing to say, to any purpose, and my mouth was very dry. The wind and the wires took up the story with a long lamenting wail.

He resumed. 'Now, sir, mark this, and judge how my mind is troubled. The spectre came back, a week ago. Ever since, it has been there, now and again, by fits and starts.'

'At the light?'

'At the Danger-light.'

'What does it seem to do?'

He repeated, if possible with increased passion and vehemence, that former gesticulation of 'For God's sake clear the way!'

Then, he went on. 'I have no peace or rest for it. It calls to me for many minutes together, in an agonized manner, "Below there! Look out! Look out!" It stands waving to me. It rings my little bell –'

I caught at that. 'Did it ring your bell yesterday evening when I was here, and you went to the door?'

'Twice.'

'Why, see,' said I, 'how your imagination misleads you. My eyes were on the bell, and my ears were open to the bell, and if I am a living man, it did *not* ring at those times. No, nor at any other time, except when it was rung in the natural course of physical things by the station communicating with you.'

He shook his head. 'I have never made a mistake as to that, yet, sir. I have never confused the spectre's ring with the man's. The ghost's ring is a strange vibration in the bell that it derives from nothing else, and I have not asserted that the bell stirs to the eye. I don't wonder that you failed to hear it. But *I* heard it.'

'And did the spectre seem to be there, when you looked out?'

'It was there.'

'Both times?'

He repeated firmly: 'Both times.'

'Will you come to the door with me, and look for it now?'

He bit his underlip as though he were somewhat unwilling, but arose. I opened the door, and stood on the step, while he stood in the doorway. There, was the Danger-light. There, was the dismal mouth of the tunnel. There, were the high wet stone walls of the cutting. There, were the stars above them.

'Do you see it?' I asked him, taking particular note of his face. His eyes were prominent and strained; but not very much more so, perhaps, than my own had been when I had directed them earnestly towards the same spot.

'No,' he answered. 'It is not there.'

'Agreed,' said I.

We went in again, shut the door, and resumed our seats. I was thinking how best to improve this advantage, if it might be called one, when he took up the conversation in such a matter of course way, so assuming that there could be no serious question of fact between us, that I felt myself placed in the weakest of positions.

'By this time you will fully understand, sir,' he said, 'that what troubles me so dreadfully, is the question, What does the spectre mean?'

I was not sure, I told him, that I did fully understand.

'What is its warning against?' he said, ruminating, with his eyes on the fire, and only by times turning them on me. 'What is the danger? Where is the danger? There is danger overhanging, somewhere on the Line. Some dreadful calamity will happen. It is not to be doubted this third time, after what has gone before. But surely this is a cruel haunting of *me*. What can *I* do?'

He pulled out his handkerchief, and wiped the drops from his heated forehead.

'If I telegraph Danger, on either side of me, or on both, I can give no reason for it,' he went on, wiping the palms of his hands. 'I should get into trouble, and do no good. They would think I was mad. This is the way it would work: Message: "Danger! Take care!" Answer: "What danger? Where?" Message: "Don't know. But for God's sake take care!" They would displace me. What else could they do?'

His pain of mind was most pitiable to see. It was the mental torture of a conscientious man, oppressed beyond endurance by an unintelligible responsibility involving life.

'When it first stood under the Danger-light,' he went on, putting his dark hair back from his head, and drawing his hands outwards across and across his temples in an extremity of feverish distress, 'why not tell me where the accident was to happen – if it must happen? Why not tell me how it could be averted – if it could have been averted? When on its second coming it hid its face, why not tell me instead: "She is going to die. Let them keep her at home"? If it came, on those two occasions, only to show me that its warnings were true, and so to prepare me for the third, why not warn me plainly now? And I, Lord help me! A mere poor signalman on this solitary station! Why not go to somebody with credit to be believed, and power to act!'

When I saw him in this state, I saw that for the poor man's sake, as well as for the public safety, what I had to do for the time was, to compose his mind. Therefore, setting aside all question of reality or unreality between us, I represented to him that whoever thoroughly discharged his duty, must do well, and that at least it was his comfort that he understood his duty, though he did not understand these confounding appearances. In this effort I succeeded far better than in the attempt to reason him out of his conviction. He became calm; the occupations incidental to his post as the night advanced, began to make larger demands on his attention; and I left him at two in the morning. I had offered to stay through the night, but he would not hear of it.

That I more than once looked back at the red light as I ascended the pathway, that I did not like the red light, and that I should have slept but poorly if my bed had been under it, I see no reason to conceal. Nor did I like the two sequences of the accident and the dead girl. I see no reason to conceal that, either.

But, what ran most in my thoughts was the consideration how ought I to act, having become the recipient of this disclosure? I had proved the man to be intelligent, vigilant, painstaking and exact; but how long might he remain so, in his state of mind? Though in a subordinate position, still he held a most important trust, and would I (for instance) like to stake my own life on the chances of his continuing to execute it with precision?

Unable to overcome a feeling that there would be something treacherous in my communicating what he had told me to his superiors in the company, without first being plain with himself and proposing a middle course to him, I ultimately resolved to offer to accompany him (otherwise keeping his secret for the present) to the wisest medical practitioner we could hear of in those parts, and to take his opinion. A change in his time of duty would come round next night, he had apprised me, and he would be off an hour or two after sunrise, and on again soon after sunset. I had appointed to return accordingly.

Next evening was a lovely evening, and I walked out early to enjoy it. The sun was not yet quite down when I traversed the field-path near the top of the deep cutting. I would extend my walk for an hour, I said to myself, half an hour on and half an hour back, and it would then be time to go to my signal-man's box.

Before pursuing my stroll, I stepped to the brink, and mechanically looked down, from the point from which I had first seen him. I cannot describe the thrill that seized upon me, when, close at the mouth of the tunnel, I saw the appearance of a man, with his left sleeve across his eyes, passionately waving his right arm.

The nameless horror that oppressed me, passed in a moment, for in a moment I saw that this appearance of a man was a man indeed, and that there was a little group of other men standing at a short distance, to whom he seemed to be rehearsing the gesture he made. The Danger-light was not yet lighted. Against its shaft, a little low hut, entirely new to me, had been made of some wooden supports and tarpaulin. It looked no bigger than a bed.

With an irresistible sense that something was wrong – with a flashing self-reproachful fear that fatal mischief had come of my leaving the man there, and causing no one to be sent to overlook or correct what he did – I descended the notched path with all the speed I could make.

'What is the matter?' I asked the men.

'Signal-man killed this morning, sir.'

'Not the man belonging to that box?'

'Yes, sir.'

'Not the man I know?'

'You will recognize him, sir, if you knew him,' said the man who spoke for the others, solemnly uncovering his own head and raising an end of the tarpaulin, 'for his face is quite composed.'

'O! how did this happen, how did this happen?' I asked, turning from one to another as the hut closed in again.

'He was cut down by an engine, sir. No man in England knew his work better. But somehow he was not clear of the outer rail. It was just at broad day. He had struck the light, and had the lamp in his hand. As the engine came out of the tunnel, his back was towards her, and she cut him down. That man drove her, and was showing how it happened. Show the gentleman, Tom.'

The man who wore a rough dark dress, stepped back to his former place at the mouth of the tunnel!

'Coming round the curve in the tunnel, sir,' he said, 'I saw him at the end, like as if I saw him down a perspective-glass. There was no time to check speed, and I knew him to be very careful. As he didn't seem to take heed of the whistle, I shut it off when we were running down upon him, and called to him as loud as I could call.'

'What did you say?'

'I said, Below there! Look out! Look out! For God's sake clear the way!'

I started.

'Ah! it was a dreadful time, sir. I never left off calling to him. I put this arm before my eyes, not to see, and I waved this arm to the last; but it was no use.'

*

Without prolonging the narrative to dwell on any one of its curious circumstances more than on any other, I may, in closing, point out the coincidence that the warning of the engine-driver included, not only the words which the unfortunate signal-man had repeated to me as haunting him, but also the words which I myself – not he – had attached, and that only in my own mind, to the gesticulation he had imitated.

# *The Old Nurse's Story*

Elizabeth Gaskell

You know, my dears, that your mother was an orphan, and an only child; and I dare say you have heard that your grandfather was a clergyman up in Westmorland, where I come from. I was just a girl in the village school, when, one day, your grandmother came in to ask the mistress if there was any scholar there who would do for a nursemaid; and mighty proud I was, I can tell ye, when the mistress called me up, and spoke to my being a good girl at my needle, and a steady honest girl, and one whose parents were very respectable, though they might be poor. I thought I should like nothing better than to serve the pretty young lady, who was blushing as deep as I was, as she spoke of the coming baby, and what I should have to do with it. However, I see you don't care so much for this part of my story, as for what you think is to come, so I'll tell you at once.

I was engaged and settled at the parsonage before Miss Rosamond (that was the baby, who is now your mother) was born. To be sure, I had little enough to do with her when she came, for she was never out of her mother's arms, and slept by her all night long; and proud enough was I sometimes when missis trusted her to me. There never was such a baby before or since, though you've all of you been fine enough in your turns; but for sweet, winning ways you've none of you come up to your mother. She took after her mother, who was a real lady born; a Miss Furnivall, a granddaughter of Lord Furnivall's, in Northumberland. I believe she had neither brother nor sister, and had been brought up in my lord's family till she had married your grand-father, who was just a curate, son to a shopkeeper in Carlisle – but a clever, fine gentleman as ever was – and one who was a right down hard-worker in his parish, which was very wide and scattered all abroad over the Westmoreland fells.

When your mother, little Miss Rosamond, was about four or five years old, both her parents died in a fortnight – one after the other. Ah! that was a sad time. My pretty young mistress and me was looking for another baby, when my master came home from one of his long rides, wet and tired, and took the fever he died of; and then she never held up her head again, but just lived to see her dear baby, and have it laid on her breast before she sighed away her life. My mistress had asked me, on her death bed, never to leave Miss Rosamond; but if she had never spoken a word, I would have gone with the little child to the end of the world.

The next thing, and before we had well stilled our sobs, the executors and guardians came to settle the affairs. They were my poor young mistress's own cousin, Lord Furnivall, and Mr Esthwaite, my master's brother, a shopkeeper in Manchester; not so well-to-do then as he was afterwards, and with a large family rising about him. Well! I don't know if it were on their settling, or because of a letter my mistress wrote on her death-bed to her cousin, my lord; but somehow it was settled that Miss Rosamond and me were to go to Furnivall Manor House, in Northumberland, and my lord spoke as if it had been her mother's wish that she should live with his family and as if he had no objections for that one or two more or less could make no difference in so grand a household. So, though that was not the way in which I should have wished the coming of my bright and pretty pet to have been looked at – who was like a sunbeam in any family, be it never so grand – I was well pleased that all the folks in the Dale should stare and admire, when they heard I was going to be young lady's maid at my Lord Furnivall's at Furnivall Manor.

But I made a mistake in thinking we were to go and live where my lord did. It turned out that the family had left Furnivall Manor House fifty years or more. I could not hear that my poor young mistress had ever been there, though she had been brought up in the family; and I was sorry for that, for I should have liked Miss Rosamond's youth to have passed where her mother's had been.

My lord's gentleman, from whom I asked as many questions as I durst, said that the Manor House was at the foot of the Cumberland Fells, and a very grand place; that an old Miss Furnivall, a great-aunt of my lord's, lived there with only a few servants but that it was a very healthy place, and my lord had thought that it would suit Miss Rosamond very well for a few years, and that her being there might perhaps amuse his old aunt.

I was bidden by my lord to have Miss Rosamond's things ready by a certain day. He was a stern proud man, as they say all the Lords Furnivall were, and he never spoke a word more than was necessary. Folk did say he had loved my young mistress; but that, because she knew that his father would object, she would never listen to him, and married Mr Esthwaite; but I don't know. He never married at any rate. But he never took much notice of Miss Rosamond; which I thought he might have done if he had cared for her dead mother. He sent his gentleman with us to the Manor House, telling him to join him at Newcastle that same evening; so there was no great length of time for him to make us known to all the strangers before he, too, shook us off; and we were left, two lonely young things (I was not eighteen), in the great old Manor House. It seems like yesterday that we drove there. We had left our own dear parsonage very early, and we had both cried as if our hearts would break, though we were travelling in my lord's carriage, which I thought so much of once. And now it was long past noon on a September day, and we stopped to change horses for the last time at a little smoky town all full of colliers and miners. Miss Rosamond had fallen asleep, but Mr Henry told me to waken her, that she might see the park and the Manor House as we drove up. I thought it rather a pity; but I did what he bade me, for fear he should complain of me to my lord. We had left all signs of a town, or even a village, and were then inside the gates of a large wild park – not like the parks here in the south, but with rocks, and the noise of running water, and gnarled thorn trees, and old oaks, all white and peeled with age.

The road went up about two miles, and then we saw a great and stately house, with many trees close around it, so close that in some places their branches dragged against the walls when the wind blew; and some hung broken down; for no one seemed to take much charge of the place; – to lop the wood or to keep the moss-covered carriage-way in order. Only in front of the house all was clear. The great oval drive was without a weed; and neither tree nor creeper was allowed to grow over the long, many-windowed front, at both sides of which a wing projected, which were each the ends of other side fronts; for the house, although it was so desolate, was even grander than I expected. Behind it rose the Fells, which seemed unenclosed and bare enough; and on the lefthand of the house as you stood facing it, was a little old-fashioned flower-garden, as I found out afterwards. A door opened out upon it from the west front; it had been scooped out of the thick dark wood for some old Lady Furnivall; but the branches of the great forest trees had grown and overshadowed it again, and there were very few flowers that would live there at that time.

When we drove up to the great front entrance, and went into the hall, I thought we should be lost – it was so large and vast, and grand. There was a chandelier, all of bronze, hung down from the middle of the ceiling; and I had never seen one before, and looked at it all in amaze. Then, at one side of the hall, was a great fire-place, as large as the sides of the houses in my country, with massy andirons and dogs to hold the wood; and by it were heavy old fashioned sofas. At the opposite end of the hall, to the left as you went in – on the western side – was an organ built into the wall, and so large that it filled up the best part of that end. Beyond it, on the same side, was a door; and opposite, on each side of the fireplace, were also doors leading to the east front; but those I never went through as long as I stayed in the house, so I can't tell you what lay beyond.

The afternoon was closing in, and the hall, which had no fire lighted in it, looked dark and gloomy, but we did not stay there a moment. The old servant, who had opened the door for us, bowed to Mr Henry, and took us in through the door at the further side of the great organ, and led us through several smaller halls and passages, in to the west drawing room, where he said that Miss Furnivall was sitting. Poor little Miss Rosamond held very tight to me, as if she were scared and lost in that great place, and as for myself, I was not much better. The west drawing room was very cheerful looking, with a warm fire in it, and plenty of good, comfortable furniture about. Miss Furnivall was an old lady, not far from eighty, I should think, but I do not know. She was thin and tall, and had a face as full of fine wrinkles as if they had been drawn all over it with a needle's point. Her eyes were very watchful, to make up, I suppose, for her being so deaf as to be obliged to use a trumpet.

Sitting with her, working at the same great piece of tapestry, was Mrs Stark, her maid and companion, and almost as old as she was. She had lived with Miss Furnivall ever since they both were young, and now she seemed more like a friend than a servant; she looked so cold and grey and stony, as if she had never loved or cared for anyone; and I don't suppose she did care for anyone, except her mistress; and, owing to the great deafness of the latter, Mrs Stark treated her very much as if she were a child. Mr Henry gave some message from my lord, and then he bowed good-bye to us all – taking no notice of my sweet little Miss Rosamond's outstretched hand – and left us standing there, being looked at by the two old ladies through their spectacles.

I was right glad when they rung for the old footman who had shown us in at first, and told him to take us to our rooms. So we went out of that great drawing-room, and into another sitting-room, and out of that, and then up a great flight of stairs, and along a broad gallery – which was something like a library, having books all down one side, and windows and writing tables all down the other – till we came to our rooms, which I was not sorry to hear were just over the kitchens; for I began to think I should be lost in that wilderness of a house. There was an old nursery, that had been used for all the little lords and ladies long ago, with a pleasant fire burning in the grate, and the kettle boiling on the hob, and tea things spread out on the table; and out of that room was the night nursery, with a little crib for Miss Rosamond close to my bed. And old James called up Dorothy, his wife, to bid us welcome; and both he and she were so hospitable and kind that, by and by, Miss Rosamond and me felt quite at home; and by the time tea was over, she was sitting on Dorothy's knee and chattering away as fast as her little tongue could go. I soon found out that Dorothy was from Westmorland, and that bound her and me together, as it were; and I would never wish to meet with kinder people than were old James and his wife. James had lived pretty nearly all his life in my lord's family, and thought there was no one so grand as they. He even looked down a little on his wife because, till he had married her, she had never lived in any but a farmer's household. But he was very fond of her, as well he might be. They had one servant under them, to do all the rough work. Agnes, they called her; and she and me, and James and Dorothy, with Miss Furnivall and Mrs Stark, made up the family; always remembering my sweet little Miss Rosamond! I used to wonder what they had done before she came, they thought so much of her now. Kitchen and drawing-room, it was all the same. The hard, sad Miss Furnivall, and the cold Mrs Stark, looked pleased when she came fluttering in like a bird playing and pranking hither and thither, with a continual murmur, and pretty prattle of gladness. I am sure they were sorry many a time when she flitted away into the kitchen, though they were too proud to ask her to stay with them, and were a little surprised at her taste; though to be sure, as Mrs Stark said, it was not to be wondered at, remembering what stock her father had come of. The great old rambling house was a famous place for little Miss Rosamond. She made expeditions all over it, with me at her heels; all, except the east wing, which was never opened, and whither we never thought of going. But in the western and northern part was many a pleasant room full of things that were curiosities to us, though they might not have been to people who had seen more. The windows were darkened by the sweeping boughs of the trees and the ivy which had overgrown them; but, in the green gloom, we could manage to see old China jars and carved ivory boxes and great, heavy books and above all, the old pictures!

Once, I remember, my darling would have Dorothy go with us to tell us who they all were; for they were all portraits of some of my lord's family, though Dorothy could not tell us the names of every one. We had gone through most of the rooms, when we came to the old state drawing-room over the hall, and there was a picture of Miss Furnivall; or, as she was called in those days, Miss Grace, for she was the younger sister. Such a beauty she must have been! But with such a set, proud look, and such scorn looking out of her handsome eyes, with her eyebrows just a little raised as if she wondered how anyone could have the impertinence to look at her, and her lip curled at us as we stood there, gazing. She had a dress on, the like of which I had never seen before, but it was all the fashion when she was young; a hat of some soft white stuff like beaver, pulled a little over her brows, and a beautiful plume of feathers sweeping round it on one side; and her gown of blue satin was open in front to a quilted white stomacher.

'Well, to be sure!' said I, when I had gazed my fill. 'Flesh is grass, they do say, but who would have thought that Miss

Furnivall had been such an out-and-out beauty, to see her now?'

'Yes,' said Dorothy, 'Folks change sadly. But if what my master's father used to say was true, Miss Furnivall, the elder sister, was handsomer than Miss Grace. Her picture is here somewhere, but if I show it to you, you must never let on, even to James, that you have seen it. Can the little lady hold her tongue, think you?' asked she.

I was not so sure, for she was such a little sweet, bold, open-spoken child, so I set her to hide herself; and then I helped Dorothy to turn a great picture that leaned with its face towards the wall, and was not hung up as the others were. To be sure, it beat Miss Grace for beauty, and, I think, for scornful pride, too, though in that matter it might be hard to choose. I could have looked at it an hour, but Dorothy seemed half-frightened at having shown it to me and hurried it back again, and bade me run and find Miss Rosamond, for that there were some ugly places about the house where she should like ill for the child to go. I was a brave, high-spirited girl, and thought little of what the old woman said, for I liked hide-and-seek as well as any child in the parish; so off I ran to find my little one.

As winter drew on, and the days grew shorter, I was sometimes almost certain that I heard a noise as if someone was playing on the great organ in the hall. I did not hear it every evening; but certainly I did very often, usually when I was sitting with Miss Rosamond, after I had put her to bed, and keeping quite still and silent in the bedroom. Then I used to hear it booming and swelling away in the distance. The first night, when I went down to my supper, I asked Dorothy who had been playing music, and James said very shortly that I was a gowk to take the wind soughing among the trees for music; but I saw Dorothy look at him very fearfully, and Bessy, the kitchen-maid, said something beneath her breath, and went quite white. I saw they did not like my question, so I held my peace till I was with Dorothy alone, when I knew I could get a good deal out of her. So, the next day, I watched my time and I coaxed and asked her who it was that played the organ, for I knew that it was the organ and not the wind, well enough, for all I had kept silence before James. But Dorothy had had her lesson, I'll warrant, and never a word could I get from her. So then I tried Bessy, though I had always held my head rather above her, as I was evened to James and Dorothy, and she was little better than their servant. So she said I must never, never tell, and if I ever told, I was never to say *she* had told me; but it was a very strange noise, and she had heard it many a time, but most of all on winter nights, and before storms; and folks did say, it was the old lord, playing on the great organ in the hall just as he used to do when he was alive; but who the old lord was, or why he played, and why he played on stormy winter evenings in particular, she either could not, or would not, tell me. Well! I told you I had a brave heart; and I thought it was rather pleasant to have that grand music rolling about the house, let who would be the player; for now it rose above the great gusts of wind, and wailed and triumphed just like a living creature, and then it fell to a softness most complete; only it was always music, and tunes, so it was nonsense to call it the wind. I thought at first that it might be Miss Furnivall who played unknown to Bessy; but one day, when I was in the hall by myself, I opened the organ and peeped all about it and around it, as I had done to the organ in Crosthwaite Church once before, and I saw it was all broken and destroyed inside, though it looked so brave and fine; and then, though it was noonday, my flesh began to creep a little, and I shut it up, and ran away pretty quickly to my own bright nursery; and I did not like hearing the music for some time after that, any more than James and Dorothy did.

All this time, Miss Rosamond was making herself more and more beloved. The old ladies liked her to dine with them at their early dinner; James stood behind Miss Furnivall's chair, and I behind Miss Rosamond's all in state; and, after dinner, she would play about in a corner of the great drawing-room, as still as any mouse, while Miss Furnivall slept, and I had my dinner in the kitchen. But she was glad enough to come to me in the nursery afterwards; for, as she said, Miss Furnivall was so sad, and Mrs Stark so dull; but she and I were merry enough; and by and by, I got not to care for that weird rolling music, which did one no harm, if we did not know where it came from.

That winter was very cold. In the middle of October the frosts began, and lasted many, many weeks. I remember, one day at dinner, Miss Furnivall lifted up her sad heavy eyes, and said to Mrs Stark, 'I am afraid we shall have a terrible winter,' in a strange kind of meaning way. But Mrs Stark pretended not to hear and talked very loud of something else. My little lady and I did not care for the frost, not we! As long as it was dry, we climbed up the steep brows, behind the house, and went up on the Fells which were bleak, and bare enough, and there we ran races in the fresh, sharp air; and once we came down by a new path that took us past the two old, gnarled holly trees, which grew about half-way down by the east side of the house. But the days grew shorter and shorter; and the old lord, if it was he, played away more and more stormily and sadly on the great organ.

One Sunday afternoon, – it must have been towards the end of November – I asked Dorothy to take charge of little Missy, when she came out of the drawing-room, after Miss Furnivall had had her nap, for it was too cold to take her with me to church, and I wanted to go. And Dorothy was glad enough to promise and was so fond of the child that all seemed well; and Bessy and I set off very briskly, though the sky hung heavy and black over the white earth, as if the night had never fully gone away; and the air, though still, was very biting and keen.

'We shall have a fall of snow,' said Bessy to me. And sure enough, even while we were in church, it came down thick, in great large flakes, so thick it almost darkened the windows. It had stopped snowing before we came out, but it lay soft, thick and deep beneath our feet, as we tramped home. Before we got to the hall, the moon rose, and I think it was lighter then – what with the moon, and what with the white, dazzling snow – than it had been when we went to church, between two and three o'clock. I have not told you that Miss Furnivall and Mrs Stark never went to church; they used to read the prayers together in their quiet, gloomy way; they seemed to feel the Sunday very long without their tapestry work to be busy at. So when I went to Dorothy in the kitchen, to fetch Miss Rosamond and take her upstairs with me, I did not much wonder when the old woman told me that the ladies had kept the child with them, and that she had never come to the kitchen, as I had bidden her, when she was tired of behaving pretty in the drawing-room. So I took off my things and went to find her, and bring her to her supper in the nursery. But when I went into the best drawing-room, there sat the two old ladies, very still and quiet, dropping out a word now and then, but looking as if nothing so bright and merry as Miss Rosamond had ever been near them. Still I thought she might be hiding from me; it was one of her pretty ways, and that she had persuaded them to look as if they knew nothing about her; so I went softly peeping under this sofa, and behind that chair, making believe I was sadly frightened at not finding her.

'What's the matter, Hester?' said Mrs Stark, sharply. I don't know if Miss Furnivall had seen me, for, as I told you, she was very deaf, and she sat quite still, idly staring into the fire, with her hopeless face.

'I'm only looking for my little Rosy-posy,' replied I, still thinking that the child was there, and near me, though I could not see her.

'Miss Rosamond is not here,' said Mrs Stark, 'She went away more than an hour ago to find Dorothy.' And she too turned and went on looking into the fire.

My heart sank at this, and I began to wish I had never left my darling. I went back to Dorothy and told her. James was gone out for the day, but she and me and Bessy took lights and went up into the nursery first and then we roamed over the great, large house, calling and entreating Miss Rosamond to come out of her hiding-place, and not frighten us to death in that way. But there was no answer; no sound.

'Oh!' said I at last, 'Can she have got into the east wing and hidden there?' But Dorothy said it was not possible, for that she herself had never been in there; that the doors were always locked, and my lord's steward had the keys, she believed; at any rate, neither she nor James had ever seen them; so I said I would go back, and see if, after all, she was not hidden in the drawing-room, unknown to the old ladies; and if I found her there, I said, I would whip her well for the fright she had given me; but I never meant to do it. Well, I went back to the west drawing-room, and I told Mrs Stark we could not find her anywhere, and asked for leave to look all about the furniture there, for I thought now, that she might have fallen asleep in some warm, hidden corner; but no! We looked, Miss Furnivall got up and looked, trembling all over, and she was nowhere there; then we set off again, every one in the house, and looked in all the places we had searched before, but we could not find her. Miss Furnivall shivered and shook so much that Mrs Stark took her back into the warm drawing-room, but not before they had made me promise to bring her to them when she was found. Well-a-day! I began to think she never would be found, when I bethought me to look out into the great, front court, all covered with snow. I was upstairs when I looked out; but, it was such clear moonlight, I could see, quite plain, two little footprints, which might be traced from the hall door, and round the corner of the east wing. I don't know how I got down, but I tugged open the great, stiff hall door; and, throwing the skirt of my gown over my head for a cloak, I ran out. I turned the east corner, and there a black shadow fell on the snow; but when I came again into the moonlight, there were the little footmarks going up – up to the Fells. It was bitter cold, so cold that the air almost took the skin off my face as I ran, but I ran on, crying to think how my poor little darling must be perished and frightened. I was within sight of the holly-trees when I saw a shepherd coming down the hill bearing something in his arms wrapped in his maud. He shouted to me, and asked me if I had lost a bairn; and, when I could not speak for crying, he bore towards me, and I saw my wee bairnie lying still, and white, and stiff, in his arms as if she had been dead. He told me he had been up the Fells to gather in his sheep, before the deep cold of night came on, and that under the holly-trees (black marks on the hillside, where no other bush was for miles around) he had found my little lady – my lamb – my queen – my darling, stiff and cold in the terrible sleep which is frost-begotten. Oh, the joy and the tears of having her in my arms again! For I would not let him carry her, but took her, maud and all, into my own arms, and held her near my own warm neck and heart, and felt the life stealing slowly back again into her little gentle limbs. But she was still insensible when we reached the hall, and I had no breath for speech. We went in by the kitchen door.

'Bring the warming-pan,' said I, and I carried her upstairs and began undressing her by the nursery fire which Bessy had kept up. I called my little lammie all the sweet and playful names I could think of – even while my eyes were blinded by my tears – and at last, oh, at length she opened her large blue eyes. Then I put her into her warm bed, and sent Dorothy down to tell Miss Furnivall that all was well; and I made up my mind to sit by my darling's bedside the live-long night. She fell away into a soft sleep as soon as her pretty head had touched the pillow and I watched by her till morning light, when she awakened up bright and clear – or so I thought at first – and, my dears, so I think now.

She said that she had fancied that she should like to go to Dorothy, for that both the old ladies were asleep, and it was very dull in the drawing-room; and that, as she was going through the west lobby, she saw the snow through the high window falling – falling, soft and steady; but she wanted to see it lying pretty and white on the ground, so she made her way into the great hall; and then, going to the window, she saw it bright and soft upon the drive; but while she stood there, she saw a little girl, not so old as she was, 'but so pretty,' said my darling, 'and this little girl beckoned to me to come out; and oh, she was so pretty and so sweet, I could not choose but go.' And then this other little girl had taken her by the hand, and side by side the two had gone round the east corner.

'Now you are a naughty little girl, and telling stories,' said I. 'What would your good Mamma, that is in heaven, and never told a story in her life, say to her little Rosamond, if she heard her – and I daresay she does – telling stories!'

'Indeed, Hester,' sobbed out my child, 'I'm telling you true, indeed I am.' 'Don't tell me,' said I very stern, 'I tracked you by your footmarks through the snow; there were only yours to be seen, and if you had had a little girl to go hand-in-hand with you up the hill, don't you think the footprints would have gone along with yours?'

'I can't help it, dear, dear Hester,' said she, crying, 'if they did not; I never looked at her feet, but she held my hand fast and tight in her little one, and it was very, very cold. She took me up the Fell path, up to the holly trees, and there I saw a lady weeping and crying; but when she saw me she hushed her weeping, and smiled very proud and grand, and took me on her knees, and began to lull me to sleep; and that's all, Hester – but that is true; and my dear Mamma knows it is,' said she, crying. So I thought the child was in a fever, and pretended to believe her, as she went over the story – over and over again, and always the same. At last Dorothy knocked at the door with Miss Rosamond's breakfast; and she told me the old ladies were down in the eating-parlour, and that they wanted to speak to me. They had both been into the night-nursery the evening before, but it was after Miss Rosamond was asleep, so they had only looked at her, not asked me any questions.

'I shall catch it,' thought I to myself, as I went along the north gallery. 'And yet,' I thought, taking courage, 'it was in their charge I left her; and it's they that'd be to blame for letting her steal away unknown and unwatched.' So I went in boldly, and told my story. I told it all to Miss Furnivall, shouting it close to her ear; but when I came to the mention of the other little girl out in the snow coaxing and tempting her out, and willing her up to the grand and beautiful lady by the holly-tree, she threw her arms up – her old and withered arms – and cried aloud, 'Oh, Heaven forgive! Have mercy!'

Mrs Stark took hold of her, roughly enough I thought, but she was past Mrs Stark's management, and spoke to me, in a kind of wild warning and authority. 'Hester! Keep her from that child! It will lure her to her death! That evil child! Tell her it is a wicked, naughty child.'

Then Mrs Stark hurried me out of the room; where indeed, I was glad enough to go. But Miss Furnivall kept shrieking out, 'Oh, have mercy! Wilt Thou never forgive! It is many a long year ago –!

I was very uneasy in my mind after that. I durst never leave Miss Rosamond, night or day, for fear lest she might slip off again, after some fancy or other; and all the more because I thought I could make out that Miss Furnivall was crazy, from their odd ways about her; and I was afraid lest something of the same kind (which might be in the family, you know) hung over my darling. And the great frost never ceased all this time; and, whenever it was a more stormy night than usual, between the gusts, and through the wind, we heard the old lord playing on the great organ. But, old lord or not, wherever Miss Rosamond went there I followed; for my love for her, pretty, helpless orphan, was stronger than my fear for the grand and terrible sound. Besides, it rested with me to keep her cheerful and merry, as beseemed her age. So we played together, and wandered together, here and there and everywhere; for I never dared to lose sight of her again in that large and rambling house.

And so it happened that, one afternoon, not long before Christmas Day, we were playing together on the billiard-table in the great hall (not that we knew the right way of playing but she liked to roll the smooth ivory balls with her pretty hands, and I liked to do whatever she did); and, by and by, without our noticing it, it grew dusk indoors, though it was still light in the open air, and I was thinking of taking her back into the nursery, when, all of a sudden, she cried out, 'Look, Hester! Look! There is my poor little girl out in the snow!'

I turned towards the long narrow windows, and there, sure enough, I saw a little girl, less than my Miss Rosamond –

dressed all unfit to be out-of-doors such a bitter night – crying, and beating against the window-panes, as if she wanted to be let in. She seemed to sob and wail, till Miss Rosamond could bear it no longer, and was flying to the door to open it, when, all of a sudden, and close upon us, the great organ pealed out so loud and thundering, it fairly made me tremble; and all the more, when I remembered me that, even in the stillness of that dead-cold weather, I had heard no sound of little battering hands upon the window-glass, although the Phantom-Child had seemed to put forth all its force; and, although I had seen it wail and cry, no faintest touch of sound had fallen upon my ears. Whether I remembered all this at the very moment, I do not know; the great organ sound had so stunned me into terror; but this I know, that I caught up Miss Rosamond before she got the hall-door opened, and clutched her, and carried her away, kicking and screaming, into the large bright kitchen, where Dorothy and Agnes were busy with their mince-pies.

'What is the matter with my sweet one?' cried Dorothy, as I bore in Miss Rosamond, who was sobbing as if her heart would break.

'She won't let me open the door for my little girl to come in; and she'll die if she is out on the Fells all night. Cruel, naughty Hester,' she said, slapping me; but she might have struck harder, for I had seen a look of ghastly terror on Dorothy's face, which made my very blood run cold.

'Shut the back kitchen door fast and bolt it well,' said she to Agnes. She said no more; she gave me raisins and almonds to quiet Miss Rosamond; but she sobbed about the little girl in the snow, and would not touch any of the good things. I was thankful when she cried herself to sleep in bed. Then I stole down to the kitchen, and told Dorothy I had made up my mind. I would carry my darling back to my father's house in Applethwaite; where, if we lived humbly, we lived at peace. I said I had been frightened enough with the old lord's organ-playing; but now that I had seen for myself this little moaning child, all decked out as no child in the neighbourhood could be, beating and battering to get in, yet always without any sound or noise – with the dark wound on its right shoulder; and that Miss Rosamond had known it again for the phantom that had nearly lured her to her death (which Dorothy knew was true); I would stand it no longer.

I saw Dorothy change colour once or twice. When I had

done, she told me she did not think I could take Miss Rosamond with me, for that she was my lord's ward, and I had no right over her; and she asked me, would I leave the child that I was so fond of, just for sounds and sights that could do me no harm; and that they had all had to get used to in their turns? I was all in a hot, trembling passion; and I said it was very well for her to talk, that knew what these sights and noises betokened, and that had, perhaps, had something to do with the Spectre-Child while it was alive. And I taunted her so, that she told me all she knew, at last; and then I wished I had never been told, for it only made me more afraid than ever.

She said she had heard the tale from old neighbours, that were alive when she was first married; when folks used to come to the hall sometimes, before it had got such a bad name on the countryside; it might not be true, or it might, what she had been told.

The old lord was Miss Furnivall's father – Miss Grace, as Dorothy called her, for Miss Maude was the elder, and Miss Furnivall, by rights. The old lord was eaten up with pride. Such a proud man was never seen or heard of; and his daughters were like him. No one was good enough to wed them, although they had choice enough; for they were the great beauties of their day, as I had seen by their portraits, where they hung in the state drawing-room.

But, as the old saying is, 'pride will have a fall'; and these two haughty beauties fell in love with the same man, and he no better than a foreign musician, whom their father had down from London to play music with him at the Manor House. For, above all things, next to his pride, the old lord loved music. He could play on nearly every instrument that ever was heard of; and it was a strange thing it did not soften him; but he was a fierce, dour old man, and had broken his poor wife's heart with his cruelty, they said. He was mad after music, and would pay any money for it. So he got this foreigner to come; who made such beautiful music, that they said the very birds on the trees stopped their singing to listen. And, by degrees, this foreign gentleman got such a hold over the old lord, that nothing would serve him but that he must come every year; and it was he that had the great organ brought from Holland, and built up in the hall, where it stood now. He taught the old lord to play on it; but many and many a time, when Lord Furnivall was thinking of nothing but his fine organ, and his finer music the dark foreigner was walking abroad in the woods with one of the young ladies; now Miss Maude, and then Miss Grace.

Miss Maude won the day and carried off the prize, such as it was; and he and she were married, all unknown to any one; and before he made his next yearly visit, she had been confined of a little girl at a farm house on the Moors, while her father and Miss Grace thought she was away at Doncaster Races. But though she was a wife and a mother, she was not a bit softened, but as haughty and as passionate as ever; and perhaps more so, for she was jealous of Miss Grace, to whom her foreign husband paid a great deal of court – by way of blinding her – as he told his wife. But Miss Grace triumphed over Miss Maude, and Miss Maude grew fiercer and fiercer, both with her husband and with her sister; and the former, who could easily shake off what was disagreeable, and hide himself in foreign countries – went away a month before his usual time that summer, and half-threatened that he would never come back again. Meanwhile, the little girl was left at the farm house, and her mother used to have her horse saddled and gallop wildly over the hills to see her once every week, at the very least – for where she loved, she loved; and where she hated, she hated. And the old lord went on playing, playing on his organ; and the servants thought the sweet music he made had soothed down his awful temper, of which (Dorothy said) some terrible tales could be told. He grew infirm too, and had to walk with a crutch; and his son – that was the present Lord Furnivall's father – was with the army in America, and the other son at sea; so Miss Maude had it pretty much her own way, and she and Miss Grace grew colder and bitterer to each other every day; till at last they hardly ever spoke, except when the old lord was by. The foreign musician came again the next summer, but it was for the last time; for they led him such a life with their jealousy and their passions, that he grew weary and went away, and never was heard of again. And Miss Maude, who had always meant to have her marriage acknowledged when her father should be dead, was left now a deserted wife – whom nobody knew to have been married – with a child that she dared not own, although she loved it to distraction; living with a father whom she feared, and a sister whom she hated. When the next summer passed over and the dark foreigner never came, both Miss Maude and Miss Grace grew gloomy and sad; they had a haggard look about them, though they looked handsome as ever. But by and by, Miss Maude brightened; for her father grew more and more infirm, and more than ever carried away by his music; and she and Miss Grace lived almost entirely apart, having separate rooms, the one on the west side, Miss Maude on the east – those very rooms which were now shut up. So she thought she might have her little girl with her, and no one need ever know except those who dared not speak about it, and were bound to believe that it was, as she said, a cottager's child she had taken a fancy to. All this, Dorothy said, was pretty well known; but what came afterwards, no one knew, except Miss Grace, and Mrs Stark, who was even then her maid, and much more of a friend to her than ever her sister had been. But the servants supposed, from words that were dropped, that Miss Maude had triumphed over Miss Grace, and told her that all the time the dark foreigner had been mocking her with pretended love – he was her own husband; the colour left Miss Grace's cheek and lips that very day for ever, and she was heard to say many a time that sooner or later she would have her revenge; and Mrs Stark was for ever spying about the east rooms.

One fearful night, just after the New Year had come in, when the snow was lying thick and deep, and the flakes were still falling – fast enough to blind anyone who might be out and abroad – there was a great and violent noise heard, and the old lord's voice above all, cursing and swearing awfully – and the cries of a little child – and the proud defiance of a fierce woman – and the sound of a blow – and a dead stillness – and moans and wailings dying away on the hillside! Then the old lord summoned all his servants, and told them, with terrible oaths, and words more terrible, that his daughter had disgraced herself, and that he had turned her out of doors – her, and her child – and that if ever they gave her help, or food, or shelter, he prayed that they might never enter Heaven. And, all the while, Miss Grace stood by him, white and still as any stone; and when he had ended, she heaved a great sigh, as much as to say her work was done, and her end was accomplished. But the old lord never touched his organ again, and died within the year; and no wonder! For, on the morrow of that wild and fearful night, the shepherds, coming down the Fell side, found Miss Maude, sitting, all crazy and smiling, under the holly-trees, nursing a dead child, with a terrible mark on its right shoulder. 'But that was not what killed it,' said Dorothy, 'it was the frost and the cold; every wild creature was in its hole, and every beast in its fold – while the child and its mother were turned out to wander on the Fells! And now you know all! And I wonder if you are less frightened now?'

I was more frightened than ever; but I said I was not. I wished myself and Miss Rosamond well out of that dreadful house for ever; but I would not leave her, and I dared not take her away. But oh, how I watched her and guarded her! We bolted the doors and shut the windows fast, an hour or more before dark, rather than leave them open five minutes too late. But my little lady still heard the weird child crying and mourning; and not all we could do or say could keep her from wanting to go to her, and let her in from the cruel wind and the snow; all this time, I kept away from Miss Furnivall and Mrs Stark, as much as ever I could; for I feared them – I knew no good could be about them, with their grey, hard faces and their dreamy eyes, looking back into the ghastly years that were gone. But, even in my fear, I had a kind of pity – for Miss Furnivall, at least. Those gone down to the pit can hardly have a more hopeless look than that which was ever on her face. At last I even got so sorry for her – who never said a word but what was forced from her – that I prayed for her; and I taught Miss Rosamond to pray for one who had done a deadly sin; but often, when she came to those words, she would listen, and start up from her knees, and say, 'I hear my little girl plaining and crying very sad – Oh, let her in, or she will die!'

One night – just after New Year's Day had come at last, and the long winter had taken a turn, as I hoped – I heard the west drawing room bell ring three times, which was the signal for me. I would not leave Miss Rosamond alone, for all she was asleep – for the old lord had been playing wilder than ever – and feared lest my darling should wake to hear the spectre child; see her I knew she could not. I had fastened the windows too well for that. So I took her out of her bed and wrapped her up in such outer clothes as were most handy, and carried her down to the drawing room, where the old ladies sat at their tapestry work as usual. They looked up when I came in, and Mrs Stark asked, quite astonished, 'Why did I bring Miss Rosamond there, out of her warm bed?' I had begun to whisper, 'Because I was afraid of her being tempted out while I was away by the wild child in the snow,' when she stopped me short (with a glance at Miss Furnivall) and said Miss Furnivall wanted me to undo some work she had done wrong, and which neither of them could see to unpick. So I laid my pretty dear on the sofa and sat down on a stool by them, and hardened my heart against them, as I heard the wind rising and howling.

Miss Rosamond slept on sound, for all the wind blew so; and Miss Furnivall said never a word, nor looked round when the gusts shook the windows. All at once, she started to her full height, and put up one hand, as if to bid us listen.

'I hear voices,' said she, 'I hear terrible screams – I hear my father's voice.'

Just at that moment, my darling wakened with a sudden start: 'My little girl is crying, oh, how she is crying,' and she tried to get up and go to her, but she got her feet entangled in the blanket, and I caught her up; for my flesh had begun to creep at these noises, which they heard while we could catch no sound. In a minute or two the noises came and gathered fast and filled our ears; we, too, heard voices and screams and no longer heard the winter's wind that raged abroad. Mrs Stark looked at me and I at her, but we dared not speak. Suddenly, Miss Furnivall went towards the door, out into the ante-room, through the west lobby, and opened the door into the great hall. Mrs Stark followed, and I durst not be left, though my heart almost stopped beating for fear. I wrapped my darling tight in my arms, and went out with them. In the hall the screams were louder than ever; they sounded to come from the east wing – nearer and nearer – close on the other side of the locked-up doors – close behind them. Then I noticed that the great bronze chandelier seemed all alight, though the hall was dim, and that a fire was blazing in the vast hearth-place, though it gave no heat; and I shuddered up with terror and folded my darling closer to me. But as I did so, the east door shook, and she, suddenly struggling to get free from me, cried, "Hester! I must go! My little girl is there; I hear her; she is coming! Hester, I must go.'

I held her tight with all my strength; with a set will I held her. If I had died, my hands would have grasped her still, I was so resolved in my mind. Miss Furnivall stood listening and paid no regard to my darling, who had got down to the ground, and whom I, upon my knees now, was holding with both my arms clasped round her neck; she was still striving and crying to get free.

All at once, the east door gave way with a thundering crash, as if torn open in a violent passion; and there came into that broad and mysterious light, the figure of a tall old man, with grey hair and gleaming eyes. He drove before him, with many a relentless gesture of abhorrence, a stern and beautiful woman with a little child clinging to her dress.

'O Hester! O Hester!' cried Miss Rosamond, 'It's the lady! The lady below the holly-trees; and my little girl is with her. Hester, Hester! Let me go to her; they are drawing me to them. I feel them, feel them. I must go.'

Again she was almost convulsed by her efforts to get away; but I held her tighter and tighter, till I feared I should do her a hurt; but rather that than let her go towards those terrible phantoms. They passed along towards the great hall door, where the winds howled and ravened for their prey; but before they reached that, the lady turned; and I could see that she defied the old man with a fierce and proud defiance; but then she quailed and then she threw up her arms wildly and piteously to save her child, her little child, from a blow from his uplifted crutch.

And Miss Rosamond was torn as by a power stronger than mine, and writhed in my arms and sobbed (for by this time the poor darling was growing faint.)

'They want me to go with them, on to the Fells, they are drawing me to them. Oh, my little girl, I would come, but cruel, wicked Hester holds me very tight.' But when she saw the uplifted crutch she swooned away, and I thanked God for it. Just at this moment, when the tall old man, his hair streaming as in the blast of a furnace, was going to strike the little, shrinking child – Miss Furnivall, the old woman by my side, cried out, 'Oh, father, father, spare the little innocent child!' But just then I saw – we all saw – another phantom shape itself, and grow clear out of the blue and misty light that filled the hall; we had not seen her till now, for it was another lady who stood by the old man, with a look of relentless hate and triumphant scorn. That figure was very beautiful to look upon, with a soft white hat drawn down over the proud brows, and a red and curling lip. It was dressed in an open robe of blue satin. I had seen that figure before. It was the likeness of Miss Furnivall in her youth; and the terrible phantoms moved on, regardless of old Miss Furnivall's wild entreaty – and the uplifted crutch fell on the right shoulder of the little child, and the younger sister looked on, stony and deadly serene. But at that moment, the dim lights, and the fire that gave no heat, went out of themselves, and Miss Furnivall lay at our feet stricken down by the palsy – death-stricken.

Yes! she was carried to her bed that night never to rise again. She lay with her face to the wall, muttering low but muttering alway, 'Alas! alas! What is done in youth can never be undone in age! What is done in youth can never be undone in age!'

# *Sir Edmund Orme*

Henry James

The statement appears to have been written, though the fragment is undated, long after the death of his wife, whom I take to have been one of the persons referred to. There is, however, nothing in the strange story to establish this point, which is, perhaps, not of importance. When I took possession of his effects I found these pages, in a locked drawer, among papers relating to the unfortunate lady's too brief career (she died in a childbirth a year after her marriage), letters, memoranda, accounts, faded photographs, cards of invitation. That is the only connection I can point to, and you may easily and will probably say that the tale is too extravagant to have had a demonstrable origin. I cannot, I admit, vouch for his having intended it as a report of real occurrence. I can only vouch for his general veracity. In any case it was written for himself, not for others. I offer it to others – having full option – precisely because it is so singular. Let them, in respect to the form of the thing, bear in mind that it was written quite for himself. I have altered nothing but the names.

*

If there's a story in the matter I recognize the exact moment at which it began. This was on a soft, still Sunday noon in November, just after church, on the sunny Parade. Brighton was full of people; it was the height of the season, and the day was even more respectable than lovely – which helped to account for the multitude of walkers. The blue sea itself was decorous; it seemed to doze, with a gentle snore (if that *be* decorum), as if nature were preaching a sermon. After writing letters all the morning I had come out to take a look at it before luncheon. I was leaning over the rail which separates the

King's Road from the beach, and I think I was smoking a cigarette, when I became conscious of an intended joke in the shape of a light walking-stick laid across my shoulders. The idea, I found, had been thrown off by Teddy Bostwick, of the Rifles, and was intended as a contribution to talk. Our talk came off as we strolled together – he always took your arm to show you he forgave your obtuseness about his humour – and looked at the people, and bowed to some of them, and wondered who others were, and differed in opinion as to the prettiness of the girls. About Charlotte Marden we agreed, however, as we saw her coming toward us with her mother; and there surely could have been no one who wouldn't have agreed with us. The Brighton air, of old, used to make plain girls pretty and pretty girls prettier still – I don't know whether it works the spell now. The place, at any rate, was rare for complexions, and Miss Marden's was one that made people turn round. It made *us* stop, heaven knows – at least, it was one of the things, for we already knew the ladies.

We turned with them, we joined them, we went where they were going. They were only going to the end and back – they had just come out of church. It was another manifestation of Teddy's humour that he got immediate possession of Charlotte, leaving me to walk with her mother. However, I was not unhappy; the girl was before me and I had her to talk about. We prolonged our walk, Mrs Marden kept me, and presently she said she was tired and must sit down. We found a place on a sheltered bench – we gossiped as the people passed. It had already struck me, in this pair, that the resemblance between the mother and the daughter was wonderful even among such resemblances – the more so that it took so little account of a difference of nature. One often hears mature mothers spoken of as warnings – signposts, more or less discouraging, of the way daughters may go. But there was nothing deterrent in the idea that Charlotte, at fifty-five, should be as beautiful, even though it were conditioned on her being as pale and preoccupied, as Mrs Marden. At twenty-two she had a kind of rosy blankness and she was admirably handsome. Her head had the charming shape of her mother's, and her features the same fine order. Then there were looks and movements and tones (movements when you could scarcely say whether it were aspect or sound), which, between the two personalities, were a reflection, a recall.

These ladies had a small fortune and a cheerful little house at Brighton, full of portraits and tokens and trophies (stuffed animals on the top of bookcases, and sallow, varnished fish under glass), to which Mrs Marden professed herself attached by pious memories. Her husband had been 'ordered' there in ill-health, to spend the last years of his life, and she had already mentioned to me that it was a place in which she felt herself still under the protection of his goodness. His goodness appeared to have been great, and she sometimes had the air of defending it against mysterious imputations. Some sense of protection, of an influence invoked and cherished, was evidently necessary to her, she had a dim wistfulness, a longing for security. She wanted friends and she had a good many. She was kind to me on our first meeting, and I never suspected her of the vulgar purpose of 'making up' to me – a suspicion, of course, unduly frequent in conceited young men. It never struck me that she wanted me for her daughter, nor yet, like some unnatural mammas, for herself. It was as if they had had a common deep, shy need and had been ready to say: 'Oh, be friendly to us and be trustful! Don't be afraid, you won't be expected to marry us.' 'Of course there's something about mamma; that's really what makes her such a dear!' Charlotte said to me, confidentially, at an early stage of our acquaintance. She worshipped her mother's appearance. It was the only thing she was vain of; she accepted the raised eyebrows as a charming ultimate fact. 'She looks as if she were waiting for the doctor, dear mamma,' she said on another occasion. 'Perhaps *you're* the doctor; do you think you are?' It appeared in the event that I had some healing power. At any rate when I learned, for she once dropped the remark, that Mrs Marden also thought there was something 'awfully strange' about Charlotte, the relation between the two ladies became extremely interesting. It was happy enough, at bottom; each had the other so much on her mind.

On the Parade the stream of strollers held its course, and Charlotte presently went by with Teddy Bostwick. She smiled and nodded and continued, but when she came back she stopped and spoke to us. Captain Bostwick positively declined to go in, he said the occasion was too jolly: might they therefore take another turn? Her mother dropped a 'Do as you like,' and the girl gave me an impertinent smile over her shoulder as they quitted us. Teddy looked at me with his glass in one eye; but I didn't mind that; it was only of Miss Marden I was thinking as I observed to my companion, laughing:

'She's a bit of a coquette, you know.'

'Don't say that – don't say that!' Mrs Marden murmured.

'The nicest girls always are – just a little,' I was magnanimous enough to plead.

'Then why are they always punished?'

The intensity of the question startled me – it had come out in such a vivid flash. Therefore I had to think a moment before I inquired: 'What do you know about it?'

'I was a bad girl myself.'

'And were you punished?'

'I carry it through life,' said Mrs Marden, looking away from me. 'Ah!' she suddenly panted, in the next breath, rising to her feet and staring at her daughter, who had reappeared again with Captain Bostwick. She stood a few seconds, with the queerest expression in her face; then she sank upon the seat again and I saw that she had blushed crimson. Charlotte, who had observed her movement, came straight up to her and, taking her hand with quick tenderness, seated herself on the other side of her. The girl had turned pale – she gave her mother a fixed, frightened look. Mrs Marden, who had had some shock which escaped our detection, recovered herself; that is she sat quiet and inexpressive, gazing at the indifferent crowd, the sunny air, the slumbering sea. My eye happened to fall, however, on the interlocked hands of the two ladies, and I quickly guessed that the grasp of the elder one was violent. Bostwick stood before them, wondering what was the matter and asking me from his little vacant disk if *I* knew; which led Charlotte to say to him after a moment, with a certain irritation:

'Don't stand there that way, Captain Bostwick; go away – *please* go away.'

I got up at this, hoping that Mrs Marden wasn't ill; but she immediately begged that we would *not* go away, that we would particularly stay and that we would presently come home to lunch. She drew me down beside her and for a moment I felt her hand pressing my arm in a way that might have been an involuntary betrayal of distress and might have been a private signal. What she might have wished to point out to me I couldn't divine: perhaps she had seen somebody or something abnormal in the crowd. She explained to us in a few minutes that she was all right; that she was only liable to palpitations – they came as quickly as they went. It was time to move, and we moved. The incident was felt to be closed. Bostwick and I lunched with our sociable friends, and when I walked away with him he declared that he had never seen such dear kind creatures.

Mrs Marden had made us promise to come back the next day to tea, and had exhorted us in general to come as often as we could. Yet the next day, when at five o'clock I knocked at the door of the pretty house, it was to learn that the ladies had gone up to town. They had left a message for us with the butler: he was to say that they had suddenly been called – were very sorry. They would be absent a few days. This was all I could extract from the dumb domestic. I went again three days later, but they were still away; and it was not till the end of a week that I got a note from Mrs Marden, saying 'We are back; do come and forgive us.' It was on this occasion, I remember (the occasion of my going just after getting the note), that she told me she had intuitions. I don't know how many people there were in England at that time in that predicament, but there were very few who would have mentioned it; so that the announcement struck me as original, especially as her point was that some of these uncanny promptings were connected with me. There were other people present – idle Brighton folk, old women with frightened eyes and irrelevant interjections – and I had but a few minutes' talk with Charlotte; but the day after this I met them both at dinner and had the satisfaction of sitting next to Miss Marden. I recall that hour as the hour on which it first completely came over me that she was a beautiful, liberal creature. I had seen her personality in patches and gleams, like a song sung in snatches, but now it was before me in a large rosy glow, as if it had been a full volume of sound – I heard the whole of the air. It was sweet, fresh music – I was often to hum it over.

After dinner I had a few words with Mrs Marden; it was at the moment, late in the evening, when tea was handed about. A servant passed near us with a tray, I asked her if she would have a cup, and, on her assenting, took one and handed it to her. She put out her hand for it and I gave it to her, safely as I supposed; but as she was in the act of receiving it she started and faltered, so that the cup and saucer dropped with a crash of porcelain and without, on the part of my interlocutress, the usual woman's movement to save her dress. I stooped to pick up the fragments and when I raised myself Mrs Marden was looking across the room at her daughter, who looked back at her smiling, but with an anxious light in her eyes. 'Dear mamma, what on earth *is* the matter with you?' the silent question seemed to say. Mrs Marden coloured, just as she had done after her strange movement on the Parade the other week, and I was therefore surprised when she said to me with unexpected assurance: 'You should really have a steadier hand!' I had begun to stammer a defence of my hand when I became aware that she had fixed her eyes upon me with an intense appeal. It was ambiguous at first and only added to my confusion; then suddenly I understood, as plainly as if she had murmured 'Make believe it was you – make believe it was you.' The servant came back to take the morsels of the cup and wipe up the spilt tea, and while I was in the midst of making believe Mrs Marden abruptly brushed away from me and from her daughter's attention and went into another room. I noticed that she gave no heed to the state of her dress.

I saw nothing more of either of them that evening, but the next morning, in the King's Road, I met Miss Marden with a roll of music in her muff. She told me she had been a little way alone, to practise duets with a friend, and I asked her if she would go a little way further in company. She gave me leave to attend her to her door, and as we stood before it I inquired if I might go in. 'No, not to-day – I don't want you,' she said, candidly, though not roughly; while the words caused me to direct a wistful, disconcerted gaze at one of the windows of the house. It fell upon the white face of Mrs Marden, who was looking out at us from the drawing-room. She stood there long enough for me to see that it *was* she and not an apparition, as I had thought for a second, and then she vanished before her daughter had observed her. The girl, during our walk, had said nothing about her. As I had been told they didn't want me I left them alone a little, after which circumstances supervened that kept us still longer apart. I finally went up to London, and while there I received a pressing invitation to come immediately down to Tranton, a pretty old place in Sussex belonging to a couple whose acquaintance I had late made.

I went to Tranton from town, and on arriving found the Mardens, with a dozen other people, in the house. The first thing Mrs Marden said was: 'Will you forgive me?' and when I asked what I had to forgive she answered: 'My throwing my tea over you.' I replied that it had gone over herself; whereupon she said: 'At any rate I was very rude; but some day I think you'll understand, and then you'll make allowances for me.' The first day I was there she dropped two or three of these references (she had already indulged in more than one), to the mystic initiation that was in store for me; so that I began, as the phrase is, to chaff her about it, to say I would rather it were less wonderful and take it out at once. She answered that when it should come to me I would have to take it out – there would be little enough option. That it *would* come was privately clear to her, a deep presentiment, which was the only reason she had ever mentioned the matter. Didn't I remember she had told me she had intuitions? From the first time of her seeing me she had been sure there were things I should not escape knowing. Meanwhile there was nothing to do but wait and keep cool, not to be precipitate. She particularly wished not to be any more nervous than she was. And I was above all not to be nervous myself – one got used to everything. I declared that though I couldn't make out what she was talking about I was terribly frightened; the absence of a clue gave such a range to one's imagination. I exaggerated on purpose; for if Mrs Marden was mystifying I can scarcely say she was alarming. I couldn't imagine what she meant, but I wondered more than I shuddered. I might have said to myself that she was a little wrong in the upper story; but that never occurred to me. She struck me as hopelessly right.

There were other girls in the house, but Charlotte Marden was the most charming; which was so generally felt to be the case that she really interfered with the slaughter of ground game. There were two or three men, and I was of the number, who actually preferred her to the society of the beaters. In short she was recognized as a form of sport superior and exquisite. She was kind to all of us – she made us go out late and come in early. I don't know whether she flirted, but several other members of the party thought *they* did. Indeed, as regards himself, Teddy Bostwick, who had come over from Brighton, was visibly sure.

The third day I was at Tranton was a Sunday, and there was a very pretty walk to morning service over the fields. It was grey, windless weather, and the bell of the little old church that nestled in the hollow of the Sussex down sounded near and domestic. We were a straggling procession, in the mild damp air (which, as always at that season, gave one the feeling that after the trees were bare there was more of it – a larger sky), and I managed to fall a good way behind with Miss Marden. I remember entertaining, as we moved together over the turf, a strong impulse to say something intensely personal, something violent and important – important for *me*, such as that I had never seen her so lovely, or that that particular moment was the sweetest of my life. But always, in youth, such words have been on the lips many times before they are spoken; and I had the sense, not that I didn't know her well enough (I cared little for that), but that she didn't know *me* well enough. In the church, where there were old Tranton tombs and brasses, the big Tranton pew was full. Several of us were scattered, and I found a seat for Miss Marden, and another for myself beside it, at a distance from her mother and from most of our friends. There were two or three decent rustics on the bench, who moved in further to make room for us, and I took my place first, to cut off my companion from our neighbours. After she was seated there was still a space left, which remained empty till service was about half over.

This at least was the moment at which I became aware that another person had entered and had taken the seat. When I noticed him he had apparently been for some minutes in the pew, for he had settled himself and put down his hat beside him, and with his hands crossed on the nob of his cane, was gazing before him at the altar. He was a pale young man in black, with the air of a gentleman. I was slightly startled on perceiving him, for Miss Marden had not attracted my attention to his entrance by moving to make room for him. After a few minutes, observing that he had no prayer-book, I reached across my neighbour and placed mine before him, on the ledge of the pew; a manoeuvre the motive of which was not unconnected with the possibility that, in my own destitution, Miss Marden would give me one side of *her* velvet volume to hold. The pretext, however, was destined to fail, for at the moment I offered him the book the intruder – whose intrusion I had so condoned – rose from his place without thanking me, stepped noiselessly out of the pew (it had no door), and, so discreetly as to attract no attention, passed down the centre of the church. A few minutes had sufficed for his devotions. His behaviour was unbecoming, his early departure even more than his late arrival; but he managed so quietly that we were not incommoded, and I perceived, on turning a little to glance after him, that nobody was disturbed by his withdrawal. I only noticed, and with surprise, that Mrs Marden had been so affected by it as to rise, involuntarily, an instant, in her place. She stared at him as he passed, but he passed very quickly, and she as quickly dropped down again, though not too soon to catch my eye across the church. Five minutes later I asked Miss Marden, in a low voice, if she would kindly pass me back my prayer-book – I had waited to see if she would spontaneously perform the act. She restored this aid to devotion, but had been so far from troubling herself about it that she could say to me as she did so: 'Why on earth did you put it there?' I was on the point of answering her when she dropped on her knees, and I held my tongue. I had only been going to say: 'To be decently civil.'

After the benediction, as we were leaving our places, I was slightly surprised, again, to see that Mrs Marden, instead of going out with her companions, had come up the aisle to join us, having apparently something to say to her daughter. She said it, but in an instant I observed that it was only a pretext – her real business was with me. She pushed Charlotte forward and suddenly murmured to me: 'Did you see him?'

'The gentleman who sat down here? How could I help seeing him?'

'Hush!' she said, with the intensest excitement; 'don't *speak* to her – don't tell her!' She slipped her hand into my arm, to keep me near her, to keep me, it seemed, away from her daughter. The precaution was unnecessary, for Teddy Bostwick had already taken possession of Miss Marden, and as they passed out of church in front of me I saw one of the other men close up on her other hand. It appeared to be considered that I had had my turn. Mrs Marden withdrew her hand from my arm as soon as we got out, but not before I felt that she had really needed the support. 'Don't speak to any one – don't tell any one!' she went on.

'I don't understand. Tell them what?'

'Why, that you saw him.'

'Surely they saw him for themselves.'

'Not one of them, not one of them.' She spoke in a tone of such passionate decision that I glanced at her – she was staring straight before her. But she felt the challenge of my eyes and she stopped short, in the old brown timber porch of the church, with the others well in advance of us, and said, looking at me now and in a quite extraordinary manner: 'You're the only person, the only person in the world.'

'But *you*, dear madam?'

'Oh me – of course. That's my curse!' And with this she moved rapidly away from me to join the body of the party. I hovered on its outskirts on the way home, for I had food for rumination. Whom had I seen and why was the apparition – it rose before my mind's eye very vividly again – invisible to the others? If an exception had been made for Mrs Marden, why did it constitute a curse, and why was I to share so questionable an advantage? This inquiry, carried on in my own locked breast, kept me doubtless silent enough during luncheon. After luncheon I went out on the old terrace to smoke a cigarette, but I had only taken a couple of turns when I perceived Mrs Marden's moulded mask at the window of one of the rooms which opened on the crooked flags. It reminded me of the same flitting presence at the window at Brighton the day I met Charlotte and walked home with her. But this time my ambiguous friend didn't vanish; she tapped on the pane and motioned me to come in. She was in a queer little apartment, one of the many reception-rooms of which the ground-floor at Tranton consisted; it was known as the Indian room and had a decoration vaguely Oriental – bamboo lounges, lacquered screens, lanterns with long fringes and strange idols in cabinets, objects not held to conduce to sociability. The place was little used, and when I went round to her we had it to ourselves. As soon as I entered she said to me: 'Please tell me this; are you in love with my daughter?'

I hesitated a moment. 'Before I answer your question will you kindly tell what gives you the idea? I don't consider that I have been very forward.'

Mrs Marden, contradicting me with her beautiful anxious eyes, gave me no satisfaction on the point I mentioned; she only went on strenuously:

'Did you say nothing to her on the way to church?'

'What makes you think I said anything?'

'The fact that you saw him.'

'Saw whom, dear Mrs Marden?'

'Oh, you know,' she answered, gravely, even a little reproachfully, as if I were trying to humiliate her by making her phrase the unphraseable.

'Do you mean the gentleman who formed the subject of your strange statement in church – the one who came into the pew?'

'You saw him, you saw him!' Mrs Marden panted, with a strange mixture of dismay and relief.

'Of course I saw him; and so did you.'

'It didn't follow. Did you feel it to be inevitable?'

I was puzzled again. 'Inevitable?'

'That you *should* see him?'

'Certainly, since I'm not blind.'

'You might have been; every one else is.' I was wonderfully at sea, and I frankly confessed it to my interlocutress; but the case was not made clearer by her presently exclaiming: 'I knew you would, from the moment you should be really in love with her! I knew it would be the test – what do I mean? – the proof.'

'Are there such strange bewilderments attached to that high state?' I asked, smiling.

'You perceive there are. You see him, you see him!' Mrs Marden announced, with tremendous exaltation. 'You'll see him again.'

'I've no objection; but I shall take more interest in him if you'll kindly tell me who he is.'

She hesitated, looking down a moment; then she said, raising her eyes: 'I'll tell you if you'll tell me first what you said to her on the way to church.'

'Has she told you I said anything?'

'Do I need that?' smiled Mrs Marden.

'Oh yes, I remember – your intuitions! But I'm sorry to see they're at fault this time; because I really said nothing to your daughter that was the least out of the way.'

'Are you very sure?'

'On my honour, Mrs Marden.'

'Then you consider that you're not in love with her?'

'That's another affair!' I laughed.

'You are – you *are*! You wouldn't have seen him if you hadn't been.'

'Who the deuce *is* he, then, madam?' I inquired with some irritation.

She would still only answer me with another question. 'Didn't you at least *want* to say something to her – didn't you come very near it?'

The question was much to the point; it justified the famous

intuitions. 'Very near it – it was the turn of a hair. I don't know what kept me quiet.'

'That was quite enough,' said Mrs Marden. 'It isn't what you say that determines it; it's what you feel. *That's* what he goes by.'

I was annoyed, at last, by her reiterated reference to an identity yet to be established, and I clasped my hands with an air of supplication which covered much real impatience, a sharper curiosity and even the first short throbs of a certain sacred dread. 'I entreat you to tell me whom you're talking about.'

She threw up her arms, looking away from me, as if to shake off both reserve and responsibility. 'Sir Edmund Orme.'

'And who is Sir Edmund Orme?'

At the moment I spoke she gave a start. 'Hush, here they come.' Then as, following the direction of her eyes, I saw Charlotte Marden on the terrace, at the window, she added, with an intensity of warning: 'Don't notice him – *never*!'

Charlotte, who had had her hands beside her eyes, peering into the room and smiling, made a sign that she was to be admitted, on which I went and opened the long window. Her mother turned away, and the girl came in with a laughing challenge: 'What plot in the world are you two hatching here?' Some plan – I forget what – was in prospect for the afternoon, as to which Mrs Marden's participation or consent was solicited – *my* adhesion was taken for granted – and she had been half over the place in her quest. I was flurried, because I saw that Mrs Marden was flurried (when she turned round to meet her daughter she covered it by a kind of extravagance, throwing herself on the girl's neck and embracing her), and to pass it off I said, fancifully, to Charlotte:

'I've been asking your mother for your hand.'

'Oh, indeed, and has she given it?' Miss Marden answered, gayly.

'She was just going to when you appeared there.'

'Well, it's only for a moment – I'll leave you free.'

'Do you like him, Charlotte?' Mrs Marden asked, with a candour I scarcely expected.

'It's difficult to say it *before* him isn't it?' the girl replied, entering into the humour of the thing, but looking at me as if she didn't like me.

She would have had to say it before another person as well,

for at that moment there stepped into the room from the terrace (the window had been left open), a gentleman who had come into sight, at least into mine, only within the instant. Mrs Marden had said 'Here *they* come,' but he appeared to have followed her daughter at a certain distance. I immediately recognized him as the personage who had sat beside us in church. This time I saw him better, saw that his face and his whole air were strange. I speak of him as a personage, because one felt, indescribably, as if a reigning prince had come into the room. He held himself with a kind of habitual majesty, as if he were different from us. Yet he looked fixedly and gravely at me, till I wondered what he expected of me. Did he consider that I should bend my knee or kiss his hand? He turned his eyes in the same way on Mrs Marden, but she knew what to do. After the first agitation produced by his approach she took no notice of him whatever; it made me remember her passionate adjuration to me. I had to achieve a great effort to imitate her, for though I knew nothing about him but that he was Sir Edmund Orme I felt his presence as a strong appeal, almost as an oppression. He stood there without speaking – young, pale, handsome, clean-shaven, decorous, with extraordinary light blue eyes and something old-fashioned, like a portrait of years ago, in his head, his manner of wearing his hair. He was in complete mourning (one immediately felt that he was very well dressed), and he carried his hat in his hand. He looked again strangely hard at me, harder than any one in the world had ever looked before; and I remember feeling rather cold and wishing he would say something. No silence had ever seemed to me so soundless. All this was of course an impression intensely rapid; but that it had consumed some instants was proved to me suddenly by the aspect of Charlotte Marden, who stared from her mother to me and back again (he never looked at her, and she had no appearance of looking at him), and then broke out with: 'What on earth is the matter with you? You've such odd faces!' I felt the colour come back to mine, and when she went on in the same tone: 'One would think you had seen a ghost!' I was conscious that I had turned very red. Sir Edmund Orme never blushed, and I could see that he had no capacity for embarrassment. One had met people of that sort, but never any one with such a grand indifference.

'Don't be impertinent; and go and tell them all that I'll join them,' said Mrs Marden with much dignity, but with a quaver in her voice.

'And will you come – *you*?' the girl asked, turning away. I made no answer, taking the question, somehow, as meant for her companion. But he was more silent than I, and when she reached the door (she was going out that way), she stopped, with her hand on the knob, and looked at me, repeating it. I assented, springing forward to open the door for her, and as she passed out she exclaimed to me mockingly: 'You haven't got your wits about you – you shan't have my hand!'

I closed the door and turned round to find that Sir Edmund Orme had during the moment my back was presented to him retired by the window. Mrs Marden stood there and we looked at each other long. It had only then – as the girl flitted away – come home to me that her daughter was unconscious of what had happened. It was *that*, oddly enough, that gave me a sudden, sharp shake, and not my own perception of our visitor, which appeared perfectly natural. It made the fact vivid to me that she had been equally unaware of him in church, and the two facts together – now that they were over – set my heart more sensibly beating. I wiped my forehead, and Mrs Marden broke out with a low distressful wail: 'Now you know my life – now you know my life!'

'In God's name who is he – *what* is he?'

'He's a man I wronged.'

'How did you wrong him?'

'Oh, awfully – years ago.'

'Years ago? When, he's very young.'

'Young – young?' cried Mrs Marden. 'He was born before *I* was!'

'Then why does he look so?'

She came nearer to me, she laid her hand on my arm, and there was something in her face that make me shrink a little. 'Don't you understand – don't you *feel*?' she murmured, reproachfully.

'I feel very queer!' I laughed; and I was conscious that my laugh betrayed it.

'He's dead!' said Mrs Marden, from her white face.

'Dead?' I panted. 'Then that gentleman was –?' I couldn't even say the word.

'Call him what you like – there are twenty vulgar names. He's a perfect presence.'

'He's a splendid presence!' I cried. 'The place is haunted – *haunted!*' I exulted in the word as if it represented the fulfilment of my dearest dream.

'It isn't the place – more's the pity! That has nothing to do with it!'

'Then it's you, dear lady?' I said, as if this were still better.

'No, nor me either – I wish it were!'

'Perhaps it's me,' I suggested with a sickly smile.

'It's nobody but my child – my innocent, innocent child!' And with this Mrs Marden broke down – she dropped into a chair and burst into tears. I stammered some question – I pressed on her some bewildered appeal, but she waved me off, unexpectedly and passionately. I persisted – couldn't I help her, couldn't I intervene?' 'You *have* intervened,' she sobbed; 'you're *in* it, you're *in* it.'

'I'm very glad to be in anything so curious,' I boldly declared.

'Glad or not, you can't get out of it.'

'I don't want to get out of it – it's too interesting.'

'I'm glad you like it. Go away.'

'But I want to know more about it.'

'You'll see all you want – go away!'

'But I want to understand what I see.'

'How can you – when I don't understand myself?'

'We'll do so together – we'll make it out.'

At this she got up, doing what she could to obliterate her tears. 'Yes, it will be better together – that's why I've liked you.'

'Oh, we'll see it through!' I declared.

'Then you must control yourself better.'

'I will, I will – with practice.'

'You'll get used to it,' said Mrs Marden, in a tone I never forgot. 'But go and join them – I'll come in a moment.'

I passed out to the terrace and felt that I had a part to play. So far from dreading another encounter with the 'perfect presence,' as Mrs Marden called it, I was filled with an excitement that was positively joyous. I desired a renewal of the sensation – I opened myself wide to the impressions, I went round the house as quickly as if I expected to overtake Sir Edmund Orme. I didn't overtake him just then, but the day was not to close without my recognizing that, as Mrs Marden had said, I should see all I wanted of him.

We took, or most of us took, the collective sociable walk

which, in the English country-house, is the consecrated pastime on Sunday afternoons. We were restricted to such a regulated ramble as the ladies were good for; the afternoons, moreover, were short, and by five o'clock we were restored to the fireside in the hall, with a sense, on my part at least, that we might have done a little more for our tea. Mrs Marden had said she would join us, but she had not appeared; her daughter, who had seen her again before we went out, only explained that she was tired. She remained invisible all the afternoon, but this was a detail to which I gave as little heed as I had given to the circumstance of my not having Miss Marden to myself during all our walk. I was too much taken up with another emotion to care; I felt beneath my feet the threshold of the strange door, in my life, which had suddenly been thrown open and out of which unspeakable vibrations played up through me like a fountain. I had heard all my days of apparitions, but it was a different thing to have seen one and to know that I should in all probability see it familiarly, as it were, again. I was on the look-out for it, as a pilot for the flash of a revolving light, and I was ready to generalize on the sinister subject, to declare that ghosts were much less alarming and much more amusing than was commonly supposed. There is no doubt that I was extremely nervous. I couldn't get over the distinction conferred upon me – the exception (in the way of mystic enlargement of vision), made in my favour. At the same time I think I did justice to Mrs Marden's absence; it was a commentary on what she had said to me – 'Now you know my life.' She had probably been seeing Sir Edmund Orme for years, and, not having my firm fibre, she had broken down under him. Her nerve was gone, though she had also been able to attest that, in a degree, one got used to him. She had got used to breaking down.

Afternoon tea, when the dusk fell early, was a friendly hour at Tranton; the firelight played into the wide, white last-century hall; sympathies almost confessed themselves, lingering together, before dressing, on deep sofas, in muddy boots, for last words, after walks; and even solitary absorption in the third volume of a novel that was wanted by some one else seemed a form of geniality. I watched my moment and went over to Charlotte Marden when I saw that she was about to withdraw. The ladies had left the place one by one, and after I had addressed myself particularly to Miss Marden the three men who were near her gradually dispersed. We had a little vague talk – she appeared preoccupied, and heaven knows *I* was – after which she said she must go: she should be late for dinner. I proved to her by book that she had plenty of time, and she objected that she must at any rate go up to see her mother: she was afraid she was unwell.

'On the contrary, she's better than she has been for a long time – I'll guarantee that,' I said. 'She has found out that she can have confidence in me, and that has done her good.' Miss Marden had dropped into her chair again. I was standing before her, and she looked up at me without a smile – with a dim distress in her beautiful eyes; not exactly as if I were hurting her, but as if she were no longer disposed to treat as a joke what had passed (whatever it was, it was at the same time difficult to be serious about it), between her mother and myself. But I could answer her inquiry in all kindness and candour, for I was really conscious that the poor lady had put off a part of her burden on me and was proportionately relieved and eased. 'I'm sure she has slept all the afternoon as she hasn't slept for years,' I went on. 'You have only to ask her.'

Charlotte got up again. 'You make yourself out very useful.'

'You've a good quarter of an hour,' I said. 'Haven't I a right to talk to you a little this way, alone, when your mother has given me your hand?'

'And is it *your* mother who has given me yours? I'm much obliged to her, but I don't want it. I think our hands are not our mothers' – they happen to be our own!' laughed the girl.

'Sit down, sit down and let me tell you!' I pleaded.

I still stood before her, urgently, to see if she wouldn't oblige me. She hesitated a moment, looking vaguely this way and that, as if under a compulsion that was slightly painful. The empty hall was quiet – we heard the loud ticking of the great clock. Then she slowly sank down and I drew a chair close to her. This made me face round to the fire again, and with the movement I perceived, disconcertedly, that we were not alone. The next instant, more strangely than I can say, my discomposure, instead of increasing, dropped, for the person before the fire was Sir Edmund Orme. He stood there as I had seen him in the Indian room, looking at me with the expressionless attention which borrowed its sternness from his sombre distinction. I knew so much more about him now that I had to check a movement of recognition, an acknowledgement of his presence. When once I was aware of it, and that it lasted, the sense that we had company, Charlotte and I, quitted me; it was impressed on me on the contrary that I was more intensely alone with Miss Marden. She evidently saw nothing to look at, and I made a tremendous and very nearly successful effort to conceal from her that my own situation was different. I say 'very nearly,' because she watched me an instant – while my words were arrested – in a way that made me fear she was going to say again, as she had said in the Indian room: 'What on earth is the matter with you?'

What the matter with me was I quickly told her, for the full knowledge of it rolled over me with the touching spectacle of her unconsciousness. It was touching that she became, in the presence of this extraordinary portent. What was portended, danger or sorrow, bliss or bane, was a minor question; all I saw, as she sat there, was that, innocent and charming, she was close to a horror, as she might have thought it, that happened to be veiled from her but that might at any moment be disclosed. I didn't mind it now, as I found, but nothing was more possible than she should, and if it wasn't curious and interesting it might easily be very dreadful. If I didn't mind it for myself, as I afterwards saw, this was largely because I was so taken up with the idea of protecting *her*. My heart beat high with this idea, on the spot; I determined to do everything I could to keep her sense sealed. What I could do might have been very obscure to me if I had not, in all this, become more aware than of anything else that I loved her. The way to save her was to love her, and the way to love her was to tell her, now and here, that I did so. Sir Edmund Orme didn't prevent me, especially as after a moment he turned his back to us and stood looking discreetly at the fire. At the end of another moment he leaned his head on his arm, against the chimney-piece, with an air of gradual dejection, like a spirit still more weary than discreet. Charlotte Marden was startled by what I said to her, and she jumped up to escape it; but she took no offence – my tenderness was too real. She only moved about the room with a deprecating murmur, and I was so busy following up any little advantage that I might have obtained that I didn't notice in what manner Sir Edmund Orme disappeared. I only observed presently that he had gone. This made no difference – he had been so small a hindrance; I only remember being struck, suddenly, with something inexorable in the slow, sweet, sad headshake that Miss Marden gave me.

'I don't ask for an answer now,' I said; 'I only want you to be sure – to know how much depends on it.'

'Oh, I don't want to give it to you, now or ever!' she replied. 'I hate the subject, please – I wish one could be let alone.' And then, as if I might have found something harsh in this irrepressible, artless cry of beauty beset, she added quickly, vaguely, kindly, as she left the room: 'Thank you, thank you – thank you so much!'

At dinner I could be generous enough to be glad, for her, that I was placed on the same side of the table with her, where she couldn't see me. Her mother was nearly opposite me, and just after we had sat down Mrs Marden gave me one long, deep look, in which all our strange communion was expressed. It meant of course 'She has told me,' but it meant other things beside. At any rate I know what my answering look to her conveyed: 'I've seen him again – I've seen him again!' This didn't prevent Mrs Marden from treating her neighbours with her usual scrupulous blandness. After dinner, when, in the drawing-room, the men joined the ladies and I went straight up to her to tell her how I wished we could have some private conversation, she said immediately, in a low tone, looking down at her fan while she opened and shut it:

'He's here – he's here.'

'Here?' I looked round the room, but I was disappointed.

'Look where *she* is,' said Mrs Marden, with just the faintest asperity. Charlotte was in fact not in the main saloon, but in an apartment into which it opened and which was known as the morning-room. I took a few steps and saw her, through a doorway, upright in the middle of the room, talking with three gentlemen whose backs were practically turned to me. For a moment my quest seemed vain; then I recognized that one of the gentlemen – the middle one – was Sir Edmund Orme. This time it *was* surprising that the others didn't see him. Charlotte seemed to be looking straight at him, addressing her conversation to him. She saw me after an instant, however, and immediately turned her eyes away. I went back to her mother with an annoyed sense that the girl would think I was watching *her*, which would be unjust. Mrs Marden had found a small sofa – a little apart – and I sat down beside her. There were some questions I had so wanted to go into that I wished we were once more in the Indian room. I presently gathered, however, that our privacy was all sufficient. We communicated so closely and completely now, and with such silent reciprocities, that it would in every circumstance be adequate.

'Oh, yes, he's there,' I said; 'and at about a quarter-past seven he was in the hall.'

'I knew it at the time, and I was so glad!'

'So glad?'

'That it was your affair, this time, and not mine. It's a rest for me.'

'Did you sleep all the afternoon?' I asked.

'As I haven't done for months. But how did you know that?'

'As *you* knew, I take it, that Sir Edmund was in the hall. We shall evidently each of us know things now – where the other is concerned.'

'Where *he* is concerned,' Mrs Marden amended. 'It's a blessing, the way you take it,' she added, with a long, mild sigh.

'I take it as a man who's in love with your daughter.'

'Of course – of course.' Intense as I now felt my desire for the girl to be, I couldn't help laughing a little at the tone of these words; and it led my companion immediately to say: 'Otherwise you wouldn't have seen him.'

'But every one doesn't see him who's in love with her, or there would be dozens.'

'They're not in love with her as you are.'

'I can, of course, only speak for myself; and I found a moment, before dinner, to do so.'

'She told me immediately.'

'And have I any hope – any chance?'

'That's what *I* long for, what I pray for.'

'Ah, how can I thank you enough?' I murmured.

'I believe it will all pass – if she loves you,' Mrs Marden continued.

'It will all pass?'

'We shall never see him again.'

'Oh, if she loves me I don't care how often I see him!'

'Ah, you take it better than I could,' said my companion. 'You have the happiness not to know – not to understand.'

'I don't indeed. What on earth does he want?'

'He wants to make me suffer.' She turned her wan face upon me with this, and I saw now for the first time, fully, how perfectly, if this had been Sir Edmund Orme's purpose, he had succeeded. 'For what I did to him,' Mrs Marden explained.

'And what did you do to him?'

She looked at me a moment. 'I killed him.' As I had seen him fifty yards away only five minutes before the words gave me a start. 'Yes, I make you jump; be careful. He's there still, but he killed himself. I broke his heart – he thought me awfully bad. We were to have been married, but I broke it off – just at the last. I saw some one I liked better; I had no reason but that. It wasn't for interest, or money, or position, or anything of that sort. All *those* things were his. It was simply that I fell in love with Captain Marden. When I saw him I felt that I couldn't marry any one else. I wasn't in love with Edmund Orme – my mother, my elder sister had brought it about. But he did love me. I told him I didn't care – that I couldn't, that I *wouldn't*. I threw him over, and he took something, some abominable drug or draught that proved fatal. It was dreadful, it was horrible, he was found that way – he died in agony. I married Captain Marden, but not for five years. I was happy, perfectly happy; time obliterates. But when my husband died I began to see him.'

I had listened intently, but I wondered. 'To see your husband?'

'Never, never *that* way, thank God! To see *him*, with Chartie – always with Chartie. The first time it nearly killed me – about seven years ago, when she first came out. Never when I'm by myself – only with her. Sometimes not for months, then every day for a week. I've tried everything to break the spell – doctors and *régimes* and climates; I've prayed to God on my knees. That day at Brighton, on the Parade with you, when you thought I was ill, that was the first for an age. And then, in the evening, when I knocked my tea over you, and the day you were at the door with Charlotte and I saw you from the window – each time he was there.'

'I see, I see.' I was more thrilled than I could say. 'It's an apparition like another.'

'Like another? Have you ever seen another?'

'No, I mean the sort of thing one has heard of. It's tremendously interesting to encounter a case.'

'Do you call me a "case"?' Mrs Marden asked, with exquisite resentment.

'I mean myself.'

'Oh, you're the right one!' she exclaimed. 'I was right when I trusted you.'

'I'm devoutly grateful you did; but what made you do it?'

'I had thought the whole thing out – I had time to in those dreadful years, while he was punishing me in my daughter.'

'Hardly that,' I objected, 'if she never knew.'

'That has been my terror, that she *will*, from one occasion to another. I've an unspeakable dread of the effect on her.'

'She shan't, she shan't!' I declared, so loud that several people looked round. Mrs Marden made me get up, and I had no more talk with her that evening. The next day I told her I must take my departure from Tranton – it was neither comfortable nor considerate to remain as a rejected suitor. She was disconcerted, but she accepted my reasons, only saying to me out of her mournful eyes: 'You'll leave me alone then with my burden?' It was of course understood between us that for many weeks to come there would be no discretion in 'worrying poor Charlotte': such were the terms in which, with odd feminine and maternal inconsistency, she alluded to an attitude on my part that she favoured. I was prepared to be heroically considerate, but it seemed to me that even this delicacy permitted me to say a word to Miss Marden before I went. I begged her, after breakfast, to take a turn with me on the terrace, and as she hesitated, looking at me distantly, I informed her that it was only to ask her a question and to say good-bye – I was leaving Tranton for *her*.

She came out with me, and we passed slowly round the house three or four times. Nothing is finer than this great airy platform, from which every look is a sweep of the country, with the sea on the furthest edge. It might have been that as we passed the windows we were conspicuous to our friends in the house, who would divine, sarcastically, why I was so significantly bolting. But I didn't care; I only wondered whether they wouldn't really this time make out Sir Edmund Orme, who joined us on one of our turns and strolled slowly on the other side of my companion. Of what transcendent essence he was composed I knew not; I have no theory about him (leaving that to others), any more than I have one about such or such another of my fellow-mortals whom I have elbowed in life. He was as positive, as individual, as ultimate a fact as any of these. Above all he was as respectable, as sensitive a fact; so that I should no more have thought of taking a liberty, of practising an experiment with him, of touching him, for instance, or speaking to him, since he set the example of silence, than I should have thought of committing any other social grossness. He had always, as I saw more fully later, the perfect propriety of his position – had always the appearance of being dressed and, in attitude and aspect, of comporting himself, as the occasion demanded. He looked strange, incontestably, but somehow he always looked *right*. I very soon came to attach an idea of beauty to his unmentionable presence, the beauty of an old story of love and pain. What I ended by feeling was that he was on my side, that he was watching over my interest, that he was looking to it that my heart shouldn't be broken. Oh, he had taken it seriously, his own catastrophe – he had certainly proved that in his day. If poor Mrs Marden, as she told me, had thought it out, I also subjected the case to the finest analysis of which my intellect was capable. It was a case of retributive justice. The mother was to pay, in suffering, for the suffering she had inflicted, and as the disposition to jilt a lover might have been transmitted to the daughter, the daughter was to be watched, so that *she* might be made to suffer should she do an equal wrong. She might reproduce her mother in character as vividly as she did in face. On the day she should transgress, in other words, her eyes would be opened suddenly and unpitiedly to the 'perfect presence,' which she would have to work as she could into her conception of a young lady's universe. I had no great fear for her, because I didn't believe she was, in any cruel degree, a coquette. We should have a good deal of ground to get over before I, at least, should be in a position to be sacrificed by her. She couldn't throw me over before she had made a little more of me.

The question I asked her on the terrace that morning was whether I might continue, during the winter, to come to Mrs Marden's house. I promised not to come too often and not to speak to her for three months of the question I had raised the day before. She replied that I might do as I liked, and on this we parted.

I carried out the vow I had made her; I held my tongue for my three months. Unexpectedly to myself there were moments of this time when she struck me as capable of playing with a man. I wanted so to make her like me that I became subtle and ingenious, wonderfully alert, patiently diplomatic. Sometimes

I thought I had earned my reward, brought her to the point of saying: 'Well, well, you're the best of them all – you may speak to me now.' Then there was a greater blankness than ever in her beauty, and on certain days a mocking light in her eyes, of which the meaning seemed to be: 'If you don't take care, I *will* accept you, to have done with you the more effectually.' Mrs Marden was a great help to me simply by believing in me, and I valued her faith all the more that it continued even though there was a sudden intermission of the miracle that had been wrought for me. After our visit to Tranton Sir Edmund Orme gave us a holiday, and I confess it was at first a disappointment to me. I felt less designated, less connected with Charlotte. 'Oh, don't cry till you're out of the wood,' her mother said; 'he has let me off sometimes for six months. He'll break out again when you least expect it – he knows what he's about.' For her these weeks were happy, and she was wise enough not to talk about me to the girl. She was so good as to assure me that I was taking the right way, that I looked as if I felt secure and that in the long run women give way to that. She had known them do it even when the man was a fool for looking so – or was a fool on any terms. For herself she felt it to be a good time, a sort of St Martin's summer of the soul. She was better than she had been for years, and she had me to thank for it. The sense of visitation was light upon her – she wasn't in anguish every time she looked round. Charlotte contradicted me very often, but she contradicted herself still more. That winter was a wonder of mildness, and we often sat out in the sun. I walked up and down with Charlotte, and Mrs Marden, sometimes on a bench, sometimes in a bath-chair, waited for us and smiled at us as we passed. I always looked out for a sign in her face – 'He's with you, he's with you' (she would see him before I should), but nothing came; the season had brought us also a sort of spiritual softness. Towards the end of April the air was so like June that, meeting my two friends one night at some Brighton sociability – an evening party with amateur music – I drew Miss Marden unresistingly out upon a balcony to which a window in one of the rooms stood open. The night was close and thick, the stars were dim, and below us, under the cliff, we heard the regular rumble of the sea. We listened to it a little and we heard mixed with it, from within the house, the sound of a violin accompanied by a piano – a performance which had been our pretext for passing out.

'Do you like me a little better?' I asked, abruptly, after a minute. 'Could you listen to me again?'

I had no sooner spoken than she laid her hand quickly, with a certain force, on my arm. 'Hush! – isn't there some one there?' She was looking into the gloom of the far end of the balcony. This balcony ran the whole width of the house, a width very great in the best of the old houses at Brighton. We were lighted a little by the open window behind us, but the other windows, curtained within, left the darkness undiminished, so that I made out but dimly the figure of a gentleman standing there and looking at us. He was in evening dress, like a guest – I saw the vague shine of his white shirt and the pale oval of his face – and he might perfectly have been a guest who had stepped out in advance of us to take the air. Miss Marden took him for one at first – then evidently, even in a few seconds, she saw that the intensity of his gaze was unconventional. What else she saw I couldn't determine; I was too taken up with my own impression to do more than feel the quick contact of her uneasiness. My own impression was in fact the strongest of sensations, a sensation of horror; for what could the thing mean but that the girl at last *saw*? I heard her give a sudden, gasping 'Ah!' and move quickly into the house. It was only afterwards that I knew that I myself had had a totally new emotion – my horror passing into anger, and my anger into a stride along the balcony with a gesture of reprobation. The case was simplified to the vision of a frightened girl whom I loved. I advanced to vindicate her security, but I found nothing there to meet me. It was either all a mistake or Sir Edmund Orme had vanished.

I followed Miss Marden immediately, but there were symptoms of confusion in the drawing-room when I passed in. A lady had fainted, the music had stopped; there was a shuffling of chairs and a pressing forward. The lady was not Charlotte, as I feared, but Mrs Marden, who had suddenly been taken ill. I remember the relief with which I learned this, for to see Charlotte stricken would have been anguish, and her mother's condition gave a channel to her agitation. It was of course all a matter for the people of the house and for the ladies, and I could have no share in attending to my friends or in conducting them to their carriage. Mrs Marden revived and insisted on going home, after which I uneasily withdrew.

I called the next morning to ask about her and was informed

that she was better, but when I asked if Miss Marden would see me the message sent down was that it was impossible. There was nothing for me to do all day but to roam about with a beating heart. But toward evening I received a line in pencil, brought by hand – 'Please come; mother wishes you.' Five minutes afterward I was at the door again and ushered into the drawing-room. Mrs Marden lay upon the sofa, and as soon as I looked at her I saw the shadow of death in her face. But the first thing she said was that she was better, ever so much better; her poor old heart had been behaving queerly again, but now it was quiet. She gave me her hand and I bent over her with my eyes in hers, and in this way I was able to read what she didn't speak – 'I'm really very ill, but appear to take what I say exactly as I say it.' Charlotte stood there beside her, looking not frightened now, but intensely grave, and not meeting my eyes. 'She has told me – she has told me!' her mother went on.

'She has told you?' I stared from one of them to the other, wondering if Mrs Marden meant that the girl had spoken to her of the circumstances on the balcony.

'That you spoke to her again – that you're admirably faithful.'

I felt a thrill of joy at this; it showed me that that memory had been uppermost, and also that Charlotte had wished to say the thing that would soothe her mother most, not the thing that would alarm her. Yet I now knew, myself, as well as if Mrs Marden had told me, that she knew and had known at the moment what her daughter had seen. 'I spoke – I spoke, but she gave me no answer,' I said.

'She will now, won't you, Chartie? I want it so, I want it!' the poor lady murmured, with ineffable wistfulness.

'You're very good to me,' Charlotte said to me, seriously and sweetly, looking fixedly on the carpet. There was something different in her, different from all the past. She had recognized something, she felt a coercion. I could see that she was trembling.

'Ah, if you would let me show you *how* good I can be!' I exclaimed, holding out my hands to her. As I uttered the words I was touched with the knowledge that something had happened. A form had constituted itself on the other side of the bed, and the form leaned over Mrs Marden. My whole being went forth into a mute prayer that Charlotte shouldn't see it and that I should be able to betray nothing. The impulse to glance towards Mrs Marden was even stronger than the involuntary movement of taking in Sir Edmund Orme; but I could resist even that, and Mrs Marden was perfectly still. Charlotte got up to give me her hand, and with the definite act she saw. She gave, with a shriek, one stare of dismay, and another sound, like a wail of one of the lost, fell at the same instant on my ear. But I had already sprung toward the girl to cover her, to veil her face. She had already thrown herself into my arms. I held her there a moment – bending over her, given up to her, feeling each of her throbs with my own and not knowing which was which; then, all of a sudden, coldly, I gathered that we were alone. She released herself. The figure beside the sofa had vanished; but Mrs Marden lay in her place with closed eyes, with something in her stillness that gave us both another terror. Charlotte expressed it in the cry of 'Mother, mother!' with which she flung herself down. I fell on my knees beside her. Mrs Marden had passed away.

Was the sound I heard when Chartie shrieked – the other and still more tragic sound I mean – the despairing cry of the poor lady's death-shock or the articulate sob (it was like a waft from a great tempest), of the exorcised and pacified spirit? Possibly the latter, for that was, mercifully, the last of Sir Edmund Orme.

# *'Oh, Whistle, And I'll Come To You, My Lad'*

M. R. James

'I suppose you will be getting away pretty soon, now Full Term is over, Professor,' said a person not in the story to the Professor of Ontography, soon after they had sat down next to each other at a feast in the hospitable hall of St James's College.

The Professor was young, neat, and precise in speech.

'Yes,' he said; 'my friends have been making me take up golf this term, and I mean to go to the East Coast – in point of fact to Burnstow – (I dare say you know it) for a week or ten days, to improve my game. I hope to get off tomorrow.'

'Oh, Parkins,' said his neighbour on the other side, 'if you are going to Burnstow, I wish you would look at the site of the Templars' preceptory, and let me know if you think it would be any good to have a dig there in the summer.'

It was, as you might suppose, a person of antiquarian pursuits who said this, but, since he merely appears in this prologue, there is no need to give his entitlements.

'Certainly,' said Parkins, the Professor: 'if you will describe to me whereabouts the site is, I will do my best to give you an idea of the lie of the land when I get back; or I could write to you about it, if you would tell me where you are likely to be.'

'Don't trouble to do that, thanks. It's only that I'm thinking of taking my family in that direction in the Long, and it occurred to me that, as very few of the English preceptories have ever been properly planned, I might have an opportunity of doing something useful on off-days.'

The Professor rather sniffed at the idea that planning out a preceptory could be described as useful. His neighbour continued:

'The site – I doubt if there is anything showing above ground – must be down quite close to the beach now. The sea has encroached tremendously, as you know, all along that bit of coast. I should think, from the map, that it must be about three-quarters of a mile from the Globe Inn, at the north end of the town. Where are you going to stay?'

'Well, *at* the Globe Inn, as a matter of fact,' said Parkins; 'I have engaged a room there. I couldn't get in anywhere else; most of the lodging houses are shut up in winter, it seems; and, as it is, they tell me that the only room of any size I can have is really a double-bedded one, and that they haven't a corner in which to store the other bed, and so on. But I must have a fairly large room, for I am taking some books down, and mean to do a bit of work; and though I don't quite fancy having an empty bed – not to speak of two – in what I may call for the time being my study, I suppose I can manage to rough it for the short time I shall be there.'

'Do you call having an extra bed in your room roughing it, Parkins?' said a bluff person opposite. 'Look here, I shall come down and occupy it for a bit; it'll be company for you.'

The Professor quivered, but managed to laugh in a courteous manner.

'By all means, Rogers; there's nothing I should like better. But I'm afraid you would find it rather dull; you don't play golf, do you?'

'No thank Heaven!' said rude Mr Rogers.

'Well, you see, when I'm not writing I shall most likely be out on the links, and that, as I say, would be rather dull for you, I'm afraid.'

'Oh, I don't know! There's certain to be somebody I know in the place; but, of course, if you don't want me, speak the word, Parkins; I shan't be offended. Truth, as you always tell us, is never offensive.'

Parkins was, indeed, scrupulously polite and strictly truthful. It is to be feared that Mr Rogers sometimes practised upon his knowledge of these characteristics. In Parkins's breast there was a conflict now raging, which for a moment or two did not allow him to answer. That interval being over, he said:

'Well, if you want the exact truth, Rogers, I was considering whether the room I speak of would really be large enough to accommodate us both comfortably; and also whether (mind, I shouldn't have said this if you hadn't pressed me) you would not constitute something in the nature of a hindrance to my work.'

Rogers laughed loudly.

'Well done, Parkins!' he said. 'It's all right. I promise not to interrupt your work; don't you disturb yourself about that. No, I won't come if you don't want me; but I thought I should do so nicely to keep the ghosts off.' Here he might have been seen to wink and to nudge his next neighbour. Parkins might also have been seen to become pink. 'I beg pardon, Parkins,' Rogers continued; 'I oughtn't to have said that. I forgot you didn't like levity on these topics.'

'Well,' Parkins said, 'as you have mentioned the matter, I freely own that I do *not* like careless talk about what you call ghosts. A man in my position,' he went on, raising his voice a little, 'cannot, I find, be too careful about appearing to sanction the current beliefs on such subjects. As you know, Rogers, or as you ought to know; for I think I have never concealed my views –'

'No, you certainly have not, old man,' put in Rogers *sotto voce*.

'– I hold that any semblance, any appearance of concession to the view that such things might exist is equivalent to a renunciation of all that I hold most sacred. But I'm afraid I have not succeeded in securing your attention.'

'Your *undivided* attention, was what Dr Blimber actually *said*,'* Rogers interrupted, with every appearance of an earnest desire for accuracy. 'But I beg your pardon, Parkins: I'm stopping you.'

'No, not at all,' said Parkins. 'I don't remember Blimber; perhaps he was before my time. But I needn't go on. I'm sure you know what I mean.'

'Yes, yes,' said Rogers, rather hastily – 'just so. We'll go into it fully at Burnstow, or somewhere.'

In repeating the above dialogue I have tried to give the impression which it made on me, that Parkins was something of an old woman – rather henlike, perhaps, in his little ways; totally destitute, alas! of the sense of humour, but at the same time dauntless and sincere in his convictions, and a man deserving of the greatest respect. Whether or not the reader has gathered so much, that was the character which Parkins had.

*

* Mr Rogers was wrong, *vide Dombey and Son*, chapter xii.

On the following day Parkins did, as he had hoped, succeed in getting away from his college, and in arriving at Burnstow. He was made welcome at the Globe Inn, was safely installed in the large double-bedded room of which we have heard, and was able before retiring to rest to arrange his materials for work in apple-pie order upon a commodious table which occupied the outer end of the room, and was surrounded on three sides by windows looking out seaward; that is to say, the central window looked straight out to sea, and those on the left and right commanded prospects along the shore to the north and south respectively. On the south you saw the village of Burnstow. On the north no houses were to be seen, but only the beach and the low cliff backing it. Immediately in front was a strip – not considerable – of rough grass, dotted with old anchors, capstans, and so forth; then a broad path; then the beach. Whatever may have been the original distance between the Globe Inn and the sea, not more than sixty yards now separated them.

The rest of the population of the inn was, of course, a golfing one, and included few elements that call for a special description. The most conspicuous figure was, perhaps that of an *ancien militaire*, secretary of a London club, and possessed of a voice of incredible strength, and of views of a pronouncedly Protestant type. These were apt to find utterance after his attendance upon the ministrations of the Vicar, an estimable man with inclinations towards a picturesque ritual, which he gallantly kept down as far as he could out of deference to East Anglian tradition.

Professor Parkins, one of whose principal characteristics was pluck, spent the greater part of the day following his arrival at Burnstow in what he had called improving his game, in company with this Colonel Wilson: and during the afternoon – whether process of improvement were to blame or not, I am not sure – the Colonel's demeanour assumed a colouring so lurid that even Parkins jibbed at the thought of walking home with him from the links. He determined, after a short and furtive look at that bristling moustache and those incarnadined features, that it would be wiser to allow the influences of tea and tobacco to do what they could with the Colonel before the dinner-hour should render a meeting inevitable.

'I might walk home tonight along the beach,' he reflected – 'yes, and take a look – there will be light enough for that – at the ruins of which Disney was talking. I don't exactly know where they are, by the way; but I expect I can hardly help stumbling on them.'

This he accomplished, I may say, in the most literal sense, for in picking his way from the links to the shingle beach his foot caught, partly in a gorse-root and partly in a biggish stone, and over he went. When he got up and surveyed his surroundings, he found himself in a patch of somewhat broken ground covered with small depressions and mounds. These latter, when he came to examine them, proved to be simply masses of flints embedded in mortar and grown over with turf. He must, he quite rightly concluded, be on the site of the preceptory he had promised to look at. It seemed not unlikely to reward the spade of the explorer; enough of the foundations was probably left at no great depth to throw a good deal of light on the general plan. He remembered vaguely that the Templars, to whom this site had belonged, were in the habit of building round churches, and he thought a particular series of the humps or mounds near him did appear to be arranged in something of a circular form. Few people can resist the temptation to try a little amateur research in a department quite outside their own, if only for the satisfaction of showing how successful they would have been had they only taken it up seriously. Our Professor, however, if he felt something of this mean desire, was also truly anxious to oblige Mr Disney. So he paced with care the circular area he had noticed, and wrote down its rough dimensions in his pocket-book. Then he proceeded to examine an oblong eminence which lay east of the centre of the circle, and seemed to his thinking likely to be the base of a platform or altar. At one end of it, the northern, a patch of the turf was gone – removed by some boy or other creature *ferae naturae*. It might, he thought, be as well to probe the soil here for evidences of masonry, and he took out his knife and began scraping away the earth. And now followed another little discovery: a portion of soil fell inward as he scraped, and disclosed a small cavity. He lighted one match after another to help him to see of what nature the hole was, but the wind was too strong for them all. By tapping and scratching the sides with his knife, however, he was able to make out that it must be an artificial hole in masonry. It was rectangular, and the sides, top, and bottom, if not actually plastered, were smooth and regular. Of course it was empty.

No! As he withdrew the knife he heard a metallic clink, and when he introduced his hand it met with a cylindrical object lying on the floor of the hole. Naturally enough, he picked it up, and when he brought it into the light, now fast fading, he could see that it, too, was of man's making – a metal tube about four inches long, and evidently of some considerable age.

By the time Parkins had made sure that there was nothing else in this odd receptacle, it was too late and too dark for him to think of undertaking any further search. What he had done had proved so unexpectedly interesting that he determined to sacrifice a little more of the daylight on the morrow to archaeology. The object which he now had safe in his pocket was bound to be of some slight value at least, he felt sure.

Bleak and solemn was the view on which he took a last look before starting homeward. A faint yellow light in the west showed the links, on which a few figures moving towards the club-house were still visible, the squat martello tower, the lights of Aldsey village, the pale ribbon of sands intersected at intervals by black wooden groynings, the dim and murmuring sea. The wind was bitter from the north, but was at his back when he set out for the Globe. He quickly rattled and clashed through the shingle and gained the sand, upon which, but for the groynings which had to be got over every few yards, the going was both good and quiet. One last look behind, to measure the distance he had made since leaving the ruined Templars' church, showed him a prospect of company on his walk, in the shape of a rather indistinct personage, who seemed to be making great efforts to catch up with him, but made little, if any, progress. I mean that there was an appearance of running about his movements, but that the distance between him and Parkins did not seem materially to lessen. So, at least, Parkins thought, and decided that he almost certainly did not know him, and that it would be absurd to wait until he came up. For all that, company, he began to think, would really be very welcome on that lonely shore, if only you could choose your companion. In his unenlightened days he had read of meetings in such places which even now would hardly bear thinking of. He went on thinking of them, however, until he reached home, and particularly of one which catches most people's fancy at some time of their childhood. 'Now I saw in my dream that Christian had gone but a very little way when he saw a foul fiend coming over the field to meet him.' 'What should I do now,' he thought, 'if I looked back and caught sight of a black figure sharply defined against the yellow sky, and saw that it had horns and wings? I wonder whether I should stand or run for it. Luckily, the gentleman behind is not of that kind, and he seems to be about as far off now as when I saw him first. Well, at this rate, he won't get his dinner as soon as I shall; and, dear me! it's within a quarter of an hour of the time now. I must run!'

Parkins had, in fact, very little time for dressing. When he met the Colonel at dinner, Peace – or as much of her as that gentleman could manage – reigned once more in the military bosom; nor was she put to flight in the hours of bridge that followed dinner, for Parkins was a more than respectable player. When, therefore, he retired towards twelve o'clock, he felt that he had spent his evening in quite a satisfactory way, and that, even for so long as a fortnight or three weeks, life at the Globe would be supportable under similar conditions – 'especially,' thought he, 'if I go on improving my game.'

As he went along the passages he met the boots of the Globe, who stopped and said:

'Beg your pardon, sir, but as I was abrushing your coat just now there was something fell out of the pocket. I put it on your chest of drawers, sir, in your room, sir – a piece of a pipe or something of that, sir. Thank you, sir. You'll find it on your chest of drawers, sir – yes, sir. Good night, sir.'

The speech served to remind Parkins of his little discovery of that afternoon. It was with some considerable curiosity that he turned it over by the light of his candles. It was of bronze, he now saw, and was shaped very much after the manner of the modern dog-whistle; in fact it was – yes, certainly it was – actually no more nor less than a whistle. He put it to his lips, but it was quite full of a fine, caked-up sand or earth, which would not yield to knocking, but must be loosened with a knife. Tidy as ever in his habits, Parkins cleared out the earth on to a piece of paper, and took the latter to the window to empty it out. The night was clear and bright, as he saw when he had opened the casement, and he stopped for an instant to look at the sea and note a belated wanderer stationed on the shore in front of the inn. Then he shut the window, a little surprised at the late hours people kept at Burnstow, and took his whistle to the light again. Why, surely there were marks on it, and not merely marks, but letters! A very little rubbing rendered the deeply-cut inscription quite legible, but the Professor had to confess, after some earnest thought, that the meaning of it was as obscure to him as the writing on the wall to Belshazzar. There were legends both on the front and on the back of the whistle. The one read thus:

FLA
FUR BIS
FLE

The other:

QUIS EST ISTE QUI VENIT

'I ought to be able to make it out,' he thought; 'but I suppose I am a little rusty in my Latin. When I come to think of it, I don't believe I even know the word for a whistle. The long one does seem simple enough. It ought to mean: "Who is this who is coming?" Well, the best way to find out is evidently to whistle for him.'

He blew tentatively and stopped suddenly, startled and yet pleased at the note he had elicited. It had a quality of infinite distance in it, and, soft as it was, he somehow felt it must be audible for miles round. It was a sound, too, that seemed to have the power (which many scents possess) of forming pictures in the brain. He saw quite clearly for a moment a vision of a wide, dark expanse at night, with a fresh wind blowing, and in the midst a lonely figure – how employed, he could not tell. Perhaps he would have seen more had not the picture been broken by the sudden surge of a gust of wind against his casement, so sudden that it made him look up, just in time to see the white glint of a sea-bird's wing somewhere outside the dark panes.

The sound of the whistle had so fascinated him that he could not help trying it once more, this time more boldly. The note was little, if at all, louder than before, and repetition broke the illusion – no picture followed, as he had half hoped it might. 'But what is this? Goodness! what force the wind can get up in a few minutes! What a tremendous gust! There! I knew that window-fastening was no use! Ah! I thought so – both candles out. It is enough to tear the room to pieces.'

The first thing was to get the window shut. While you might count twenty Parkins was struggling with the small casement, and felt almost as if he were pushing back a sturdy burglar, so strong was the pressure. It slackened all at once, and the window banged to and latched itself. Now to relight the candles and see what damage, if any, had been done. No, nothing seemed amiss; no glass even was broken in the casement. But the noise had evidently roused at least one member of the household: the Colonel was to be heard stumping in his stockinged feet on the floor above, and growling.

Quickly as it had risen, the wind did not fall at once. On it went, moaning and rushing past the house, at times rising to a cry so desolate that, as Parkins disinterestedly said, it might have made fanciful people feel quite uncomfortable; even the unimaginative, he thought after a quarter of an hour, might be happier without it.

Whether it was the wind, or the excitement of golf, or of the researches in the preceptory that kept Parkins awake, he was not sure. Awake he remained, in any case, long enough to fancy (as I am afraid I often do myself under such conditions) that he was the victim of all manner of fatal disorders: he would lie counting the beats of his heart, convinced that it was going to stop work every moment, and would entertain grave suspicions of his lungs, brain, liver, etc. – suspicions which he was sure would be dispelled by the return of daylight, but which until then refused to be put aside. He found a little vicarious comfort in the idea that someone else was in the same boat. A near neighbour (in the darkness it was not easy to tell his direction) was tossing and rustling in his bed, too.

The next stage was that Parkins shut his eyes and determined to give sleep every chance. Here again over-excitement asserted itself in another form – that of making pictures. *Experto crede*, pictures do come to the closed eyes of one trying to sleep, and are often so little to his taste that he must open his eyes and disperse them.

Parkins's experience on this occasion was a very distressing one. He found that the picture which presented itself to him was continuous. When he opened his eyes, of course, it went; but when he shut them once more it framed itself afresh, and acted itself out again, neither quicker nor slower than before. What he saw was this:

A long stretch of shore – shingle edged by sand, and intersected at short intervals with black groynes running down to the water – a scene, in fact, so like that of his afternoon's walk that, in the absence of any landmark, it could not be distinguished therefrom. The light was obscure, conveying an impression of gathering storm, late winter evening, and slight cold rain. On this bleak stage at first no actor was visible. Then, in the distance, a bobbing black object appeared; a moment more, and it was a man running, jumping, clambering over the groynes, and every few seconds looking eagerly back. The nearer he came the more obvious it was that he was not only anxious, but even terribly frightened, though his face was not to be distinguished. He was, moreover, almost at the end of his strength. On he came; each successive obstacle seemed to cause him more difficulty than the last. 'Will he get over this next one?' thought Parkins; 'it seems a little higher than the others.' Yes; half climbing, half throwing himself, he did get over, and fell all in a heap on the other side (the side nearest to the spectator). There, as if really unable to get up again, he remained crouching under the groyne, looking up in an attitude of painful anxiety.

So far no cause whatever for the fear of the runner had been shown; but now there began to be seen, far up the shore, a little flicker of something light-coloured moving to and fro with great swiftness and irregularity. Rapidly growing larger, it, too, declared itself as a figure in pale, fluttering draperies, ill-defined. There was something about its motion which made Parkins very unwilling to see it at close quarters. It would stop, raise arms, bow itself towards the sand, then run stooping across the beach to the water-edge and back again; and then, rising upright, once more continue its course forward at a speed that was startling and terrifying. The moment came when the pursuer was hovering about from left to right only a few yards beyond the groyne where the runner lay in hiding. After two or three ineffectual castings hither and thither it came to a stop, stood upright, with arms raised high, and then darted straight forward towards the groyne.

It was at this point that Parkins always failed in his resolution to keep his eyes shut. With many misgivings as to incipient failure of eyesight, overworked brain, excessive smoking, and so on, he finally resigned himself to light his candle, get out a book, and pass the night waking, rather than be tormented by this persistent panorama, which he saw clearly enough could only be a morbid reflection of his walk and his thoughts on that very day.

The scraping of match on box and the glare of light must have startled some creatures of the night – rats or what not – which he heard scurry across the floor from the side of his bed with much rustling. Dear, dear! the match is out! Fool that it is! But the second one burnt better, and a candle and book were duly procured, over which Parkins pored till sleep of a wholesome kind came upon him, and that in no long space. For about the first time in his orderly and prudent life he forgot to blow out the candle, and when he was called next morning at eight there was still a flicker in the socket and a sad mess of guttered grease on the top of the little table.

After breakfast he was in his room, putting the finishing touches to his golfing costume – fortune had again allotted the Colonel to him for a partner – when one of the maids came in.

'Oh, if you please,' she said, 'would you like any extra blankets on your bed, sir?'

'Ah! thank you,' said Parkins. 'Yes, I think I should like one. It seems likely to turn rather colder.'

In a very short time the maid was back with the blanket.

'Which bed should I put it on, sir?' she asked.

'What? Why, that one – the one I slept in last night,' he said, pointing to it.

'Oh yes! I beg your pardon, sir, but you seemed to have tried both of 'em; leastways, we had to make 'em both up this morning.'

'Really? How very absurd!' said Parkins. 'I certainly never touched the other, except to lay some things on it. Did it actually seem to have been slept in?'

'Oh yes, sir!' said the maid. 'Why, all the things was crumpled and throwed about all ways, if you'll excuse me, sir – quite as if anyone 'adn't passed but a very poor night, sir.'

'Dear me,' said Parkins. 'Well, I may have disordered it more than I thought when I unpacked my things. I'm very sorry to have given you the extra trouble, I'm sure. I expect a friend of mine soon, by the way – a gentleman from Cambridge – to come and occupy it for a night or two. That will be all right, I suppose, won't it?'

'Oh yes, to be sure, sir. Thank you, sir. It's no trouble, I'm sure,' said the maid, and departed to giggle with her colleagues.

Parkins set forth, with a stern determination to improve his game.

I am glad to be able to report that he succeeded so far in this enterprise that the Colonel, who had been rather repining at the prospect of a second day's play in his company, became quite chatty as the morning advanced; and his voice boomed out over the flats, as certain also of our own minor poets have said, 'like some great bourdon in a minster tower'.

'Extraordinary wind, that, we had last night,' he said. 'In my old home we should have said someone had been whistling for it.'

'Should you, indeed!' said Parkins. 'Is there a superstition of that kind still current in your part of the country?'

'I don't know about superstition,' said the Colonel. 'They believe in it all over Denmark and Norway, as well as on the Yorkshire coast; and my experience is, mind you, that there's generally something at the bottom of what these country-folk hold to, and have held to for generations. But it's your drive' (or whatever it might have been: the golfing reader will have to imagine appropriate digressions at the proper intervals).

When conversation was resumed, Parkins said, with a slight hesitancy:

'Apropos of what you were saying just now, Colonel, I think I ought to tell you that my own views on such subjects are very strong. I am, in fact, a convinced disbeliever in what is called the "supernatural".'

'What!' said the Colonel, 'do you mean to tell me you don't believe in second-sight, or ghosts, or anything of that kind?'

'In nothing whatever of that kind,' returned Parkins firmly.

'Well,' said the Colonel, 'but it appears to me at that rate, sir, that you must be little better than a Sadducee.'

Parkins was on the point of answering that, in his opinion, the Sadducees were the most sensible persons he had ever read of in the Old Testament; but, feeling some doubt as to whether much mention of them was to be found in that work, he preferred to laugh the accusation off.

'Perhaps I am,' he said; 'but – Here, give me my cleek, boy! – Excuse me one moment, Colonel.' A short interval. 'Now, as to whistling for the wind, let me give you my theory about it. The laws which govern winds are really not at all perfectly known – to fisherfolk and such, of course, not known at all. A man or woman of eccentric habits, perhaps, or a stranger, is seen repeatedly on the beach at some unusual hour, and is heard whistling. Soon afterwards a violent wind rises; a man who could read the sky perfectly or who possessed a barometer could have foretold that it would. The simple people of a fishing-village have no barometers, and only a few rough rules for prophesying weather. What more natural than that the eccentric personage I postulated should be regarded as having raised the wind, or that he or she should clutch eagerly at the reputation of being able to do so? Now, take last night's wind: as it happens, I myself was whistling. I blew a whistle twice, and the wind seemed to come absolutely in answer to my call. If anyone had seen me –'

The audience had been a little restive under this harangue, and Parkins had, I fear, fallen somewhat into the tone of a lecturer; but at the last sentence the Colonel stopped.

'Whistling, were you?' he said. 'And what sort of whistle did you use? Play this stroke first.' Interval.

'About that whistle you were asking, Colonel. It's rather a curious one. I have it in my – No; I see I've left it in my room. As a matter of fact, I found it yesterday.'

And then Parkins narrated the manner of his discovery of the whistle, upon hearing which the Colonel grunted, and opined that, in Parkins's place, he should himself be careful about using a thing that had belonged to a set of Papists, of whom, speaking generally, it might be affirmed that you never knew what they might not have been up to. From this topic he diverged to the enormities of the Vicar, who had given notice on the previous Sunday that Friday would be the Feast of St Thomas the Apostle, and that there would be service at eleven o'clock in the church. This and other similar proceedings constituted in the Colonel's view a strong presumption that the Vicar was a concealed Papist, if not a Jesuit; and Parkins, who could not very readily follow the Colonel in this region, did not disagree with him. In fact, they got on so well together in the morning that there was not talk on either side of their separating after lunch.

Both continued to play well during the afternoon, or at least, well enough to make them forget everything else until the light began to fail them. Not until then did Parkins remember that he had meant to do some more investigating at the preceptory; but it was of no great importance, he reflected. One day was as good as another; he might as well go home with the Colonel.

As they turned the corner of the house, the Colonel was almost knocked down by a boy who rushed into him at the very top of his speed, and then, instead of running away, remained hanging on to him and panting. The first words of the warrior were naturally those of reproof and objurgation, but he very quickly discerned that the boy was almost speechless with fright. Inquiries were useless at first. When the boy got his breath he began to howl, and still clung to the Colonel's legs. He was at last detached, but continued to howl.

'What in the world *is* the matter with you? What have you been up to? What have you seen?' said the two men.

'Ow, I seen it wive at me out of the winder,' wailed the boy, 'and I don't like it.'

'What window?' said the irritated Colonel. 'Come pull yourself together, my boy.'

'The front winder it was, at the 'otel,' said the boy.

At this point Parkins was in favour of sending the boy home, but the Colonel refused; he wanted to get to the bottom of it, he said; it was most dangerous to give a boy such a fright as this one had had, and if it turned out that people had been playing jokes, they should suffer for it in some way. And by a series of questions he made out this story: The boy had been playing about on the grass in front of the Globe with some others; then they had gone home to their teas, and he was just going, when he happened to look up at the front winder and see it a-wiving at him. *It* seemed to be a figure of some sort, in white as far as he knew – couldn't see its face; but it wived at him, and it warn't a right thing – not to say not a right person. Was there a light in the room? No, he didn't think to look if there was a light. Which was the window? Was it the top one or the second one? The seckind one it was – the big winder what got two little uns at the sides.

'Very well, my boy,' said the Colonel, after a few more questions. 'You run away home now. I expect it was some person trying to give you a start. Another time, like a brave English boy, you just throw a stone – well, no, not that exactly, but you go and speak to the waiter, or to Mr Simpson, the landlord, and – yes – and say that I advised you to do so.'

The boy's face expressed some of the doubt he felt as to the likelihood of Mr Simpson's lending a favourable ear to his complaint, but the Colonel did not appear to perceive this, and went on:

'And here's a sixpence – no, I see it's a shilling – and you be off home, and don't think any more about it.'

The youth hurried off with agitated thanks, and the Colonel and Parkins went round to the front of the Globe and reconnoitred. There was only one window answering to the description they had been hearing.

'Well, that's curious,' said Parkins; 'it's evidently my window the lad was talking about. Will you come up for a moment, Colonel Wilson? We ought to be able to see if anyone has been taking liberties in my room.'

They were soon in the passage, and Parkins made as if to open the door. Then he stopped and felt in his pockets.

'This is more serious than I thought,' was his next remark. 'I remember now that before I started this morning I locked the door. It is locked now, and, what is more, here is the key.' And he held it up. 'Now,' he went on, 'if the servants are in the habit of going into one's room during the day when one is away, I can only say that – well, that I don't approve of it at all.' Conscious of a somewhat weak climax, he busied himself in opening the door (which was indeed locked) and in lighting candles. 'No,' he said, 'nothing seems disturbed.'

'Except your bed,' put in the Colonel.

'Excuse me, that isn't my bed,' said Parkins. 'I don't use that one. But it does look as if someone had been playing tricks with it.'

It certainly did: the clothes were bundled up and twisted together in a most tortuous confusion. Parkins pondered.

'That must be it,' he said at last. 'I disordered the clothes last night in unpacking, and they haven't made it since. Perhaps they came in to make it, and that boy saw them through the window; and then they were called away and locked the door after them. Yes, I think that must be it.'

'Well, ring and ask,' said the Colonel, and this appealed to Parkins as practical.

The maid appeared, and, to make a long story short, deposed that she had made the bed in the morning when the gentleman was in the room, and hadn't been there since. No, she hadn't no other key. Mr Simpson, he kep' the keys; he'd be able to tell the gentleman if anyone had been up.

This was a puzzle. Investigation showed that nothing of value had been taken, and Parkins remembered the disposition of the small objects on tables and so forth well enough to be pretty sure that no pranks had been played with them. Mr and Mrs Simpson furthermore agreed that neither of them had given the duplicate key of the room to any person whatever during the day. Nor could Parkins, fair-minded man as he was, detect anything in the demeanour of master, mistress, or maid that indicated guilt. He was much more inclined to think that the boy had been imposing on the Colonel.

The latter was unwontedly silent and pensive at dinner and throughout the evening. When he bade goodnight to Parkins, he murmured in a gruff undertone:

'You know where I am if you want me during the night.'

'Why, yes, thank you, Colonel Wilson, I think I do; but there isn't much prospect of my disturbing you, I hope. By the way,' he added, 'did I show you that old whistle I spoke of? I think not. Well, here it is.'

The Colonel turned it over gingerly in the light of the candle.

'Can you make anything of the inscription?' asked Parkins, as he took it back.

'No, not in this light. What do you mean to do with it?'

'Oh, well, when I get back to Cambridge I shall submit it to some of the archaeologists there, and see what they think of it; and very likely, if they consider it worth having, I may present it to one of the museums.'

'M!' said the Colonel. 'Well, you may be right. All I know is that, if it were mine, I should chuck it straight into the sea. It's no use talking, I'm well aware, but I expect that with you it's a case of live and learn. I hope so, I'm sure, and I wish you a good night.'

He turned away, leaving Parkins in act to speak at the bottom of the stair, and soon each was in his own bedroom.

By some unfortunate accident, there were neither blinds nor curtains to the windows of the Professor's room. The previous night he had thought little of this, but tonight there seemed every prospect of a bright moon rising to shine directly on his bed, and probably wake him later on. When he noticed this he was a good deal annoyed, but, with an ingenuity which I can only envy, he succeeded in rigging up, with the help of a railway-rug, some safety-pins, and a stick and umbrella, a screen which, if it only held together, would completely keep the moonlight off his bed. And shortly afterwards he was comfortably in that bed. When he had read a somewhat solid work for long enough to produce a decided wish for sleep, he cast a drowsy glance round the room, blew out the candle, and fell back upon the pillow.

He must have slept soundly for an hour or more, when a sudden clatter shook him up in a most unwelcome manner. In a moment he realized what had happened: his carefully-constructed screen had given way, and a very bright frosty moon was shining directly on his face. This was highly annoying. Could he possibly get up and reconstruct the screen? or could he manage to sleep if he did not?

For some minutes he lay and pondered over the possibilities; then he turned over sharply, and with all his eyes open lay breathlessly listening. There had been a movement, he was sure, in the empty bed on the opposite side of the room. Tomorrow he would have it moved, for there must be rats or something playing about in it. It was quiet now. No! the commotion began again. There was a rustling and shaking: surely more than any rat could cause.

I can figure to myself something of the Professor's bewilderment and horror, for I have in a dream thirty years back seen the same thing happen; but the reader will hardly, perhaps, imagine how dreadful it was to him to see a figure suddenly sit up in what he had known was an empty bed. He was out of his own bed in one bound, and made a dash towards the window, where lay his only weapon, the stick with which he had propped the screen. This was, as it turned out, the worst thing he could have done, because the personage in the empty bed, with a sudden smooth motion, slipped from the bed and took up a position, with outspread arms, between the two beds, and in front of the door. Parkins watched it in a horrid perplexity. Somehow, the idea of getting past it and escaping through the door was intolerable to him; he could not have borne – he didn't know why – to touch it; and as for its touching him, he would sooner dash himself through the window than have that happen. It stood for the moment in a band of dark shadow, and he had not seen what its face was like. Now it began to move, in a stooping posture, and all at once the spectator realized, with some horror and some relief, that it must be blind, for it seemed to feel about it with its muffled arms in a groping and random fashion. Turning half away from him, it became suddenly conscious of the bed he had just left, and darted towards it, and bent and felt over the pillows in a way which made Parkins shudder as he had never in his life thought it possible. In a very few moments it seemed to know that the bed was empty, and then, moving forward into the area of light and facing the window, it showed for the first time what manner of thing it was.

Parkins, who very much dislikes being questioned about it, did once describe something of it in my hearing, and I gathered that what he chiefly remembers about it is a horrible, an intensely horrible, face *of crumpled linen*. What expression he read upon it he could not or would not tell, but that the fear of it went nigh to maddening him is certain.

But he was not at leisure to watch it for long. With formidable quickness it moved into the middle of the room, and as it groped and waved, one corner of its draperies swept across Parkins's face. He could not, though he knew how perilous a sound was – he could not keep back a cry of disgust, and this gave the searcher an instant clue. It leapt towards him upon the instant, and the next moment he was half-way through the window backwards, uttering cry upon cry at the utmost pitch of his voice, and the linen face was thrust close into his own. At this, almost the last possible second, deliverance came, as you will have guessed: the Colonel burst the door open, and was just in time to see the dreadful group at the window. When he reached the figures only one was left. Parkins sank forward into the room in a faint, and before him on the floor lay a tumbled heap of bed-clothes.

Colonel Wilson asked no questions, but busied himself in keeping everyone else out of the room and in getting Parkins back to his bed; and himself, wrapped in a rug, occupied the other bed, for the rest of the night. Early on the next day Rogers arrived, more welcome than he would have been a day before, and the three of them held a very long consultation in the Professor's room. At the end of it the Colonel left the hotel door carrying a small object between his finger and thumb, which he cast as far into the sea as a very brawny arm could send it. Later on the smoke of a burning ascended from the back premises of the Globe.

Exactly what explanation was patched up for the staff and visitors at the hotel I must confess I do not recollect. The Professor was somehow cleared of the ready suspicion of delirium tremens, and the hotel of the reputation of a troubled house.

There is not much question as to what would have happened to Parkins if the Colonel had not intervened when he did. He would either have fallen out of the window or else lost his wits.

But it is not so evident what more the creature that came in answer to the whistle could have done than frighten. There seemed to be absolutely nothing material about it save for the bedclothes of which it had made itself a body. The Colonel, who remembered a not very dissimilar occurrence in India, was of the opinion that if Parkins had closed with it it could really have done very little, and that its one power was that of frightening. The whole thing, he said, served to confirm his opinion of the Church of Rome.

There is really nothing more to tell, but, as you may imagine, the Professor's views on certain points are less clear cut than they used to be. His nerves, too, have suffered: he cannot even now see a surplice hanging on a door quite unmoved, and the spectacle of a scarecrow in a field late on a winter afternoon has cost him more than one sleepless night.

# *'They'*

## Rudyard Kipling

One view called me to another; one hill-top to its fellow, half across the county, and since I could answer at no more trouble than the snapping forward of a lever, I let the country flow under my wheels. The orchid-studded flats of the East gave way to the thyme, ilex, and grey grass of the Downs; these again to the rich cornland and fig-trees of the lower coast, where you carry the beat of the tide on your left hand for fifteen level miles; and when at last I turned inland through a huddle of rounded hills and woods I had run myself clean out of my known marks. Beyond that precise hamlet which stands god-mother to the capital of the United States, I found hidden villages where bees, the only things awake, boomed in eighty-foot lindens that overhung grey Norman churches; miraculous brooks diving under stone bridges built for heavier traffic than would ever vex them again; tithe-barns larger than their churches, and an old smithy that cried out aloud how it had once been a hall of the Knights of the Temple. Gipsies I found on a common where the gorse, bracken, and heath fought it out together up a mile of Roman road; and a little farther on I disturbed a red fox rolling dog-fashion in the naked sunlight.

As the wooded hills closed about me I stood up in the car to take the bearings of that great Down whose ringed head is a landmark for fifty miles across the low countries. I judged that the lie of the country would bring me across some westward-running road that went to his feet, but I did not allow for the confusing veils of the woods. A quick turn plunged me first into a green cutting brim-full of liquid sunshine, next into a gloomy tunnel where last year's dead leaves whispered and scuffled about my tyres. The strong hazel stuff meeting overhead had not been cut for a couple of generations at least, nor had any axe helped the moss-cankered oak and beech to spring above them. Here the road changed frankly into a carpeted ride on whose brown velvet spent primrose-clumps showed like jade, and a few sickly, white-stalked bluebells nodded together. As the slope favoured I shut off the power and slid over the whirled leaves, expecting every moment to meet a keeper; but I only heard a jay, far off, arguing against the silence under the twilight of the trees.

Still the track descended, I was on the point of reversing and working my way back on the second speed ere I ended in some swamp, when I saw sunshine through the tangle ahead and lifted the brake.

It was down again at once. As the light beat across my face my fore-wheels took the turf of a great still lawn from which sprang horsemen ten feet high with levelled lances, monstrous peacocks, and sleek round-headed maids of honour – blue, black, and glistening – all of clipped yew. Across the lawn – the marshalled woods besieged it on three sides – stood an ancient house of lichened and weather-worn stone, with mullioned windows and roofs of rose-red tile. It was flanked by semi-circular walls, also rose-red, that closed the lawn on the fourth side, and at their feet a box hedge grew man-high. There were doves on the roof about the slim brick chimneys, and I caught a glimpse of an octagonal dove-house behind the screening wall.

'If I am not packed off for a trespasser, or if this knight does not ride a wallop at me,' thought I, 'Shakespeare and Queen Elizabeth at least must come out of that half-open garden door and ask me to tea.'

A child appeared at an upper window, and I thought the little thing waved a friendly hand. But it was to call a companion, for presently another bright head showed. Then I heard a laugh among the yew-peacocks, and turning to make sure (till then I had been watching the house only) I saw the silver of a fountain behind a hedge thrown up against the sun. The doves on the roof cooed to the cooing water; but between the two notes I caught the utterly happy chuckle of a child absorbed in some light mischief.

The garden door – heavy oak sunk deep in the thickness of the wall – opened further: a woman in a big garden hat set foot slowly on the time-hollowed stone step and as slowly walked across the turf. I was forming some apology when she lifted up her head and I saw that she was blind.

'I heard you,' she said. 'Isn't that a motor car?'

'I'm afraid I've made a mistake in my road. I should have turned off up above – I never dreamed –' I began.

'But I'm very glad. Fancy a motor car coming into the garden! It will be such a treat –' She turned and made as though looking about her. 'You – you haven't seen any one, have you – perhaps?'

'No one to speak to, but the children seemed interested at a distance.'

'Which?'

'I saw a couple up at the window just now, and I think I heard a little chap in the grounds.'

'Oh, lucky you!' she cried, and her face brightened. 'I hear them, of course, but that's all. You've seen them and heard them?'

'Yes,' I answered. 'And if I know anything of children, one of them's having a beautiful time by the fountain yonder. Escaped, I should imagine.'

'You're fond of children?'

I gave her one or two reasons why I did not altogether hate them.

'Of course, of course,' she said. 'Then you understand. Then you won't think it foolish if I ask you to take your car through the gardens, once or twice – quite slowly. I'm sure they'd like to see it. They see so little, poor things. One tries to make their life pleasant, but –' she threw out her hands towards the woods. 'We're so out of the world here.'

'That will be splendid,' I said. 'But I can't cut up your grass.'

She faced to the right. 'Wait a minute,' she said. 'We're at the South gate, aren't we? Behind those peacocks there's a flagged path. We call it the Peacocks' Walk. You can't see it from here, they tell me, but if you squeeze along by the edge of the wood you can turn at the first peacock and get on to the flags.'

It was sacrilege to wake that dreaming house-front with the clatter of machinery, but I swung the car to clear the turf, brushed along the edge of the wood and turned in on the broad stone path where the fountain-basin lay like one star-sapphire.

'May I come too?' she cried. 'No, please don't help me. They'll like it better if they see me.'

She felt her way lightly to the front of the car, and with one foot on the step she called: 'Children, oh, children! Look and see what's going to happen!'

The voice would have drawn lost souls from the Pit, for the yearning that underlay its sweetness, and I was not surprised to hear an answering shout beyond the yews. It must have been the child by the fountain, but he fled at our approach, leaving a little toy boat in the water. I saw the glint of his blue blouse among the still horsemen.

Very disposedly we paraded the length of the walk and at her request backed again. This time the child had got the better of his panic, but stood far off and doubting.

'The little fellow's watching us,' I said. 'I wonder if he'd like a ride.'

'They're very shy still. Very shy. But, oh, lucky you to be able to see them! Let's listen.'

I stopped the machine at once, and the humid stillness, heavy with the scent of box, cloaked us deep. Shears I could hear where some gardener was clipping; a mumble of bees and broken voices that might have been the doves.

'Oh, unkind!' she said weariedly.

'Perhaps they're only shy of the motor. The little maid at the window looks tremendously interested.'

'Yes?' She raised her head. 'It was wrong of me to say that. They are really fond of me. It's the only thing that makes life worth living – when they're fond of you, isn't it? I daren't think what the place would be without them. By the way, is it beautiful?'

'I think it is the most beautiful place I have ever seen.'

'So they all tell me. I can feel it, of course, but that isn't quite the same thing.'

'Then have you never –?' I began, but stopped abashed.

'Not since I can remember. It happened when I was only a few months old, they tell me. And yet I must remember something, else how could I dream about colours. I see light in my dreams, and colours, but I never see *them*. I only hear them just as I do when I'm awake.'

'It's difficult to see faces in dreams. Some people can, but most of us haven't the gift,' I went on, looking up at the window where the child stood all but hidden.

'I've heard that too,' she said. 'And they tell me that one never sees a dead person's face in a dream. Is that true?'

'I believe it is – now I come to think of it.'

'But how is it with yourself – yourself?' The blind eyes turned towards me.

'I have never seen the faces of my dead in any dream,' I answered.

'Then it must be as bad as being blind.'

The sun had dipped behind the woods and the long shades were possessing the insolent horsemen one by one. I saw the light die from off the top of a glossy-leafed lance and all the brave hard green turn to soft black. The house, accepting another day at end, as it had accepted an hundred thousand gone, seemed to settle deeper into its rest among the shadows.

'Have you ever wanted to?' she said after the silence.

'Very much sometimes,' I replied. The child had left the window as the shadows closed upon it.

'Ah! So've I, but I don't suppose it's allowed. . . . Where d'you live?'

'Quite the other side of the county – sixty miles and more, and I must be going back. I've come without my big lamps.'

'But it's not dark yet. I can feel it.'

'I'm afraid it will be by the time I get home. Could you lend me someone to set me on my road at first? I've utterly lost myself.'

'I'll send Madden with you to the cross-roads. We are so out of the world, I don't wonder you were lost! I'll guide you round to the front of the house; but you will go slowly, won't you, till you're out of the grounds? It isn't foolish, do you think?'

'I promise you I'll go like this,' I said, and let the car start herself down the flagged path.

We skirted the left wing of the house, whose elaborately cast lead guttering alone was worth a day's journey; passed under a great rose-grown gate in the red wall, and so round to the high front of the house, which in beauty and stateliness as much excelled the back as that all others I had seen.

'Is it so very beautiful?' she said wistfully when she heard my raptures. 'And you like the lead figures too? There's the old azalea garden behind. They say that this place must have been made for children. Will you help me out, please? I should like to come with you as far as the cross-roads, but I mustn't leave them. Is that you, Madden? I want you to show this gentleman the way to the cross-roads. He has lost his way, but – he has seen them.'

A butler appeared noiselessly at the miracle of old oak that must be called the front door, and slipped aside to put on his hat. She stood looking at me with open blue eyes in which no sight lay, and I saw for the first time that she was beautiful.

'Remember,' she said quietly, 'if you are fond of them you will come again,' and disappeared within the house.

The butler in the car said nothing till we were nearly at the lodge gates, where catching a glimpse of a blue blouse in a shrubbery I swerved amply lest the devil that leads little boys to play should drag me into child-murder.

'Excuse me,' he asked of a sudden, 'but why did you do that, Sir?'

'The child yonder.'

'Our young gentleman in blue?'

'Of course.'

'He runs about a good deal. Did you see him by the fountain, Sir?'

'Oh, yes, several times. Do we turn here?'

'Yes, Sir. And did you 'appen to see them upstairs too?'

'At the upper window? Yes.'

'Was that before the mistress come out to speak to you, Sir?'

'A little before that. Why d'you want to know?'

He paused a little. 'Only to make sure that – that they had seen the car, Sir, because with children running about, though I'm sure you're driving particularly careful, there might be an accident. That was all, Sir. Here are the cross-roads. You can't miss your way from now on. Thank you, Sir, but that isn't *our* custom, not with –'

'I beg your pardon,' I said, and thrust away the British silver.

'Oh, it's quite right with the rest of 'em as a rule. Good-bye, Sir.'

He retired into the armour-plated conning-tower of his caste and walked away. Evidently a butler solicitous for the honour of his house, and interested, probably through a maid, in the nursery.

Once beyond the signposts at the cross-roads I looked back, but the crumpled hills interlaced so jealously that I could not see where the house had lain. When I asked its name at a cottage along the road, the fat woman who sold sweetmeats there gave me to understand that people with motor cars had small right to live – much less to 'go about talking like carriage folk'. They were not a pleasant-mannered community.

When I retraced my route on the map that evening I was

little wiser. Hawkin's Old Farm appeared to be the Survey title of the place, and the old *County Gazetteer*, generally so ample, did not allude to it. The big house of those parts was Hodnington Hall, Georgian with early Victorian embellishments, as an atrocious steel engraving attested. I carried my difficulty to a neighbour – a deep-rooted tree of that soil – and he gave me a name of a family which conveyed no meaning.

A month or so later – I went again, or it may have been that my car took the road on her own volition. She over-ran the fruitless Downs, threaded every turn of the maze of lanes below the hills, drew through the high-walled woods, impenetrable in their full leaf, came out at the cross-roads where the butler had left me, and a little farther on developed an internal trouble which forced me to turn her in on a grass way-waste that cut into a summer-silent hazel wood. So far as I could make sure by the sun and a six-inch Ordnance map, this should be the road flank of that wood which I had first explored from the heights above. I made a mighty serious business of my repairs and a glittering shop of my repair kit, spanners, pump, and the like, which I spread out orderly upon a rug. It was a trap to catch all childhood, for on such a day, I argued, the children would not be far off. When I paused in my work I listened, but the wood was so full of the noises of summer (though the birds had mated) that I could not at first distinguish these from the tread of small cautious feet stealing across the dead leaves. I rang my bell in an alluring manner, but the feet fled, and I repented, for to a child a sudden noise is very real terror. I must have been at work half an hour when I heard in the wood the voice of the blind woman crying: 'Children, oh, children! Where are you?' and the stillness made slow to close on the perfection of that cry. She came towards me, half feeling her way between the tree boles, and though a child, it seemed, clung to her skirt, it swerved into the leafage like a rabbit as she drew nearer.

'Is that you?' she said, 'from the other side of the county?'

'Yes, it's me from the other side of the county.'

'Then why didn't you come through the upper woods? They were there just now.'

'They were here a few minutes ago. I expect they knew my car had broken down, and came to see the fun.'

'Nothing serious, I hope? How do cars break down?'

'In fifty different ways. Only mine has chosen the fifty-first.'

She laughed merrily at the tiny joke, cooed with delicious laughter, and pushed her hat back.

'Let me hear,' she said.

'Wait a moment,' I cried, 'and I'll get you a cushion.'

She set her foot on the rug all covered with spare parts, and stooped above it eagerly. 'What delightful things!' The hands through which she saw glanced in the chequered sunlight. 'A box here – another box! Why, you've arranged them like playing shop!'

'I confess now that I put it out to attract them. I don't need half those things really.'

'How nice of you! I heard your bell in the upper wood. You say they were here before that?'

'I'm sure of it. Why are they so shy? That little fellow in blue who was with you just now ought to have got over his fright. He's been watching me like a Red Indian.'

'It must have been your bell,' she said. 'I heard one of them go past me in trouble when I was coming down. They're shy – so shy even with me.' She turned her face over her shoulder and cried again: 'Children, oh, children! Look and see!'

'They must have gone off together on their own affairs,' I suggested, for there was a murmur behind us of lowered voices broken by the sudden squeaking giggles of childhood. I returned to my tinkerings and she leaned forward, her chin on her hand, listening interestedly.

'How many are they?' I said at last. The work was finished, but I saw no reason to go.

Her forehead puckered a little in thought. 'I don't quite know,' she said simply. 'Sometimes more – sometimes less. They come and stay with me because I love them, you see.'

'That must be very jolly,' I said, replacing a drawer, and as I spoke I heard the inanity of my answer.

'You – you aren't laughing at me?' she cried. 'I – I haven't any of my own. I never married. People laugh at me sometimes about them because – because –'

'Because they're savages,' I returned. 'It's nothing to fret for. That sort laugh at everything that isn't in their own fat lives.'

'I don't know. How should I? I only don't like being laughed at about *them*. It hurts; and when one can't see. . . . I don't want to seem silly,' her chin quivered like a child's as she spoke, 'but we blindies have only one skin, I think. Everything outside hits straight at our souls. It's different with you.

You've such good defences in your eyes – looking out – before anyone can really pain you in your soul. People forget that with us.'

I was silent, reviewing that inexhaustible matter – the more than inherited (since it is also carefully taught) brutality of the Christian peoples, besides which the mere heathendom of the West Coast nigger is clean and restrained. It led me a long distance into myself.

'Don't do that!' she said of a sudden, putting her hands before her eyes.

'What?'

She made a gesture with her hand.

'That! It's – it's all purple and black. Don't! That colour hurts.'

'But how in the world do you know about colours?' I exclaimed, for here was a revelation indeed.

'Colours as colours?' she asked.

'No. *Those* Colours which you saw just now.'

'You know as well as I do,' she laughed, 'else you wouldn't have asked that question. They aren't in the world at all. They're in *you* – when you went so angry.'

'D'you mean a dull purplish patch, like port wine mixed with ink?' I said.

'I've never seen ink or port wine, but the colours aren't mixed. They can separate – all separate.'

'Do you mean black streaks and jags across the purple?'

She nodded. 'Yes – if they are all like this,' and zig-zagged her finger again, 'but it's more red than purple – that bad colour.'

'And what are the colours at the top of the – whatever you see?'

Slowly she leaned forward and traced on the rug the figure of the Egg itself.

'I see them so,' she said, pointing with a grass stem, 'white, green, yellow, red, purple, and when people are angry or bad, black across the red – as you were just now.'

'Who told you anything about it – in the beginning?' I demanded.

'About the colours? No one. I used to ask what colours were when I was little – in tablecovers and curtains and carpets you see – because some colours hurt me and some made me happy. People told me; and when I got older that was how I saw people.' Again she traced the outline of the Egg which it is given to very few of us to see.

'All by yourself?' I repeated.

'All by myself. There wasn't anyone else. I only found out afterwards that other people did not see the Colours.'

She leaned against the tree-bole plaiting and unplaiting chance-plucked grass stems. The children in the wood had drawn nearer. I could see them with the tail of my eye frolicking like squirrels.

'Now I am sure you will never laugh at me,' she went on after a long silence. 'Nor at *them*.'

'Goodness! No!' I cried, jolted out of my train of thought. 'A man who laughs at a child – unless the child is laughing too – is a heathen!'

'I didn't meant that, of course. You'd never laugh *at* children, but I thought – I used to think – that perhaps you might laugh about *them*. So now I beg your pardon. . . . What are you going to laugh at?'

I had made no sound, but she knew.

'At the notion of your begging my pardon. If you had done your duty as a pillar of the State and a landed proprietress you ought to have summoned me for trespass when I barged through your woods the other day. It was disgraceful of me – inexcusable.'

She looked at me, her head against the tree-trunk – long and steadfastly – this woman who could see the naked soul.

'How curious,' she half whispered. 'How very curious.'

'Why, what have I done?'

'You don't understand . . . and yet you understood about the Colours. Don't you understand?'

She spoke with a passion that nothing had justified, and I faced her bewilderedly as she rose. The children had gathered themselves in a roundel behind a bramble bush. One sleek head bent over something smaller, and the set of the little shoulders told me that fingers were on lips. They, too, had some child's tremendous secret. I alone was hopelessly astray there in the broad sunlight.

'No,' I said, and shook my head as though the dead eyes could note. 'Whatever it is, I don't understand yet. Perhaps I shall later – if you'll let me come again.'

'You will come again,' she answered. 'You will surely come again and walk in the wood.'

'Perhaps the children will know me well enough by that time to let me play with them – as a favour. You know what children are like.'

'It isn't a matter of favour but of right,' she replied, and while I wondered what she meant, a dishevelled woman plunged round the bend of the road, loose-haired, purple, almost lowing with agony as she ran. It was my rude, fat friend of the sweetmeat shop. The blind woman heard and stepped forward. 'What is it, Mrs Madehurst?' she asked.

The woman flung her apron over her head and literally grovelled in the dust, crying that her grandchild was sick to death, that the local doctor was away fishing, that Jenny the mother was at her wits' end, and so forth, with repetitions and bellowings.

'Where's the nearest doctor?' I asked between paroxysms.

'Madden will tell you. Go round to the house and take him with you. I'll attend to this. Be quick!' She half supported the fat woman into the shade. In two minutes I was blowing all the horns of Jericho under the front of the House Beautiful, and Madden, in the pantry, rose to the crisis like a butler and a man.

A quarter of an hour at illegal speeds caught us a doctor five miles away. Within the half-hour we had decanted him, much interested in motors, at the door of the sweetmeat shop, and drew up the road to await the verdict.

'Useful things, cars,' said Madden, all man and no butler. 'If I'd had one when mine took sick she wouldn't have died.'

'How was it?' I asked.

'Croup. Mrs Madden was away. No one knew what to do. I drove eight miles in a tax-cart for the doctor. She was choked when we came back. This car'd ha' saved her. She'd have been close on ten now.'

'I'm sorry,' I said. 'I thought you were rather fond of children from what you told me going to the cross-roads the other day.'

'Have you seen 'em again, Sir – this mornin'?'

'Yes, but they're well broke to cars. I couldn't get any of them within twenty yards of it.'

He looked at me carefully as a scout considers a stranger – not as a menial should lift his eyes to his divinely appointed superior.

'I wonder why,' he said just above the breath that he drew.

We waited on. A light wind from the sea wandered up and down the long lines of the woods, and the wayside grasses, whitened already with summer dust, rose and bowed in sallow waves.

A woman, wiping the suds off her arms, came out of the cottage next the sweetmeat shop.

'I've be'n listenin' in de back-yard,' she said cheerily. 'He says Arthur's unaccountable bad. Did ye hear him shruck just now? Unaccountable bad. I reckon t'will come Jenny's turn to walk in de wood nex' week along, Mr Madden.'

'Excuse me, Sir, but your lap-robe is slipping,' said Madden deferentially. The woman started, dropped a curtsey, and hurried away.

'What does she mean by "walking in the wood"?' I asked.

'It must be some saying they use hereabouts. I'm from Norfolk myself,' said Madden. 'They're an independent lot in this county. She took you for a chauffeur, Sir.'

I saw the Doctor come out of the cottage followed by a draggle-tailed wench who clung to his arm as though he could make treaty for her with Death. 'Dat sort,' she wailed – 'dey're just as much to us dat has 'em as if dey was lawful born. Just as much – just as much! An' God he'd be just as pleased if you saved 'un, Doctor. Don't take it from me, Miss Florence will tell ye de very same. Don't leave 'im, Doctor!'

'I know, I know,' said the man; 'but he'll be quiet for a while now. We'll get the nurse and the medicine as fast as we can.' He signalled me to come forward with the car, and I strove not to be privy to what followed; but I saw the girl's face, blotched and frozen with grief, and I felt the hand without a ring clutching at my knees when we moved away.

The Doctor was a man of some humour, for I remember he claimed my car under the Oath of Aesculapius, and used it and me without mercy. First we convoyed Mrs Madehurst and the blind woman to wait by the sick-bed till the nurse should come. Next we invaded a neat county town for prescriptions (the Doctor said the trouble was cerebro-spinal meningitis), and when the County Institute, banked and flanked with scared market cattle, reported itself out of nurses for the moment we literally flung ourselves loose upon the county. We conferred with the owners of great houses – magnates at the ends of overarching avenues whose big-boned women folk strode away from their tea-tables to listen to the imperious

Doctor. At last a white-haired lady sitting under a cedar of Lebanon and surrounded by a court of magnificent Borzois – all hostile to motors – gave the Doctor, who received them as from a princess, written orders which we bore many miles at top speed, through a park, to a French nunnery, where we took over in exchange a pallid-faced and trembling Sister. She knelt at the bottom of the tonneau telling her beads without pause till, by short cuts of the Doctor's invention, we had her to the sweetmeat shop once more. It was a long afternoon crowded with mad episodes that rose and dissolved like the dust of our wheels; cross-sections of remote and incomprehensible lives through which we raced at right angles; and I went home in the dusk, wearied out, to dream of the clashing horns of cattle; round-eyed nuns walking in a garden of graves; pleasant tea-parties beneath shady trees; the carbolic-scented, grey-painted corridors of the County Institute; the steps of shy children in the wood, and the hands that clung to my knees as the motor began to move.

*

I had intended to return in a day or two, but it pleased Fate to hold me from that side of the county, on many pretexts, till the elder and the wild rose had fruited. There came at last a brilliant day, swept clear from the south-west, that brought the hills within hand's reach – a day of unstable airs and high filmy clouds. Through no merit of my own I was free, and set the car for the third time on that known road. As I reached the crest of the Downs I felt the soft air change, saw it glaze under the sun; and, looking down at the sea, in that instant beheld the blue of the Channel turn through polished silver and dulled steel to dingy pewter. A laden collier hugging the coast steered outward for deeper water, and, across copper-coloured haze, I saw sails rise one by one on the anchored fishing-fleet. In a deep dene behind me an eddy of sudden wind drummed through sheltered oaks, and spun aloft the first dry sample of autumn leaves. When I reached the beach road the sea-fog fumed over the brickfields, and tide was telling all the groynes of the gale beyond Ushant. In less than an hour summer England vanished in chill grey. We were again the shut island of the North, all the ships of the world bellowing at our perilous gates; and between their outcries ran the piping of bewildered gulls. My cap dripped moisture, the folds of the rug held it in pools or sluiced it away in runnels, and the salt-rime stuck to my lips.

Inland the smell of autumn loaded the thickened fog among the trees, and the drip became a continuous shower. Yet the late flowers – mallow of the wayside, scabious of the field, and dahlia of the garden – showed gay in the mist, and beyond the sea's breath there was little sign of decay in the leaf. Yet in the villages the house doors were all open, and bare-legged, bare-headed children sat at ease on the damp doorsteps to shout 'pip-pip' at the stranger.

I made bold to call at the sweetmeat shop, where Mrs Madehurst met with a fat woman's hospitable tears. Jenny's child, she said, had died two days after the nun had come. It was, she felt, best out of the way, even though insurance offices, for reasons which she did not pretend to follow, would not willingly insure such stray lives. 'Not but what Jenny didn't tend to Arthur as though he'd come all proper at de end of de first year – like Jenny herself.' Thanks to Miss Florence, the child had been buried with a pomp which, in Mrs Madehurst's opinion, more than covered the small irregularity of its birth. She described the coffin, within and without, the glass hearse, and the evergreen lining of the grave.

'But how's the mother?' I asked.

'Jenny? Oh, she'll get over it. I've felt dat way with one or two o' my own. She'll get over. She's walkin' in de wood now.'

'In this weather?'

Mrs Madehurst looked at me with narrowed eyes across the counter.

'I dunno but it opens de 'eart like. Yes, it opens de 'eart. Dat's where losin' and bearin' comes so alike in de long run we do say.'

Now the wisdom of the old wives is greater than that of all the Fathers, and this last oracle sent me thinking so extendedly as I went up the road, that I nearly ran over a woman and a child at the wooded corner by the lodge gates of the House Beautiful.

'Awful weather!' I cried, as I slowed dead for the turn.

'Not so bad,' she answered placidly out of the fog. 'Mine's used to 'un. You'll find yours indoors, I reckon.'

Indoors, Madden received me with professional courtesy, and kind inquiries for the health of the motor, which he would put under cover.

I waited in a still, nut-brown hall, pleasant with late flowers and warmed with a delicious wood fire – a place of good influence and great peace. (Men and women may sometimes, after great effort, achieve a creditable lie; but the house, which is their temple, cannot say anything save the truth of those who have lived in it.) A child's cart and a doll lay on the black-and-white floor, where a rug had been kicked back. I felt that the children had only just hurried away – to hide themselves, most like – in the many turns of the great adzed staircase that climbed steadily out of the hall, or to crouch and gaze behind the lions and roses of the carven gallery above. Then I heard her voice above me, singing as the blind sing – from the soul:

'In the pleasant orchard-closes.'

And all my early summer came back at the call.

'In the pleasant orchard-closes,
God bless all our gains say we –
But may God bless all our losses,
Better suits with our degree.'

She dropped the marring fifth line, and repeated –

'Better suits with our degree!'

I saw her lean over the gallery, her linked hands white as pearl against the oak.

'Is that you – from the other side of the county?' she called.

'Yes, me – from the other side of the county,' I answered, laughing.

'What a long time before you had to come here again.' She ran down the stairs, one hand lightly touching the broad rail. 'It's two months and four days. Summer's gone!'

'I meant to come before, but Fate prevented.'

'I knew it. Please do something to that fire. They won't let me play with it, but I can feel it's behaving badly. Hit it!'

I looked on either side of the deep fireplace, and found but a half-charred hedge-stake with which I punched a black log into flame.

'It never goes out, day or night,' she said, as though explaining. 'In case any one comes in with cold toes, you see.'

'It's even lovelier inside than it was out,' I murmured. The red light poured itself along the age-polished dusky panels till the Tudor roses and lions of the gallery took colour and motion. An old eagle-topped convex mirror gathered the picture into its mysterious heart, distorting afresh the distorted shadows, and curving the gallery lines into the curves of a ship. The day was shutting down in half a gale as the fog turned to stringy scud. Through the uncurtained mullions of the broad window I could see the valiant horsemen of the lawn rear and recover against the wind that taunted them with legions of dead leaves.

'Yes, it must be beautiful,' she said. 'Would you like to go over it? There's still light enough upstairs.'

I followed her up the unflinching, wagon-wide staircase to the gallery whence opened the thin fluted Elizabethan doors.

'Feel how they put the latch low down for the sake of the children.' She swung a light door inward.

'By the way, where are they?' I asked. 'I haven't even heard them today.'

She did not answer at once. Then, 'I can only hear them,' she replied softly. 'This is one of their rooms – everything ready, you see.'

She pointed into a heavily-timbered room. There were little low gate tables and children's chairs. A doll's house, its hooked front half open, faced a great dappled rocking-horse, from whose padded saddle it was but a child's scramble to the broad window-seat overlooking the lawn. A toy gun lay in a corner beside a gilt wooden cannon.

'Surely they've only just gone,' I whispered. In the failing light a door creaked cautiously. I heard the rustle of a frock and the patter of feet – quick feet through a room beyond.

'I heard that,' she cried triumphantly. 'Did you? Children, oh, children! Where are you?'

The voice filled the walls that held it lovingly to the last perfect note, but there came no answering shout such as I had heard in the garden. We hurried on from room to oak-floored room; up a step here, down three steps there; among a maze of passages; always mocked by our quarry. One might as well have tried to work an unstopped warren with a single ferret. There were bolt-holes innumerable – recesses in walls, embrasures of deep-slitten windows now darkened, whence they could start up behind us; and abandoned fire-places, six feet deep in the masonry, as well as the tangle of communicating doors. Above all, they had the twilight for their helper in our game. I had caught one or two joyous chuckles of evasion, and once or twice had seen the silhouette of a child's frock against some darkening window at the end of a passage; but we returned empty-handed to the gallery, just as a middle-aged woman was setting a lamp in its niche.

'No, I haven't seen her either this evening, Miss Florence,' I heard her say, 'but that Turpin he says he wants to see you about his shed.'

'Oh, Mr Turpin must want to see me very badly. Tell him to come to the hall, Mrs Madden.'

I looked down into the hall whose only light was that dulled fire, and deep in the shadow I saw them at last. They must have slipped down while we were in the passages, and now thought themselves perfectly hidden behind an old gilt leather screen. By child's law, my fruitless chase was as good as an introduction, but since I had taken so much trouble I resolved to force them to come forward later by the simple trick, which children detest, of pretending not to notice them. They lay close, in a little huddle, no more than shadows except when a quick flame betrayed an outline.

'And now we'll have some tea,' she said. 'I believe I ought to have offered it you at first, but one doesn't arrive at manners somehow when one lives alone and is considered – h'm – peculiar.' Then with very pretty scorn, 'Would you like a lamp to see to eat by?'

'The firelight's much pleasanter, I think.' We descended into that delicious gloom and Madden brought tea.

I took my chair in the direction of the screen ready to surprise or be surprised as the game should go, and at her permission, since a hearth is always sacred, bent forward to play with the fire.

'Where do you get these beautiful short faggots from?' I asked idly. 'Why, they are tallies!'

'Of course,' she said. 'As I can't read or write I'm driven back on the early English tally for my accounts. Give me one and I'll tell you what it meant.'

I passed her an unburned hazel-tally, about a foot long, and she ran her thumb down the nicks.

'This is the milk-record for the home farm for the month of April last year, in gallons,' said she. 'I don't know what I should have done without tallies. An old forester of mine taught me the system. It's out of date now for every one else;

but my tenants respect it. One of them's coming now to see me. Oh, it doesn't matter. He has no business here out of office hours. He's a greedy, ignorant man – very greedy, or – he wouldn't come here after dark.'

'Have you much land then?'

'Only a couple of hundred acres in hand, thank goodness. The other six hundred are nearly all let to folk who knew my folk before me, but this Turpin is quite a new man – and a highway robber.'

'But are you sure I shan't be – ?'

'Certainly not. You have the right. He hasn't any children.'

'Ah, the children!' I said, and slid my low chair back till it nearly touched the screen that hid them. 'I wonder whether they'll come out for me.'

There was a murmur of voices – Madden's and a deeper note – at the low, dark side door, and a ginger-headed, canvas-gaitered giant of the unmistakable tenant-farmer type stumbled or was pushed in.

'Come to the fire, Mr Turpin,' she said.

'If – if you please, Miss, I'll – I'll be quite as well by the door.' He clung to the latch as he spoke like a frightened child. Of a sudden I realized that he was in the grip of some almost overpowering fear.

'Well?'

'About that new shed for the young stock – that was all. These first autumn storms settin' in . . . but I'll come again, Miss.' His teeth did not chatter much more than the door-latch.

'I think not,' she answered levelly. 'The new shed – m'm. What did my agent write you on the 15th?'

'I – fancied p'raps that if I came to see you – ma – man to man like, Miss. But –'

His eyes rolled into every corner of the room wide with horror. He half opened the door through which he had entered, but I noticed it shut again – from without and firmly.

'He wrote what I told him,' she went on. 'You are over-stocked already. Dunnett's Farm never carried more than fifty bullocks – even in Mr Wright's time. And *he* used cake. You've sixty-seven, and you don't cake. You've broken the lease in that respect. You're dragging the heart out of the farm.'

'I'm – I'm getting some minerals – superphosphates – next week. I've as good as ordered a truck-load already. I'll go down to the station tomorrow about 'em. Then I can come and see you man to man like, Miss, in the daylight. . . . That gentleman's not going away, is he?' He almost shrieked.

I had only slid the chair a little farther back, reaching behind me to tap on the leather of the screen, but he jumped like a rat.

'No. Please attend to me, Mr Turpin.' She turned in her chair and faced him with his back to the door. It was an old and sordid little piece of scheming that she forced from him – his plea for the new cow-shed at his landlady's expense, that he might with the covered manure pay his next year's rent out of the valuation after, as she made clear, he had bled the enriched pastures to the bone. I could not but admire the intensity of his greed, when I saw him outfacing for its sake whatever terror it was that ran wet on his forehead.

I ceased to tap the leather – was, indeed, calculating the cost of the shed – when I felt my relaxed hand taken and turned softly between the soft hands of a child. So at last I had triumphed. In a moment I would turn and acquaint myself with those quick-footed wanderers . . .

The little brushing kiss fell in the centre of my palm – as a gift on which the fingers were, once, expected to close: as the all-faithful half-reproachful signal of a waiting child not used to neglect even when grown-ups were busiest – a fragment of the mute code devised very long ago.

Then I knew. And it was as though I had known from the first day when I looked across the lawn at the high window.

I heard the door shut. The woman turned to me in silence, and I felt that she knew.

What time passed after this I cannot say. I was roused by the fall of a log, and mechanically rose to put it back. Then I returned to my place in the chair very close to the screen.

'Now you understand,' she whispered, across the packed shadows.

'Yes, I understand – now. Thank you.'

'I – I only hear them.' She bowed her head in her hands. 'I have no right, you know – no other right. I have neither borne nor lost – neither borne nor lost!'

'Be very glad then,' said I, for my soul was torn open within me.

'Forgive me!'

She was still, and I went back to my sorrow and my joy.

'It was because I loved them so,' she said at last, brokenly.

'*That* was why it was, even from the first – even before I knew that they – they were all I should ever have. And I loved them so!'

She stretched out her arms to the shadows and the shadows within the shadow.

'They came because I loved them – because I needed them. I – I must have made them come. Was that wrong, think you?'

'No – no.'

'I – I grant you that the toys and – and all that sort of thing were nonsense, but – but I used to so hate empty rooms myself when I was little.' She pointed to the gallery. 'And the passages all empty. . . . And how could I ever bear the garden door shut? Suppose –'

'Don't! For pity's sake, don't!' I cried. The twilight had brought a cold rain with gusty squalls that plucked at the leaded windows.

'And the same thing with keeping the fire in all night. *I* don't think it so foolish – do you?'

I looked at the broad brick hearth, saw, through tears, I believe, that there was no unpassable iron on or near it, and bowed my head.

'I did all that and lots of other things – just to make believe. Then they came. I heard them, but I didn't know that they were not mine by right till Mrs Madden told me –'

'The butler's wife? What?'

'One of them – I heard – she saw. And knew Hers! *Not* for me. I didn't know at first. Perhaps I was jealous. Afterwards, I began to understand that it was only because I loved them, not because _ . . . Oh, you *must* bear or lose,' she said piteously. 'There is no other way – and yet they love me. They must! Don't they?'

There was no other sound in the room except the lapping voices of the fire, but we two listened intently, and she at least took comfort from what she heard. She recovered herself and half rose. I sat still in my chair by the screen.

'Don't think me a wretch to whine about myself like this, but – but I'm all in the dark, you know, and *you* can see.'

In truth I could see, and my vision confirmed me in my resolve, though that was like the very parting of spirit and flesh. Yet a little longer I would stay since it was the last time.

'You think it is wrong, then?' she cried sharply, though I had said nothing.

'Not for you. A thousand times no. For you it is right. . . . I am grateful to you beyond words. For me it would be wrong. For me only . . .'

'Why?' she said, but passed her hand before her face as she had done at our second meeting in the wood. 'Oh, I see,' she went on simply as a child. 'For you it would be wrong.' Then with a little indrawn laugh. 'And, d'you remember, I called you lucky – once – at first. You who must never come here again!'

She left me to sit a little longer by the screen, and I heard the sound of her feet die out along the gallery above.

# *Green Tea*

J. S. Le Fanu

## CHAPTER I

### DR HESSELIUS RELATES HOW HE MET THE REV. MR JENNINGS

The Rev. Mr Jennings is tall and thin. He is middle-aged, and dressed with a natty, old-fashioned high-church precision. He is naturally a little stately, but not at all stiff. His features, without being handsome, are well formed, and their expression extremely kind, but also shy.

I met him one evening at Lady Mary Heyduke's. The modesty and benevolence of his countenance are extremely prepossessing.

We were but a small party, and he joined agreeably enough in the conversation. He seems to enjoy listening very much more than contributing to the talk; but what he says is always to the purpose and well said. He is a great favourite of Lady Mary's, who it seems, consults him upon many things, and thinks him the most happy and blessed person on earth. Little knows she about him.

The Rev. Mr Jennings is a bachelor, and has, they say, sixty thousand pounds in the funds. He is a charitable man. He is most anxious to be actively employed in his sacred profession, and yet, though always tolerably well elsewhere, when he goes down to his vicarage in Warwickshire, to engage in the actual duties of his sacred calling, his health soon fails him, and in a very strange way. So says Lady Mary.

There is no doubt that Mr Jennings' health does break down in generally a sudden and mysterious way, sometimes in the very act of officiating in his old and pretty church at Kenlis. It may be his heart, it may be his brain. But so it has happened, three or four times or oftener, that after proceeding a certain way in the service, he has on a sudden stopped short; and after a silence, apparently quite unable to resume, he has fallen into solitary, inaudible prayer, his hands and his eyes uplifted, and then pale as death, and in the agitation of a strange shame and horror, descended trembling, and got into the vestry-room, leaving his congregation, without explanation, to themselves. This occurred when his curate was absent. When he goes down to Kenlis now, he always takes care to provide a clergyman to share his duty, and to supply his place on the instant should he become thus suddenly incapacitated.

When Mr Jennings breaks down quite, and beats a retreat from the vicarage, and returns to London – where, in a dark street off Piccadilly, he inhabits a very narrow house – Lady Mary says that he is always perfectly well. I have my own opinion about that. There are degrees, of course. We shall see.

Mr Jennings is a perfectly gentlemanlike man. People, however, remark something odd. There is an impression a little ambiguous. One thing which certainly contributes to it, people I think don't remember or, perhaps, distinctly remark. But I did, almost immediately. Mr Jennings has a way of looking side-long upon the carpet, as if his eye followed the movements of something there. This, of course, is not always. It occurs only now and then. But often enough to give a certain oddity, as I have said, to his manner, and in this glance travelling along the floor there is something both shy and anxious.

A medical philosopher, as you are good enough to call me, elaborating theories by the aid of cases sought out by himself, and by him watched and scrutinized with more time at command, and consequently infinitely more minuteness than the ordinary practitioner can afford, falls insensibly into habits of observation, which accompany him everywhere, and are exercised, as some people would say, impertinently, upon every subject that presents itself with the least likelihood of rewarding inquiry.

There was a promise of this kind in the slight, timid, kindly, but reserved gentleman, whom I met for the first time at this agreeable little evening gathering. I observed, of course, more than I here set down; but I reserve all that borders on the technical for a strictly scientific paper.

I may remark that when I here speak of medical science, I do so, as I hope some day to see it more generally understood, in a much more comprehensive sense than its generally material treatment would warrant. I believe the entire natural world is but the ultimate expression of that spiritual world from which, and in which alone, it has its life. I believe that the essential man is a spirit, that the spirit is an organized substance, but as different in point of material from what we ordinarily understand by matter, as light or electricity is; that the material body is, in the most literal sense, a vesture, and death consequently no interruption of the living man's existence, but simply his extrication from the natural body – a process which commences at the moment of what we term death, and the completion of which, at furthest a few days later, is the resurrection 'in power'.

The person who weighs the consequences of these positions will probably see their practical bearing upon medical science. This is, however, by no means the proper place for displaying the proofs and discussing the consequences of this too generally unrecognized state of facts.

In pursuance of my habit, I was covertly observing Mr Jennings with all my caution – I think he perceived it – and I saw plainly that he was as cautiously observing me. Lady Mary happening to address me by my name, as Dr Hesselius, I saw that he glanced at me more sharply, and then became thoughtful for a few minutes.

After this, as I conversed with a gentleman at the other end of the room, I saw him look at me more steadily, and with an interest which I thought I understood. I then saw him take an opportunity of chatting with Lady Mary, and was, as one always is, perfectly aware of being the subject of a distant inquiry and answer.

This tall clergyman approached me by-and-by; and in a little time we had got into conversation. When two people who like reading, and know books and places, having travelled, wish to discourse, it is very strange if they can't find topics. It was not accident that brought him near me, and led him into conversation. He knew German, and had read my *Essays on Metaphysical Medicine*, which suggest more than they actually say.

This courteous man, gentle, shy, plainly a man of thought and reading, who, moving and talking among us, was not altogether of us, and whom I already suspected of leading a life whose transactions and alarms were carefully concealed, with an impenetrable reserve from, not only the world, but his best beloved friends – was cautiously weighing in his own mind the idea of taking a certain step with regard to me.

I penetrated his thoughts without his being aware of it, and was careful to say nothing which could betray to his sensitive vigilance my suspicions respecting his position, or my surmises about his plans respecting myself.

We chatted upon different subjects for a time, but at last he said:

'I was very much interested by some papers of yours, Dr Hesselius, upon what you term Metaphysical Medicine – I read them in German, ten or twelve years ago – have they been translated?'

'No, I'm sure they have not – I should have heard. They would have asked my leave, I think.'

'I asked the publishers here, a few months ago, to get the book for me in the original German; but they tell me it is out of print.'

'So it is, and has been for some years; but it flatters me as an author to find that you have not forgotten my little book, although,' I added laughing, 'ten or twelve years is a considerable time to have managed without it; but I suppose you have been turning the subject over again in your mind, or something has happened lately to revive your interest in it.'

At this remark, accompanied by a glance of inquiry, a sudden embarrassment disturbed Mr Jennings, analogous to that which makes a young lady blush and look foolish. He dropped his eyes, and folded his hands together uneasily, and looked oddly, and you would have said guiltily, for a moment.

I helped him out of his awkwardness in the best way, by appearing not to observe it; and going straight on, I said: 'Those revivals of interest in a subject happen to me often; one book suggests another, and often sends me back a wild-goose chase over an interval of twenty years. But if you still care to possess a copy, I shall be only too happy to provide you; I have still got two or three by me – and if you allow me to present one I shall be very much honoured.'

'You are very good indeed,' he said, quite at his ease again, in a moment: 'I almost despaired – I don't know how to thank you.'

'Pray don't say a word; the thing is really so little worth that I am only ashamed of having offered it, and if you thank me any more I shall throw it into the fire in a fit of modesty.'

Mr Jennings laughed. He inquired where I was staying in London, and after a little more conversation on a variety of subjects he took his departure.

## CHAPTER II

### THE DOCTOR QUESTIONS LADY MARY, AND SHE ANSWERS

'I like your vicar so much, Lady Mary,' said I, as soon as he was gone. 'He has read, travelled, and thought, and having also suffered, he ought to be an accomplished companion.'

'So he is, and, better still, he is a really good man,' said she. 'His advice is invaluable about my schools, and all my little undertakings at Dawlbridge, and he's so painstaking, he takes so much trouble – you have no idea – wherever he thinks he can be of use; he's so good-natured and so sensible.'

'It is pleasant to hear so good an account of his neighbourly virtues. I can only testify to his being an agreeable and gentle companion, and in addition to what you have told me, I think I can tell you two or three things about him,' said I.

'Really!'

'Yes, to begin with, he's unmarried.'

'Yes, that's right – go on.'

'He has been writing, that is he *was*; but for two or three years, perhaps, he has not gone on with his work; and the book was upon some rather abstract subject – perhaps theology.'

'Well, he was writing a book, as you say; I'm not quite sure what it was about, but only that it was nothing that I cared for; very likely you are right, and he certainly did stop – yes.'

'And although he only drank a little coffee here to-night, he likes tea, at least did like it, extravagantly.'

'Yes, that's *quite* true.'

'He drank green tea a good deal, didn't he?' I pursued.

'Well, that's very odd! Green tea was a subject on which we used almost to quarrel.'

'But he has quite given that up,' said I.

'So he has.'

'And now, one more fact. His mother or his father, did you know them?'

'Yes, both; his father is only ten years dead, and their place is near Dawlbridge. We knew them very well,' she answered.

'Well, either his mother or his father – I should rather think his father, saw a ghost,' said I.

'Well, you really are a conjurer, Dr Hesselius.'

'Conjurer or no, haven't I said right?' I answered merrily.

'You certainly have, and it *was* his father: he was a silent, whimsical man, and he used to bore my father about his dreams, and at last he told him a story about a ghost he had seen and talked with; and a very odd story it was. I remember it particularly, because I was so afraid of him. This story was long before he died – when I was quite a child – and his ways were so silent and moping, and he used to drop in sometimes, in the dusk, when I was alone in the drawing-room, and I used to fancy there were ghosts about him.'

I smiled and nodded.

'And now, having established my character as a conjurer, I think I must say goodnight,' said I.

'But how *did* you find it out?'

'By the planets, of course, as the gipsies do,' I answered, and so, gaily, we said good-night.

Next morning I sent the little book he had been inquiring after, and a note, to Mr Jennings, and on returning late that evening, I found that he had called at my lodgings and left his card. He asked whether I was at home, and asked at what hour he would be most likely to find me.

Does he intend opening his case, and consulting me 'professionally,' as they say? I hope so. I have already conceived a theory about him. It is supported by Lady Mary's answers to my parting questions. I should like much to ascertain from his own lips. But what can I do consistently with good breeding to invite a confession? Nothing. I rather think he meditates one. At all events, my dear Van L., I shan't make myself difficult of access; I mean to return his visit to-morrow. It will be only civil, in return for his politeness, to ask to see him. Perhaps something may come of it. Whether much, little, or nothing, my dear Van L., you shall hear.

## CHAPTER III

### DR HESSELIUS PICKS UP SOMETHING IN LATIN BOOKS

Well, I have called at Blank Street.

On inquiring at the door, the servant told me that Mr Jennings was engaged very particularly with a gentleman, a clergyman from Kenlis, his parish in the country. Intending to reserve my privilege, and to call again, I merely intimated that I should try another time, and had turned to go, when the servant begged my pardon, and asked me, looking at me a little more attentively than well-bred persons of his order usually do, whether I was Dr Hesselius; and, on learning that I was, he said, 'Perhaps then, sir, you would allow me to mention it to Mr Jennings, for I am sure he wishes to see you.'

The servant returned in a moment, with a message from Mr Jennings asking me to go into his study, which was in effect his back drawing-room, promising to be with me in a very few minutes.

This was really a study – almost a library. The room was lofty, with two tall slender windows, and rich dark curtains. It was much larger than I had expected, and stored with books on every side, from the floor to the ceiling. The upper carpet – for to my tread it felt that there were two or three – was a Turkey carpet. My steps fell noiselessly. The book-cases standing out, placed the windows, particularly narrow ones, in deep recesses. The effect of the room was, although extremely comfortable, and even luxurious, decidedly gloomy and, aided by the silence, almost oppressive. Perhaps, however, I ought to have allowed something for association. My mind has connected peculiar ideas with Mr Jennings. I stepped into this perfectly silent room, of a very silent house, with a peculiar foreboding; and its darkness and solemn clothing of books – for except where two narrow looking-glasses were set in the wall they were everywhere – helped this sombre feeling.

While awaiting Mr Jennings' arrival, I amused myself by looking into some of the books with which his shelves were laden. Not among these, but immediately under them, with the backs upwards, on the floor, I lighted upon a complete set of Swedenborg's *Arcana Cælestia*, in the original Latin, a very fine folio set, bound in the natty livery which theology affects, pure vellum namely, gold letters, and carmine edges. There were paper markers in several of these volumes; I raised and placed them, one after the other, upon the table, and opening where these papers were placed, I read in the solemn Latin phraseology a series of sentences indicated by a pencilled line at the margin. Of these I copy here a few, translating them into English:

'When man's interior sight is opened, which is that of his spirit, then there appear the things of another life, which cannot possibly be made visible to the bodily sight. . . .'

'By the internal sight it has been granted me to see the things that are in the other life, more clearly than I see those that are in the world. From these considerations it is evident that external vision exists from interior vision, and this from a vision still more interior, and so on. . . .'

'There are with every man at least two evil spirits. . . .'

'With wicked genii there is also a fluent speech, but harsh and grating. There is also among them a speech which is not fluent, wherein the dissent of the thoughts is perceived as something secretly creeping along within it. . . .'

'The evil spirits associated with man are, indeed, from the hells, but when with man they are not then in hell, but are taken out thence. The place where they then are is in the midst between heaven and hell, and is called the world of spirits – when the evil spirits who are with man, are in that world, they are not in any infernal torment, but in every thought and affection of the man, and so, in all that the man himself enjoys. But when they are remitted into their hell, they return to their former state. . . .'

'If evil spirits could perceive that they were associated with man, and yet that they were spirits separate from him, and if they could flow in into the things of his body, they would attempt by a thousand means to destroy him; for they hate man with a deadly hatred. . . .'

'Knowing, therefore, that I was a man in the body, they were continually striving to destroy me, not as to the body only, but especially as to the soul; for to destroy any man or spirit is the very delight of the life of all who are in hell; but I have been continually protected by the Lord. Hence it appears how dangerous it is for man to be in a living consort with spirits, unless he be in the good of faith. . . .'

'Nothing is more carefully guarded from the knowledge of associate spirits than their being thus conjoint with a man, for if they knew it they would speak to him, with the intention to destroy him. . . .'

'The delight of hell is to do evil to man, and to hasten his eternal ruin. . . .'

A long note, written with a very sharp and fine pencil, in Mr Jennings' neat hand, at the foot of the page, caught my eye. Expecting his criticism upon the text, I read a word or two, and stopped; for it was something quite different, and began with these words, *Deus misereatur mei* – 'May God compassionate me.' Thus warned of its private nature, I averted my eyes, and shut the book, replacing all the volumes as I had found them, except one which interested me, and in which, as men studious and solitary in their habits will do, I grew so absorbed as to take no cognizance of the outer world, nor to remember where I was.

I was reading some pages which refer to 'representatives' and 'correspondents,' in the technical language of Swedenborg, and had arrived at a passage, the substance of which is that evil spirits, when seen by other eyes than those of their infernal associates, present themselves, by 'correspondence,' in the shape of the beast (*fera*) which represents their particular lust and life, in aspect direful and atrocious. This is a long passage, and particularizes a number of those bestial forms.

## CHAPTER IV

### FOUR EYES WERE READING THE PASSAGE

I was running the head of my pencil-case along the line as I read it, and something caused me to raise my eyes.

Directly before me was one of the Mirrors I have mentioned, in which I saw reflected the tall shape of my friend Mr Jennings, leaning over my shoulder, and reading the page at which I was busy, and with a face so dark and wild that I should hardly have known him.

I turned and rose. He stood erect also, and with an effort laughed a little, saying:

'I came in and asked you how you did, but without succeeding in awaking you from your book; so I could not restrain my curiosity, and very impertinently, I'm afraid, peeped over your shoulder. This is not your first time of looking into those pages. You have looked in Swedenborg, no doubt, long ago?'

'Oh dear, yes! I owe Swedenborg a great deal; you will discover traces of him in the little book on *Metaphysical Medicine*, which you were so good as to remember.'

Although my friend affected a gaiety of manner, there was a slight flush in his face, and I could perceive that he was inwardly much perturbed.

'I'm scarcely yet qualified, I know so little of Swedenborg. I've only had them a fortnight,' he answered, 'and I think they are rather likely to make a solitary man nervous – that is, judging from the very little I have read – I don't say that they have made me so,' he laughed; 'and I'm so very much obliged for the book. I hope you got my note?'

I made all proper acknowledgments and modest disclaimers.

'I never read a book that I go with, so entirely, as that of yours,' he continued. 'I saw at once there is more in it than is quite unfolded. Do you know Dr Harley?' he asked, rather abruptly.

[In passing, the editor remarks that the physician here named was one of the most eminent who had ever practised in England.]

I did, having had letters to him, and had experienced from him great courtesy and considerable assistance during my visit to England.

'I think that man one of the very greatest fools I ever met in my life,' said Mr Jennings.

This was the first time I had ever heard him say a sharp thing of anybody, and such a term applied to so high a name a little startled me.

'Really! and in what way?' I asked.

'In his profession,' he answered.

I smiled.

'I mean this,' he said: 'he seems to me, one half, blind – I mean one half of all he looks at is dark – preternaturally bright and vivid all the rest; and the worst of it is, it seems *wilful*. I can't get him – I mean he won't – I've had some experience of him as a physician, but I look on him as, in that sense, no better than a paralytic mind, an intellect half dead. I'll tell you – I know I shall some time – all about it,' he said, with a little agitation. 'You stay some months longer in England. If I should be out of town during your stay for a little time, would you allow me to trouble you with a letter?'

'I should be only too happy,' I assured him.

'Very good of you. I am utterly dissatisfied with Harley.'

'A little leaning to the materialistic school,' I said.

'A *mere* materialist,' he corrected me; 'you can't think how that sort of thing worries one who knows better. You won't tell anyone – any one of my friends you know – that I am hippish; now, for instance, no one knows – not even Lady Mary – that I have seen Dr Harley, or any other doctor. So pray don't mention it; and, if I should have any threatening of an attack, you'll kindly let me write, or, should I be in town, have a little talk with you.'

I was full of conjecture, and unconsciously I found I had fixed my eyes gravely on him, for he lowered his for a moment, and he said:

'I see you think I might as well tell you now, or else you are forming a conjecture; but you may as well give it up. If you were guessing all the rest of your life, you will never hit on it.'

He shook his head smiling, and over that wintry sunshine a black cloud suddenly came down, and he drew his breath in through his teeth, as men do in pain.

'Sorry, of course, to learn that you apprehend occasion to consult any of us; but command me when and how you like, and I need not assure you that your confidence is sacred.'

He then talked of quite other things, and in a comparatively cheerful way, and after a little time I took my leave.

## CHAPTER V

### DR HESSELIUS IS SUMMONED TO RICHMOND

We parted cheerfully, but he was not cheerful, nor was I. There are certain expressions of that powerful organ of spirit – the human face – which, although I have seen them often, and possess a doctor's nerve, yet disturb me profoundly. One look of Mr Jennings haunted me. It had seized my imagination with so dismal a power that I changed my plans for the evening, and went to the opera, feeling that I wanted a change of ideas.

I heard nothing of or from him for two or three days, when a note in his hand reached me. It was cheerful, and full of hope.

He said that he had been for some little time so much better – quite well, in fact – that he was going to make a little experiment, and run down for a month or so to his parish, to try whether a little work might not quite set him up. There was in it a fervent religious expression of gratitude for his restoration, as he now almost hoped he might call it.

A day or two later I saw Lady Mary, who repeated what his note had announced, and told me that he was actually in Warwickshire, having resumed his clerical duties at Kenlis; and she added, 'I begin to think that he is really perfectly well, and that there never was anything the matter, more than nerves and fancy; we are all nervous, but I fancy there is nothing like a little hard work for that kind of weakness, and he has made up his mind to try it. I should not be surprised if he did not come back for a year.'

Notwithstanding all this confidence, only two days later I had this note, dated from his house off Piccadilly:

> 'Dear Sir – I have returned disappointed. If I should feel at all able to see you, I shall write to ask you kindly to call. At present I am too low and, in fact, simply unable to say all I wish to say. Pray don't mention my name to my friends. I can see no one. By-and-by, please God, you shall hear from me. I mean to take a run into Shropshire, where some of my people are. God bless you! May we, on my return, meet more happily than I can now write.'

About a week after this I saw Lady Mary at her own house, the last person, she said, left in town and just on the wing for Brighton, for the London season was quite over. She told me that she had heard from Mr Jennings' niece, Martha, in Shropshire. There was nothing to be gathered from her letter, more than he was low and nervous. In those words, of which healthy people think so lightly, what a world of suffering is sometimes hidden!

Nearly five weeks had passed without any further news of Mr Jennings. At the end of that time I received a note from him. He wrote:

'I have been in the country, and have had change of air, change of scene, change of faces, change of everything and in everything – but *myself*. I have made up my mind, so far as the most irresolute creature on earth can do it, to tell my case fully to you. If your engagements will permit, pray come to me to-day, to-morrow, or the next day; but, pray defer as little as possible. You know not how much I need help. I have a quiet house at Richmond, where I now am. Perhaps you can manage to come to dinner, or to luncheon, or even to tea. You shall have no trouble in finding me out. The servant at Blank Street, who takes this note, will have a carriage at your door at any hour you please; and I am always to be found. You will say that I ought not to be alone. I have tried everything. Come and see.'

I called up the servant, and decided on going out the same evening, which accordingly I did.

He would have been much better in a lodging-house, or hotel, I thought, as I drove up through a short double row of sombre elms to a very old-fashioned brick house, darkened by the foliage of these trees, which overtopped and nearly surrounded it. It was a perverse choice, for nothing could be imagined more triste and silent. The house, I found, belonged to him. He had stayed for a day or two in town, and, finding it for some cause insupportable, had come out here, probably because, being furnished and his own, he was relieved of the thought and delay of selection, by coming here.

The sun had already set, and the red reflected light of the western sky illuminated the scene with the peculiar effect with which we are all familiar. The hall seemed very dark, but, getting to the back drawing-room, whose windows command the west, I was again in the same dusky light.

I sat down, looking out upon the richly-wooded landscape that glowed in the grand and melancholy light which was every moment fading. The corners of the room were already dark; all was growing dim, and the gloom was insensibly toning my mind, already prepared for what was sinister. I was waiting alone for his arrival, which soon took place. The door communicating with the front room opened, and the tall figure of Mr Jennings, faintly seen in the ruddy twilight, came, with quiet stealthy steps, into the room.

We shook hands, and, taking a chair to the window, where there was still light enough to enable us to see each other's faces, he sat down beside me, and, placing his hand upon my arm, with scarcely a word of preface began his narrative.

## CHAPTER VI

### HOW MR JENNINGS MET HIS COMPANION

The faint glow of the west, the pomp of the then lonely woods of Richmond, were before us, behind and about us the darkening room, and on the stony face of the sufferer – for the character of his face, though still gentle and sweet, was changed – rested that dim, odd glow which seems to descend and produce, where it touches, lights, sudden though faint, which are lost, almost without gradation, in darkness. The silence, too, was utter; not a distant wheel, or bark, or whistle from without; and within the depressing stillness of an invalid bachelor's house.

I guessed well the nature, though not even vaguely the particulars of the revelations I was about to receive, from that fixed face of suffering that, so oddly flushed, stood out, like a portrait of Schalken's, before its background of darkness.

'It began,' he said, 'on the 15th of October, three years and eleven weeks ago, and two days – I keep very accurate count, for every day is torment. If I leave anywhere a chasm in my narrative tell me.

'About four years ago I began a work which had cost me very much thought and reading. It was upon the religious metaphysics of the ancients.'

'I know,' said I; 'the actual religion of educated and thinking paganism, quite apart from symbolic worship? A wide and very interesting field.'

'Yes; but not good for the mind – the Christian mind, I mean. Paganism is all bound together in essential unity, and, with evil sympathy, their religion involves their art, and both their manners, and the subject is a degrading fascination and the Nemesis sure. God forgive me!

'I wrote a great deal; I wrote late at night. I was always thinking on the subject, walking about, wherever I was, everywhere. It thoroughly infected me. You are to remember that all the material ideas connected with it were more or less of the beautiful, the subject itself delightfully interesting, and I, then, without a care.'

He sighed heavily.

'I believe that every one who sets about writing in earnest does his work, as a friend of mine phrased it, *on* something –

tea, or coffee, or tobacco. I suppose there is a material waste that must be hourly supplied in such occupations, or that we should grow too abstracted, and the mind, as it were, pass out of the body, unless it were reminded often of the connection by actual sensation. At all events I felt the want, and I supplied it. Tea was my companion – first the ordinary black tea, made in the usual way, not too strong: but I drank a good deal, and increased its strength as I went on. I never experienced an uncomfortable symptom from it. I began to take a little green tea. I found the effect pleasanter, it cleared and intensified the power of thought so. I had come to take it frequently, but not stronger than one might take it for pleasure. I wrote a great deal out here, it was so quiet, and in this room. I used to sit up very late, and it became a habit with me to sip my tea – green tea – every now and then as my work proceeded. I had a little kettle on my table, that swung over a lamp, and made tea two or three times between eleven o'clock and two or three in the morning, my hours of going to bed. I used to go into town every day. I was not a monk, and, although I spent an hour or two in a library hunting up authorities and looking out lights upon my theme, I was in no morbid state as far as I can judge. I met my friends pretty much as usual and enjoyed their society, and, on the whole, existence had never been, I think, so pleasant before.

'I had met with a man who had some odd old books, German editions in mediæval Latin, and I was only too happy to be permitted access to them. This obliging person's books were in the City, a very out-of-the-way part of it. I had rather out-stayed my intended hour, and, on coming out, seeing no cab near, I was tempted to get into the omnibus which used to drive past this house. It was darker than this by the time the 'bus had reached an old house you may have remarked, with four poplars at each side of the door, and there the last passenger but myself got out. We drove along rather faster. It was twilight now. I leaned back in my corner next the door, ruminating pleasantly.

'The interior of the omnibus was nearly dark. I had observed in the corner opposite to me at the other side, and at the end next the horses, two small circular reflections, as it seemed to me of a reddish light. They were about two inches apart, and about the size of those small brass buttons that yachting men used to put upon their jackets. I began to speculate, as listless men will, upon this trifle, as it seemed. From what centre did that faint but deep red light come, and from what – glass beads, buttons, toy decorations – was it reflected? We were lumbering along gently, having nearly a mile still to go. I had not solved the puzzle, and it became in another minute more odd, for these two luminous points, with a sudden jerk, descended nearer the floor, keeping still their relative distance and horizontal position, and then, as suddenly, they rose to the level of the seat on which I was sitting, and I saw them no more.

'My curiosity was now really excited, and, before I had time to think, I saw again these two dull lamps, again together near the floor; again they disappeared, and again in their old corner I saw them.

'So, keeping my eyes upon them, I edged quietly up my own side, towards the end at which I still saw these tiny discs of red.

'There was very little light in the 'bus. It was nearly dark. I leaned forward to aid my endeavour to discover what these little circles really were. They shifted their position a little as I did so. I began now to perceive an outline of something black, and I soon saw, with tolerable distinctness, the outline of a small black monkey, pushing its face forward in mimicry to meet mine; those were its eyes, and I now dimly saw its teeth grinning at me. I drew back, not knowing whether it might not meditate a spring. I fancied that one of the passengers had forgot this ugly pet, and wishing to ascertain something of its temper, though not caring to trust my fingers to it, I poked my umbrella softly towards it. It remained immovable – up to it – *through* it. For through it, and back and forward it passed, without the slightest resistance.

'I can't, in the least, convey to you the kind of horror that I felt. When I had ascertained that the thing was an illusion, as I then supposed, there came a misgiving about myself and a terror that fascinated me in impotence to remove my gaze from the eyes of the brute for some moments. As I looked it made a little skip back, quite into the corner, and I, in a panic, found myself at the door, having put my head out, drawing deep breaths of the outer air, and staring at the lights and trees we were passing, too glad to reassure myself of reality.

'I stopped the 'bus and got out. I perceived the man look oddly at me as I paid him. I daresay there was something unusual in my looks and manner, for I had never felt so strangely before.

## CHAPTER VII

### THE JOURNEY: FIRST STAGE

'When the omnibus drove on, and I was along upon the road, I looked carefully round to ascertain whether the monkey had followed me. To my indescribable relief I saw it nowhere. I can't describe easily what a shock I had received, and my sense of genuine gratitude on finding myself, as I supposed, quite rid of it.

'I had got out a little before we reached this house, two or three hundred steps. A brick wall runs along the footpath, and inside the wall is a hedge of yew, or some dark evergreen of that kind, and within that again the row of fine trees which you may have remarked as you came.

'This brick wall is about as high as my shoulder, and happening to raise my eyes I saw the monkey, with that stooping gait, on all fours, walking or creeping, close beside me on top of the wall. I stopped, looking at it with a feeling of loathing and horror. As I stopped so did it. It sat up on the wall with its long hands on its knees looking at me. There was not light enough to see it much more than in outline, nor was it dark enough to bring the peculiar light of its eyes into strong relief. I still saw, however, that red foggy light plainly enough. It did not show its teeth, nor exhibit any sign of irritation, but seemed jaded and sulky, and was observing me steadily.

'I drew back into the middle of the road. It was an unconscious recoil, and there I stood, still looking at it. It did not move.

'With an instinctive determination to try something – anything, I turned about and walked briskly towards town, with askance look, all the time watching the movements of the beast. It crept swiftly along the wall, at exactly my pace.

'Where the wall ends, near the turn of the road, it came down, and with a wiry spring or two brought itself close to my feet, and continued to keep up with me as I quickened my pace. It was at my left side, so close to my leg that I felt every moment as if I should tread upon it.

'The road was quite deserted and silent, and it was darker every moment. I stopped dismayed and bewildered, turning, as I did so, the other way – I mean towards this house, away from which I had been walking. When I stood still the monkey drew back to a distance of, I suppose, about five or six yards, and remained stationary, watching me.

'I had been more agitated than I have said. I had read, of course, as everyone has, something about "spectral illusions," as you physicians term the phenomena of such cases. I considered my situation, and looked my misfortune in the face.

'These affections, I had read, are sometimes transitory and sometimes obstinate. I had read of cases in which the appearance, at first harmless, had, step by step, degenerated into something direful and insupportable, and ended by wearing its victim out. Still, as I stood there, but for my bestial companion quite alone, I tried to comfort myself by repeating again and again the assurance, "the thing is purely disease, a well-known physical affection, as distinctly as small-pox or neuralgia. Doctors are all agreed on that, philosophy demonstrates it. I must not be a fool. I've been sitting up too late, and I daresay my digestion is quite wrong, and, with God's help, I shall be all right, and this is but a symptom of nervous dyspepsia." Did I believe all this? Not one word of it, no more than any other miserable being ever did who is once seized and riveted in this satanic captivity. Against my convictions, I might say my knowledge, I was simply bullying myself into a false courage.

'I now walked homeward. I had only a few hundred yards to go. I had forced myself into a sort of resignation, but I had not got over the sickening shock and the flurry of the first certainty of my misfortune.

'I made up my mind to pass the night at home. The brute moved close beside me, and I fancied there was the sort of anxious drawing toward the house, which one sees in tired horses or dogs, sometimes, as they come toward home.

'I was afraid to go into town, I was afraid of any one's seeing and recognizing me. I was conscious of an irrepressible agitation in my manner. Also, I was afraid of any violent change in my habits, such as going to a place of amusement, or walking from home in order to fatigue myself. At the hall door it waited till I mounted the steps, and when the door was opened entered with me.

'I drank no tea that night. I got cigars and some brandy and water. My idea was that I should act upon my material system, and by living for a while in sensation apart from thought, send myself forcibly, as it were, into a new groove. I came up here to this drawing-room. I sat just here. The monkey then got upon a small table that then stood *there*. It looked dazed and languid. An irrepressible uneasiness as to its movements kept my eyes always upon it. Its eyes were half closed, but I could see them glow. It was looking steadily at me. In all situations, at all hours, it is awake and looking at me. That never changes.

'I shall not continue in detail my narrative of this particular night. I shall describe, rather, the phenomena of the first year, which never varied essentially. I shall describe the monkey as it appeared in daylight. In the dark, as you shall presently hear, there are peculiarities. It is a small monkey, perfectly black. It had only one peculiarity – a character of malignity – unfathomable malignity. During the first year it looked sullen and sick. But this character of intense malice and vigilance was always underlying that surly languor. During all that time it acted as if on a plan of giving me as little trouble as was consistent with watching me. Its eyes were never off me. I have never lost sight of it, except in my sleep, light or dark, day or night, since it came here, excepting when it withdraws for some weeks at a time, unaccountably.

'In total dark it is visible as in daylight. I do not mean merely its eyes. It is *all* visible distinctly in a halo that resembles a glow of red embers, and which accompanies it in all its movements.

'When it leaves me for a time it is always at night, in the dark, and in the same way. It grows at first uneasy, and then furious, and then advances towards me, grinning and shaking, its paws clenched, and, at the same time, there comes the appearance of fire in the grate. I never have any fire. I can't sleep in the room where there is any – and it draws nearer and nearer to the chimney, quivering, it seems, with rage, and when its fury rises to the highest pitch it springs into the grate, and up the chimney, and I see it no more.

'When first this happened I thought I was released. I was now a new man. A day passed – a night – and no return, and a blessed week – a week – another week. I was always on my knees, Dr Hesselius, always, thanking God and praying. A whole month passed of liberty; but, on a sudden it was with me again.

## CHAPTER VIII

## THE SECOND STAGE

'It was with me, and the malice which before was torpid under a sullen exterior was now active. It was perfectly unchanged in every other respect. This new energy was apparent in its activity and its looks, and soon in other ways.

'For a time, you will understand, the change was shown only in an increased vivacity, and an air of menace, as if it were always brooding over some atrocious plan. Its eyes, as before, were never off me.'

'Is it here now?' I asked.

'No,' he replied, 'it has been absent exactly a fortnight and a day – fifteen days. It has sometimes been away so long as nearly two months, once for three. Its absence always exceeds a fortnight, although it may be but by a single day. Fifteen days having past since I saw it last, it may return now at any moment.'

'Is its return,' I asked, 'accompanied by any peculiar manifestation?'

'Nothing – no,' he said. 'It is simply with me again. On lifting my eyes from a book, or turning my head, I see it, as usual, looking at me, and then it remains, as before, for its appointed time. I have never told so much and so minutely before to anyone.'

I perceived that he was agitated, and looking like death, and he repeatedly applied his handkerchief to his forehead; I suggested that he might be tired, and told him that I would call, with pleasure, in the morning, but he said:

'No, if you don't mind hearing it all now. I have got so far, and I should prefer making one effort of it. When I spoke to Dr Harley, I had nothing like so much to tell. You are a philosophic physician. You give spirit its proper rank. If this thing is real –'

He paused, looking at me with agitated inquiry.

'We can discuss it by-and-by, and very fully. I will give you all I think,' I answered, after an interval.

'Well – very well. If it is anything real, I say, it is prevailing, little by little, and drawing me more interiorly into hell. Optic nerves, he talked of. Ah! well – there are other nerves of communication. May God Almighty help me! You shall hear.

‘Its power of action, I tell you, had increased. Its malice became, in a way, aggressive. About two years ago, some questions that were pending between me and the bishop having been settled, I went down to my parish in Warwickshire, anxious to find occupation in my profession. I was not prepared for what happened, although I have since thought I might have apprehended something like it. The reason for my saying so is this –’

He was beginning to speak with a great deal more effort and reluctance, and sighed often, and seemed at times nearly overcome. But at this time, his manner was not agitated. It was more like that of a sinking patient, who has given himself up.

‘Yes, but I will first tell you about Kenlis, my parish.

‘It was with me when I left this place for Dawlbridge. It was my silent travelling companion, and it remained with me at the vicarage. When I entered on the discharge of my duties, another change took place. The thing exhibited an atrocious determination to thwart me. It was with me in the church – in the reading-desk – in the pulpit – within the communion rails. At last it reached this extremity, that while I was reading to the congregation it would spring upon the open book and squat there, so that I was unable to see the page. This happened more than once.

‘I left Dawlbridge for a time. I placed myself in Dr Harley’s hands. I did everything he told me. He gave my case a great deal of thought. It interested him, I think. He seemed successful. For nearly three months I was perfectly free from a return. I began to think I was safe. With his full assent I returned to Dawlbridge.

‘I travelled in a chaise. I was in good spirits. I was more – I was happy and grateful. I was returning, as I thought, delivered from a dreadful hallucination, to the scene of duties which I longed to enter upon. It was a beautiful sunny evening, everything looked serene and cheerful, and I was delighted. I remember looking out of the window to see the spire of my church at Kenlis among the trees, at the point where one has the earliest view of it. It is exactly where the little stream that bounds the parish passes under the road by a culvert; and where it emerges at the road-side a stone with an old inscription is placed. As we passed this point I drew my head in and sat down, and in the corner of the chaise was the monkey.

‘For a moment I felt faint, and then quite wild with despair and horror. I called to the driver, and got out, and sat down at the road-side, and prayed to God silently for mercy. A despairing resignation supervened. My companion was with me as I re-entered the vicarage. The same persecution followed. After a short struggle I submitted, and soon I left the place.

'I told you,' he said, 'that the beast has before this become in certain ways aggressive. I will explain a little. It seemed to be actuated by intense and increasing fury whenever I said my prayers, or even meditated prayer. It amounted at last to a dreadful interruption. You will ask, how could a silent immaterial phantom effect that? It was thus, whenever I meditated praying; it was always before me, and nearer and nearer.

'It used to spring on a table, on the back of a chair, on the chimney-piece, and slowly to swing itself from side to side, looking at me all the time. There is in its motion an indefinable power to dissipate thought, and to contract one's attention to that monotony, till the ideas shrink, as it were, to a point, and at last to nothing – and unless I had started up, and shook off the catalepsy, I have felt as if my mind were on the point of losing itself. There are other ways,' he sighed heavily; 'thus, for instance, while I pray with my eyes closed, it comes closer and closer, and I see it. I know it is not to be accounted for physically, but I do actually see it, though my lids are closed, and so it rocks my mind, as it were, and overpowers me, and I am obliged to rise from my knees. If you had ever yourself known this, you would be acquainted with desperation.'

## CHAPTER IX

## THE THIRD STAGE

'I see, Dr Hesselius, that you don't lose one word of my statement. I need not ask you to listen specially to what I am now going to tell you. They talk of the optic nerves, and of spectral illusions, as if the organ of sight was the only point assailable by the influences that have fastened upon me – I know better. For two years in my direful case that limitation prevailed. But as food is taken in softly at the lips, and then brought under the teeth, as the tip of the little finger caught in a mill crank will draw in the hand, and the arm, and the whole body, so the miserable mortal who has been once caught firmly by the end of the finest fibre of his nerve is drawn in and in, by the enormous machinery of hell, until he is as I am. Yes, Doctor, as *I* am, for while I talk to you, and implore relief, I feel that my prayer is for the impossible, and my pleading with the inexorable.'

I endeavoured to calm his visibly increasing agitation, and told him that he must not despair.

While we talked the night had overtaken us. The filmy moonlight was wide over the scene which the window commanded, and I said:

'Perhaps you would prefer having candles. This light, you know, is odd. I should wish you, as much as possible, under your usual conditions, while I make my diagnosis, shall I call it – otherwise I don't care.'

'All lights are the same to me,' he said. 'Except when I read or write, I care not if night were perpetual. I am going to tell you what happened about a year ago. The thing began to speak to me.'

'Speak! How do you mean – speak as a man does, do you mean?'

'Yes; speak in words and consecutive sentences, with perfect coherence and articulation; but there is a peculiarity. It is not like the tone of a human voice. It is not by my ears it reaches me – it comes like a singing through my head.

'This faculty, the power of speaking to me, will be my undoing. It won't let me pray, it interrupts me with dreadful blasphemies. I dare not go on, I could not. Oh! Doctor, can the skill, and thought, and prayers of man avail me nothing!'

'You must promise me, my dear sir, not to trouble yourself with unnecessarily exciting thoughts; confine yourself strictly to the narrative of *facts*; and recollect, above all, that even if the thing that infests you be, as you seem to suppose, a reality with an actual independent life and will, yet it can have no power to hurt you, unless it be given from above: its access to your senses depends mainly upon your physical condition – this is, under God, your comfort and reliance: we are all alike environed. It is only that in your case, the "*paries*," the veil of the flesh, the screen, is a little out of repair, and sights and sounds are transmitted. We must enter on a new course, sir – be encouraged. I'll give to-night to the careful consideration of the whole case.'

'You are very good, sir; you think it worth trying, you don't give me quite up; but, sir, you don't know, it is gaining such an influence over me: it orders me about, it is such a tyrant, and I'm growing so helpless. May God deliver me!'

'It orders you about – of course you mean by speech?'

'Yes, yes; it is always urging me to crimes, to injure others, or myself. You see, Doctor, the situation is urgent, it is indeed. When I was in Shropshire, a few weeks ago' (Mr Jennings was speaking rapidly and trembling now, holding my arm with one hand, and looking in my face), 'I went out one day with a party of friends for a walk: my persecutor, I tell you, was with me at the time. I lagged behind the rest: the country near the Dee, you know, is beautiful. Our path happened to lie near a coal mine, and at the verge of the wood is a perpendicular shaft, they say, a hundred and fifty feet deep. My niece had remained behind with me – she knows, of course, nothing of the nature of my sufferings. She knew, however, that I had been ill, and was low, and she remained to prevent my being quite alone. As we loitered slowly on together, the brute that accompanied me was urging me to throw myself down the shaft. I tell you now – oh, sir, think of it! – the one consideration that saved me from that hideous death was the fear lest the shock of witnessing the occurrence should be too much for the poor girl. I asked her to go on and take her walk with her friends, saying I could go no further. She made excuses, and the more I urged her the firmer she became. She looked doubtful and frightened. I suppose there was something in my looks or manner that alarmed her; but she would not go, and that literally saved me. You had no idea, sir, that a living man could be made so abject a slave of Satan,' he said, with a ghastly groan and a shudder.

There was a pause here, and I said, 'You *were* preserved nevertheless. It was the act of God. You are in His hands and in the power of no other being: be therefore confident for the future.'

## CHAPTER X

## HOME

I made him have candles lighted, and saw the room looking cheery and inhabited before I left him. I told him that he must regard his illness strictly as one dependent on physical, though *subtle* physical causes. I told him that he had evidence of God's care and love in the deliverance which he had just described, and that I had perceived with pain that he seemed to regard its peculiar features as indicating that he had been delivered over to spiritual reprobation. Than such a conclusion nothing could be, I insisted, less warranted; and not only so, but more contrary to facts, as disclosed in his mysterious deliverance from that murderous influence during his Shropshire excursion. First, his niece had been retained by his side without his intending to keep her near him; and secondly, there had been infused into his mind an irresistible repugnance to execute the dreadful suggestion in her presence.

As I reasoned this point with him, Mr Jennings wept. He seemed comforted. One promise I exacted, which was that should the monkey at any time return, I should be sent for immediately; and, repeating my assurance that I would give neither time nor thought to any other subject until I had thoroughly investigated his case, and that to-morrow he should hear the result, I took my leave.

Before getting into the carriage I told the servant that his master was far from well, and that he should make a point of frequently looking into his room.

My own arrangements I made with a view to being quite secure from interruption.

I merely called at my lodgings, and with a travelling-desk and carpet-bag set off in a hackney carriage for an inn, about two miles out of town, called 'The Horns,' a very quiet and comfortable house with good thick walls. And there I resolved, without the possibility of intrusion or distraction, to devote some hours of the night, in my comfortable sitting-room, to Mr Jennings' case, and so much of the morning as it might require.

[There occurs here a careful note of Dr Hesselius' opinion upon the case, and of the habits, dietary, and medicines which he prescribed. It is curious – some persons would say mystical. But, on the whole, I doubt whether it would sufficiently interest a reader of the kind I am likely to meet with, to warrant its being here reprinted. The whole letter was plainly written at the inn where he had hid himself for the occasion. The next letter is dated from his town lodgings.]

I left town for the inn where I slept last night at half-past nine, and did not arrive at my room in town until one o'clock this afternoon. I found a letter in Mr Jennings' hand upon my table. It had come by post, and, on inquiry, I learned that Mr Jennings' servant had brought it, and, on learning that I was not to return until to-day and that no one could tell him my address, he seemed very uncomfortable, and said that his orders from his master were that he was not to return without an answer.

I opened the letter and read:

> 'DEAR DR HESSELIUS. – It is here. You had not been an hour gone when it returned. It is speaking. It knows all that has happened. It knows everything – it knows you, and is frantic and atrocious. It reviles. I send you this. It knows every word I have written – I write. This I promised, and I therefore write, but I fear very confused, very incoherently. I am so interrupted, disturbed.
>
> Ever yours, sincerely yours,
> ROBERT LYNDER JENNINGS.'

'When did this come?' I asked.

'About eleven last night: the man was here again, and has been here three times to-day. The last time is about an hour since.'

Thus answered, and with the notes I had made upon his case in my pocket, I was in a few minutes driving towards Richmond to see Mr Jennings.

I by no means, as you perceive, despaired of Mr Jennings' case. He had himself remembered and applied, though quite in a mistaken way, the principle which I lay down in my *Metaphysical Medicine*, and which governs all such cases. I was about to apply it in earnest. I was profoundly interested, and very anxious to see and examine him while the 'enemy' was actually present.

I drove up to the sombre house, and ran up the steps and knocked. The door, in a little time, was opened by a tall woman in black silk. She looked ill, and as if she had been crying. She curtseyed, and heard my question, but she did not answer. She turned her face away, extending her hand towards two men who were coming downstairs; and thus having, as it were, tacitly made me over to them, she passed through a side-door hastily and shut it.

The man who was nearest the hall, I at once accosted, but

being now close to him I was shocked to see that both his hands were covered with blood.

I drew back a little, and the man, passing downstairs, merely said in a low tone, 'Here's the servant, sir.'

The servant had stopped on the stairs, confounded and dumb at seeing me. He was rubbing his hands in a handkerchief, and it was steeped in blood.

'Jones, what is it? what has happened?' I asked, while a sickening suspicion overpowered me.

The man asked me to come up to the lobby. I was beside him in a moment, and, frowning and pallid, with contracted eyes, he told me the horror which I already half guessed.

His master had made away with himself.

I went upstairs with him to the room – what I saw there I won't tell you. He had cut his throat with his razor. It was a frightful gash. The two men had laid him on the bed, and composed his limbs. It had happened, as the immense pool of blood on the floor declared, at some distance between the bed and the window. There was carpet round his bed, and a carpet under his dressing-table, but none on the rest of the floor, for the man said he did not like a carpet in his bedroom. In this sombre and now terrible room, one of the great elms that darkened the house was slowly moving the shadow of one of its great boughs upon this dreadful floor.

I beckoned to the servant, and we went downstairs together. I turned off the hall into an old-fashioned panelled room, and there standing, I heard all the servant had to tell. It was not a great deal.

'I concluded, sir, from your words, and looks, sir, as you left last night, that you thought my master seriously ill. I thought it might be that you were afraid of a fit, or something. So I attended very close to your directions. He sat up late, till past three o'clock. He was not writing or reading. He was talking a great deal to himself, but that was nothing unusual. At about that hour I assisted him to undress, and left him in his slippers and dressing-gown. I went back softly in about half-an-hour. He was in his bed, quite undressed, and a pair of candles lighted on the table beside his bed. He was leaning on his elbow, and looking out at the other side of the bed when I came in. I asked him if he wanted anything, and he said "No."

'I don't know whether it was what you said to me, sir, or

something a little unusual about him, but I was uneasy, uncommon uneasy about him last night.

'In another half hour, or it might be a little more, I went up again. I did not hear him talking as before. I opened the door a little. The candles were both out, which was not usual. I had a bedroom candle, and I let the light in, a little bit, looking softly round. I saw him sitting in that chair beside the dressing-table with his clothes on again. He turned round and looked at me. I thought it strange he should get up and dress, and put out the candles to sit in the dark, that way. But I only asked him again if I could do anything for him. He said, "No," rather sharp, I thought. I asked if I might light the candles, and he said, "Do as you like, Jones." So I lighted them, and I lingered about the room, and he said, "Tell me truth, Jones; why did you come again – you did not hear anyone cursing?" "No, sir," I said, wondering what he could mean.

'"No," said he, after me, "of course, no"; and I said to him, "Wouldn't it be well, sir, you went to bed? It's just five o'clock"; and he said nothing but, "Very likely; good-night, Jones." So I went, sir, but in less than an hour I came again. The door was fast, and he heard me, and called as I thought from the bed to know what I wanted, and he desired me not to disturb him again. I lay down and slept for a little. It must have been between six and seven when I went up again. The door was still fast, and he made no answer, so I did not like to disturb him, and thinking he was asleep I left him till nine. It was his custom to ring when he wished me to come, and I had no particular hour for calling him. I tapped very gently, and getting no answer I stayed away a good while, supposing he was getting some rest then. It was not till eleven o'clock I grew really uncomfortable about him – for at the latest he was never, that I could remember, later than half-past ten. I got no answer. I knocked and called, and still no answer. So not being able to force the door, I called Thomas from the stables, and together we forced it, and found him in the shocking way you saw.'

Jones had no more to tell. Poor Mr Jennings was very gentle and very kind. All his people were fond of him. I could see that the servant was very much moved.

So, dejected and agitated, I passed from that terrible house, and its dark canopy of elms, and I hope I shall never see it more. While I write to you I feel like a man who has but half waked from a frightful and monotonous dream. My memory rejects the picture with incredulity and horror. Yet I know it is true. It is the story of the process of a poison, a poison which excites the reciprocal action of spirit and nerve, and paralyses the tissue that separates those cognate functions of the senses, the external and the interior. Thus we find strange bed-fellows, and the mortal and immortal prematurely make acquaintance.

# *The White Cat of Drumgunniol*

J. S. Le Fanu

There is a famous story of a white cat, with which we all become acquainted in the nursery. I am going to tell a story of a white cat very different from the amiable and enchanted princess who took that disguise for a season. The white cat of which I speak was a more sinister animal.

The traveller from Limerick toward Dublin, after passing the hills of Killaloe upon the left, as Keeper Mountain rises high in view, finds himself gradually hemmed in, up the right, by a range of lower hills. An undulating plain that dips gradually to a lower level than that of the road interposes, and some scattered hedgerows relieve its somewhat wild and melancholy character.

One of the few human habitations that send up their films of turf-smoke from that lonely plain, is the loosely-thatched, earth-built dwelling of a 'strong farmer,' as the more prosperous of the tenant-farming classes are termed in Munster. It stands in a clump of trees near the edge of a wandering stream, about half-way between the mountains and the Dublin road, and had been for generations tenanted by people named Donovan.

In a distant place, desirous of studying some Irish records which had fallen into my hands, and inquiring for a teacher capable of instructing me in the Irish language, a Mr Donovan, dreamy, harmless, and learned, was recommended to me for the purpose.

I found that he had been educated as a Sizar in Trinity College, Dublin. He now supported himself by teaching, and the special direction of my studies, I suppose, flattered his national partialities, for he unbosomed himself of much of his long-reserved thoughts, and recollections about his country and his early days. It was he who told me this story, and I mean to repeat it, as nearly as I can, in his own words.

I have myself seen the old farm-house, with its orchard of huge mossgrown apple trees. I have looked round on the peculiar landscape; the roofless, ivied tower, that two hundred years before had afforded a refuge from raid and rapparee, and which still occupies its old place in the angle of the haggard; the bush-grown 'liss,' that scarcely a hundred and fifty steps away records the labours of a bygone race; the dark and towering outline of old Keeper in the background; and the lonely range of furze and heath-clad hills that form a nearer barrier, with many a line of grey rock and clump of dwarf oak or birch. The pervading sense of loneliness made it a scene not unsuited for a wild and unearthly story. And I could quite fancy how, seen in the grey of a wintry morning, shrouded far and wide in snow, or in the chill splendour of a moonlight night, it might have helped to tone a dreamy mind like honest Dan Donovan's to superstition and a proneness to the illusions of fancy. It is certain, however, that I never anywhere met with a more simple-minded creature, or one on whose good faith I could more entirely rely.

When I was a boy, said he, living at home at Drumgunniol, I used to take my Goldsmith's *Roman History* in my hand and go down to my favourite seat, the flat stone, sheltered by a hawthorn tree beside the little lough, a large and deep pool, such as I have heard called a tarn in England. It lay in the gentle hollow of a field that is overhung towards the north by the old orchard, and being a deserted place was favourable to my studious quietude.

One day reading here, as usual, I wearied at last, and began to look about me, thinking of the heroic scenes I had just been reading of. I was as wide awake as I am at this moment, and I saw a woman appear at the corner of the orchard and walk down the slope. She wore a long, light grey dress, so long that it seemed to sweep the grass behind her, and so singular was her appearance in a part of the world where female attire is so inflexibly fixed by custom, that I could not take my eyes off her. Her course lay diagonally from corner to corner of the field, which was a large one, and she pursued it without swerving.

When she came near I could see that her feet were bare, and

that she seemed to be looking steadfastly upon some remote object for guidance. Her route would have crossed me – had the tarn not interposed – about ten or twelve yards below the point at which I was sitting. But instead of arresting her course at the margin of the lough, as I had expected, she went on without seeming conscious of its existence, and I saw her, as plainly as I see you, sir, walk across the surface of the water, and pass, without seeming to see me, at about the distance I had calculated.

I was ready to faint from sheer terror. I was only thirteen years old then, and I remember every particular as if it had happened this hour.

The figure passed through the gap at the far corner of the field, and there I lost sight of it. I had hardly strength to walk home, and was so nervous, and ultimately so ill, that for three weeks I was confined to the house, and could not bear to be alone for a moment. I never entered that field again, such was the horror with which from that moment every object in it was clothed. Even at this distance of time I should not like to pass through it.

This apparition I connected with a mysterious event; and, also, with a singular liability, that has for nearly eight years distinguished, or rather afflicted, our family. It is no fancy. Everybody in that part of the country knows all about it. Everybody connected what I had seen with it.

I will tell it all to you as well as I can.

When I was about fourteen years old – that is about a year after the sight I had seen in the lough field – we were one night expecting my father home from the fair of Killaloe. My mother sat up to welcome him home, and I with her, for I liked nothing better than such a vigil. My brothers and sisters, and the farm servants, except the men who were driving home the cattle from the fair, were asleep in their beds. My mother and I were sitting in the chimney corner chatting together, and watching my father's supper, which was kept hot over the fire. We knew that he would return before the men who were driving home the cattle, for he was riding, and told us that he would only wait to see them fairly on the road, and then push homeward.

At length we heard his voice and the knocking of his loaded whip at the door, and my mother let him in. I don't think I ever saw my father drunk, which is more than most men of my age, from the same part of the country, could say of theirs. But he could drink his glass of whisky as well as another, and he usually came home from fair or market a little merry and mellow, and with a jolly flush in his cheeks.

To-night he looked sunken, pale and sad. He entered with the saddle and bridle in his hand, and he dropped them against the wall, near the door, and put his arms round his wife's neck, and kissed her kindly.

'Welcome home, Meehal,' said she, kissing him heartily.

'God bless you, mavourneen,' he answered.

And hugging her again, he turned to me, who was plucking him by the hand, jealous of his notice. I was little, and light of my age, and he lifted me up in his arms, and kissed me, and my arms being about his neck, he said to my mother:

'Draw the bolt, acuishla.'

She did so, and setting me down very dejectedly, he walked to the fire and sat down on a stool, and stretched his feet toward the glowing turf, leaning with his hands on his knees.

'Rouse up, Mick, darlin',' said my mother, who was growing anxious, 'and tell me how did the cattle sell, and did everything go lucky at the fair, or is there anything wrong with the landlord, or what in the world is it that ails you, Mick, jewel?'

'Nothin', Molly. The cows sould well, thank God, and there's nothin' fell out between me an' the landlord, an' everything's the same way. There's no fault to find anywhere.'

'Well, then, Mickey, since so it is, turn round to your hot supper, and ate it, and tell us is there anything new.'

'I got my supper, Molly, on the way, and I can't ate a bit,' he answered.

'Got your supper on the way, an' you knowin' 'twas waiting for you at home, an' your wife sittin' up an' all!' cried my mother, reproachfully.

'You're takin' a wrong meanin' out of what I say,' said my father. 'There's something happened that leaves me that I can't ate a mouthful, and I'll not be dark with you, Molly, for, maybe, it ain't very long I have to be here, an' I'll tell you what it was. It's what I've seen, the white cat.'

'The Lord between us and harm!' exclaimed my mother, in a moment as pale and as chap-fallen as my father; and then, trying to rally, with a laugh, she said: 'Ha! 'tis only funnin' me you are. Sure a white rabbit was snared a Sunday last, in

Grady's wood; an' Teigue seen a big white rat in the haggard yesterday.'

''Twas neither rat nor rabbit was in it. Don't ye think but I'd know a rat or a rabbit from a big white cat, with green eyes as big as halfpennies, and its back riz up like a bridge, trottin' on and across me, and ready, if I dar' stop, to rub its sides against my shins, and maybe to make a jump and seize my throat, if that it's a cat, at all, an' not something worse?'

As he ended his description in a low tone, looking straight at the fire, my father drew his big hand across his forehead once or twice, his face being damp and shining with the moisture of fear, and he sighed, or rather groaned, heavily.

My mother had relapsed into panic, and was praying again in her fear. I, too, was terribly frightened, and on the point of crying, for I knew all about the white cat.

Clapping my father on the shoulder, by way of encouragement, my mother leaned over him, kissing him, and at last began to cry. He was wringing her hands in his, and seemed in great trouble.

'There was nothin' came into the house with me?' he asked, in a very low tone, turning to me.

'There was nothin', father,' I said, 'but the saddle and bridle that was in your hand.'

'Nothin' white kem in at the doore wid me,' he repeated.

'Nothin' at all,' I answered.

'So best,' said my father, and making the sign of the cross, he began mumbling to himself, and I knew he was saying his prayers.

Waiting for a while, to give him time for this exercise, my mother asked him where he first saw it.

'When I was riding up the bohereen,' – the Irish term meaning a little road, such as leads up to a farm-house – 'I bethought myself that the men was on the road with the cattle, and no one to look to the horse barrin' myself, so I thought I might as well leave him in the crooked field below, an' I tuck him there, he bein' cool, and not a hair turned, for I rode him aisy all the way. It was when I turned, after lettin' go – the saddle and bridle bein' in my hand – that I saw it, pushin' out o' the long grass at the side o' the path, an' it walked across it, in front of me, an' then back again, before me, the same way, an' sometimes at one side, an' then at the other, lookin' at me wid them shinin' eyes; and I consayted I heard it growlin' as it kep' beside me – as close as ever you see – till I kem up to the doore, here, an' knocked an' called, as ye heard me.'

Now, what was it, in so simple an incident, that agitated my father, my mother, myself, and finally, every member of this rustic household, with a terrible foreboding? It was this that we, one and all, believed that my father had received, in thus encountering the white cat, a warning of his approaching death.

The omen had never failed hitherto. It did not fail now. In a week after my father took the fever that was going, and before a month he was dead.

My honest friend, Dan Donovan, paused here; I could perceive that he was praying, for his lips were busy, and I concluded that it was for the repose of that departed soul.

In a little while he resumed.

It is eighty years now since that omen first attached to my family. Eighty years? Ay, is it. Ninety is nearer the mark. And I have spoken to many old people, in those earlier times, who had a distinct recollection of everything connected with it.

It happened in this way.

My grand-uncle, Connor Donovan, had the old farm of Drumgunniol in his day. He was richer than ever my father was, or my father's father either, for he took a short lease of Balraghan, and made money of it. But money won't soften a hard heart, and I'm afraid my grand-uncle was a cruel man – a profligate man he was, surely, and that is mostly a cruel man at heart. He drank his share, too, and cursed and swore, when he was vexed, more than was good for his soul, I'm afraid.

At that time there was a beautiful girl of the Colemans, up in the mountains, not far from Capper Cullen. I'm told that there are no Colemans there now at all, and that family has passed away. The famine years made great changes.

Ellen Coleman was her name. The Colemans were not rich. But, being such a beauty, she might have made a good match. Worse than she did for herself, poor thing, she could not.

Con Donovan – my grand-uncle, God forgive him! – sometimes in his rambles saw her at fairs or patterns, and he fell in love with her, as who might not?

He used her ill. He promised her marriage, and persuaded her to come away with him; and, after all, he broke his word. It was just the old story. He tired of her, and he wanted to push himself in the world; and he married a girl of the Collopys, that had a great fortune – twenty-four cows, seventy sheep, and a hundred and twenty goats.

He married this Mary Collopy, and grew richer than before; and Ellen Coleman died broken-hearted. But that did not trouble the strong farmer much.

He would have liked to have children, but he had none, and this was the only cross he had to bear, for everything else went much as he wished.

One night he was returning from the fair at Nenagh. A shallow stream at that time crossed the road – they have thrown a bridge over it, I am told, some time since – and its channel was often dry in summer weather. When it was so, as it passes close by the old farm-house of Drumgunniol, without a great deal of winding, it makes a sort of road, which people then used as a short cut to reach the house by. Into this dry channel, as there was plenty of light from the moon, my grand-uncle turned his horse, and when he had reached the two ash-trees at the meering of the farm he turned his horse short into the river-field, intending to ride through the gap at the other end, under the oak-tree, and so he would have been within a few hundred yards of his door.

As he approached the 'gap' he saw, or thought he saw, with a slow motion, gliding along the ground toward the same point, and now and then with a soft bound, a white object, which he described as being no bigger than his hat, but what it was he could not see, as it moved along the hedge and disappeared at the point to which he was himself tending.

When he reached the gap the horse stopped short. He urged and coaxed it in vain. He got down to lead it through, but it recoiled, snorted, and fell into a wild trembling fit. He mounted it again. But its terror continued, and it obstinately resisted his caresses and his whip. It was bright moonlight, and my grand-uncle was chafed by the horse's resistance, and, seeing nothing to account for it, and being so near home, what little patience he possessed forsook him, and, plying his whip and spur in earnest, he broke into oaths and curses.

All on a sudden the horse sprang through, and Con Donovan, as he passed under the broad branch of the oak, saw clearly a woman standing on the bank beside him, her arm extended, with the hand of which, as he flew by, she struck him a blow upon the shoulders. It threw him forward upon the neck of the horse, which, in wild terror, reached the door at a gallop, and stood there quivering and steaming all over.

Less alive than dead, my grand-uncle got in. He told his story, at least, as much as he chose. His wife did not quite know what to think. But that something very bad had happened she could not doubt. He was very faint and ill, and begged that the priest should be sent for forthwith. When they were getting him to his bed they saw distinctly the marks of five fingerpoints on the flesh of his shoulder, where the spectral blow had fallen. These singular marks – which they said resembled in tint the hue of a body struck by lightning – remained imprinted on his flesh, and were buried with him.

When he had recovered sufficiently to talk with the people about him – speaking, like a man at his last hour, from a burdened heart, and troubled conscience – he repeated his story, but said he did not see, or, at all events, know, the face of the figure that stood in the gap. No one believed him. He told more about it to the priest than to others. He certainly had a secret to tell. He might as well have divulged it frankly, for the neighbours all knew well enough that it was the face of dead Ellen Coleman that he had seen.

From that moment my grand-uncle never raised his head. He was a scared, silent, broken-spirited man. It was early summer then, and at the fall of the leaf in the same year he died.

Of course there was a wake, such as beseemed a strong farmer so rich as he. For some reason the arrangements of this ceremonial were a little different from the usual routine.

The usual practice is to place the body in the great room, or kitchen, as it is called, of the house. In this particular case there was, as I told you, for some reason, an unusual arrangement. The body was placed in a small room that opened upon the greater one. The door of this, during the wake, stood open. There were candles about the bed, and pipes and tobacco on the table, and stools for such guests as chose to enter, the door standing open for their reception.

The body, having been laid out, was left alone, in this smaller room, during the preparations for the wake. After nightfall one of the women, approaching the bed to get a chair which she had left near it, rushed from the room with a scream, and, having recovered her speech at the further end of the 'kitchen,' and surrounded by a gaping audience, she said, at last:

'May I never sin, if his face bain't riz up again the back o' the bed, and he starin' down to the doore, wid eyes as big as pewter plates, that id be shinin' in the moon!'

'Arra, woman! Is it cracked you are?' said one of the farm boys as they are termed, being men of any age you please.

'Agh, Molly, don't be talkin', woman! 'Tis what ye con-sayted it, goin' into the dark room, out o' the light. Why didn't ye take a candle in your fingers, ye aumadhaun?' said one of her female companions.

'Candle, or no candle; I seen it,' insisted Molly. 'An' what's more, I could a'most tak' my oath I seen his arum, too, stretchin' out o' the bed along the flure, three times as long as it should be, to take hould o' me be the fut.'

'Nansinse, ye fool, what id he want o' yer fut?' exclaimed one scornfully.

'Gi' me the candle, some o' yez – in the name o' God,' said old Sal Doolan, that was straight and lean, and a woman that could pray like a priest almost.

'Give her a candle,' agreed all.

But whatever they might say, there wasn't one among them that did not look pale and stern enough as they followed Mrs Doolan, who was praying as fast as her lips could patter, and leading the van with a tallow candle, held like a taper, in her fingers.

The door was half open, as the panic-stricken girl had left it; and holding the candle on high the better to examine the room, she made a step or so into it.

If my grand-uncle's hand had been stretched along the floor, in the unnatural way described, he had drawn it back again under the sheet that covered him. And tall Mrs Doolan was in no danger of tripping over his arm as she entered. But she had not gone more than a step or two with her candle aloft, when, with a drowning face, she suddenly stopped short, staring at the bed which was now fully in view.

'Lord, bless us, Mrs Dollan, ma'am, come back,' said the woman next her, who had fast hold of her dress, or her 'coat,' as they call it, and drawing her backwards with a frightened pluck, while a general recoil among her followers betokened the alarm which her hesitation had inspired.

'Whisht, will yez?' said the leader, peremptorily, 'I can't hear my own ears wid the noise ye're makin', an' which iv yez let the cat in here, an' whose cat is it?' she asked, peering suspiciously at a white cat that was sitting on the breast of the corpse.

'Put it away, will yez?' she resumed, with horror at the profanation. 'Many a corpse as I sthretched and crossed in the bed, the likes o' that I never seen yet. The man o' the house, wid a brute baste like that mounted on him, like a phooka, Lord forgi' me for namin' the like in this room. Dhrive it away, some o' yez! out o' that, this minute, I tell ye.'

Each repeated the order, but no one seemed inclined to execute it. They were crossing themselves, and whispering their conjectures and misgivings as to the nature of the beast, which was no cat of that house, nor one that they had ever seen before. On a sudden, the white cat placed itself on the pillow over the head of the body, and having from that place glared for a time at them over the features of the corpse, it crept softly along the body towards them, growling low and fiercely as it drew near.

Out of the room they bounced, in dreadful confusion, shutting the door fast after them, and not for a good while did the hardiest venture to peep in again.

The white cat was sitting in its old place, on the dead man's breast, but this time it crept quietly down the side of the bed, and disappeared under it, the sheet which was spread like a coverlet, and hung down nearly to the floor, concealing it from view.

Praying, crossing themselves, and not forgetting a sprinkling of holy water, they peeped, and finally searched, poking spades, 'wattles,' pitchforks and such implements under the bed. But the cat was not to be found, and they concluded that it had made its escape among their feet as they stood near the threshold. So they secured the door carefully, with hasp and padlock.

But when the door was opened next morning they found the white cat sitting, as if it had never been disturbed, upon the breast of the dead man.

Again occurred very nearly the same scene with a like result, only that some said they saw the cat afterwards lurking under a big box in a corner of the outer-room, where my grand-uncle kept his leases and papers, and his prayer-book and beads.

Mrs Doolan heard it growling at her heels wherever she went; and although she could not see it, she could hear it spring on the back of her chair when she sat down, and growl in her ear, so that she would bounce up with a scream and a prayer, fancying that it was on the point of taking her by the throat.

And the priest's boy, looking round the corner, under the branches of the old orchard, saw a white cat sitting under the little window of the room where my grand-uncle was laid out and looking up at the four small panes of glass as a cat will watch a bird.

The end of it was that the cat was found on the corpse again, when the room was visited, and do what they might, whenever the body was left alone, the cat was found again in the same ill-omened contiguity with the dead man. And this continued, to the scandal and fear of the neighbourhood, until the door was opened finally for the wake.

My grand-uncle being dead, and, with all due solemnities, buried, I have done with him. But not quite yet with the white cat. No banshee ever yet was more inalienably attached to a family than this ominous apparition is to mine. But there is this difference. The banshee seems to be animated with an affectionate sympathy with the bereaved family to whom it is hereditarily attached, whereas this thing has about it a suspicion of malice. It is the messenger simply of death. And its taking the shape of a cat – the coldest, and they say, the most vindictive of brutes – is indicative of the spirit of its visit.

When my grandfather's death was near, although he seemed quite well at the time, it appeared not exactly, but very nearly in the same way in which I told you it showed itself to my father.

The day before my Uncle Teigue was killed by the bursting of his gun, it appeared to him in the evening, at twilight, by the lough, in the field where I saw the woman who walked across the water, as I told you. My uncle was washing the barrel of his gun in the lough. The grass is short there, and there is no cover near it. He did not know how it approached; but the first he saw of it, the white cat was walking close round his feet, in the twilight, with an angry twist of its tail, and a green glare in its eyes, and do what he would, it continued walking round and round him, in larger or smaller circles, till he reached the orchard, and there he lost it.

My poor Aunt Peg – she married one of the O'Brians, near Oolah – came to Drumgunniol to go to the funeral of a cousin who died about a mile away. She died herself, poor woman, only a month after.

Coming from the wake, at two or three o'clock in the morning, as she got over the style into the farm of Drumgunniol, she saw the white cat at her side, and it kept close beside her, she ready to faint all the time, till she reached the door of the house, where it made a spring up into the white-thorn tree that grows close by, and so it parted from her. And my little brother Jim saw it also, just three weeks before he died. Every member of our family who dies, or takes his death-sickness, at Drumgunniol, is sure to see the white cat, and no one of us who sees it need hope for long life after.

1869

# *The Story of the Inexperienced Ghost*

H. G. Wells

The scene amidst which Clayton told his last story comes back very vividly to my mind. There he sat, for the greater part of the time, in the corner of the authentic settle by the spacious open fire, and Sanderson sat beside him smoking the Broseley clay that bore his name. There was Evans, and that marvel among actors, Wish, who is also a modest man. We had all come down to the Mermaid Club that Saturday morning, except Clayton, who had slept there overnight – which indeed gave him the opening of his story. We had golfed until golfing was invisible; we had dined, and we were in that mood of tranquil kindliness when men will suffer a story. When Clayton began to tell one, we naturally supposed he was lying. It may be that indeed he was lying – of that the reader will speedily be able to judge as well as I. He began, it is true, with an air of matter-of-fact anecdote, but that we thought was only the incurable artifice of the man.

'I say!' he remarked, after a long consideration of the upward rain of sparks from the log that Sanderson had thumped, 'you know I was alone here last night?'

'Except for the domestics,' said Wish.

'Who sleep in the other wing,' said Clayton.

'Yes. Well –' He pulled at his cigar for some little time as though he still hesitated about his confidence. Then he said, quite quietly, 'I caught a ghost!'

'Caught a ghost, did you?' said Sanderson. 'Where is it?'

And Evans, who admires Clayton immensely and has been four weeks in America, shouted, '*Caught* a ghost, did you, Clayton? I'm glad of it! Tell us all about it right now.'

Clayton said he would in a minute, and asked him to shut the door.

He looked apologetically at me. 'There's no eavesdropping of course, but we don't want to upset our very excellent service with any rumours of ghosts in the place. There's too much shadow and oak panelling to trifle with that. And this, you know, wasn't a regular ghost. I don't think it will come again – ever.'

'You mean to say you didn't keep it?' said Sanderson.

'I hadn't the heart to,' said Clayton.

And Sanderson said he was surprised.

We laughed, and Clayton looked aggrieved. 'I know,' he said, with the flicker of a smile, 'but the fact is it really *was* a ghost, and I'm as sure of it as I am that I am talking to you now. I'm not joking. I mean what I say.'

Sanderson drew deeply at his pipe, with one reddish eye on Clayton, and then emitted a thin jet of smoke more eloquent than many words.

Clayton ignored the comment. 'It is the strangest thing that has ever happened in my life. You know I never believed in ghosts or anything of the sort, before, ever; and then, you know, I bag one in a corner; and the whole business is in my hands.'

He meditated still more profoundly and produced and began to pierce a second cigar with a curious little stabber he affected.

'You talked to it?' asked Wish.

'For the space, probably, of an hour.'

'Chatty?' I said, joining the party of the sceptics.

'The poor devil was in trouble,' said Clayton, bowed over his cigar end and with the very faintest note of reproof.

'Sobbing?' some one asked.

Clayton heaved a realistic sigh at the memory. 'Good Lord!' he said; 'yes.' And then, 'Poor fellow! yes.'

'Where did you strike it?' asked Evans, in his best American accent.

'I never realised,' said Clayton, ignoring him, 'the poor sort of thing a ghost might be,' and he hung us up again for a time, while he sought for matches in his pocket and lit and warmed to his cigar.

'I took an advantage,' he reflected at last.

We were none of us in a hurry. 'A character,' he said, 'remains just the same character for all that it's been disembodied. That's a thing we too often forget. People with a certain strength or fixity of purpose may have ghosts of a certain strength and fixity of purpose – most haunting ghosts, you know, must be as one-idea'd as monomaniacs and as obstinate as mules to come back again and again. This poor creature wasn't.' He suddenly looked up rather queerly, and his eye went round the room. 'I say it,' he said, 'in all kindliness, but that is the plain truth of the case. Even at the first glance he struck me as weak.'

He punctuated with the help of his cigar.

'I came upon him, you know, in the long passage. His back was towards me and I saw him first. Right off I knew him for a ghost. He was transparent and whitish; clean through his chest I could see the glimmer of the little window at the end. And not only his physique but his attitude struck me as being weak. He looked, you know, as though he didn't know in the slightest whatever he meant to do. One hand was on the panelling and the other fluttered to his mouth. Like – *so!*'

'What sort of physique?' said Sanderson.

'Lean. You know that sort of young man's neck that has two great flutings down the back, here and here – so! And a little, meanish head with scrubby hair and rather bad ears. Shoulders bad, narrower than the hips; turndown collar, ready-made short jacket, trousers baggy and a little frayed at the heels. That's how he took me. I came very quietly up the staircase. I did not carry a light, you know – the candles are on the landing table and there is that lamp – and I was in my list slippers, and I saw him as I came up. I stopped dead at that – taking him in. I wasn't a bit afraid. I think that in most of these affairs one is never nearly so afraid or excited as one imagines one would be. I was surprised and interested. I thought, "Good Lord! Here's a ghost at last! And I haven't believed for a moment in ghosts during the last five-and-twenty years." '

'Um,' said Wish.

'I suppose I wasn't on the landing a moment before he found out I was there. He turned on me sharply, and I saw the face of an immature young man, a weak nose, a scrubby little moustache, a feeble chin. So for an instant we stood – he looking over his shoulder at me – and regarded one another. Then he seemed to remember his high calling. He turned round, drew himself up, projected his face, raised his arms, spread his hands in approved ghost fashion – came towards me. As he did so his little jaw dropped, and he emitted a faint, drawn-out "Boo."

No, it wasn't – not a bit dreadful. I'd dined. I'd had a bottle of champagne, and being all alone, perhaps two or three – perhaps even four or five – whiskies, so I was as solid as rocks and no more frightened than if I'd been assailed by a frog. "Boo!" I said. "Nonsense. You don't belong to *this* place. What are you doing here?"

'I could see him wince. "Boo-oo," he said.

' "Boo – be hanged! Are you a member?" I said; and just to show I didn't care a pin for him I stepped through a corner of him and made to light my candle. "Are you a member?" I repeated, looking at him sideways.

'He moved a little so as to stand clear of me, and his bearing became crestfallen. "No," he said, in answer to the persistent interrogation of my eye; "I'm not a member. I'm a ghost."

' "Well, that doesn't give you the run of the Mermaid Club. Is there any one you want to see, or anything of that sort?" And doing it as steadily as possible for fear that he should mistake the carelessness of whisky for the distraction of fear, I got my candle alight. I turned on him, holding it. "What are you doing here?" I said.

'He had dropped his hands and stopped his booing, and there he stood, abashed and awkward, the ghost of a weak, silly, aimless young man. "I'm haunting," he said.

' "You haven't any business to," I said in a quiet voice.

' "I'm a ghost," he said, as if in defence.

' "That may be, but you haven't any business to haunt here. This is a respectable private club; people often stop here with nursemaids and children, and, going about in the careless way you do, some poor little mite could easily come upon you and be scared out of her wits. I suppose you didn't think of that?"

' "No, sir," he said. "I didn't."

' "You should have done. You haven't any claim on the place, have you? Weren't murdered here, or anything of that sort?"

' "None, sir; but I thought as it was old and oak-panelled –"

' "That's *no* excuse." I regarded him firmly. "Your coming here is a mistake," I said, in a tone of friendly superiority. I feigned to see if I had my matches, and then looked up at him frankly. "If I were you I wouldn't wait for cock-crow – I'd vanish right away."

'He looked embarrassed. "The fact *is*, sir –" he began.

' "I'd vanish," I said, driving it home.

' "The fact is, sir, that – somehow – I can't."

' "You *can't?*"

' "No, sir. There's something I've forgotten. I've been hanging about here since midnight last night, hiding in the cupboards of the empty bedrooms and things like that. I'm flurried. I've never come haunting before, and it seems to put me out."

' "Put you out?"

' "Yes, sir. I've tried to do it several times, and it doesn't come off. There's some little thing has slipped me, and I can't get back."

'That, you know, rather bowled me over. He looked at me in such an abject way that for the life of me I couldn't keep up quite the high, hectoring vein I had adopted. "That's queer," I said, and as I spoke I fancied I heard some one moving about down below. "Come into my room and tell me more about it," I said. I didn't, of course, understand this, and I tried to take him by the arm. But, of course, you might as well have tried to take hold of a puff of smoke! I had forgotten my number, I think; anyhow, I remember going into several bedrooms – it was lucky I was the only soul in that wing – until I saw my traps. "Here we are," I said, and sat down in the arm-chair; "sit down and tell me all about it. It seems to me you have got yourself into a jolly awkward position, old chap."

'Well, he said he wouldn't sit down; he'd prefer to flit up and down the room if it was all the same to me. And so he did, and in a little while we were deep in a long and serious talk. And presently, you know, something of those whiskies and sodas evaporated out of me, and I began to realise just a little what a thundering rum and weird business it was that I was in. There he was, semi-transparent – the proper conventional phantom, and noiseless except for his ghost of a voice – flitting to and fro in that nice, clean, chintz-hung old bedroom. You could see the gleam of the copper candlesticks through him, and the lights on the brass fender, and the corners of the framed engravings on the wall, and there he was telling me all about this wretched little life of his that had recently ended on earth. He hadn't a particularly honest face, you know, but being transparent, of course, he couldn't avoid telling the truth.'

'Eh?' said Wish, suddenly sitting up in his chair.

'What?' said Clayton.

'Being transparent – couldn't avoid telling the truth – I don't see it,' said Wish.

'*I* don't see it,' said Clayton, with inimitable assurance. 'But it *is* so, I can assure you nevertheless. I don't believe he got once a nail's breadth off the Bible truth. He told me how he had been killed – he went down into a London basement with a candle to look for a leakage of gas – and described himself as a senior English master in a London private school when that release occurred.'

'Poor wretch!' said I.

'That's what I thought, and the more he talked the more I thought it. There he was, purposeless in life and purposeless out of it. He talked of his father and mother and his schoolmaster, and all who had ever been anything to him in the world, meanly. He had been too sensitive, too nervous; none of them had ever valued him properly or understood him, he said. He had never had a real friend in the world, I think; he had never had a success. He had shirked games and failed examinations. "It's like that with some people," he said; "whenever I got into the examination-room or anywhere everything seemed to go." Engaged to be married of course – to another over-sensitive person, I suppose – when the indiscretion with the gas escape ended his affairs. "And where are you now?" I asked. "Not in –?"

'He wasn't clear on that point at all. The impression he gave me was of a sort of vague, intermediate state, a special reserve for souls too non-existent for anything so positive as either sin or virtue. *I* don't know. He was much too egotistical and unobservant to give me any clear idea of the kind of place, kind of country, there is on the Other Side of Things. Wherever he was, he seems to have fallen in with a set of kindred spirits: ghosts of weak Cockney young men, who were on a footing of Christian names, and among these there was certainly a lot of talk about "going haunting" and things like that. Yes – going haunting! They seemed to think "haunting" a tremendous adventure, and most of them funked it all the time. And so primed, you know, he had come.'

'But really!' said Wish to the fire.

'These are the impressions he gave me, anyhow,' said Clayton, modestly. 'I may, of course, have been in a rather uncritical state, but that was the sort of background he gave to himself. He kept flitting up and down, with his thin voice going

– talking, talking about his wretched self, and never a word of clear, firm statement from first to last. He was thinner and sillier and more pointless than if he had been real and alive. Only then, you know, he would not have been in my bedroom here – if he *had* been alive. I should have kicked him out.'

'Of course,' said Evans, 'there *are* poor mortals like that.'

'And there's just as much chance of their having ghosts as the rest of us,' I admitted.

'What gave a sort of point to him, you know, was the fact that he did seem within limits to have found himself out. The mess he had made of haunting had depressed him terribly. He had been told it would be a "lark"; he had come expecting it to be a "lark," and here it was, nothing but another failure added to his record! He proclaimed himself an utter out-and-out failure. He said, and I can quite believe it, that he had never tried to do anything all his life that he hadn't made a perfect mess of – and through all the wastes of eternity he never would. If he had had sympathy, perhaps –. He paused at that, and stood regarding me. He remarked that, strange as it might seem to me, nobody, not any one, ever, had given him the amount of sympathy I was doing now. I could see what he wanted straight away, and I determined to head him off at once. I may be a brute, you know, but being the Only Real Friend, the recipient of the confidences of one of these egotistical weaklings, ghost or body, is beyond my physical endurance. I got up briskly. "Don't you brood on these things too much," I said. "The thing you've got to do is to get out of this – get out of this sharp. You pull yourself together and *try*." "I can't," he said. "You try," I said, and try he did.'

'Try!' said Sanderson. *'How?'*

'Passes,' said Clayton.

'Passes?'

'Complicated series of gestures and passes with the hands. That's how he had come in and that's how he had to get out again. Lord! what a business I had!'

'But how could *any* series of passes –' I began.

'My dear man,' said Clayton, turning on me and putting a great emphasis on certain words, 'you want *everything* clear. *I* don't know *how*. All I know is that you *do* – that *he* did, anyhow, at least. After a fearful time, you know, he got his passes right and suddenly disappeared.'

'Did you,' said Sanderson, slowly, 'observe the passes?'

'Yes,' said Clayton, and seemed to think. 'It was tremendously queer,' he said. 'There we were, I and this thin vague ghost, in that silent room, in this silent, empty inn, in this silent little Friday-night town. Not a sound except our voices and a faint panting he made when he swung. There was the bedroom candle, and one candle on the dressing-table alight, that was all – sometimes one or other would flare up into a tall, lean, astonished flame for a space. And queer things happened. "I can't," he said; "I shall never –!" And suddenly he sat down on a little chair at the foot of the bed and began to sob and sob. Lord! what a harrowing, whimpering thing he seemed!

' "You pull yourself together," I said, and tried to pat him on the back, and . . . my confounded hand went through him! By that time, you know, I wasn't nearly so – massive as I had been on the landing. I got the queerness of it full. I remember snatching back my hand out of him, as it were, with a little thrill, and walking over to the dressing-table. "You pull yourself together," I said to him, "and try." And in order to encourage and help him I began to try as well.'

'What!' said Sanderson, 'the passes?'

'Yes, the passes.'

'But –' I said, moved by an idea that eluded me for a space.

'This is interesting,' said Sanderson, with his finger in his pipe-bowl. 'You mean to say this ghost of yours gave away –'

'Did his level best to give away the whole confounded barrier? *Yes.*'

'He didn't,' said Wish; 'he couldn't. Or you'd have gone there too.'

'That's precisely it,' I said, finding my elusive idea put into words for me.

'That *is* precisely it,' said Clayton, with thoughtful eyes upon the fire.

For just a little while there was silence.

'And at last he did it?' said Sanderson.

'At last he did it. I had to keep him up to it hard, but he did it at last – rather suddenly. He despaired, we had a scene, and then he got up abruptly and asked me to go through the whole performance, slowly, so that he might see. "I believe," he said, "if I could *see* I should spot what was wrong at once." And he did. "*I* know," he said. "What do you know?" said I. "*I* know," he repeated. Then he said, peevishly, "I *can't* do it if you look at me – I really *can't*; it's been that, partly, all along.

I'm such a nervous fellow that you put me out." Well, we had a bit of an argument. Naturally I wanted to see; but he was as obstinate as a mule, and suddenly I had come over as tired as a dog – he tired me out. "All right," I said, "*I* won't look at you," and turned towards the mirror, on the wardrobe, by the bed.

'He started off very fast. I tried to follow him by looking in the looking-glass, to see just what it was had hung. Round went his arms and his hands, so, and so, and so, and then with a rush came to the last gesture of all – you stand erect and open out your arms – and so, don't you know, he stood. And then he didn't! He didn't! He wasn't! I wheeled round from the looking-glass to him. There was nothing! I was alone, with the flaring candles and a staggering mind. What had happened? Had anything happened? Had I been dreaming? . . . And then, with an absurd note of finality about it, the clock upon the landing discovered the moment was ripe for striking *one*. So! – Ping! And I was as grave and sober as a judge, with all my champagne and whisky gone into the vast serene. Feeling queer, you know – confoundedly *queer*! Queer! Good Lord!'

He regarded his cigar-ash for a moment. 'That's all that happened,' he said.

'And then you went to bed?' asked Evans.

'What else was there to do?'

I looked Wish in the eye. We wanted to scoff, and there was something, something perhaps in Clayton's voice and manner, that hampered our desire.

'And about these passes?' said Sanderson.

'I believe I could do them now.'

'Oh!' said Sanderson, and produced a penknife and set himself to grub the dottel out of the bowl of his clay.

'Why don't you do them now?' said Sanderson, shutting his pen-knife with a click.

'That's what I'm going to do,' said Clayton.

'They won't work,' said Evans.

'If they do –' I suggested.

'You know, I'd rather you didn't,' said Wish, stretching out his legs.

'Why?' asked Evans.

'I'd rather he didn't,' said Wish.

'But he hasn't got 'em right,' said Sanderson, plugging too much tobacco into his pipe.

'All the same, I'd rather he didn't,' said Wish.

We argued with Wish. He said that for Clayton to go through those gestures was like mocking a serious matter. 'But you don't believe –?' I said. Wish glanced at Clayton, who was staring into the fire, weighing something in his mind. 'I do – more than half, anyhow, I do,' said Wish.

'Clayton,' said I, 'you're too good a liar for us. Most of it was all right. But that disappearance . . . happened to be convincing. Tell us, it's a tale of cock and bull.'

He stood up without heeding me, took the middle of the hearthrug, and faced me. For a moment he regarded his feet thoughtfully, and then for all the rest of the time his eyes were on the opposite wall, with an intent expression. He raised his two hands slowly to the level of his eyes and so began. . . .

Now, Sanderson is a Freemason, a member of the lodge of the Four Kings, which devotes itself so ably to the study and elucidation of all the mysteries of Masonry past and present, and among the students of this lodge Sanderson is by no means the least. He followed Clayton's motions with a singular interest in his reddish eye. 'That's not bad,' he said, when it was done. 'You really do, you know, put things together, Clayton, in a most amazing fashion. But there's one little detail out.'

'I know,' said Clayton. 'I believe I could tell you which.'

'Well?'

'This,' said Clayton, and did a queer little twist and writhing and thrust of the hands.

'Yes.'

'That, you know, was what *he* couldn't get right,' said Clayton. 'But how do *you* –?'

'Most of this business, and particularly how you invented it, I don't understand at all,' said Sanderson, 'but just that phase – I do.' He reflected. 'These happen to be a series of gestures – connected with a certain branch of esoteric Masonry – Probably you know. Or else – *How?*' He reflected still further. 'I do not see I can do any harm in telling you just the proper twist. After all, if you know, you know; if you don't, you don't.'

'I know nothing,' said Clayton, 'except what the poor devil let out last night.'

'Well, anyhow,' said Sanderson, and placed his churchwarden very carefully upon the shelf over the fireplace. Then very rapidly he gesticulated with his hands.

'So?' said Clayton, repeating.

'So,' said Sanderson, and took his pipe in hand again.

'Ah, *now*,' said Clayton, 'I can do the whole thing – right.'

He stood up before the waning fire and smiled at us all. But I think there was just a little hesitation in his smile. 'If I begin –' he said.

'I wouldn't begin,' said Wish.

'It's all right!' said Evans. 'Matter is indestructible. You don't think any jiggery-pokery of this sort is going to snatch Clayton into the world of shades. Not it! You may try, Clayton, so far as I'm concerned, until your arms drop off at the wrists.'

'I don't believe that,' said Wish, and stood up and put his arm on Clayton's shoulder. 'You've made me half believe in that story somehow, and I don't want to see the thing done.'

'Goodness!' said I, 'here's Wish frightened!'

'I am,' said Wish, with real or admirably feigned intensity. 'I believe that if he goes through these motions right he'll *go*.'

'He'll not do anything of the sort,' I cried. 'There's only one way out of this world for men, and Clayton is thirty years from that. Besides . . . And such a ghost! Do you think –?'

Wish interrupted me by moving. He walked out from among our chairs and stopped beside the table and stood there. 'Clayton,' he said, 'you're a fool.'

Clayton, with a humorous light in his eyes, smiled back at him. 'Wish,' he said, 'is right and all you others are wrong. I shall go. I shall get to the end of these passes, and as the last swish whistles through the air, Presto! – this hearthrug will be vacant, the room will be blank amazement, and a respectably dressed gentleman of fifteen stone will plump into the world of shades. I'm certain. So will you be. I decline to argue further. Let the thing be tried.'

'*No*,' said Wish, and made a step and ceased, and Clayton raised his hands once more to repeat the spirit's passing.

By that time, you know, we were all in a state of tension – largely because of the behaviour of Wish. We sat all of us with our eyes on Clayton.

I, at least, with a sort of tight, stiff feeling about me as though from the back of my skull to the middle of my thighs my body had been changed to steel. And there, with a gravity that was imperturbably serene, Clayton bowed and swayed and waved his hands and arms before us. As he drew towards the end one piled up, one tingled in one's teeth. The last gesture, I have said, was to swing the arms out wide open, with the face held up. And when at last he swung out to this closing gesture I ceased even to breathe. It was ridiculous, of course, but you know that ghost-story feeling. It was after dinner, in a queer, old shadowy house. Would he, after all –?

There he stood for one stupendous moment, with his arms open and his upturned face, assured and bright, in the glare of the hanging lamp. We hung through that moment as if it were an age, and then came from all of us something that was half a sigh of infinite relief and half a reassuring '*No!*' For visibly – he wasn't going. It was all nonsense. He had told an idle story, and carried it almost to conviction, that was all!. . . And then in that moment the face of Clayton changed.

It changed. It changed as a lit house changes when its lights are suddenly extinguished. His eyes were suddenly eyes that were fixed, his smile was frozen on his lips, and he stood there still. He stood there, very gently swaying.

That moment, too, was an age. And then, you know, chairs were scraping, things were falling, and we were all moving. His knees seemed to give, and he fell forward, and Evans rose and caught him in his arms. . . .

It stunned us all. For a minute I suppose no one said a coherent thing. We believed it, yet could not believe it. . . . I came out of a muddled stupefaction to find myself kneeling beside him, and his vest and shirt were torn open, and Sanderson's hand lay on his heart. . . .

Well – the simple fact before us could very well wait our convenience; there was no hurry for us to comprehend. It lay there for an hour; it lies athwart my memory, black and amazing still, to this day. Clayton had, indeed, passed into the world that lies so near to and so far from our own, and he had gone thither by the only road that mortal man may take. But whether he did indeed pass there by that poor ghost's incantation, or whether he was stricken suddenly by apoplexy in the midst of an idle tale – as the coroner's jury would have us believe – is no matter for my judging; it is just one of those inexplicable riddles that must remain unsolved until the final solution of all things shall come. All I certainly know is that, in the very moment, in the very instant, of concluding those passes, he changed, and staggered, and fell down before us – dead!

# *All Souls*

## Edith Wharton

Queer and inexplicable as the business was, on the surface it appeared fairly simple – at the time, at least; but with the passing of years, and owing to there not having been a single witness of what happened except Sara Clayburn herself, the stories about it have become so exaggerated, and often so ridiculously inaccurate, that it seems necessary that someone connected with the affair, though not actually present – I repeat that when it happened my cousin was (or thought she was) quite alone in her house – should record the few facts actually known.

In those days I was often at Whitegates (as the place had always been called) – I was there, in fact, not long before, and almost immediately after, the strange happenings of those thirty-six hours. Jim Clayburn and his widow were both my cousins, and because of that, and of my intimacy with them, both families think I am more likely than anybody else to be able to get at the facts, as far as they can be called facts, and as anybody can get at them. So I have written down, as clearly as I could, the gist of the various talks I had with cousin Sara, when she could be got to talk – it wasn't often – about what occurred during that mysterious weekend.

*

I read the other day in a book by a fashionable essayist that ghosts went out when electric light came in. What nonsense! The writer, though he is fond of dabbling, in a literary way, in the supernatural, hasn't even reached the threshold of his subject. As between turreted castles patrolled by headless victims with clanking chains, and the comfortable suburban house with a refrigerator and central heating where you feel, as soon as you're in it, *that there's something wrong*, give me the latter for sending a chill down the spine! And, by the way, haven't you noticed that it's generally not the high-strung and imaginative who see ghosts, but the calm matter-of-fact people who don't believe in them, and are sure they wouldn't mind if they did see one? Well, that was the case with Sara Clayburn and her house. The house, in spite of its age – it was built, I believe, about 1780 – was open, airy, high-ceilinged, with electricity, central heating and all the modern appliances: and its mistress was – well, very much like her house. And, anyhow, this isn't exactly a ghost story and I've dragged in the analogy only as a way of showing you what kind of woman my cousin was, and how unlikely it would have seemed that what happened at Whitegates should have happened just there – or to her.

When Jim Clayburn died the family all thought that, as the couple had no children, his widow would give up Whitegates and move either to New York or Boston – for being of good Colonial stock, with many relatives and friends, she would have found a place ready for her in either. But Sara Clayburn seldom did what other people expected, and in this case she did exactly the contrary; she stayed at Whitegates.

'What, turn my back on the old house – tear up all the family roots, and go and hang myself up in a bird-cage flat in one of those new skyscrapers in Lexington Avenue, with a bunch of chickweed and a cuttlefish to replace my good Connecticut mutton? No, thank you. Here I belong, and here I stay till my executors hand the place over to Jim's next-of-kin – that stupid fat Presley boy. . . . Well, don't let's talk about him. But I tell you what – I'll keep him out of here as long as I can.' And she did – for being still in the early fifties when her husband died, and a muscular, resolute figure of a woman, she was more than a match for the fat Presley boy, and attended his funeral a few years ago, in correct mourning, with a faint smile under her veil.

Whitegates was a pleasant hospitable-looking house, on a height overlooking the stately windings of the Connecticut River; but it was five or six miles from Norrington, the nearest town, and its situation would certainly have seemed remote and lonely to modern servants. Luckily, however, Sara Clayburn had inherited from her mother-in-law two or three old stand-bys who seemed as much a part of the family tradition as the roof they lived under; and I never heard of her having any trouble in her domestic arrangements.

The house, in Colonial days, had been foursquare, with four spacious rooms on the ground floor, an oak-floored hall dividing them, the usual kitchen extension at the back, and a good attic under the roof. But Jim's grandparents, when interest in the 'Colonial' began to revive, in the early eighties, had added two wings, at right angles to the south front, so that the old 'circle' before the front door became a grassy court, enclosed on three sides, with a big elm in the middle. Thus the house was turned into a roomy dwelling, in which the last three generations of Clayburns had exercised a large hospitality; but the architect had respected the character of the old house, and the enlargement made it more comfortable without lessening its simplicity. There was a lot of land about it, and Jim Clayburn, like his fathers before him, farmed it, not without profit, and played a considerable and respected part in state politics. The Clayburns were always spoken of as a 'good influence' in the county, and the townspeople were glad when they learned that Sara did not mean to desert the place – 'though it must be lonesome, winters, living all alone up there atop of that hill' – they remarked as the days shortened, and the first snow began to pile up under the quadruple row of elms along the common.

Well, if I've given you a sufficiently clear idea of Whitegates and the Clayburns – who shared with their old house a sort of reassuring orderliness and dignity – I'll efface myself, and tell the tale, not in my cousin's words, for they were too confused and fragmentary, but as I built it up gradually out of her half-avowals and nervous reticences. If the thing happened at all – and I must leave you to judge of that – I think it must have happened in this way. . . .

## I

The morning had been bitter, with a driving sleet – though it was only the last day of October – but after lunch a watery sun showed for a while through banked-up woolly clouds, and tempted Sara Clayburn out. She was an energetic walker, and given, at that season, to tramping three or four miles along the valley road, and coming back by way of Shaker's wood. She had made her usual round, and was following the main drive to the house when she overtook a plainly-dressed woman walking in the same direction. If the scene had not been so lonely – the way to Whitegates at the end of an autumn day was not a frequented one – Mrs Clayburn might not have paid any attention to the woman, for she was in no way noticeable; but when she caught up with the intruder my cousin was surprised to find that she was a stranger – for the mistress of Whitegates prided herself on knowing, at least by sight, most of her country neighbors. It was almost dark, and the woman's face was hardly visible, but Mrs Clayburn told me she recalled her as middle-aged, plain and rather pale.

Mrs Clayburn greeted her, and then added: 'You're going to the house?'

'Yes, ma'am,' the woman answered, in a voice that the Connecticut Valley in old days would have called 'foreign,' but that would have been unnoticed by ears used to the modern multiplicity of tongues. 'No, I couldn't say where she came from,' Sara always said. 'What struck me as queer was that I didn't know her.'

She asked the woman, politely, what she wanted, and the woman answered: 'Only to see one of the girls.' The answer was natural enough, and Mrs Clayburn nodded and turned off from the drive to the lower part of the gardens, so that she saw no more of the visitor then or afterward. And, in fact, a half hour later something happened which put the stranger entirely out of her mind. The brisk and light-footed Mrs Clayburn, as she approached the house, slipped on a frozen puddle, turned her ankle and lay suddenly helpless.

*

Price, the butler, and Agnes, the dour old Scottish maid whom Sara had inherited from her mother-in-law, of course knew exactly what to do. In no time they had their mistress stretched out on a lounge, and Dr Selgrove had been called up from Norrington. When he arrived, he ordered Mrs Clayburn to bed, did the necessary examining and bandaging, and shook his head over her ankle, which he feared was fractured. He thought, however, that if she would swear not to get up, or even shift the position of her leg, he could spare her the discomfort of putting it in plaster. Mrs Clayburn agreed, the more promptly as the doctor warned her that any rash movement would prolong her immobility. Her quick imperious nature made the prospect trying, and she was annoyed with herself for having been so clumsy. But the mischief was done, and she immediately thought what an opportunity she would have for going over her accounts and catching up with her correspondence. So she settled down resignedly in her bed.

'And you won't miss much, you know, if you have to stay there a few days. It's beginning to snow, and it looks as if we were in for a good spell of it,' the doctor remarked, glancing through the window as he gathered up his implements. 'Well, we don't often get snow here as early as this; but winter's got to begin sometime,' he concluded philosophically. At the door he stopped to add: 'You don't want me to send up a nurse from Norrington? Not to nurse you, you know; there's nothing much to do till I see you again. But this is a pretty lonely place when the snow begins, and I thought maybe –'

Sara Clayburn laughed. 'Lonely? With my old servants? You forget how many winters I've spent here alone with them. Two of them were with me in my mother-in-law's time.'

'That's so,' Dr Selgrove agreed. 'You're a good deal luckier than most people, that way. Well, let me see; this is Saturday. We'll have to let the inflammation go down before we can X-ray you. Monday morning, first thing, I'll be here with the X-ray man. If you want me sooner, call me up.' And he was gone.

## II

The foot at first, had not been very painful; but towards the small hours Mrs Clayburn began to suffer. She was a bad patient, like most healthy and active people. Not being used to pain she did not know how to bear it, and the hours of wakefulness and immobility seemed endless. Agnes, before leaving her, had made everything as comfortable as possible. She had put a jug of lemonade within reach, and had even (Mrs Clayburn thought it odd afterward) insisted on bringing in a tray with sandwiches and a thermos of tea. 'In case you're hungry in the night, madam.'

'Thank you; but I'm never hungry in the night. And I certainly shan't be tonight – only thirsty. I think I'm feverish.'

'Well, there's the lemonade, madam.'

'That will do. Take the other things away, please.' (Sara had always hated the sight of unwanted food 'messing about' in her room.)

'Very well, madam. Only you might –'

'Please take it away,' Mrs Clayburn repeated irritably.

'Very good, madam.' But as Agnes went out, her mistress heard her set the tray down softly on a table behind the screen which shut off the door.

'Obstinate old goose!' she thought, rather touched by the old woman's insistence.

Sleep, once it had gone, would not return, and the long black hours moved more and more slowly. How late the dawn came in November! 'If only I could move my leg,' she grumbled.

She lay still and strained her ears for the first steps of the servants. Whitegates was an early house, its mistress setting the example; it would surely not be long now before one of the women came. She was tempted to ring for Agnes, but refrained. The woman had been up late, and this was Sunday morning, when the household was always allowed a little extra time. Mrs Clayburn reflected restlessly: 'I was a fool not to let her leave the tea beside the bed, as she wanted to. I wonder if I could get up and get it?' But she remembered the doctor's warning, and dared not move. Anything rather than risk prolonging her imprisonment. . . .

Ah, there was the stable clock striking. How loud it sounded in the snowy stillness! One – two – three – four – five. . . .

What? Only five? Three hours and a quarter more before she could hope to hear the door handle turned. . . . After a while she dozed off again, uncomfortably.

Another sound aroused her. Again the stable clock. She listened. But the room was still in deep darkness, and only six strokes fell. . . . She thought of reciting something to put her to sleep; but she seldom read poetry, and being naturally a good sleeper, she could not remember any of the usual devices against insomnia. The whole of her leg felt like lead now. The bandages had grown terribly tight – her ankle must have swollen. . . . She lay staring at the dark windows, watching for the first glimmer of dawn. At last she saw a pale filter of daylight through the shutters. One by one the objects between the bed and the window recovered first their outline, then their bulk, and seemed to be stealthily regrouping themselves, after goodness knows what secret displacements during the night. Who that has lived in an old house could possibly believe that the furniture in it stays still all night? Mrs Clayburn almost fancied she saw one little slender-legged table slipping hastily back into its place.

'It knows Agnes is coming, and it's afraid,' she thought whimsically. Her bad night must have made her imaginative for such nonsense as that about the furniture had never occurred to her before. . . .

At length, after hours more, as it seemed, the stable clock struck eight. Only another quarter of an hour. She watched the hand moving slowly across the face of the little clock beside her bed . . . ten minutes . . . five . . . only five! Agnes was as punctual as destiny . . . in two minutes now she would come. The two minutes passed, and she did not come. Poor Agnes – she had looked pale and tired the night before. She had overslept herself, no doubt – or perhaps she felt ill, and would send the housemaid to replace her. Mrs Clayburn waited.

She waited half an hour; then she reached up to the bell at the head of the bed. Poor old Agnes – her mistress felt guilty about waking her. But Agnes did not appear – and after a considerable interval Mrs Clayburn, now with a certain impatience, rang again. She rang once; twice; three times – but still no one came.

Once more she waited; then she said to herself: 'There must be something wrong with the electricity.' Well – she could find out by switching on the bed lamp at her elbow (how admirably the room was equipped with every practical appliance!). She switched it on – but no light came. Electric current cut off; and it was Sunday, and nothing could be done about it till the next morning. Unless it turned out to be just a burnt-out fuse, which Price could remedy. Well, in a moment now some one would surely come to her door.

It was nine o'clock before she admitted to herself that something uncommonly strange must have happened in the house. She began to feel a nervous apprehension; but she was not the woman to encourage it. If only she had had the telephone put in her room, instead of out on the landing! She measured mentally the distance to be travelled, remembered Dr Selgrove's admonition, and wondered if her broken ankle would carry her there. She dreaded the prospect of being put in plaster, but she had to get to the telephone, whatever happened.

She wrapped herself in her dressing gown, found a walking

stick, and, resting heavily on it, dragged herself to the door. In her bedroom the careful Agnes had closed and fastened the shutters, so that it was not much lighter there than at dawn; but outside in the corridor the cold whiteness of the snowy morning seemed almost reassuring. Mysterious things – dreadful things – were associated with darkness; and here was the wholesome prosaic daylight come again to banish them. Mrs Clayburn looked about her and listened. Silence. A deep nocturnal silence in that day-lit house, in which five people were presumably coming and going about their work. It was certainly strange. . . . She looked out of the window, hoping to see someone crossing the court or coming along the drive. But no one was in sight, and the snow seemed to have the place to itself: a quiet steady snow. It was still falling, with a business-like regularity, muffling the outer world in layers on layers of thick white velvet, and intensifying the silence within. A noiseless world – were people so sure that absence of noise was what they wanted? Let them first try a lonely country house in a November snowstorm!

She dragged herself along the passage to the telephone. When she unhooked the receiver she noticed that her hand trembled.

She rang up the pantry – no answer. She rang again. Silence – more silence! It seemed to be piling itself up like the snow on the roof and in the gutters. Silence. How many people that she knew had any idea what silence was – and how loud it sounded when you really listened to it?

Again she waited: then she rang up 'Central.' No answer. She tried three times. After that she tried the pantry again. . . . The telephone was cut off, then; like the electric current. Who was at work downstairs, isolating her thus from the world? Her heart began to hammer. Luckily there was a chair near the telephone, and she sat down to recover her strength – or was it her courage?

Agnes and the housemaid slept in the nearest wing. She would certainly get as far as that when she had pulled herself together. Had she the courage –? Yes, of course she had. She had always been regarded as a plucky woman; and had so regarded herself. But this silence –

It occurred to her that by looking from the window of a neighbouring bathroom she could see the kitchen chimney. There ought to be smoke coming from it at that hour; and if there were she thought she would be less afraid to go on. She got as far as the bathroom and looking through the window saw that no smoke came from the chimney. Her sense of loneliness grew more acute. Whatever had happened below-stairs must have happened before the morning's work had begun. The cook had not had time to light the fire, the other servants had not yet begun their round. She sank down on the nearest chair, struggling against her fears. What next would she discover if she carried on her investigations?

The pain in her ankle made progress difficult; but she was aware of it now only as an obstacle to haste. No matter what it cost her in physical suffering, she must find out what was happening belowstairs – or had happened. But first she would go to the maid's room. And if that were empty – well, somehow she would have to get herself downstairs.

She limped along the passage, and on the way steadied herself by resting her hand on a radiator. It was stone-cold. Yet in that well-ordered house in winter the central heating, though damped down at night, was never allowed to go out, and by eight in the morning a mellow warmth pervaded the rooms. The icy chill of the pipes startled her. It was the chauffeur who looked after the heating – so he too was involved in the mystery, whatever it was, as well as the house servants. But this only deepened the problem.

## III

At Agnes's door Mrs Clayburn paused and knocked. She expected no answer, and there was none. She opened the door and went in. The room was dark and very cold. She went to the window and flung back the shutters; then she looked slowly around, vaguely apprehensive of what she might see. The room was empty but what frightened her was not so much its emptiness as its air of scrupulous and undisturbed order. There was no sign of anyone having lately dressed in it – or undressed the night before. And the bed had not been slept in.

Mrs Clayburn leaned against the wall for a moment; then she crossed the floor and opened the cupboard. That was where Agnes kept her dresses; and the dresses were there, neatly hanging in a row. On the shelf above were Agnes's few and unfashionable hats, rearrangements of her mistress's old ones. Mrs Clayburn, who knew them all, looked at the shelf, and saw that one was missing. And so was also the warm winter coat she had given to Agnes the previous winter.

The woman was out, then; had gone out, no doubt, the night before, since the bed was unslept in, the dressing and washing appliances untouched. Agnes, who never set foot out of the house after dark, who despised the movies as much as she did the wireless, and could never be persuaded that a little innocent amusement was a necessary element in life, had deserted the house on a snowy winter night, while her mistress lay upstairs, suffering and helpless! Why had she gone, and where had she gone? When she was undressing Mrs Clayburn the night before, taking her orders, trying to make her more comfortable, was she already planning this mysterious nocturnal escape? Or had something – the mysterious and dreadful Something for the clue of which Mrs Clayburn was still groping – occurred later in the evening, sending the maid downstairs and out of doors into the bitter night? Perhaps one of the men at the garage – where the chauffeur and gardener lived – had been suddenly taken ill, and someone had run up to the house for Agnes. Yes – that must be the explanation. . . . Yet how much it left unexplained.

Next to Agnes's room was the linen room; beyond that was the housemaid's door. Mrs Clayburn went to it and knocked. 'Mary!' No one answered, and she went in. The room was in the same immaculate order as her maid's, and here too the bed was unslept in, and there were no signs of dressing or undressing. The two women had no doubt gone out together – gone where?

More and more the cold unanswering silence of the house weighed down on Mrs Clayburn. She had never thought of it as a big house, but now, in this snowy winter light, it seemed immense, and full of ominous corners around which one dared not look.

Beyond the housemaid's room were the back stairs. It was the nearest way down, and every step that Mrs Clayburn took was increasingly painful; but she decided to walk slowly back, the whole length of the passage, and go down by the front stairs. She did not know why she did this; but she felt that at the moment she was past reasoning, and had better obey her instinct.

More than once she had explored the ground floor in the

small hours, in search of unwonted midnight noises; but now it was not the idea of noises that frightened her, but that inexorable and hostile silence, the sense that the house had retained in full daylight its nocturnal mystery, and was watching her as she was watching it; that in entering those empty orderly rooms she might be disturbing some unseen confabulation on which beings of flesh-and-blood had better not intrude.

The broad oak stairs were beautifully polished, and so slippery that she had to cling to the rail and let herself down tread by tread. And as she descended, the silence descended with her – heavier, denser, more absolute. She seemed to feel its steps just behind her, softly keeping time with hers. It had a quality she had never been aware of in any other silence, as though it were not merely an absence of sound, a thin barrier between the ear and the surging murmur of life just beyond, but an impenetrable substance made out of the worldwide cessation of all life and all movement.

Yes, that was what laid a chill on her: the feeling that there was no limit to this silence, no outer margin, nothing beyond it. By this time she had reached the foot of the stairs and was limping across the hall to the drawing room. Whatever she found there, she was sure, would be mute and lifeless; but what would it be? The bodies of her dead servants, mown down by some homicidal maniac? And what if it were her turn next – if he were waiting for her behind the heavy curtains of the room she was about to enter? Well, she must find out – she must face whatever lay in wait. Not impelled by bravery – the last drop of courage had oozed out of her – but because anything, anything was better than to remain shut up in that snowbound house without knowing whether she was alone in it or not, 'I must find that out, I must find that out,' she repeated to herself in a sort of meaningless sing-song.

The cold outer light flooded the drawing room. The shutters had not been closed, nor the curtains drawn. She looked about her. The room was empty, and every chair in its usual place. Her armchair was pushed up by the chimney, and the cold hearth was piled with the ashes of the fire at which she had warmed herself before starting on her ill-fated walk. Even her empty coffee cup stood on a table near the armchair. It was evident that the servants had not been in the room since she had left it the day before after luncheon. And suddenly the conviction entered into her that, as she found the drawing room, so she would find the rest of the house; cold, orderly – and empty. She would find nothing, she would find no one. She no longer felt any dread of ordinary human dangers lurking in those dumb spaces ahead of her. She knew she was utterly alone under her own roof. She sat down to rest her aching ankle, and looked slowly about her.

There were the other rooms to be visited, and she was determined to go through them all – but she knew in advance that they would give no answer to her question. She knew it, seemingly, from the quality of the silence which enveloped her. There was no break, no thinnest crack in it anywhere. It had the cold continuity of the snow which was still falling steadily outside.

She had no idea how long she waited before nerving herself to continue her inspection. She no longer felt the pain in her ankle, but was only conscious that she must not bear her weight on it, and therefore moved very slowly, supporting herself on each piece of furniture in her path. On the ground floor no shutter had been closed, no curtain drawn, and she progressed without difficulty from room to room: the library, her morning room, the dining room. In each of them, every piece of furniture was in its usual place. In the dining room, the table had been laid for her dinner of the previous evening, and the candelabra, with candles unlit, stood reflected in the dark mahogany. She was not the kind of woman to nibble a poached egg on a tray when she was alone, but always came down to the dining room, and had what she called a civilized meal.

The back premises remained to be visited. From the dining room she entered the pantry, and there too everything was in irreproachable order. She opened the door and looked down the back passage with its neat linoleum floor covering. The deep silence accompanied her; she still felt it moving watchfully at her side, as though she were its prisoner and it might throw itself upon her if she attempted to escape. She limped on toward the kitchen. That of course would be empty too, and immaculate. But she must see it.

She leaned a minute in the embrasure of a window in the passage. 'It's like the "Mary Celeste" – a "Mary Celeste" on *terra firma*,' she thought, recalling the unsolved sea mystery of her childhood. 'No one ever knew what happened on board the "Mary Celeste." And perhaps no one will ever know what has happened here. Even I shan't know.'

At the thought her latent fear seemed to take on a new quality. It was like an icy liquid running through every vein, and lying in a pool about her heart. She understood now that she had never before known what fear was, and that most of the people she had met had probably never known either. For this sensation was something quite different. . . .

It absorbed her so completely that she was not aware how long she remained leaning there. But suddenly a new impulse pushed her forward, and she walked on toward the scullery. She went there first because there was a service slide in the wall, through which she might peep into the kitchen without being seen; and some indefinable instinct told her that the kitchen held the clue to the mystery. She still felt strongly that whatever had happened in the house must have its source and centre in the kitchen.

In the scullery, as she had expected, everything was clean and tidy. Whatever had happened, no one in the house appeared to have been taken by surprise; there was nowhere any sign of confusion or disorder: 'It looks as if they'd known beforehand, and put everything straight,' she thought. She glanced at the wall facing the door, and saw that the slide was open. And then, as she was approaching it, the silence was broken. A voice was speaking in the kitchen – a man's voice, low but emphatic, and which she had never heard before.

She stood still, cold with fear. But this fear was again a different one. Her previous terrors had been speculative, conjectural, a ghostly emanation of the surrounding silence. This was a plain everyday dread of evildoers. Oh, God, why had she not remembered her husband's revolver, which ever since his death had lain in a drawer in her room?

She turned to retreat across the smooth slippery floor but halfway her stick slipped from her, and crashed down on the tiles. The noise seemed to echo on and on through the emptiness, and she stood still, aghast. Now that she had betrayed her presence, flight was useless. Whoever was beyond the kitchen door would be upon her in a second. . . .

But to her astonishment the voice went on speaking. It was as though neither the speaker nor his listeners had heard her. The invisible stranger spoke so low that she could not make out what he was saying, but the tone was passionately earnest, almost threatening. The next moment she realized that he was speaking in a foreign language, a language unknown to her. Once more her terror was surmounted by the urgent desire to know what was going on, so close to her yet unseen. She crept to the slide, peered cautiously through into the kitchen, and saw that it was as orderly and empty as the other rooms. But in the middle of the carefully scoured table stood a portable wireless, and the voice she heard came out of it. . . .

She must have fainted then, she supposed; at any rate she felt so weak and dizzy that her memory of what next happened remained indistinct. But in the course of time she groped her way back to the pantry, and there found a bottle of spirits – brandy or whisky, she could not remember which. She found a glass, poured herself a stiff drink, and while it was flushing through her veins, managed, she never knew with how many shuddering delays, to drag herself through the deserted ground floor, up the stairs, and down the corridor to her own room. There, apparently, she fell across the threshold, again unconscious. . . .

When she came to, she remembered, her first care had been to lock herself in; then to recover her husband's revolver. It was not loaded, but she found some cartridges, and succeeded in loading it. Then she remembered that Agnes, on leaving her the evening before, had refused to carry away the tray with the tea and sandwiches, and she fell on them with a sudden hunger. She recalled also noticing that a flask of brandy had been put beside the thermos, and being vaguely surprised. Agnes's departure, then, had been deliberately planned, and she had known that her mistress, who never touched spirits, might have need of a stimulant before she returned. Mrs Clayburn poured some of the brandy into her tea, and swallowed it greedily.

After that (she told me later) she remembered that she had managed to start a fire in her grate, and after warming herself, had got back into her bed, piling on it all the coverings she could find. The afternoon passed in a haze of pain, out of which there emerged now and then a dim shape of fear – the fear that she might lie there alone and untended till she died of cold, and of the terror of her solitude. For she was sure by this time that the house was empty – completely empty, from garret to cellar. She knew it was so, she could not tell why; but again she felt that it must be because of the peculiar quality of the silence – the silence which had dogged her steps wherever she went, and was now folded down on her like a pall. She was sure that the nearness of any other human being, however dumb and secret, would have made a faint crack in the texture of that silence, flawed it as a sheet of glass is flawed by a pebble thrown against it. . . .

IV

'Is that easier?' the doctor asked, lifting himself from bending over her ankle. He shook his head disapprovingly. 'Looks to me as if you'd disobeyed orders – eh? Been moving about, haven't you? And I guess Dr Selgrove told you to keep quiet till he saw you again, didn't he?'

The speaker was a stranger, whom Mrs Clayburn knew only by name. Her own doctor had been called away that morning to the bedside of an old patient in Baltimore, and had asked this young man, who was beginning to be known at Norrington, to replace him. The newcomer was shy, and somewhat familiar, as the shy often are, and Mrs Clayburn decided that she did not much like him. But before she could convey this by the tone of her reply (and she was past mistress of the shades of disapproval) she heard Agnes speaking – yes, Agnes, the same, the usual Agnes, standing behind the doctor, neat and stern-looking as ever. 'Mrs Clayburn must have got up and walked about in the night instead of ringing for me, as she'd ought to,' Agnes intervened severely.

This was too much! In spite of the pain, which was now exquisite, Mrs Clayburn laughed. 'Ringing for you? How could I, with the electricity cut off?'

'The electricity cut off?' Agnes's surprise was masterly. 'Why, when was it cut off?' she pressed her finger on the bell beside the bed, and the call tinkled through the quiet room. 'I tried that bell before I left you last night, madam, because if there'd been anything wrong with it I'd have come and slept in the dressing room sooner than leave you here alone.'

Mrs Clayburn lay speechless, staring up at her. 'Last night? But last night I was all alone in the house.'

Agnes's firm features did not alter. She folded her hands resignedly across her trim apron. 'Perhaps the pain's made you a little confused, madam.' She looked at the doctor, who nodded.

'The pain in your foot must have been pretty bad,' he said.

'It was,' Mrs Clayburn replied. 'But it was nothing to the horror of being left alone in this empty house since the day before yesterday, with the heat and the electricity cut off, and the telephone not working.'

The doctor was looking at her in evident wonder. Agnes's sallow face flushed slightly, but only as if in indignation at an unjust charge. 'But, madam, I made up your fire with my own hands last night – and look, it's smouldering still. I was getting ready to start it again just now, when the doctor came.'

'That's so. She was down on her knees before it,' the doctor corroborated.

Again Mrs Clayburn laughed. Ingeniously as the tissue of lies was being woven about her, she felt she could still break through it. 'I made up the fire myself yesterday – there was no one else to do it,' she said, addressing the doctor, but keeping her eyes on her maid. 'I got up twice to put on more coal, because the house was like a sepulchre. The central heating must have been out since Saturday afternoon.'

At this incredible statement Agnes's face expressed only a polite distress; but the new doctor was evidently embarrassed at being drawn into an unintelligible controversy with which he had no time to deal. He said he had brought the X-ray photographer with him, but that the ankle was too much swollen to be photographed at present. He asked Mrs Clayburn to excuse his haste, as he had all Dr Selgrove's patients to visit besides his own, and promised to come back that evening to decide whether she could be X-rayed then, and whether, as he evidently feared, the ankle would have to be put in plaster. Then, handing his prescriptions to Agnes, he departed.

Mrs Clayburn spent a feverish and suffering day. She did not feel well enough to carry on the discussion with Agnes; she did not ask to see the other servants. She grew drowsy, and understood that her mind was confused with fever. Agnes and the housemaid waited on her as attentively as usual, and by the time the doctor returned in the evening her temperature had fallen; but she decided not to speak of what was on her mind until Dr Selgrove reappeared. He was to be back the following evening; and the new doctor preferred to wait for him before deciding to put the ankle in plaster – though he feared this was now inevitable.

## V

That afternoon Mrs Clayburn had me summoned by telephone, and I arrived at Whitegates the following day. My cousin, who looked pale and nervous, merely pointed to her foot, which had been put in plaster, and thanked me for coming to keep her company. She explained that Dr Selgrove had been taken suddenly ill in Baltimore, and would not be back for several days, but that the young man who replaced him seemed fairly competent. She made no allusion to the strange incidents I have set down, but I felt at once that she had received a shock which her accident, however painful, could not explain.

Finally, one evening, she told me the story of her strange weekend, as it had presented itself to her unusually clear and accurate mind, and as I have recorded it above. She did not tell me this till several weeks after my arrival; but she was still upstairs at the time, and obliged to divide her days between her bed and a lounge. During those endless intervening weeks, she told me, she had thought the whole matter over: and though the events of the mysterious thirty-six hours were still vivid to her, they had already lost something of their haunting terror, and she had finely decided not to reopen the question with Agnes, or to touch on it in speaking to the other servants. Dr Selgrove's illness had been not only serious but prolonged. He had not yet returned, and it was reported that as soon as he was well enough he would go on a West Indian cruise, and not resume his practice at Norrington till the spring. Dr Selgrove, as my cousin was perfectly aware, was the only person who could prove that thirty-six hours had elapsed between his visit and that of his successor; and the latter, a shy young man, burdened by the heavy additional practice suddenly thrown on his shoulders, told me (when I risked a little private talk with him) that in the haste of Dr Selgrove's departure the only instructions he had given about Mrs Clayburn were summed up in the brief memorandum: 'Broken ankle. Have X-rayed.'

Knowing my cousin's authoritative character, I was surprised at her decision not to speak to the servants of what had happened; but on thinking it over I concluded she was right. They were all exactly as they had been before that unexplained episode: efficient, devoted, respectful and respectable. She was dependent on them and felt at home with them, and she evidently preferred to put the whole matter out of her mind, as far as she could. She was absolutely certain that something strange had happened in her house, and I was more than ever convinced that she had received a shock which the accident of a broken ankle was not sufficient to account for; but in the end I agreed that nothing was to be gained by cross-questioning the servants or the new doctor.

I was at Whitegates off and on that winter and during the following summer, and when I went home to New York for good early in October I left my cousin in her old health and spirits. Dr Selgrove had been ordered to Switzerland for the summer, and this further postponement of his return to his practice seemed to have put the happenings of the strange weekend out of her mind. Her life was going on as peacefully and normally as usual, and I left her without anxiety, and indeed without a thought of the mystery, which was now nearly a year old.

I was living then in a small flat in New York by myself, and I had hardly settled into it when, very late one evening – on the last day of October – I heard my bell ring. As it was my maid's evening out, and I was alone, I went to the door myself, and on the threshold, to my amazement, I saw Sara Clayburn. She was wrapped in a fur cloak, with a hat drawn down over her forehead, and a face so pale and haggard that I saw something dreadful must have happened to her. 'Sara,' I gasped, not knowing what I was saying, 'where in the world have you come from at this hour?'

'From Whitegates. I missed the last train and came by car.' She came in and sat down on the bench near the door. I saw that she could hardly stand, and sat down beside her, putting my arm about her. 'For heaven's sake, tell me what's happened.'

She looked at me without seeming to see me. 'I telephoned to Nixon's and hired a car. It took me five hours and a quarter to get here.' She looked about her. 'Can you take me in for the night? I've left my luggage down stairs.'

'For as many nights as you like. But you look so ill –'

She shook her head. 'No; I'm not ill. I'm only frightened – deathly frightened,' she repeated in a whisper.

Her voice was so strange, and the hands I was pressing between mine were so cold, that I drew her to her feet and led her straight to my little guest room. My flat was in an old-fashioned building, not many stories high, and I was on more human terms with the staff than is possible in one of the modern Babels. I telephoned down to have my cousin's bags brought up, and meanwhile I filled a hot water bottle, warmed the bed, and got her into it as quickly as I could. I had never seen her as unquestioning and submissive, and that alarmed me even more than her pallor. She was not the woman to let herself be undressed and put to bed like a baby; but she submitted without a word, as though aware that she had reached the end of her tether.

'It's good to be here,' she said in a quieter tone, as I tucked her up and smoothed the pillows. 'Don't leave me yet, will you – not just yet.'

'I'm not going to leave you for more than a minute – just to get you a cup of tea,' I reassured her; and she lay still. I left the door open, so that she could hear me stirring about in the little pantry across the passage, and when I brought her the tea she swallowed it gratefully, and a little colour came into her face. I sat with her in silence for some time; but at last she began: 'You see it's exactly a year –'

I should have preferred to have her put off till the next morning whatever she had to tell me; but I saw from her burning eyes that she was determined to rid her mind of what was burdening it, and that until she had done so it would be useless to proffer the sleeping draft I had ready.

'A year since what?' I asked stupidly, not yet associating her precipitate arrival with the mysterious occurrences of the previous year at Whitegates.

She looked at me in surprise. 'A year since I met that woman. Don't you remember – the strange woman who was coming up the drive the afternoon when I broke my ankle? I didn't think of it at the time, but it was on All Souls' eve that I met her.'

Yes, I said, I remembered that it was.

'Well – and this is All Souls' eve, isn't it? I'm not as good as you are on Church dates, but I thought it was.'

'Yes. This is All Souls' eve.'

'I thought so. . . . Well, this afternoon I went out for my usual walk. I'd been writing letters, and paying bills, and didn't start till late; not till it was nearly dusk. But it was a lovely clear evening. And as I got near the gate, there was the woman coming in – the same woman . . . going toward the house. . . .'

I pressed my cousin's hand, which was hot and feverish now.

'If it was dusk, could you be perfectly sure it was the same woman?' I asked.

'Oh, perfectly sure, the evening was so clear. I knew her and she knew me; and I could see she was angry at meeting me. I stopped her and asked: "Where are you going?" just as I had asked her last year. And she said, in the same queer half-foreign voice: "Only to see one of the girls," as she had before. Then I felt angry all of a sudden, and I said: "You shan't set foot in my house again. Do you hear me? I order you to leave." And she laughed; yes, she laughed – very low, but distinctly. By that time it had got quite dark, as if a sudden storm was sweeping up over the sky, so that though she was so near me I could hardly see her. We were standing by the clump of hemlocks at the turn of the drive, and as I went up to her, furious at her impertinence, she passed behind the hemlocks, and when I followed her she wasn't there. . . . No; I swear to you she wasn't there. . . . And in the darkness I hurried back to the house, afraid that she would slip by me and get there first. And the queer thing was that as I reached the door the black cloud vanished, and there was the transparent twilight again. In the house everything seemed as usual, and the servants were busy about their work; but I couldn't get it out of my head that the woman, under the shadow of that cloud, had somehow got there before me.' She paused for breath, and began again. 'In the hall I stopped at the telephone and rang up Nixon, and told him to send me a car at once to go to New York, with a man he knew to drive me. And Nixon came with the car himself. . . .'

Her head sank back on the pillow and she looked at me like a frightened child. 'It was good of Nixon,' she said.

'Yes; it was very good of him. But when they saw you leaving – the servants, I mean. . . .'

'Yes. Well, when I got upstairs to my room I rang for Agnes. She came, looking just as cool and quiet as usual. And when I told her I was starting for New York in half an hour – I said it was on account of a sudden business call – well, then her presence of mind failed her for the first time. She forgot to look surprised, she even forgot to make an objection – and you know what an objector Agnes is. And as I watched her I could see a little secret spark of relief in her eyes, though she was so on her guard. And she just said: 'Very well, madam,' and asked me what I wanted to take with me. Just as if I were in the habit of dashing off to New York after dark on an autumn night to meet a business engagement! No, she made a mistake not to show any surprise – and not even to ask me why I didn't take my own car. And her losing her head in that way frightened me more than anything else. For I saw she was so thankful I was going that she hardly dared speak, for fear she should betray herself, or I should change my mind.'

After that Mrs Clayburn lay a long while silent, breathing less unrestfully; and at last she closed her eyes, as though she felt more at ease now that she had spoken, and wanted to sleep. As I got up quietly to leave her, she turned her head a little and murmured: 'I shall never go back to Whitegates again.' Then she shut her eyes and I saw that she was falling asleep.

I have set down above, I hope without omitting anything essential, the record of my cousin's strange experience as she told it to me. Of what happened at Whitegates that is all I can personally vouch for. The rest – and of course there is a rest – is pure conjecture; and I give it only as such.

My cousin's maid, Agnes, was from the isle of Skye, and the Hebrides, as everyone knows, are full of the supernatural – whether in the shape of ghostly presences, or the almost ghostlier sense of unseen watchers peopling the long nights of those stormy solitudes. My cousin, at any rate, always regarded Agnes as the – perhaps unconscious, at any rate irresponsible – channel through which communications from the other side of the veil reached the submissive household at Whitegates. Though Agnes had been with Mrs Clayburn for a long time without any peculiar incident revealing this affinity with the unknown forces, the power to communicate with them may all the while have been latent in the woman, only awaiting a kindred touch; and that touch may have been given by the unknown visitor whom my cousin, two years in succession, had met coming up the drive at Whitegates on the eve of All Souls'. Certainly the date bears out my hypothesis; for I suppose that, even in this unimaginative age, a few people still remember that All Souls' eve is the night when the dead can walk – and when, by the same token, other spirits, piteous or malevolent, are also freed from the restrictions which secure the earth to the living on the other days of the year.

If the recurrence of this date is more than a coincidence – and for my part I think it is – then I take it that the strange woman who twice came up the drive at Whitegates on All Souls' eve was either a 'fetch,' or else, more probably, and more alarmingly, a living woman inhabited by a witch. The history of witchcraft, as is well known, abounds in such cases, and such a messenger might well have been delegated by the powers who rule in these matters to summon Agnes and her fellow servants to a midnight 'Coven' in some neighbouring solitude. To learn what happens at Covens, and the reason of the irresistible fascination they exercise over the timorous and superstitious, one need only address oneself to the immense body of literature dealing with these mysterious rites. Anyone who has once felt the faintest curiosity to assist at a Coven apparently soon finds the curiosity increase to desire, the desire to an uncontrollable longing, which, when the opportunity presents itself, breaks down all inhibitions; for those who have once taken part in a Coven will move heaven and earth to take part again.

Such is my – conjectural – explanation of the strange happenings at Whitegates. My cousin always said she could not believe that incidents which might fit into the desolate landscape of the Hebrides could occur in the cheerful and populous Connecticut Valley; but if she did not believe, she at least feared – such moral paradoxes are not uncommon – and though she insisted that there must be some natural explanation of the mystery, she never returned to investigate it.

'No, no,' she said with a little shiver, whenever I touched on the subject of her going back to Whitegates, 'I don't want ever to risk seeing that woman again. . . .' And she never went back.